Cheyenne Sunrise

Montana Gold Series

Book One: Hills of Nevermore
Book Two: Cheyenne Sunrise
Book Three: Stagecoach to Liberty

Cheyenne Sunrise

Montana Gold Series

By

Janalyn Voigt

Cheyenne Sunrise
Published by Mountain Brook Ink
White Salmon, WA U.S.A.

The website addresses shown in this book are not intended in any way to be or imply an endorsement on the part of Mountain Brook Ink, nor do we vouch for their content.

This story is a work of fiction. All characters and events are the product of the author's imagination other than those stated in the author notes as based on historical characters. Any other resemblance to any person, living or dead, is coincidental.

Scripture quotations are taken from the King James Version of the Bible. Public domain.

ISBN 9781-943959-37-2

The Team: Miralee Ferrell, Susan K Marlow, Nikki Wright, Cindy Jackson
Cover Design: Indie Cover Design, Lynnette Bonner Designer

Mountain Brook Ink is an inspirational publisher offering fiction you can believe in.

Printed in the United States of America

Reader Bonuses

For a map showing locations in this story plus exclusive features
to enhance reading this book, go here:
http://janalynvoigt.com/hills-of-nevermore-readers.

Dedication

This book is dedicated to the memory of my father,
Carl Thomas Weise, who lived nobly and well.

Acknowledgments

A historical fiction novel doesn't spring, fully clothed, from the author's imagination. I must give credit where it is due.

Many thanks to historian Jim Peterson for his help in understanding Montana history.

Those who advised me during development of this story include Sarah Joy Freese, my talented and inspiring agent at Wordserve Literary; Barbara Johnson, celebrated editor and my first agent and mentor; and authors Lynnette Bonner and Lesley Ann McDaniel.

Miralee Ferrell of Mountain Brook Ink, publisher of this book and a celebrated author in her own right, deserves special thanks for her tireless contributions to this book. Judy Vandiver applied her copywriting skills to make *Cheyenne Sunrise* a better novel. Thanks to all those who proofread this book.

Lynnette Bonner of Indie Cover Design created the beautiful cover and made working with her fun.

Special thanks go to my family for enduring my distraction when deadlines loomed and for supporting me while I worked on this book.

CHAPTER ONE

Boston, May 1865

AN ARM CLAMPED BRY'S WAIST AND hauled her backward into an unyielding embrace. Her heartbeat surged in her ears. The carved rosewood door gaped tauntingly ajar mere steps away. She twisted, her fingernails gouging flesh.

Her assailant rasped in a breath. "Fight if it helps your pride, *Irish.*" Jeffrey Wainwright's familiar voice snarled in her ear. He gripped her tighter. "We both know you want this."

Bry turned her head to give her employer's son the glare he deserved. "You flatter yourself."

He slid moist lips over her cheek, but she ducked her head before they reached her mouth. "Let me go." She struggled to free herself. "This minute!"

"Never mind trying to cozy up, now." He laughed at his own joke and turned her toward him, his hold loosening. With his blond head tilted and shadows carving hollows in his cheeks, he appeared older than his nineteen years. He stroked her back. "I've seen the way you look at me."

He must have noticed her keeping an eye on him, something she'd done since he'd started watching her. "What would your mother say?" She spoke without conviction. They both knew that Audra Wainwright exerted little control over her son.

"Who's going to tell her? Not you if you want your job." Jeffrey pulled her closer. "Slip away to my bed now and again. I promise you'll never find yourself cast upon the road."

"Like Deirdre?" Bry shoved against his chest. "Shame on you for what you did to her, Master Wainwright!"

He tugged her closer. "My, but you're a little shrew, aren't you?"

"And you're a bully."

"That's not what Deirdre said."

Bry drove her heel down Jeffrey's instep. He grunted, his arms slackening. She wrenched free but spun back. Her slap echoed through the bedchamber. She closed her stinging hand into a fist. Tremors ran down her spine. "Never touch me again." The sharp words matched her staccato footsteps as she put distance between them. She whirled to look back from the doorway.

"Harpy!" He rubbed his cheek. "That will cost you."

Bry tossed her head. "Deirdre Connery told me more than you'd care to have your mother know. Keep that in mind."

The smile that spread over his face made him look *almost* charming. "If you think she'd take your word over mine, you're a fool."

Bry slammed the door between them.

The bedchamber belonging to his mother stood blessedly empty. Bry sagged against the tall door and clasped her arms about herself. Tears trembled on her lashes, but she brushed them away with a sigh. Why cry over Jeffrey Wainwright's misbehavior when she'd shed her share of tears over a man more worthless than him.

Bry caught sight of herself in the gilded mirror above the dressing table. A pale woman stared back, eyes sparking green fire. Fresh alarm jangled through her. She looked a fright. How would she ever conceal what had happened? And yet she must to keep her job. Jeffrey had spoken the truth. His mother would never take her word against his. She hastened to tuck her tumbled black hair into her cap and smooth her serviceable frock.

The door burst open. As if conjured by Bry's thought of her, Audra Wainwright swept into the room. Her gaze locked on Bry's. Mrs. Wainwright halted abruptly, and her silk faille day dress swung about an ample figure. "What are you doing? You should have finished the bedrooms by now. Instead, I find you admiring yourself in my mirror."

Bry gaped at her employer, too stunned by her hostile tone to answer.

"Stay, however. I want a word with you." Audra settled into a rose velvet chair in front of draperies in the same unfortunate shade, which clashed with the woman's determinedly red hair.

"Yes, Ma'am." Bry waited with as much patience as she could muster, but she yearned to shut herself into her little room in the attic.

Audra folded her hands in her lap and looked Bry up and down. "My son tells me you've made improper advances toward him."

Bry started. Jeffrey had lost no time in seeking his revenge. "*I* made advances?"

"Yes, well. . ." Audra smoothed her skirt. "Under the circumstances, I no longer require your services."

"But I'm innocent."

"That's not what Jeffrey tells me."

"Mrs. Wainwright, you are mistaken. Your son—" Bry choked on her outrage. "Your son—"

"Mind you, as another widow, I understand loneliness. And Jeffrey is handsome enough to tempt a saint. However that may be, I won't allow you to seduce my boy."

The urge to laugh burbled up within Bry. She fought to quell it.

Audra waved a plump hand. "That's all I have to say. Leave me."

"But--"

Audra's face turned as red as the handprint had on Jeffrey's cheek. "You are dismissed!"

Bry straightened her spine. She would leave all right, but not before she spoke the truth. "Your son made improper advances to *me*, Mrs. Wainwright, and I'm not the first to draw his eye. *He's* the one who ruined Deirdre and made Mary run away."

"*Liar!*" The veins stood out in Audra's temples and her face turned red.

"Mrs. Wainwright!" Bry feared she would suffer a stroke.

Her employer waved a hand. "Go this minute, or I'll have Grayson put you out. And don't think you'll receive a reference from me."

"I'll pack my things." Bry flung open the door and stumbled down the corridor to the back stairs. She climbed the two steep flights to the bedchamber she'd shared with Mary, the quiet blonde scullery maid from County Kerry who had run away to escape Jeffrey's advances. Bry had always found the view from the dormer window fascinating, but today she didn't linger to watch tall ships ply the sparkling waters of Boston Harbor. Holding back tears, she placed a clean shift, a change of clothes, and a few oddments in her satchel. She glanced around the small room she'd called home for more than two years, then slipped down the stairs and let herself out by the servant's door.

The harbor wind scoured her face in an icy blast. Bry turned her back on the manor that had seemed a haven when she'd first come to it in the days after Ian's death. The disastrous marriage she'd made to escape a life of squalor had left her battered and destitute. But she'd survived to stand over Ian's grave, delivered by his death from the violence of his life. She would endure now, even if it meant returning to the slums of Manhattan.

CHAPTER TWO

A FRECKLED YOUNG BOY WITH CLEAR blue eyes challenged Nick with his hands fisted. "You gonna scalp us in our sleep, *Injun*?"

"Whoa, there!" Nick smiled and held up his own hands in mock surrender, although the question made his gut ache.

Caroline Keller looked back from the group walking ahead of her son on the trail. "George, come here at once!"

The boy ran to his mother with such speed Nick might have smiled in other circumstances. Caroline collared the boy while sending Nick an uneasy glance over the top of her son's head. No need to wonder where the boy had come up with his question. Nick's gut ached. How could he have thought things would be different this time?

The Kellers stopped at a wide place in the trail where Ty Davis waited, his Stetson clutched against his chest. Behind the wagon master, sagebrush and grass covered the ground all the way to the distant mountains painted shades of blue.

Beside the shallow grave in the middle of the trail, Ty bowed his head. "Ashes to ashes. Dust to dust. May the Lord God Almighty have mercy on their souls. Amen."

A chorus of voices echoed the wagon master's last word. Clods of dirt, cast by many hands, clattered over a row of crude coffins. Nick had helped build them from wagon boxes no longer needed by those who had died. Nick looked away from the smaller coffins, but that didn't stop the memories. He saw again the young victims, scalped and mutilated, sprawled among the carnage of the wagon massacre he'd stumbled upon while scouting.

Meadowlarks trilled and a few early wildflowers nodded among the grasses. However, when Nick took up the spade an icy wind numbed his fingers. The others looked on with solemn faces until he and Ty finished shoveling the mounded soil over the coffins, then one by one turned away.

Ty drove his spade into the ground and dusted off his hands. "We'll ride over the grave in the morning to pack down the dirt against Indians and wolves."

Nick laid his shovel down and picked up his slouch hat without comment. Indians didn't care to steal from the dead and nothing would keep out the wolves, but some things were better left unspoken.

"Nick—" Ty cleared his throat. "Stay a moment."

Nick tensed but waited.

Ty's lazy eye squinted, and he pulled the brim of his Stetson lower. "There ain't no good way to tell you this, so I'll just say it. No offense now, but I got to let you go."

"Why?"

Ty frowned. "Nothing agin you, like I said, but the wagon captains voted you out."

"Do they expect to reach Oregon without a scout?"

"Well now." Ty's ears turned red. "Jed Mills volunteered to take over, at least until Fort Hall, where I can look for someone else."

The notion of Jedidiah Mills, an apothecary's son, guiding a wagon train made Nick want to laugh.

"Mind you, I got nothing against you." Ty added hastily. "But folks on the trail are plumb nervous these days, and rightly so. It's natural to ask whether you came across that massacre or were part of it."

"Those were Sioux arrows. My mother's people are Cheyenne, and I don't even have a bow."

"Doesn't matter to men looking to protect their families. I know and like you on account of your father, but they don't share my feelings. They're bent on your leaving, and there'd be trouble if you stayed."

"Then I guess there's nothing more to say."

Ty tossed him a leather pouch that clinked when he caught it, although it didn't weigh much in his hand. "Here's your pay so far." His smile looked more like a grimace. "Maybe next year things will settle down, and I can hire you on again."

Nick shrugged as he backed away. "Sure. Next year."

"Hold up, now. You don't have to go until morning."

"Thanks all the same but I make it a point not to stay where I'm not welcome." Nick turned away.

"Suit yourself," Ty called after him. "Take enough food to see you home, why don't you?"

"Thank you kindly." Nick accepted Ty's guilt offering, more for the wagon master's sake than his own. He always kept his saddlebags packed and ready but added a little jerked buffalo and hardtack from the camp's supplies. Slinging his father's Henry repeating rifle over his shoulder, he carried his saddle and bridle into the wagon circle which formed a makeshift corral. Nick whistled for his horse. Mo'kôhtavo'ha, 'black horse' in the Cheyenne tongue, lifted his dark head and trotted to him. Nick bridled and saddled Tavo, the nickname he'd given his horse. The awareness of someone watching settled between his shoulder blades. He peered behind him, but nothing stirred in the quiet camp. He bent and tightened the girth with the back of his neck prickling, certain that the sooner he lit out of here, the better.

At the chink of metal, he slowly turned his head and looked into the muzzle of a rifle.

"Lay down your weapon nice and easy." Jonathon Keller growled.

Nick sucked in a breath. "This is my rifle, Jon. I need it to hunt, same as you need yours."

"I don't think you understand, Injun. If you lay down your weapon, I might let you live."

Nick didn't miss the tension rising in Jonathon's voice. He'd be a fool to try anything. If he killed a white man, he'd be as good as dead himself. No one would care that he'd done it in self-defense. The fact that he was half white wouldn't keep him from being lynched any more than it had saved his job. He eased the Henry away from his shoulder and dropped it to the sod.

"Smart man."

Nick stepped backward, his gaze trained on Jonathon's trigger finger.

"I did say, 'might'."

Nick snapped his attention to Jonathon's smirking face.

Footsteps thudded behind Nick.

Tavo neighed and reared. Jonathon whipped around to stare with startled eyes at the horse.

Nick spun about and caught sight of Jonathon's brother an instant before Amos' fist slammed into his stomach. Amos' momentum carried them down. Nick curled around the agony in his belly and clenched his teeth against the urge to vomit. Amos pushed to his knees and pulled back a fist.

Nick raised his arms in time to deflect the blow.

Amos lunged for his throat.

Nick rolled sideways and locked his hands around Amos's wrists. He staggered to his feet, pulling him upright. His stomach throbbed, and his knees shook, but by a miracle he stayed upright. "If you plan on shooting me, you'd better make good and sure of your aim." He ground out. "You wouldn't want to hit your brother by mistake."

"Don't do it." Amos pleaded in a thin voice.

Jonathon's rifle wavered, then lowered. "Your Injun brothers teach you to fight like that?"

Nick refused to be drawn. "Let's call it even."

Ty walked around the end of a wagon, his Winchester leveled at Jonathon's chest. "Lay down your weapon, Keller."

Jonathon cursed. "What's this, Ty? You ready to shoot me on account of a savage?"

"He's a man, Jon, not a savage. He's leaving same as you wanted. Now put down your Winchester, move off, and let him go."

"Have it your way." Jonathon laid his rifle on the ground.

Nick released his hold on Amos, who lurched toward the

wagons behind his brother.

Ty picked up the Henry and raised a brow at Nick. "Best get out of here while you can."

Nick whistled for Tavo. "I don't envy you, traveling with those two."

"I'll get by."

Nick pulled himself into the saddle, gasping with pain. Ty handed him his rifle, and Nick shouldered the Henry. "Thanks for looking after me."

"I did it for your Pa. He saved my life once. Reckon now we're even."

His father had told him how he'd rescued Ty from the Cheyenne. He'd have been glad to know his good deed had helped his son. Nick pointed Tavo eastward along the north side of the Snake. The loneliness of the less-traveled trail suited him just fine. He kept Tavo to a walk to spare his throbbing belly although he'd rather ride like the wind across the plain. He needed to hire on with another wagon train. That is, if he found one that wasn't dead set against a half-Cheyenne guide.

CHAPTER THREE

PARSON PEABODY PEERED AT BRY WITH watery blue eyes. "Mrs. Brennan, I wish I could help you. Unfortunately, the timing of your request in the middle of the church's poverty relief drive prevents that." His frown pulled down the corners of his white mustache. "I am but one man."

Bry recognized her mistake. She shouldn't have asked Parson Peabody for a reference, not after hearing Mrs. Wainwright brag about her generosity to his church. If he believed what she'd told him about her dismissal, he was bound to feel conflicted.

"I thank you for your time." She clutched her reticule and rose from the chair. "Good day."

"Certainly." He saw her out but lingered in the doorway of his office. "Yesterday I received a visitor who asked about you."

"Really?"

"He presented himself as Con Walsh. Said you were his sister."

Bry struggled to speak. Con had run off several years ago after an argument with their father. She'd wondered whether she would ever see her brother again. "Con! Here in Boston? Did he give an address?"

Parson Peabody flushed. "I'm afraid I forgot to ask. I had heard—that is to say, Mrs. Wainwright stopped by earlier in the day—for comfort, you see. She happened to mention that you are no longer situated with her. I assumed you'd left town, gone back to your family. Under the circumstances, I could give your brother no assistance in finding you."

His words struck her like a blow. To have Con so near only to lose him again made her mind reel. Aware of Parson Peabody's stare, she unclenched her gloved fists and schooled her features.

"Thank you, Parson. If my brother returns, please direct him to Mrs. Slattery's Boarding House on Caraway Street."

"But, that's an unsavory part of town."

"My circumstances are considerably reduced." Pride stopped her from calling them desperate.

He backed into his office. "Perhaps your brother can help you. If he returns, I'll direct him to you." He shut the tall mahogany door between them.

Parson Peabody's secretary was not at the desk in the outer office, removing the worry that Bry's visit would provide fodder for gossip. Few people in Boston cared what she did, but the household servants would speculate on the reason she'd left the Wainwrights. She doubted Parson Peabody would tell anyone he had turned her away, and Mrs. Wainwright would probably keep her dismissal quiet to shield Jeffrey. Her former employer's silence would protect Bry, but it wouldn't help her secure another position. That required the reference Parson Peabody had no time to give her.

Bry opened the multi-paned entrance door, exchanging the pungent scent of furniture oil for the fragrance of hyacinths. A purple ribbon of the fragrant blossoms flanked the brick walkway. A robin dipped its beak into newly-turned soil in a garden bed beneath a bay window. Her spirits lifted, despite everything. No matter how harsh the winter, spring always came. She had to believe that. A pair of matched bay Hackney horses clopped by, pulling a phaeton. The man and woman leaning together behind the driver looked so carefree that Bry couldn't deny a twinge of envy. What did privileged people know of hunger, broken promises, and death?

She started down the street toward Tremont Bank, chiding herself for giving way to jealousy. God forbid that the young couple she'd seen should bear the hardships she'd known. She entered the bank with a lighter step. Her circumstances had not changed, but her mindset had.

A gentleman who had attended parties at the Wainwright

mansion was leaving as she entered. Did she imagine disapproval in the tilt of his head? It had only been a day since her dismissal. Surely gossip about her couldn't have already made the rounds. Maybe it had, though. It struck her with horrifying clarity that Jeffrey might punish her for rejecting his advances by making up stories to ruin her reputation.

A clerk wearing a visor, waistcoat, and banded sleeves waited behind the gleaming mahogany counter. Her footsteps echoed as she crossed the marble floor to stand before him. "I need to close my account."

He adjusted his spectacles. "You'd be better off coming back another day. It's fifty cents on the dollar for withdrawals until further notice."

She gripped her reticule tighter. "I don't understand."

He cleared his throat. "Of late, this bank has suffered from bad investments."

"What?" She wanted to shake him. "How could the owners be so careless with my hard-earned wages?"

"They apologize for any inconvenience, of course."

She stared at him. "Apologies? What good are those to me?"

"Truly, I'm sorry, but we've had to lower our payouts. Many of our customers lost confidence and withdrew their funds, leaving us without sufficient funds to meet new demands."

The door behind her opened and shut. Boots thumped on the floorboards.

The teller cleared his throat. "Ma'am, I must ask you to make your decision or step aside while I wait on another customer."

Bry could scarcely think, let alone decide such an urgent matter, and yet she must. Emmaline Slattery required payment from her boarders in advance. The cost had been higher than Bry had anticipated, and she'd barely had enough cash to pay for last night's lodging. If she returned without payment tonight, she'd be evicted. No. Waiting for better terms from her bank was out of the question. What would she do if the doors closed for good, leaving her with nothing? If she took her money out today, she'd at least have enough to return to her family. However, gone was any hope of spending a week in Boston searching for work, perhaps as a laundress or seamstress. She would have to purchase a train ticket and leave town at once.

Her decision made, she squared her shoulders. "I'd like to close my account."

"Very well."

Bry signed the necessary documents, and the clerk counted out a paltry sum. He pushed the small stack across the counter to her. "You'll find all in order."

She riffled through the bills. "The amount is correct, but it's not fair."

He flushed. "I'm sorry, but it's the best we can do."

"I must take it or risk receiving nothing, but I'm not pleased to be cheated in this way." She snapped her reticule shut. "Good day." She turned her back on the clerk and marched to the door, which she shut smartly behind her. An oriole whistled, a scrap of black and orange flashing through the treetops in the small park across the street. With no escort and carrying all her material wealth, Bry resisted the impulse to slip into its leafy solace. Instead, she directed her steps eastward toward the railway station, where she purchased a ticket on a train departing in the morning. She would return to Five Points, the slum in lower Manhattan where she belonged.

On her way back to the boarding house, she noticed the doors to Parson Peabody's church standing ajar. Peering through the opening, she found the sanctuary empty. She could spare a few minutes for prayer, not that she expected much from the Almighty. He seemed to have forgotten her, but it wouldn't hurt to try.

The thick carpet muffled her footfalls. Shadows obscured the vaulted ceiling overhead, but on either side stained glass windows glowed with jewel colors. Bry knelt at the altar rail, met by the tangy scent of pine oil. She released her breath on a sigh and let the peace of this quiet place cool her feverish thoughts.

"God, I don't want to go back to the slum." Bry prayed quietly, but her voice echoed in the stillness. She swallowed against the tears scratching her throat. "Please, if you care about me at all, help me."

"He cares, Bryanna, and so do I."

Her eyes flew open. She knew that voice.

Her brother stood at the rear of the church near the open double doors. Dressed in the western manner with a leather vest, brimmed hat, and boots, he looked older than when he'd left, a man fully grown. His dark hair was longer than before, and his face leaner, but she knew him. "Con!" She ran to embrace him.

"Careful!" He laughed. "You'll bowl me over for sure." His arms enfolded her.

"I can't believe you're here!" Bry's laughter gave way to tears. "We thought you died."

He frowned. "I shouldn't have left the way I did."

"Why did you?"

"Did Da never tell you?"

"All he said was that you weren't coming back anytime soon, maybe never." She hated the wobble in her voice.

"Oh, Bry! I never meant to hurt you." The sorrow in Con's voice echoed the ache in her own heart. "I should have written."

She pushed out of his embrace. "Why didn't you?"

His green gaze shifted away from hers. "I had to leave, to make something of myself. But I never meant to stay away so long. And then I—well, it's hard to explain. The West utterly consumes a man. When you're trying to keep body and soul together, it's hard to think of letter writing." He met her eyes at last. "I'm sorry, Sis. Will you forgive me?"

"I can, but you'll find Da harder to convince."

Tears formed in Con's eyes. "I arrived in Five Points last week after riding there from my ranch. There's news, Bry, about Da. It's not good."

Her pulse thrummed in her ears. "Tell me."

"Look, why don't you sit down?"

"Tell me what's wrong with Da!"

"I'm sorry, Bry. He was killed a year ago during the draft riots."

She stared at her brother in horror. Da had seemed so strong, so solid, as if he would always be there. "What happened?" She couldn't picture her father involved in the draft protest certain troublemakers had used as an excuse to attack Negroes.

"He died in the fire at the Colored Orphan Asylum while helping the matron remove the children. Rob couldn't find either of us to let us know."

After Ian's death, she had put off sending her father word of her whereabouts, and she'd had no money to visit. No, that wasn't right. She could have found a way, if she'd wanted to go. The truth condemned her. Fearful that Da and her second-oldest brother Rob would insist she remain, she'd stayed away from Five Points on purpose. Bry pressed the back of her hand against her mouth. Only moments ago, she had begged God not to make her return home. "What have I done?"

"You're no more to blame than I am," Con's voice shook. "I keep asking myself if I had been there, whether it would have happened differently."

She slid her arms around him. "Why torture yourself by asking a question with no answer?"

His arms tightened around her, and his body shook as he wept. She let her own tears fall. It wasn't fair! Why couldn't things have happened differently? Mam, Da, and Liam might still be alive. Now only Con and Rob remained of her family.

She scrubbed at her cheeks. "How did you find me?"

He offered her a handkerchief and passed a hand across his damp face. "It wasn't easy, I'll tell you. When I went back to the tenement to find you, I didn't know you'd married. Rob gave me information that led me to Hartford. I learned from your minister that you'd gone to Boston. He even gave me the name of your employer, except you weren't there when I called." His brow furrowed. "What happened? They said you no longer lived there and all but threw me off the premises."

Con was hot-headed enough to go after Jeffrey if he learned

what had happened. "I'd rather not say."

He frowned but didn't pursue the matter. "I asked after you at most of the churches in Boston, but the one minister who knew you assured me you'd left town for parts unknown. I was walking down the street trying to decide where to look next when I saw you go into this church."

She twisted the handkerchief in her hands. "Why were you searching for me in the first place?"

"I came back to rescue what remains of my family from that hell hole of a slum. I've built a ranch from the money I made mining. I want you and Rob to help run the place."

"Where is Rob, then? Have you not brought him with you?"

"I sent him ahead to watch over my ranch while I searched for you."

She pressed her hands to her cheeks. "May God keep him on the journey."

He caught her hand. "Come home with me, Bry. There's a valley in Montana Territory, a place where a person can settle down to honest work. Gold gives out eventually but never the need for food."

His words stirred a familiar ache. How she longed for a new start. She'd tried to give herself one by marrying her way out of Five Points. What a lot of misery she'd have avoided if she'd trusted her instincts and refused Ian's proposal.

Con touched her cheek. " To have both you and Rob near would seem a miracle."

CHAPTER FOUR

THE S.S. RIVER BELLE, ITS WIDE paddles churning in steady rhythm, cut through the lacquered brown water. Bry curled her gloved hands around the hurricane deck railing and watched the sternwheeler's wake intersect ripples made by insects and jumping fish. Behind her, the pilot house perched above quarters for the captain and crew while steam puffed in alternating bursts from twin smokestacks.

A brisk wind tugged at the wide ribbons she'd tied beneath her chin to secure her new spoon bonnet. She shivered despite her wool jacket.

Con frowned. "You're cold. We should go inside."

"Oh please, not yet! I'd rather suffer the cold than confinement to the ladies' cabin all the long day. At least here I can breathe fresh air and enjoy your company."

"How is it that I always indulge you?" His smile smoothed over his exasperation.

She summoned her most angelic smile. "And well you should."

Con pushed his Stetson back on his head. His plain duck trousers and leather vest were casual, but an elegant string cravat secured his collar.

"Just a little longer. You may want to freeze, but I don't."

"I'm much warmer than I might have been, thanks to my new clothes." After confinement to widow's black for more than two years, she felt lighter in her ready-made traveling costume woven of wool in shades of blue. Con had bought her another gown of mustard watered silk trimmed with lace, as well as a brown calico and rose dimity, both of which she would save for warmer weather.

"That's only a start." Con winked at her. "You won't have to wear that horrible dress I found you in ever again."

She made a face at his lack of tact. "My duties left me little time to sew a new gown at the end of mourning, and black suited my station." She'd donated her widow's weeds to charity, grateful to vanquish her last tie to Ian.

"Did you have nothing else to wear?"

"Only another black dress, shabbier than the first. After Ian died, I was forced to sell my clothing to meet his debts."

Con's smile faded. "I wish I could have spared you that much."

"Never mind." She touched his arm. "We're together now."

He covered her hand with his own. "Sweet Bryanna. Do you feel overwhelmed? You're a long way from Boston or Manhattan. "

Her smile withered. "I wish we might have visited Da's grave before we left."

"Da's buried in a ditch somewhere in Potter's Field with no stone to mark him. Going back to Five Points wouldn't have been a good idea anyway."

"What do you mean?"

"Let's just say that Uncle Seamus didn't welcome me with open arms."

"He can't blame you!" Bry looked around in chagrin, having spoken more loudly than she'd intended. They were alone on the hurricane deck, thankfully.

"Tell that to Uncle Seamus." The bleak look in Con's eyes belied his light tone.

Bry stared at him. What sort of greeting might she have received if she returned to the house on Orange Street? Would Uncle Seamus have blamed her for staying away too long?

"Don't think about it, Bry. Uncle Seamus grieves about more than Da's passing. He'd rather have stayed in Ireland when the tatties gave out. That way we could have starved all at once and together in our homeland instead of wasting away, one by one, in the land of promise."

Bry blinked at tears. It was true, all of it, but she hated to hear it said.

"Ah, but listen to me. I mean to make you smile, not cry."

She threaded her arm through his. "You're on edge, I think, after too many days aboard steamboats. I'll be grateful when we can walk on dry land again." It had been a long journey from the Ohio River to the Mississippi and now along the Missouri westward.

"I won't argue about that at all. Too much can go wrong on one of these steam-driven contraptions. If stagecoach travel wasn't dusty and miserable, I'd have booked passage by that route."

"Too much can go wrong?"

"You can stop squeezing my arm, Bry. We'll have to trust in God to protect us."

She'd never heard Con talk about having faith, but he seemed to have acquired some. If only she could do the same. Ian had beaten all hopefulness out of her long ago, and she doubted she'd find it again.

With a chattering cry, a pheasant burst from a partially-submerged bush along what, when the water level fell, would become the riverbank. The bird's flapping wings carried it downriver.

Bry turned back to Con. "You mentioned a place called Alder Gulch. Is that where your ranch is located?"

"Perish the thought. Alder Gulch is a hard ride eastward. That's for the best. Miners can be a rough lot. My ranch is near Fort Owen."

"There's a fort near your ranch?"

"It's not much, only a few adobe-and-log buildings, but it's a place to trade."

"How civilized. I'll feel safer with a fort nearby. That is, if we don't perish on this riverboat or on the wagon journey."

"It has no soldiers, more's the pity. John Owens declared the place a fort and named it after himself which was perhaps a stretch, but the man is well-liked. Don't frown, darlin'. Remember, I'll be keeping you safe."

Bry laughed at Con's quizzical expression and exaggerated brogue. The lilt of their native country still colored his speech, as it did hers, but had softened for both of them over time. Feeling more alive than she had in quite a while, she dashed across the deck and turned with her hand on the stairwell rail. "Well then, me *bráthair*— you can start by delivering me from this cold and wind."

Surprise crossed Con's face, followed by a mischievous expression. She laughed and turned to flee down the stairs.

"Watch yourself!" A blond gentleman in a gray frock coat pulled an equally blonde female out of her path.

Bry brought herself up, narrowly avoiding a collision.

A smile lurked at the corners of the woman's mouth and touched her steel-gray eyes, although her smooth-complexioned face remained composed.

"I-I'm sorry!" Bry stuttered.

Con's running footsteps drew up behind Bry, and the woman transferred her attention to him, her expression changing from bemusement to a look of appraisal.

The blond man's gaze slid over Bry, lingering insultingly on her curves.

Con's hand slid around her elbow, and he shifted her behind him. "Move on your way."

The man shoved past them, scowling, and dragged the woman with him.

Jaw set, her brother glared at the stranger's back. "I could thrash him for being rude to you."

She laid a hand on his chest. "That would accomplish the wrong things."

"More's the pity."

Bry tossed her head. "What do you expect? You can't dress us in fine clothes and pretend we're other than we are. All the gold in Montana Territory will never change the truth."

He raised his brows. "That, being Irish, we're less than worthy? Thick-headed lout that I am, I still believe in America's freedom."

The aroma of bacon, beans and johnnycake made Nick's stomach growl. He'd spent long days in the saddle to reach Brett Colter's camp on the banks of the Missouri outside Independence. It had been a while since he'd enjoyed a hot supper, and he hoped Brett had a portion to spare.

"What happened to you?" The wagon master paused to stare at him, ignoring the steaming ladle in his hand.

Nick slid from Tavo's back to stand on unsteady legs. "Do I look that bad?"

Brett dropped the ladle into the cast iron kettle filled with bubbling beans. He'd hung the pot over his campfire from three poles lashed together. Brett ran an assessing glance over Nick. "Trouble?"

The soft word blended sympathy and understanding, almost ruining Nick's composure. He gave a curt nod.

Brett pushed his black Stetson back on his head, causing a mass of unruly brown hair to fall across his brow. "Hungry?"

Nick managed a weak smile. "Yes, thank you."

"No trouble." Brett nodded toward a barrel lashed to a prairie schooner. "Help yourself to a bit of grain for your horse, and I'll get a couple of plates." He sprang up the rear steps and inside the wagon.

Nick located Tavo's feed bag and then hobbled to the barrel. After days in the saddle, the pain in his belly had subsided, but whenever he twisted, his ribs ached. He scooped grain into the canvas sack and fitted it over Tavo's head.

Brett stepped down from the wagon and gave Nick one of the tin plates. "Go ahead. You first."

Nick bent over the pot. Steam warmed his cheeks as he heaped his plate full. He waited for Brett to do the same before digging in. His mother had taught him manners, saying he'd need them more than most. Before he'd known anything about the color of his skin, he'd wondered what she'd meant by that. Now he knew.

The beans warmed Nick as they went down, and he ate two

platefuls. Brett crouched at the fire, and then passed him a tin cup brimming with coffee. Nick took a sip, but the brew was too hot to drink. He looked up and caught Brett watching him. The wagon master had probably already guessed the reason for his visit, so Nick might as well come out with it. "I'm looking for work. Need a guide?"

Brett's brow puckered. "I wish I'd known you wanted a job before this. Just hired Matt Wilson, but I'd rather have you."

The wagon master didn't need to say more. Besides having a weakness for the bottle, Matt Wilson wasn't the best guide. Nick had known that finding a position with Brett would be a long shot at this late date, but when he'd heard his father's friend was about to take a wagon train west, he'd had to try. Of all the wagon masters he could name, he liked working with Brett best. "Too bad."

Brett gave him a level look. "I'm sorry, Nick."

"Ah well, it can't be helped."

"You'll find another train to take you on."

Nick shrugged. "Maybe, or I might just give up until next year."

"Can't say as I blame you. With the summer coming on, there's time to hunt, fish, and bait enough game to survive the winter in your father's cabin."

Nick considered the idea. Earning money supplied more variety in his diet as well as a few luxuries. It also provided him with company. During camp gatherings, he could listen to the chatter from the edge of the firelight, so as not to call attention to himself, yet still feel like he belonged.

Brett scratched the dark stubble on his chin. "Sorry I can't take you on. You're welcome to spend the night by the fire."

"I'm obliged." With feeble light slanting through the trees and a whippoorwill already calling, Nick felt no urge to push on. At Brett's fireside, he could forget the differences that set him apart, if only for a little while.

He drank his coffee while Brett finished whittling a pipe and told stories from his trapping days. "I'll never forget when Anton and I found ourselves stranded on an island in the Missouri River.

We both thought the other had tied up the boat, and it washed away." Brett chuckled. "It's funny now but sure wasn't then. The river was too wide to swim across, so we had to lash saplings together to make a raft. Taught us to talk more."

Nick swallowed against the lump that formed in his throat as the longing to hear his father's voice again gripped him. Nothing remained in his cup but dregs. He threw them out and stood. "I'd better water my horse."

He led Tavo away from the sprawling wagon camp and along a short path toward a place where bullfrogs droned. At a shallow spot Tavo waded in to drink, becoming a dark shape against the rosy surface of the river at sunset.

Nick returned to camp with his eyelids closing of their own accord. He ought to stay awake and decide where to go tomorrow, but after removing Tavo's saddle and tack and turning his horse loose in the makeshift corral the chained wagons formed, he couldn't think of anything but sleep. He turned his steps toward Brett's campfire, ready to lay out his bedroll.

A red-headed bear of a man stood beside Brett in the light of his fire. With a sinking feeling, Nick recognized Matt Wilson.

Matt's eyes met Nick's, but he continued his conversation without acknowledging him.

Brett didn't let the snub pass but turned to Nick with exaggerated politeness. "You and Matt know each other?"

"I reckon we do," Matt spoke before he could respond, which was just as well. Nick didn't know what he would have said. He'd first seen Matt, filthy and stinking of alcohol, lying in the rain alongside the trail near Independence Rock. He'd dragged the unconscious man onto Tavo and revived him at his campfire. The next day, Matt had rewarded Nick by accusing him of stealing his money and his horse. Matt might have succeeded in getting him hanged for his imagined crimes if the wagon master hadn't come looking for him with his horse in tow and a witness who said it had run off when he'd fallen from its back.

Nick stood beside Brett, never taking his eyes from Matt. If he'd learned anything in life, it was that people rarely changed.

Matt's smile was almost a sneer. "I thought you headed out with Ty Davis's train, Injun."

Brett stiffened at the slur, but Nick touched his arm. He'd fight his own battles. He wished Matt hadn't known his whereabouts. Hard telling what Matt would make of his return to Independence. "As you can see, I'm not with Ty's train."

Matt stroked his grizzled red beard. "Funny, I could have sworn—"

Brett shifted beside Nick. "It's late and morning comes early. Why don't we call it a night?" His tone brooked no argument.

Matt looked about to argue anyway, but then seemed to remember who his employer was and backed away, all the while pinning Nick with a cold gaze.

Nick figured he'd better sleep light.

CHAPTER FIVE

Bry stepped past Con, who held open the Bellweather Hotel's carved oak doors. Her feet sank into plush red carpet. Linen-covered tables set with crystal and silver ranked down either side of the dining room. The brass chandelier dominating the entrance dripped prisms in which the flames of candles danced. Having catered to Audra Wainwright's guests during her society gatherings, Bry was familiar with luxury. However, it was one thing to serve others and quite another to be waited upon.

A waiter greeted them and led the way to a table beside a tall window overlooking the street. Con held her ring-backed chair, then sat across from her. He opened the corded and tasseled menu. "What will you have, Sis? Name anything you like."

He'd enjoyed saying that, judging by his smug smile. How much gold had he found? A day of spending more money than she'd seen in a lifetime seemed not to have pinched his resources. She didn't know half of the foods on the menu, so she laid it down without reading further. "What do you recommend?"

Con's face lit with wry humor. "You won't go wrong ordering the chicken. Unless you prefer the cold tongue."

"Chicken is fine."

When the waiter returned, Con ordered for them both.

Bry glanced around at the other diners. It was early, barely past five, but customers already crowded into the high-ceilinged room. "The food must be good here, or else there aren't many places in town to eat."

Con laughed. "Your first guess was correct. Independence boasts many fine restaurants." He picked up his water goblet and took a sip. "Enjoy your supper. After this it will be camp fare until we reach the ranch."

"When do we leave?"

"Our wagon train pulls out bright and early Friday morning. We'll need to pack the wagon I had built tomorrow."

An odd mixture of exhilaration and fear shot through her. "I wasn't quite ready for that news."

He smiled and reached across the table to pat her hand. "You'll adjust, I'm certain." He looked past her, and his smile froze.

The blonde female she'd nearly run into on the steamboat entered on the arm of the man who had snubbed them. The opulence of the green velvet gown that swathed the woman's delicate figure made Bry glad she'd worn her watered silk and troubled to tame her hair into a loose coil at her nape. As the waiter led them to a nearby table, the woman's tawny gaze slipped sideways to Con, where it lingered a little too long before flitting away. Dressed in a frock coat and cravat, her companion carried his derby hat under his arm. After a start of recognition, he looked straight ahead without otherwise acknowledging them.

Heat rose into Bry's cheeks. Being ignored by the man was preferable to being addressed, but she didn't like the way her brother's jaw tightened. To make matters worse, the waiter seated the pair at the table behind Con. Perhaps she should suggest to Con that they leave.

Con, on the other hand, seemed in no hurry to go. He ate his porterhouse steak with apparent relish while Bry picked at her roasted chicken.

Con arched his brows. "Waste not, want not, sister of mine. We're in for a steady diet of beans, bacon, and cornpone that will make you wish for a plate of chicken."

She picked up her fork but poked at her food. "I'm sorry to be such poor company. My head aches." Against her better judgment, she flicked a glance toward the newcomers.

Concern lit her brother's green eyes. "Perhaps you should retire to your room. I can have your food sent up."

"Oh no, Con. I don't want to spoil your supper. *Please.*"

"All right, if you're certain you wish to remain."

Con looked so like his younger self in that moment that she smiled. "I'm already feeling better." She decided the matter out loud. To prove her point, she lifted a forkful of chicken to her mouth.

Con swirled the water in his glass. "Being Irish, I have a fair notion how that headache came about."

Her cheeks heated again. "Being Irish, I should be used to unkindness."

"Ah, no. I wouldn't want you hardened."

The woman behind Con laughed at something the man said, a musical sound. Con's face took on a bemused expression.

Bry leaned forward and kept her voice low. "She's beautiful."

Con's smile lit his face. "That she is, but a world apart."

"She'll be married anyway."

"There's no ring on her finger."

She grinned. "Of course, you would notice that. Her companion is probably her brother, then. They look too respectable for anything else."

"Never mind about them. I want to know what you think of Independence."

"It's a bustling city for sure." She allowed Con to lead their conversation down safer paths. "There's an excitement here that's something special."

"As a major jumping-off place for trails west, that's only natural."

"Tell me about your ranch."

"I built a cabin and a barn in the Bitterroot Valley, one of the loveliest grasslands you'll find. I'm building my herd by trading pioneers one fattened cow for two trail-worn ones. They're only too glad to strike the bargain, I'm paid for my trouble, and it allows me to provide beef to the mining camps."

"You've started quite a business."

He shrugged. "It's not as easy as it might sound. I take the risk that the cattle I trade for will sicken and die. On the open range, they can fall prey to predators, some of them on two feet. And of course, there's the work of rounding up the herd to brand the calves in the spring and cull them in the fall. Not that I'm complaining. It's profitable, and I love the work."

"I'm glad." The enthusiasm in Con's voice announced that he'd found a passion to pursue. Contrasting the troubled youth he'd been with the man he'd become, she could tell that western life agreed with her brother. She hoped to take to it as well. "What's it like, living in Montana Territory?"

He flashed a smile. "With the wide sky above, the good earth below, and clear waters flowing, I'd say it feels like freedom. However, there is a cost—in lawlessness."

"Is it as violent as the dime novels say?"

"And what were you doing, reading dime novels?" He winked at her. "Your face is a picture. Never mind trying to bluster." He nodded to her empty plate. "I'm glad you found your appetite. Shall we go?" He stood and pulled back her chair as she rose.

Bry started for the door and almost stepped on a handkerchief lying in the aisle. Con bent to retrieve the lacy scrap of embroidered fabric. She caught her breath as her brother turned to the blonde woman at the next table. "Pardon me, but I believe you dropped this."

The blond man from the steamboat picked up his wine glass without looking up. "Leave it lay."

The woman glanced at Con then back to her companion. "Miles. . .”

"Quiet, Alicia. I said leave it lay!" He sipped his wine, set his glass down, and dabbed his napkin to his lips. "It's sullied now."

Bry sucked in her breath. The man's meaning could not be clearer.

Con stiffened. "Say that again—outside."

"Come away, Con." Bry took hold of his arm, but he shook off her hand.

The man's gaze slid over Bry's figure with insolent thoroughness. "Listen to your *woman*, Irish."

Con went still. "Come outside."

Bry choked back a rush of alarm. "Con, no!"

"Are you threatening me? If so, this is a matter for the law." Miles' voice rose on his final sentence.

Their waiter hurried toward them.

Bry pulled her brother toward the door.

Miles jumped to his feet. "Apprehend that fellow."

Alicia stood and placed a hand on his chest. "Dear heaven, Miles, let them go."

Con pulled Bry out the door. As it banged shut a chill draught laden with the river's scent breathed over her. She ran across the porch beside Con, their feet thudding on its wooden boards. Raised voices followed them. Someone flung open the door. Con turned Bry to face him. "You used to outrun me, as I recall. Might be a good time to discover if you still can."

In the split skirt and knickerbockers that made up the riding costume Con had bought her, Bry rode astride the dun quarter horse Con had saddled for her at the livery. Her horse answered to Kilkenny, he'd informed her with a lilt in his voice. She'd exclaimed in wonder. Con would have sought out an Irish trader in Independence since no one knew horses like the Irish. Even so, finding a horse named after the county of her birth could only be a rarity. She blinked away tears, touched all over again by what seemed a gift from the hand of God.

Her brother drove the mules they'd purchased for drawing the wagon by a jerk line from the back of one of the rear mules. His sorrel horse followed, tied behind the wagon, which swayed and creaked along.

Bry shivered in a sudden blast of cold. "It's a sorry time of night to be about." Her thoughts turned to the hotel bed with the lovely feather tick she wouldn't sink into tonight. After they'd left the restaurant, Con had insisted on joining the wagon camp at once. They'd returned to their rooms only long enough to gather their belongings and for her to change into riding clothes. She sighed. "But I suppose it's better than seeing you jailed."

"I doubt it'd have come to that, but better safe than sorry. Hard telling what Miles had in mind."

"I don't know what got into you in the restaurant." Well, maybe she did. That beautiful blonde woman probably had something to do with it.

"I'll not apologize for defending your honor, if that's what you're driving at." Con spoke sharply. "I'm surprised you object."

Bry hesitated, unwilling to wound her brother for taking up for her, but he needed to understand. "That's not what troubles me. I want you to protect me, indeed I do. If only you could manage it less boisterously, though. I lived with enough violence at Five Points and during my marriage to know the wretchedness it causes. I can scarcely stand to see more."

"I'm sorry for that, Bry, but when called upon, I must fight on your behalf."

She nodded and changed the subject. "In case you didn't notice, brother of mine, you fell for that woman's ruse."

"Ruse?" Con asked in a baffled voice.

She shook her head at his thickness. Con had obviously learned nothing about women during his years in the West. "Surely you don't think she dropped that handkerchief by accident."

"What d'you mean?"

"I saw that ploy more than once during my service in Boston."

A long silence followed her words. "To what purpose?"

"Go on with you!" She rounded on him, but kindly. "I'm sure you can guess. It's to draw the notice of an interesting man. You can wipe that smirk off your face."

"How can you know in the dark that I'm smirking?"

"By the light of the moon, of course." Nearly full, it shone down so brightly they hadn't needed a lantern to show them the path. She laughed. "Besides, I can hear it in your voice."

"Well, I won't deny being flattered, but I've a notion that *cailin* would bring me trouble."

"You're probably right, but I doubt she realized what would happen when she dropped her handkerchief."

"Are you sure of that? Maybe she was trying to irritate Miles. She could be something other than his sister."

"I guess we'll never know. It's just as well that we're leaving town."

"My point exactly."

Poor Con. His pride must have taken a beating. She wouldn't complain again. The road unfurled like a blue ribbon to the banks of the Missouri where campfires flickered. "Tell me more about your ranch."

"Let's see. . . the well draws some of the best drinking water you'll ever taste. The weather is hot as blazes in the summer but cold as death in the winter."

"How pleasant."

"You'll get used to it."

"Mind you, I won't complain about having a roof over my head…"

"We're nearing a camp."

"Even if that roof is a wagon bonnet."

Con laughed. "I hope living out of a wagon won't be too vexing. When I wired the wagon builder before leaving Boston I asked him to build a false floor to fit above our supplies. I'm happy to sleep outside in my tent, but there's a feather tick awaiting you inside."

She smiled. "I'm touched you would take such pains over my comfort."

They pulled into a grassy patch at the edge of camp. Several shapes huddled near a campfire, and Bry made out an older couple.

"New to the train?" The man's long face shone in the light of the lantern he carried.

Con removed his hat. "We are. I'm Conner Walsh and this is my sister, Mrs. Brennan. When we reach Fort Hall, we'll head north into Montana Territory."

"Pleased to make your acquaintance." He raised his bowler hat. "I'm Martin Wallers. You won't be alone when you turn north. Lots of folks are going after gold. My wife and I will continue westward. Mrs. Wallers has a sister in Oregon she hasn't seen since fifty-two."

Bry smiled, thankful to be welcomed by such a friendly couple. "It's nice to meet you both."

"Likewise." Mr. Wallers beamed at them. "There's room to camp alongside us. Unless you prefer to set up somewhere else, o' course."

Con glanced at Bry, and she nodded. "This will do." Con's voice held a relieved note.

Mr. Wallers watched Con settle the wagon, then stepped forward. "Can I help you settle your livestock?"

"I wouldn't want to trouble you." Surprise lifted Con's voice.

"It's no bother."

"Well, then. I'll take you up on that offer with thanks."

Mrs. Wallers gave Bry a quiet smile. "Come and warm yourself by our fire."

"Thank you. I'm chilled through." Bry let her brother swing her down and lead Kilkenny away.

"It's a might cold of late." Mrs. Wallers pulled her shawl tighter about her. "Would you like a cup of tea and perhaps a slice of dried apple pie?"

It was much later before Bry sank, with a contented sigh, into the feathered tick. It wasn't the Bellweather's finery, but she preferred a makeshift bed in a wagon box if it meant she could sleep in peace.

A lever clicked, wrenching Nick awake in the weak light before dawn.

"Time to clear out, Injun." Matt slurred.

Nick turned his head. A rifle muzzle filled his vision. He repressed a start.

"Easy does it!" Matt chuckled. "Leastways, if you want to keep body and soul together. As for me, it don't matter which way it goes. No one's gonna string me up for shooting an Injun these days. Take my meaning?"

Nick gave a slow nod.

"All right, then." Matt turned his head and spat. "You probably stole that horse, but I'm gonna let you take it. I want you out of here afore Brett wakes up. He can be soft-headed sometimes, but it's up to me to look after him. Now go."

Look after your job, you mean. Nick rolled to his side, ready to push to his feet while keeping an eye on Matt's trigger finger.

"For your information, Wilson, I don't need looking after." Brett spoke from behind him.

Matt's eyes widened, then narrowed.

Nick dove sideways before the rifle went off. The bullet zinged into the ground, and dirt pelted him. Sharp exclamations came from nearby wagons. Running feet pounded toward them. Nick stood and backed with slow steps.

"Stop it right now!" Brett snarled. "You're drunk and bigoted besides. But I'm even more of a fool for hiring you."

Matt turned his rifle on Brett. "*Injun lover.* If you weren't a white man, I'd have killed you already."

Nick eased his fingers into his boot. He straightened with his knife balanced in his hand.

"Back away." A man in a slouch hat came up behind Matt, his rifle trained on him.

Nick waited, tensed to spring.

Matt's rifle wavered and went down. He pierced Nick with a glare. "Don't ever cross my path again."

"Clear out, Wilson." Brett's voice brooked no argument. "You're lucky I don't have you arrested."

Matt spat and, without so much as a glance at the man who had challenged him, strode off.

"I'm obliged to you, Billy." Brett spoke above the hubbub in camp.

"No trouble a'tall." The man in the slouch hat slanted a look sideways to Nick. "What about this one?"

"He's all right. This is Nick Laramie. He and I are old friends. Nick, meet Billy Masters."

Billy grunted but didn't lower his rifle. He waited until Nick returned his knife to its sheath before turning away.

"Well then." Brett threw an arm around Nick's shoulders. "I guess you have yourself a job."

CHAPTER SIX

BRY DODGED SMOKE FROM THE CAMPFIRE, then passed Con a plate laden with bacon stew and cornpone. She sat on an overturned crate across from him with a sigh. "My feet hurt."

He nodded. "That's natural after our first day on the trail."

"Adjusting to life in a wagon camp might prove more difficult than I expected."

"Give it time."

"I'll never get used to being thrust rudely from sleep by gunshots. Must the wagon master use that method to rouse the camp?"

Con grinned. "I'll inform him that from now on you prefer to be summoned from bed by the strumming of a harp."

She made a face at him, then glanced around, hoping no one had seen the childish gesture. Her pulse kicked up a notch. "Isn't that an Indian over there?"

A raven-haired man across the wagon circle turned his head, as if he'd heard her question. Surely he'd been out of earshot. His gleaming eyes met hers, and heat uncurled in her stomach. She hadn't meant to stare, but she'd never seen an Indian before. The man wore trousers, a buckskin vest, and boots similar to Con's, but his chestnut skin, high cheekbones, and dark eyes proclaimed his heritage.

"Don't mind him, Bry." Con's voice woke her from what felt like a dream. "According to Brett Colter, Nick Laramie is one of the best trail guides living. Since our wagon master trusts him, I'm sure there's nothing to worry about."

She stole another glance at the intriguing man. "Laramie? That doesn't sound like an Indian name."

"His father, Anton LaRamee, was a French trapper who took a native wife. I guess he Americanized his last name. Many do."

"His father is no longer living?"

Con took a bite and watched her while he chewed. He swallowed then swigged steaming coffee from a tin cup. "You're a mite curious."

She resisted the urge to glance away from her brother's penetrating gaze. "Of course I am. This is all new to me."

His eyes sparkled. "Will you be asking questions all the way to Virginia City, little sister?"

She laughed. "Indeed I will."

"What am I in for?" He smiled, but then sobered. "Since you insist on knowing, Anton LaRamee died a few years back. I can't remember the particulars, but I believe Indians killed him."

She drew a breath, but he held up a hand for silence.

"Before you ask, I don't know what happened to his wife."

"How did you know what I was going to ask?"

He laughed. "Have you forgotten that we used to play Riddle?"

"Do you think I ever could?" In case Con planned to continue playing the thought-guessing game they'd invented in childhood, Bry clamped down on her interest in the mysterious man across the wagon circle. Maybe she should distract her brother. "That woman we met in Independence—what was her name? Oh, yes, Alicia."

The pained expression that crossed Con's face made her regret bringing the memory back to him. "What about her?" he asked a casual voice.

"I wonder what she'd make of traveling in a wagon train."

He smiled. "I can't picture her doing so, nor Miles either."

Bry nodded. Despite the nice clothing Con had bought her, she'd felt like a fraud beside Alicia's elegance. "They're mighty fine compared to the likes of us. And yet…" She shook her head. "They acted in ways that didn't match their breeding. Their behavior seemed—"

"Common?" He lifted an eyebrow. "The upper classes would like to hide that we're all the same under the skin." He polished off the last of his stew, set his plate down, and stood up. "I'd better look after Guss or we'll lose the use of our best lead mule. I noticed a rash around one of his hooves before turning him out today." He strode off.

Bry brought a forkful of beans to her mouth. She'd better hurry if she wanted to have her camp chores done before dark. Already the sky smudged its edges, a breeze breathed across the water while shaggy oxen and long-eared mules lay down to rest in the wagon circle.

They would camp another night beside the Missouri and strike out westward in the morning. According to Con, their wagon train wasn't as large as some, but at thirty strong its size overwhelmed her all the same. Everyone at the wagon camp seemed to know one another, but with unfamiliar faces all around, she felt lost in a group of strangers.

She finished her supper and gathered the plates for washing. Something bumped against her knees, and she looked down into shining blue eyes. A girl of perhaps three smiled up at her. Golden curls brushed the collar of the child's blue plaid dress, and scuffs marred her black high-top shoes.

Bry bent until her eyes were on a level with the child's. "And who are you?"

Con frowned. "So young a child shouldn't wander about alone."

Bry held out her arms, and the little girl walked into them without reservation. "She must have wandered off. Do you know who her mother is?"

"*Phoebe!*" A frantic note infused the call.

Con set his plate aside and stood. "Unless I miss my guess, we're about to meet her."

A woman with dark hair coiled at her nape and wearing brown linsey-woolsey hurried toward them. Chest heaving, she quickened her step.

Little Phoebe squirmed, and Bry lowered her onto her feet, thinking the child wanted to go to her mother. Instead, Phoebe giggled and darted away.

"Catch her!" the woman called.

"Hold up there." Con stepped in front of the girl, but she veered to the side.

Bry dashed after the errant child and managed to catch her by one arm. Phoebe squealed with obvious delight and wriggled when scooped up but then nestled her head against Bry's shoulder. Holding her baby brother, Liam, had felt like this. At the thought, Bry held Phoebe a little closer.

The woman reached them, clutching her side and panting. Phoebe leaned toward the woman with her arms out. "Ma."

"Phoebe! You know better . . . than to run off," the woman cradled her child even as she scolded her. "I can't turn my back . . . for a minute these days."

The image of Liam, chubby legs pumping as he ran down the road away from their farm, came alive for Bry. He'd given them fits that day, and all because he'd wanted to work with Da. The bittersweet memory sucked the wind from her lungs. "I know how willful children can be."

Con frowned. "You'll want to take more care in the future. A lot can happen to a child in camp. There's always danger from livestock."

The woman's smile vanished. "I'll keep that in mind." She turned away, but then looked back. "Where are my manners? I'm Maisey Wilcox, wife to Avery. You've already met our daughter, Phoebe."

"I'm Conner Walsh, and this is my sister, Bryanna Brennan. I met your husband earlier while watering the mules."

Bry smiled at her. "You have a lovely daughter, Mrs. Wilcox."

"Thank you, but please call me Maisey."

"And I'm Bry." She extended her hand.

Maisey shifted the child in her arms and shook Bry's hand. "Nice to meet you. I hope we can become friends."

"I'd like that." She hesitated. "Let me know if you need help minding that little one."

"Thanks. I may accept your offer." Phoebe squirmed in her mother's arms, but Maisey held her close. "I'd better get back to my chores. There's talk of dancing later."

"How fun. Con should strike up his fiddle."

"Don't mind if I do."

Maisey smiled. "I'll see you later, then."

Bry waited until Maisey was out of earshot. "I meant that the evening will be fun for others. I'll take to my bed early."

"Oh? I'd hoped to dance with my darlin' sister."

"I don't care to dance."

"Then I'm doomed to become a wallflower."

She laughed. "Such blarney. You've a friend wherever you go."

"Honestly, you should come. It's a chance to get to know the people in our wagon train from the start."

"I'll have no choice but to meet them soon."

"What is it, Bry?" Con stepped closer and lowered his voice. "Sorrow for your husband?"

"No!" She hadn't meant to spit out the word. She took a breath. "I observed a proper mourning period. I'll not do more."

"Then why not join in tonight's fun?"

"I've no heart for such things anymore, Con."

He touched her shoulder. "I'm sorry you feel that way. I didn't mean to stir bad memories."

She nodded. Memories of Ian needed no stirring, for they returned daily.

"What did Ian do to make you hate him?"

Hate? The word startled her, but yes. Hatred was one of the strands of emotion that snarled together when she thought of Ian. She'd given up on untangling them all.

Nick retreated into the shadow of a lone oak. A kingfisher chided him from its branches and flew away in a flurry of feathers. The day had gentled toward evening, and the bird hovered above the river, batting its wings like a dragonfly. In the background, the wash and flow of water sang a rippling harmony. Music gusted from the wagon camp, a poor substitute for the cadences of nature. The kingfisher swooped to the painted surface, and then flapped upward with a fish in its beak.

The woman he'd seen earlier—was she among the dancers? Her eyes had narrowed as they met his, her face taking on the expression of distrust he'd come to recognize. He should be used to it by now, but somehow, this time it mattered. He couldn't deny that she'd caught his interest. Even from across the wagon circle, he'd read strength and vulnerability in her face, an intriguing combination. Who was she?

Why he should dwell on this woman, he did not know. Perhaps the beauty of her dark hair and creamy skin attracted him. Although he never intended to marry, he still had a man's interest in a beautiful woman. He hadn't missed the intelligence in her expression or the modest way she'd averted her eyes from his stare. He'd only known one other who bloomed like a rare flower in the high desert, and she had gone from this world.

Determined to shake off thoughts of a woman he could never pursue, he turned his back on the wagon camp and followed a deer trail along the banks of the Missouri. He cut through tangled underbrush beneath oaks, hickories, and maples and breathed in the scent of water. He didn't slow until the creaking drone of bullfrogs drowned all sounds from the camp.

He watched a floating log bob under, only to come up downriver. Uneasiness tugged at him—a bad feeling about this wagon train crossing he couldn't suppress. Coming upon the remains of the massacre had spooked him, but it was more than that. Now that the War Between the States was drawing to a close, conflicts with the Sioux, Cheyenne, and Arapaho were escalating. Having lived among his mother's people, Nick knew of the atrocities and treaty violations that angered the young men in particular. But his father had raised him to embrace Christianity. Taking the life of innocents, no matter who did the killing, was wrong.

Honi, his mother, whose full name, Honiahaka, meant "Little Wolf," had accepted her husband's Christianity, a fact that later brought her ridicule when she returned to her tribe after his father's death. His mother had loved the Missouri River. Nick's earliest memories were of sitting between his parents in a dugout canoe as the bow parted the sparkling waters. He could still see his mother's bright eyes crinkling at the corners as her lips lifted in a ready smile. Although it had been many years since she had gone to Ma'heo'o, the creator of all life, sometimes he imagined he heard her voice in the wind, whispering his Cheyenne name.

Ho'neheameohtse...

She'd named him "Wolf Walking" after a lone buffalo wolf which sometimes visited the small cabin his father had built on a hilltop above the river. Large and white, the beautiful animal appeared at their door in lean times to beg scraps from his mother's hand. Father discouraged her from feeding it, but her love for the wolf kept him from shooting it outright. He chased the wolf away whenever it came around while he was home. The wolf always returned, gazing at the cabin with hungry eyes.

Nick shook off his thoughts much as he'd seen that buffalo wolf shake the rain from its coat after a storm. Remembering his parents only brought home to him that they were gone forever. Thinking of his mother's people reminded him of why he would never return to them.

The night wind pushed his hair back from his forehead and sprinkled his cheeks with droplets of moisture that felt like tears.

CHAPTER SEVEN

A WHIPPOORWILL CALLED FROM SOMEWHERE NEAR, and Maisey opened her eyes in pitch blackness. A sick feeling clutched her stomach. *Where am I?* Wind shook the wagon bonnet while Phoebe stirred beside her on the feather tick. Maisey let out her breath. When would she grow used to sleeping in the wagon?

Her husband thrashed on her other side, moaning. "Avery." She shook his shoulder, whispering to avoid disturbing their daughter. "You're dreaming."

Avery sat up, shouting at a phantom intruder.

Phoebe startled awake and let out a cry.

Maisey gathered her daughter's small body into her arms and held her close while she wailed. Avery's breathing rasped and hitched as sobs wrenched from him. Maisey longed to comfort her husband, but nothing eased him during one of his spells. He'd fought spectral battles since Gettysburg. Discharged with his mangled arm in a sling, he spoke of the torments that gouged his soul more deeply than of the gash marring his face.

Avery's sobs slowed at last, and Phoebe settled back into slumber. Maisey eased away and turned to her husband. Avery caught her against him with his good arm and buried his face in her neck. With his breath feathering her skin, she sighed into sleep.

Rifle shots jerked Maisey from slumber. She sat up with her heart pounding at the wagon camp's signal to wake. This morning it came too soon. Phoebe crawled into her arms for an embrace while Avery rolled out of bed. He pulled duck trousers from a peg in the dimness.

Maisey rose and lit a lantern. Her daughter tugged on her shift, begging to be picked up. "Hush, little one."

With his fair hair sleep-tousled and new growth shadowing his chin, Avery resembled the boy he'd been when she'd first met him, so long ago. He dropped a quick kiss on top of her head. "What would I do without you?"

"Let's hope you never have to answer that."

He gusted a sigh. "Not that again."

"I can't help it." Her husband well knew her misgivings about leaving the familiar world behind and venturing into the western wilderness, a place no civilized person belonged. Anything could happen.

"Countless people before us have done this same crossing."

And left graves strung along the trail. She didn't speak the words that pressed her lips. What was the use? Avery needed to go west, and badly. He would make a new start or die trying. With his left arm hanging useless at his side, she couldn't ask him to sacrifice what remained of his manhood on the altar of her fears.

Phoebe begged to be picked up, but Maisey laid a quieting hand on her golden head. "Patience, little lamb." Maisey took her linsey-woolsey gown and the petticoat that went beneath it from their hooks and dressed quickly. Phoebe clutched her legs and giggled when her mother's skirts fell around her. Maisey detached her daughter and lifted her out from under her skirts. She couldn't resist the temptation to tickle her, much to Phoebe's delight.

Avery loosened the pickle string to widen the gap at the rear of the bonnet and stepped out of the wagon.

Maisey dressed her squirming daughter and snatched up a piece of cold cornpone with which to soothe her before following Avery outside.

Dawn light struggled to overcome the dark of night, but the camp already swarmed with activity. Women bent over campfires, children gathered firewood, and men yoked bawling oxen or hitched mules. Expectancy rode the air, for today their journey began.

Mornings, with everyone hurrying to break camp, would be hardest for her and Avery. Her husband couldn't handle the mules alone with any speed as yet, and the train wouldn't wait long for members unable to keep up. The thought of Phoebe wandering off terrified Maisey, so she watched her daughter constantly while helping Avery with the mules. She set her daughter down on a large rock beside the wagon with firm instructions to stay put and went into the wagon circle where Avery was roping Jack, one of the lead mules. Avery held Jack while Maisey buckled on the mule's collar and fastened the harness assembly. She stepped back and glanced at Phoebe, finding her daughter contentedly gnawing her cornpone.

Maisey held Jack while Avery went after Buttercup, the other lead mule.

"Ma." Phoebe called to her from beside the rock.

"I told you to stay put." Maisey shouted to her daughter. Phoebe's face puckered, and she dissolved into tears. Maisey looked to Avery, but he was chasing down Buttercup. Another glance toward Phoebe confirmed her fears. Her small daughter had ventured farther into the wagon circle. "No, Phoebe. Stop!"

One of the mules thudded toward her daughter.

"Avery," Maisey called, her pulse pounding. He didn't turn his head. Busy roping Buttercup, he probably hadn't heard. Maisey let go of Jack and rushed toward her daughter.

She'd never reach her in time.

"Haw!" Conner Walsh sprang from between the wagons, waving his arms. Braying, the mule turned barely in time. The Irishman lifted Phoebe and patted her back. "There now, darling."

Maisey's face flamed. "Mr. Walsh, I'm in your debt again."

"Never mind that. Here's your daughter, safe and sound." He transferred Phoebe to her.

Maisey held her trembling child in arms that shook and buried her face in her unruly hair.

Conner Walsh looked past her to Avery. The expression on his face softened, and she knew he'd seen Avery's handicap. "You and your husband have your hands full with those mules, I see. I need to yoke my team, but then I'll come and help you. Meanwhile, I'm sure my sister would be more than happy to watch Phoebe while you help your husband."

"I'm sure she's busy," Maisey protested.

"I can do it." Natty, the Davis's oldest daughter spoke from the other side of chained wagon wheels. "We're almost packed. I'd love to watch Phoebe, if you don't mind lending her to me."

The oldest girl of the seven children belonging to Marsh and Ginny Davis, Natty must be fourteen or so. "I'd be obliged. Go and ask your Ma if she wants you watching a three-year-old."

"She sent me to ask."

"Thank you, then." Maisey needed no more prodding. She kissed Phoebe's forehead and transferred her to the girl. Phoebe went without a protest. "She's taken a shine to you."

Natty jostled Phoebe in her arms. "Children usually do."

"You'll be a good mother someday." Maisey exchanged a smile with the girl, then walked away with a sense of relief.

Avery stood with Buttercup's rope in his hand, eying the Irishman and his sister while Maisey hurried toward her husband. "Who was that man you were talking with?" he asked when she reached him.

"Connor Walsh? I met him and his sister Bryanna Brennan when Phoebe wandered away yesterday. Did you see Mr. Walsh rescue Phoebe? Charley bolted when you roped Buttercup." She glanced at the wheeler mule, already settling down. "Phoebe came into the circle trying to reach me, and he nearly ran her over."

Avery's forehead furrowed. "I'm sorry, Maisey. Going west hasn't worked out very well for us."

"It's bound to be rough in the beginning." Her bright tone belied her true feelings. "Thankfully, Natty Davis volunteered to watch Phoebe while we hitch the mules."

"Isn't she a mite young for the job?"

"I don't think so."

"I hope you're right. Phoebe's a lively one."

"It's only for a short while, and we can see right into the Marsh's camp from here."

"All right, I suppose, but I wish we had no need of assistance. " He looked around. "Where's Jack?"

"I let go of him when I ran to Phoebe, but he can't have strayed far."

Nick Laramie strode their way with Jack pacing like a domesticated dog beside him.

Avery nodded his head when the wagon guide reached them. "Much obliged."

Nick touched the brim of his hat to Maisey and turned his attention on her husband. "Looks like you could use some help."

"Thank you." Avery's face reddened. "Your offer frees my wife to tend our daughter." He nodded to Maisey, his meaning clear.

Bry reined in Kilkenny, restraining the mare's natural urge to run, which she'd held in check during the day's long ride. She knew more about horses than mules. Ian had bought her a paint mare early in their marriage. When Ian had sold Patches to settle his gambling debts, she'd been inconsolable. She pulled in a breath, then pushed the memory away on a long sigh. High time to think of pleasant things instead of dwelling on past hurts. Never mind that her body ached from too long in the saddle. She didn't have to walk, as some of the other women did.

Con, guiding the team from the back of one of the heeler mules, flicked a glance at her. "How are you holding up?"

"I'm fine, thank you very much." She stuck her tongue out at him.

He laughed. "You haven't lost your sass, I see."

"You bring it out in me."

"Well, in case you wondered, we should break for the night soon." He winked at her. "There'll be dancing later."

A smile tugged at her mouth. "Is that so?"

"Save me one, will you?"

"What, a dance?" Her smile escaped. "You'll be at the top of my list."

He sobered. "I'll hold you to that."

"Now you're meddling." She kept her tone light.

"And if I am? You'll never find another husband if you hide away like a nun. I want to be an uncle someday."

Her smile fled. "Your wish is doomed to failure, if you're counting on me."

They crested a rise and turned a bend as it started down the other side, diverting Con's attention while he called commands to their mule team.

"Don't speak too soon, Bry. A comely woman has trouble remaining single in the west." He treated her to his most impish smile. "But then again, giving such venomous looks may help you find a way."

At the sparkle in his eyes, her irritation vanished. "Such blarney! Tell me again why you haven't yet married."

"As I informed you, I haven't found anyone to ask. Most sensible women remain in the east."

"Instead of haring off to heaven knows where with their charming brothers? How wise."

Hoofbeats thudded behind them. Bry turned to see who approached, but the rise cut off her view. The side of a horse running past flashed across her vision. Mud splattered her skirts. Kilkenny flinched and shuddered. Bry curbed her mare, but just barely.

"Have a care!" Con shouted after the intruder.

The man rode back to them and doffed his hat, revealing hair the same chestnut as his horse's coat above a boyish face with a cleft chin. "Sorry, Ma'am."

"You startled my sister's horse." Con glared at the man. "What's the hurry?"

The man rode alongside them. "The Davis wagon had to stop for repairs. They asked me to tell the wagon master."

"Yes, well, easy does it," Con cautioned him. "There are

children about, and you might have injured my sister."

The intruder's gray gaze traveled over Bry, then slipped over her curves and upward to her eyes. "That would have been a crying shame." The corners of his mouth quirked into a slow smile that left her in no doubt where his mind had gone.

Bry looked away from him. Had the man no decency?

"Name's Thaddeus Taylor, but folks call me Thad."

Bry tightened her lips and made no answer.

A grin spread over her brother's face. "I'm Con Walsh, and my sister is the widow Brennan."

Bry's face flamed with an odd mixture of annoyance and embarrassment. Con's desire to be an uncle seemed to have blinded him to Thad Taylor's faults. From his bold looks and heedless riding, the man was obviously a rogue.

"Pleased to meet you both, and I hope to further our acquaintance." Thad Taylor's gaze swept over her again. He donned his hat and rode off in a spray of mud.

"Did a whirlwind just blow past?" Bry huffed.

Con laughed. "He's a force to be reckoned with, for certain. By the way he looked at you, he's smitten."

"Is that what you call it?" She quirked an eyebrow at her brother and bent to brush the mud from her skirts.

Con whistled. "Looks like he's stuck in your craw."

She gave up on her skirts and instead patted Kilkenny's neck to soothe her. "In case you wonder, I won't be getting any ideas about Mr. Taylor. I'm not interested in him or any other, for that matter." Weariness made her short-tempered, and she couldn't keep the edge from her tone. Con had her reaction to Thad Taylor all wrong, but she doubted he'd listen if she tried to set him straight. Fortunately, whether she courted again wasn't up to her bull-headed brother.

Thad Taylor had better keep well away from her.

CHAPTER EIGHT

NICK STOOD BESIDE BRETT COLTER'S WAGON watching Avery Wilcox fumble to remove the harness from one of his mules. Although he could accomplish the task in a few moments, Nick restrained the urge to assist. Once, in the winter, his mother's wolf had become caught in one of his father's traps. Nick had freed the wounded creature, but the wolf had run off before he could help it. He'd spotted it afterward, running with such strength and grace he hadn't at first noticed that its front leg hung useless. Avery's fierce determination to overcome his handicap reminded Nick of that wolf.

Coddling a crippled man would do him no favor. The very frustration that drew lines across Avery's forehead as the mule flicked its long ears and stomped in ill temper would teach him to endure. If time were short Nick would have stepped in, but now, as shadows lengthened and women called their families to supper, there was time to allow the crippled man to teach himself how to survive. The mule bolted with the bridle partly unfastened. Avery let loose an oath but went after him.

Much later, with the mules unhitched and Avery gathering harnesses from the ground where he'd dropped them, Nick strode to him.

"I suppose you saw all that." Avery spoke over his shoulder as he started for his wagon.

Nick picked up the rest of the collars and caught up with him. "Why'd you decide on mules anyway?" Nick wouldn't have chosen the long-eared animals for the crippled man. Although oxen were heavier, their docile natures made for easier handling. But then sometimes a man bought livestock to meet his future needs. If

Avery planned to mine, mules were the better choice. For farming, oxen served better.

"We're headed for Alder Gulch." Avery's face lit. "Folks say there's a powerful lot of gold for the taking there still."

Nick hesitated, but men consumed by gold fever seldom wanted advice. He could offer his experience, though. "I've heard the same stories, but I've also seen down-and-out miners come and go. There seem to be more lately from Alder Gulch."

"I reckon it'll take hard work."

"Stay away from the whiskey, and you'll improve your chances."

Avery smiled. "I'll steer clear. I have a family to think of."

Mention of Avery's family brought to mind the bruised look in his wife's eyes and the golden-haired child who scampered beneath her skirts. Nick spoke on impulse. "A mining camp isn't the best place to bring a wife and child."

Avery's face took on a determined look. "We'll adjust."

Nick shrugged. "I hope it works out. Meanwhile, I can help with the mules once in a while in the mornings, if I'm in camp. Sometimes I have to ride ahead."

The light in Avery's eyes died. "I appreciate the offer, but I can't pay you."

"Do you think I want your money?"

"Don't take it that way. I only meant that I would like to pay you out of gratitude. At least let me invite you to supper."

Nick set his jaw. "You don't want to do that."

Avery jutted out his chin. "I guess I know what I do and don't want to do."

Nick squinted in the low rays of the sun that snagged the branches of the cottonwoods along the Big Blue River. "But I'm half-Cheyenne."

Avery swung toward him. "What does that have to do with anything?"

Nick couldn't hold back his smile. "Nothing, I guess."

Bry set Phoebe Wilcox on her feet in the meadow at the edge of the wagon camp. The little darling danced in the sunshine, her golden curls bouncing.

Con, watching her from beside Bry, chuckled. "She's a fairy, I'm certain."

Phoebe sent Con a beckoning glance and scampered away on chubby legs. He surged after her, roaring like a bear, while she squealed with laughter. Con flung Phoebe's flailing body over his shoulder and stomped the meadow grass in a circle.

Bry put her hands on her hips as if to scold, but a smile tugged her mouth. "So, brother of mine, I see you've found a playmate."

Con gave her a glinting look out of his blue eyes. "You're quick with your tongue, as ever." He tossed Phoebe into the air above his head to the child's delighted screams.

Bry's heart pounded. "Have a care! I'm sure Phoebe's mother would like her back in one piece."

Con twirled Phoebe, and the little girl's giggles rose and fell. He set her down. After several wobbling steps, she thumped onto her bottom. Beyond Phoebe, picketed horses and mules tore at the tender spring grasses threaded with wild mint and clover.

Bry put a hand to the small of her back and stretched her aching muscles. My, she was tired. They'd taken few rests on today's journey.

Con stretched. "I'd better put up my tent and fill our water barrel. Guess you won't need to cook tonight. It was nice of you to take Phoebe off Maisey's hands and get us invited for supper."

Bry's cheeks warmed. She could read the truth behind Con's humor. He was undoubtedly relieved to have a break from her attempts at cooking. "Go on with you. That's not why I offered. Maisey had dark circles under her eyes today. It must be hard traveling with so young a child."

Con frowned, and his gaze searched her face. "This trip hasn't been easy on you, either."

She waved a hand. "I'm used to hardship." A year spent as a chamber maid hadn't prepared her for the rigors of life on the trail, but she didn't mention that. Neither of them could change the situation, so why cause Con to feel bad? She had to ride to spare the mules. Even if the wagon had been lighter and not crammed with supplies, the ruts in the trail would have made travel in the wagon uncomfortable. She was becoming used to long days in the saddle, but when she crawled into bed at night, she couldn't sleep until the cramping in her muscles lessened.

Con shouldered the water barrel and strode toward the river. Phoebe tottered behind him. Bry dashed after her. The little girl shrieked and broke into a run, but Bry chased her down and distracted her with a game of peek-a-boo.

The water barrel thunked into place on the wagon's sideboard. Phoebe watched with wide eyes as Con drove tent pegs into the ground. He finished pitching the tent and lifted the little girl to his shoulders. The Wilcoxes were only a few wagons away, but Con walked slowly, jouncing Phoebe with every step. Her hands covered his eyes, and Con pretended to stagger. Phoebe rewarded him with ecstatic screams.

Laughing at their antics behind her, Bry rounded the rear of the Wilcox's wagon. She caught a look of surprise on Nick Laramie's face before slamming into his chest. His strong arms caught and steadied her while his heart thudded beneath her ear. The aroma of wood smoke rose from his buckskin vest.

"Are you all right?" His husky voice vibrated in her ear.

"Yes." She tilted her head to look at him and felt her hairpins slip. He caught at her hair as if to arrest its slide. His fingers tangled in her tresses and lingered against her scalp.

A heady sensation swept over Bry. She should pull away but somehow didn't. He seemed more dangerous close up than he had at a distance. Despite the shortness of his dark hair, its sleekness proclaimed his wild heritage. His features appeared etched from mahogany, and he scanned her face with dark eyes. His gaze melted into hers. It seemed that, in a place beyond sight, their spirits touched. Without the strength of his arms, she might have sunk to the ground. Bry pulled in a breath and struggled to form words. *"Please."* She desperately needed to feel safe in her emotions, and the emotions this man roused in her did the opposite.

"Take your hands off my sister!" Con's voice thundered.

Bry jumped. She'd forgotten all about her brother.

Nick released her so quickly she almost fell, but his gaze clung to hers.

With an effort of will, she turned away from Nick and toward her brother. "It's my fault, Con. I should have looked where I was going."

"I saw what happened." Maisey called from beside the campfire, where she stirred a steaming pot with a long-handled spoon. "It was a pure accident."

Avery nodded from beside her. "That's a fact, Con."

"He has no call to take advantage of the situation." Con refused to back down. Phoebe fussed, and he swung her down from his shoulders, lowering her onto her feet. Phoebe ran to Maisey. Turning startled eyes on Con, she buried her face in her mother's skirts.

Bry captured her wayward hair with hands that shook. Blood rushed into her cheeks, making them tingle. *Had* Nick Laramie taken advantage of the situation? It hadn't felt that way, but she had no words for what had passed between them.

Con clenched his fists, going into the fighting stance she knew well from their childhood. At first she'd patched up his bruises and bloodied lips, but eventually he'd returned home with only his knuckles needing care.

Nick stood still, but tension radiated from him.

The last thing Bry wanted was for the two men to come to blows on her account. She pulled in a slow breath and racked her brain for something to say that would distract them.

"Maisey told you what happened, Con." Avery's quiet voice cut through the silence. "I'll thank you not to make trouble with a guest at my fireside. You've already frightened my daughter."

Relief washed through Bry at Avery's intervention.

Con seared Nick with a glare. "Apologize, and we can let the matter drop."

Avery opened his mouth to speak again.

"No, he's right." Nick looked to Con, and his throat moved as he swallowed. "Your sister is a beautiful woman, and I must have lost my head. It won't happen again."

"All right." Con eased into a more relaxed posture.

Nick Laramie's dark eyes fastened on Bry's. "I'm sorry."

Bry dipped her head by way of answer, her cheeks now burning in earnest. Even if she had known what to say, she couldn't have spoken around the lump in her throat.

"Come and eat." Maisey's voice sounded overly bright.

Nick held up his hands. "Thank you, but I'd better go."

Avery's forehead creased. "I'd like you to stay."

Nick shook his head. "That's not a good idea."

Bry waited for Con to speak, but he stood silent. She wanted to shake her brother. It wouldn't have hurt him to extend a little grace, especially after Nick's apology. She wished she could add her own invitation to Avery's, but doing so would make her seem forward.

Nick stepped backward. "I should try and get some sleep, anyway. I have sentry duty tonight."

"At least take a piece of cornbread away with you." Maisey pressed him.

"Thank you, Mrs. Wilcox, but I seem to have lost my appetite."

"Well, for later then." Maisey cut a slice from the cornbread loaf and wrapped it in a gingham napkin.

"Thank you, Ma'am. I appreciate your hospitality." Nick accepted her offering without further protest. "Good evening." He swept a glance to them all then cut across the wagon circle toward his tent.

The memory of being in his arms returned to Bry, unbidden. What would it be like to belong there? She shouldn't think such thoughts, especially since she wasn't likely to find out. Hadn't he promised it wouldn't happen again? Besides, she had her own reasons to avoid being trapped in a man's arms again.

She sat beside Con as they ate buffalo stew and cornbread, but the joy had gone out of the evening for her. Although she tried, she could think of little to say. Con also kept quiet while Avery and Maisey both looked strained and tired. Even little Phoebe fell asleep in her mother's lap.

Maisey rose to carry her daughter to bed. Bry stretched and stood as well. "I confess I'm ready to turn in. I suppose I'm not used to watching a three-year-old." She picked up her unwashed plate and reached for Con's. "Let me help with the washing up before I retire."

"Don't trouble yourself." Maisey reached for the stack of plates in Bry's hands.

She held on with a smile. "It's no trouble. I'm sure you're as exhausted as I am."

Maisey smiled right back. "All right, my friend. I can see your mind is made up. You can help."

Bry dried and stacked dishes on the trunk that Maisey used for a table. The men's voices, joined in conversation at the fireside, washed over her. She accepted another wet plate from Maisey and swiped it with her towel. "I hope you won't think badly of Con." She kept her voice low to avoid embarrassing her brother. "He wouldn't frighten Phoebe on purpose, but he can be hot-headed sometimes."

"Don't let it trouble you." Maisey handed her another wet plate. "Your brother didn't see what happened before he arrived, and I imagine he's protective of you."

Bry grimaced, releasing her pent feelings. "He is at that."

Maisey sighed. "Sometimes I wish I had a brother to look after me."

"Have you none?"

"I did once." Maisey's hands lay idle in the dishwater. "I was a disappointment to my family."

With the last dish dried and put away, Bry and Con took their leave from the Wilcoxes. Bry walked beside her brother toward their wagon with tree branches dark against a steely sky. Somewhere, a harmonica wailed. Bry waved to the Wallers, the older couple who had greeted them when they first arrived, but neither she nor Con stopped to talk with them.

"I'm going to bed." Bry told Con when they reached their camp. She made tracks for the wagon.

"Hold up," he said. "I want a word with you, if I may."

She frowned but turned to him. It wasn't hard to guess her brother's thoughts, but she wouldn't make this easy for him. She arched a brow. "Can't it wait until morning?"

"It's best to have this out now."

She sighed. "Must we?"

"Don't go getting ideas about Nick Laramie."

She tossed her head. "If I thought it was any of your business I'd set you straight, brother of mine."

"I'm making it my business," he ground out. "You're my only sister, Bry. I mean to watch out for you."

"Don't worry." She crossed her arms against a chill breeze that ran fingers along her skin. "I don't expect to remarry."

"I can tell you're not pining for Ian." He cocked his head. "Why would you want to deny me the chance to become an uncle?"

"I'll never pine for Ian." She heaved a steadying breath. "My husband used his fists on me whenever he was home long enough to notice me."

"Ah, I'm sorry, Sis. That's horrible. I should never have gone away."

"You can't blame yourself for Ian's wrongs. If you hadn't gone, you'd have no ranch to take me to now."

"But I'd have a sister who didn't fear men."

"I wouldn't call wisdom fear."

Her brother scowled. "I wish Ian were still alive so I could teach him a thing or two."

"Oh, Con." She put a hand on his arm. "Don't hate Ian on my account."

"Don't *you* hate him?"

"He gave me no reason to love him. His gambling stole the home out from under me, but that wasn't the worst thing he did to me." She tipped back her head and gazed at the faint outline of the full moon in the darkening sky. "He stomped every ounce of hope I owned under his boots. But I should let go of hating him. It only hurts me inside, as if he has never stopped hurting me."

"How can you find the heart to forgive the man?"

"I'm not sure I can. He took so much when I had so little—" She paused until the thickness in her throat cleared. "But I want to be free of what happened, not live it over and over. I'm trying to let go of the past."

"I'd still like to teach him how to treat a woman."

She gave him a tender smile. "Thank you."

His arms enfolded her, and his voice grumbled beneath her ear. "For what?"

"For wanting to protect me."

"I'm your brother, Bryanna. It comes with the territory."

She laughed and pushed against his chest. "Now, let me go before you crush me."

He released her. "I hope you find a man to trust. You're too young to remain a widow."

"Good night, Con."

His lips quirked. "I haven't given up on having lots of nieces and nephews to bounce on my knee."

"You've made that clear, but I'm thinking you need children of your own." She climbed the wagon steps.

"Bry!" Con's soft call followed her.

She turned back to him. "What now?"

"Tell me if anyone tries to bother you, all right?"

Irritation shot through her. "Of course, you mean Nick Laramie."

"It's not hard to tell that he's interested in you. It almost seemed that you liked him too. But remember, he's half Cheyenne."

She jammed her hands on her hips. "What I don't understand is how you can be so prejudiced, and you're Irish."

"Maybe that's why I know you're better off with your own kind. It's bad enough being from another country, let alone from another race. Life with Nick Laramie could only bring you misery."

She closed her mouth, which had dropped open. "You're taking this too far! I told you I have no interest in him."

"I hope that's true."

Long after she sank into the softness of her feather tick, Con's last words rang in her ears. How had he guessed her fascination with Nick Laramie? She'd kept it hidden. And if Con knew, could Nick know, too? What if he thought she'd run into him on purpose? Maybe that's why he'd responded as he had. The possibility mortified her. She'd never be able to look him in the eye again.

Memories of Ian flashed through her mind—his flushed face right before his fist bashed her eye. He'd hit her the first time for being late with supper, and it had taken days for her eye to open. Bewildered, she'd sobbed at his feet but believed his promise to never hurt her again.

The second time he struck her, she decided to leave him, but he'd begged for forgiveness with such passion she'd begun to hope he'd changed. Gathering her in his arms, he'd carried her to bed to comfort her. Relieved that she didn't have to figure out what to do without money or a place to go, she'd stayed with him, pretending for a little while longer that he would turn into the man she thought she'd married.

As the night wore on, the cramps in her legs from the day's long ride eased but her thoughts didn't let up. When an owl hooted outside the wagon, she knelt and parted the flaps to look out. The night breeze cooled her cheeks. Stars burned in a clear sky, and moonlight mantled the meadow. She couldn't locate the owl, which flitted from tree to tree, elusive as sleep.

Her conversation with Con had stirred things best left alone. She shouldn't have told him of Ian. He would only worry about her needlessly. She'd learned never to fully trust anyone, least of all herself. Bry sighed. She'd have to guard her own heart well, and she could do that best by avoiding Nick Laramie.

Nick stepped into a cottonwood's long shadow to avoid alarming Bryanna Brennan. He'd been on his way back when she peered from her wagon in the moonlight, wearing only a shift. Her hair framed her face and lay against the curve of her neck before falling over her shoulders. Nick's pulse picked up as the yearning to run his hands through her hair again kicked through him. A hooting owl recalled him, and he dragged his gaze away. Mindful that she didn't know he was there, he kept his gaze from straying back, even when she sighed. Strange. It sounded almost as if she wept. Had his behavior caused her pain? In the face of her brother's anger, he hadn't considered that idea.

What had come over him anyway? He'd held her longer than warranted and, with her softness in his arms, forgotten all sense.

Leaning against the cottonwood's trunk, he drank in the cooling night air. In the river beyond the wagons, a fish arched, raining silver droplets. Nick caught the glint of wings, and an owl glided to a perch above him. Horses picketed in the meadow stirred and thumped the ground with their hooves.

Bry's weeping faded. He turned his head to find that she'd backed away from the opening. At the loss of her presence, a curious ache assailed him. Nick strode toward the horses. He had other things to think about than Bry Brennan. For his own peace of mind, the sooner they parted ways, the better.

CHAPTER NINE

"COME ON, SIS. YOU WON'T FIND a better chance to kick up your heels." Con tilted his head toward the small crowd knotted around the wagon train's musicians at the edge of the encampment. Prairie grass waved in a gold and green tide about the laughing group. Above them, evening washed across the sky, and the setting sun dyed distant hills in shades of mauve.

Bry shook her head. "My feet are so cramped I can't imagine prancing about on them." She bit her lip, sorry to have called attention to her discomfort. Her legs still troubled her at night, but less than before. After weeks of riding fifteen or twenty miles a day, her stamina had improved.

Con winked at her. "Likely excuse! You don't have to dance if you don't want to, and you'd feel better with a little company."

"I'm not making it up," she answered him, stung. "I've said nothing about hurting until now because I didn't want you to fret over me. Now I see how wrong that was."

Con's smile slid away. "I know it's hard, Bryanna, but you'll toughen up."

"Stop that!" She blinked at the mist before her eyes.

"Stop what?"

"Looking at me with pity."

His smile crept back. "I don't always do as I'm bid."

"Neither do I." She scowled at him, but a smile tugged her lips.

He gusted a sigh. "You've grown into a cheeky *cailin*, and that's a fact."

It had been a while since anyone had called her a girl in Gaelic or English. Her smile broke free. "However that may be, this night I'll seek my bed early."

"Well, I won't twist your arm, but a little fun wouldn't hurt you any."

She shook her head at him. "Now you're meddling."

Con picked up his fiddle. "Seems like you could use a little help making up your mind now and again."

She laughed at the doleful look he gave her. "Good night to you."

He bowed elaborately then strode toward the gathering, but the slump of his shoulders betrayed his disappointment.

A shaft of remorse pierced Bry. "Con, wait!"

He shrugged without looking back.

She started after him but then stopped and turned into the wagon. Appeasing her brother would be a mistake. Hadn't the two years she'd tiptoed around Ian's moods taught her anything? She sat on the feather tick and massaged her aching limbs. Con would have to understand her hesitation to join in the merrymaking.

She could explain her withdrawal to him better if she understood it herself. All she knew was that being alone soothed her while time spent with others enjoying life reminded her of everything she'd missed in life.

Music and laughter drifted into the wagon, vibrating a chord of longing within her. Con was right. She needed people more than she'd realized. On impulse, she emerged from her wagon and picked her way in the fading light to the crowd circled around the dancers. Con's head came up, and he stopped playing his fiddle to bow to her while the banjo and harmonica carried on playing, "She is a Winsome Wee Thing."

Bry returned a playful smiled and dropped into a curtsy. She spotted Maisey beside Avery and went to her side.

"Where's Phoebe?" She raised her voice above the music.

Maisey smiled. "Mrs. Taylor took Phoebe under her wing." Bry followed her gaze across the dancers to where a trim woman with graying hair jostled Phoebe in her arms while speaking with a man Bry recognized. Thad Taylor and the graying woman both looked her way. Bry couldn't escape the feeling that she had been the topic of their conversation.

She leaned toward Maisey and spoke near her ear. "Is that mother and son?"

"They do look alike, don't they? Thad and Martha Taylor *are* mother and son. His father, Theo, should be somewhere near, as well as his uncle and sister"—Maisey sent her a bright glance—"but no wife."

Bry's cheeks warmed. "I fear I've given you the wrong impression."

Maisey laughed. "Noticing a comely man is normal. A woman ripe for marriage doesn't remain single for very long in the West, you know."

Bry frowned. "I'm not in need of a husband."

Maisey sobered. "Oh, I am sorry. I didn't think—"

"Please, don't trouble yourself—" Bry couldn't go on. How could she explain her hatred for Ian's memory and herself for marrying him? "It's not that." She protested feebly. She should have gone to bed after all, instead of letting the music and laughter draw her.

"Are you thirsty?" Maisey took advantage of a lull in the music to ask the question. "I made switchel, if you want some." She held up a ring-shaped canteen.

Bry had grown used to the ginger and molasses beverage some called "haymaker's punch." During the daily ordeal on the trail, she found its warmth comforting. The drink slaked her dry throat without cramping her stomach.

"Thanks for the offer. Perhaps later?"

"Of course. You'll work up a thirst dancing."

"Oh, I really don't think—" Bry's skin prickled with the sensation of someone watching her. She turned her head.

Thad's lips twitched into a crooked smile, and he closed one eye in a signal that spelled trouble. Bry jerked her gaze away. His blatant appraisal from across the circle made her skin crawl, and no man winked at a woman he thought proper.

"Bry! Whatever's wrong?" Maisey asked near her ear.

"It's nothing—a headache. Begging your pardon, but I need to lie down."

"I'll walk with you."

"That's not necessary." The space between Maisey's eyebrows puckered, and Bry softened her tone. "I—I'm fine. I only need to get away from the noise."

Maisey's frown deepened, but as Bry turned away, she made no move to stop her. "Sweet dreams."

Bry summoned a smile for Maisey, who couldn't know what it meant to be a widow or Irish. "Good night to you." She skirted the meadow in the direction of her wagon with her conscience smiting her. She shouldn't have worried Maisey that way, although her fabricated headache had become real.

She stopped to breathe in the cool night air and watch the dancers sashay in the firelight. A part of her wanted to return, but she ignored the urge. Maybe another day.

"Well, well." A hand circled her upper arm. "Waiting for me?"

Nick rolled onto his side and settled deeper into his furs, trying to shut out the sounds from the meadow in Ash Hollow. If only the merrymakers would quiet so he could sleep, but he couldn't blame them for celebrating the chance to rest from the journey, especially after the arduous descent of Windlass Hill. The previous day had been hard on body, soul, and mind. Tonight, they would sleep beneath tall trees and beside budding roses in a green meadow where sweet waters flowed.

He'd yet to meet anyone who knew for certain how Windlass Hill came by its name. Some folks swore it described the fact that they'd need a windlass to lower their wagons, whereas others believed a windlass had once perched there. This group had come down the steep incline without incident, but as a trail guide, he'd witnessed countless mishaps. Even with wheels locked and all available hands holding onto ropes to slow them, sometimes wagons busted loose. While women screamed and men shouted, panicked livestock hurtled downward. When the pall of dust lifted men, beasts, and wagons lay broken beyond repair.

Nick turned on his back to dispel the memories. Such thoughts did nothing to encourage sleep. Starlight blazed in the sky. The meadow grasses stirred, and wind sighed across his face. Wolves howled on the edge of hearing.

The many choruses of "Oh! Susanna" rang out amid laughter.

Was Bry lying awake too? An image of her looking out from her wagon by moonlight rose in his mind's eye. He'd watched her despite himself, captivated by her beauty but also by the sadness that clung to her. He'd never seen her join the wagon encampment's celebrations. Why? Brett had told him she was a widow. She must grieve for her husband. Would she someday leave sorrow behind and marry again? What would it be like to have the right to taste her kisses?

Nick groaned. Such thoughts could get him whipped or worse. He shoved them away, but the fierce longing to hold her remained to torment him.

He shifted onto his side again. Tomorrow he'd scout ahead—anything to remove himself from temptation.

A flicker of movement at the edge of the meadow captured his attention as Bry walked along the edge of the meadow. Moonlight pearled her face and gleamed in the dark hair rippling down her back. She glanced around as if nervous, then stepped into a shadow beneath the ash trees.

A man followed her with furtive movements.

Nick crept toward the two figures outlined in dappled moonlight.

The man hauled Bry toward him, but she jerked away. "What do you think you're doing?"

"Come on darlin'," Thad Taylor's voice growled. "Don't make me beg."

Nick hesitated. Maybe he'd been wrong about Bry grieving her husband. Had he stumbled onto a lover's spat?

"Let go of me!" Bry pushed away from Thad.

"Why play coy? I saw you watching me across the dancers."

She edged farther from him. "I'm afraid you have mistaken my interest, Mr. Taylor."

"I reckon so." Thad adopted a rueful tone. "But honestly, when you waltzed off after staring at me, I thought you meant me to follow."

Bry put her hands on her hips. "Well, I didn't."

Thad shifted closer to her. "There's no call to get on your high horse, Madam. I know when a woman admires me."

"And I know when a man insults me."

"Listen to you." Thad leaned toward her intimidatingly. "Anyone would think you were a society lady instead of a—"

"That's enough." Nick stepped out of the shadows.

Thad grunted. "This explains things, I guess."

"Back away from the lady." Nick barely managed to keep his tone civil.

"She's no more a lady than you're a white man."

Nick restrained the urge to drive a fist into Thad's mouth. "Better move on."

Thad's gaze raked Bry, now poised to flee. "Can't a man come a-courtin'?"

Bry tossed her head. "I want nothing to do with you."

"Let's see if I can't change your mind." Thad turned without warning and landed a punch to Nick's jaw. "Touch her, and I'll see you hanged."

Nick picked himself up from the ground but held his tongue. He'd learned long ago to watch and wait when faced with a rattlesnake.

Thad spun on his heel and strode off.

"Thank you." Bry's voice trembled. "Are you all right?"

"I think so." Nick worked his jaw to make sure it wasn't broken. "Did he hurt you?"

"No. At least, not in ways that matter." Her laugh held a bitter note. "It's always the same. Men think because I'm a widow I'll welcome advances. And since I'm Irish I must be a—a fancy woman."

Nick gazed at her, mystified. "What does being Irish have to do with, well with—"

She stared at him. "You really don't know. In the slums Irish women sometimes go astray to feed their families."

He frowned. "What are slums?"

Her eyes widened, and she laughed.

Nick stiffened. He was used to unkindness, but her laughter wounded him. Had he somehow made a fool of himself?

Her mirth died, and she touched his arm. "I'm sorry. I didn't mean to offend you. It surprised me that you know nothing about slums. I wish I could say the same. They are cruel prisons that cage the poor."

He ached to soothe the sorrow her voice revealed but resisted the urge to cover her hand with his own. "What do *you* know of slums?" He should have kept his tone neutral, but instead it caressed her. He heard the hitch of her breath, and her hand withdrew.

"I should go." She set off beneath the trees.

He'd gone too far, and she'd had the good sense to flee. Why then, did he object to her wise solution? "Wait."

She looked back to him in the shifting moonlight filtering through the cottonwoods. "Thank you for defending me, but I always seem to get you into trouble. You really should stay away from me."

He agreed but trailed her until she reached the safety of her wagon anyway.

CHAPTER TEN

NICK HEAVED HIS SADDLE ONTO TAVO'S back. At the thud of footsteps behind him, he glanced over his shoulder.

Brett walked toward him in the wagon circle, one eye squinted against the morning sun. "You look like a plate of yesterday's dinner."

"That so?" Nick ignored the pain from his cut lip and bent to tighten Tavo's girth strap.

Brett scratched his whiskers. "Want to tell me where that bruiser on your jaw came from?"

"Not especially." Nick lifted his saddlebags and fastened them into place. When Brett made no answer, he turned his head and discovered the wagon master still watching him.

"It's my business, you know," Brett said in a quiet voice.

Nick picked up his canteen and tied it to the saddle without replying. He wouldn't willingly say anything that could compromise Bry's reputation.

The wagon master came around Tavo and spoke across the horse's back. "This doesn't have anything to do with the fact that Thad Taylor is grouchy as an old bear this morning, now does it?"

"Ask him that question."

Brett narrowed his steely eyes. "I'm talking to you."

Nick raked a hand through his hair. "All right, yes. It does."

"Now we're getting somewhere." Brett nodded approvingly. "So, what happened between you two?"

Nick dusted off his hat before answering. "We didn't see eye-to-eye."

"That's clear. And?"

Nick hadn't meant to snap. "Look, can we just leave it at that?"

"I'd like to, but I don't abide fighting in my camp."

"I know, I know."

"You got a grievance with someone, bring it to me."

"All right." Nick put on his hat and pulled the brim down to shade his eyes.

"I suspect I know what this was all about, anyway."

"What do you mean?" Nick kept his voice even.

"I got eyes in my head."

Nick slanted a glance to him and waited as Brett chewed his lip.

"Least said, soonest mended, I expect," the wagon master muttered. "But no more fighting, you hear?"

"You can't mean that!" Bry stared at Con. "Tell me you're joking."

Her brother, seated before the fire, looked up from his plate of wilted cabbage, bacon, and potatoes. "Do you dislike Thad Taylor, for some reason?"

"I don't trust him."

"He's a bit rough, but he handles a horse well. He asked for a job, and I need a ranch hand. Exactly why do you object to my hiring him?"

"I just do, that's all."

His eyebrows shot upward. "You seem to have a strong reaction to Thad for no reason at all. Want to tell me something?"

"There's nothing to tell." She answered quickly and regretted her haste when a knowing look crept over Con's face.

"Well, well. Like that, is it?"

Con had the wrong idea, but Bry murmured something vague in response. If she told him what had happened, he might pick a fight with Thad. She had little doubt that her street-hardened brother could win such a confrontation, but she preferred not to be the object of one. Folks would come to their own conclusions about her as a result. Ugly rumors would fly. Nick might be dragged into the mess. Why she cared so much about protecting the trail guide was a question she wouldn't ask herself.

The notion of Thad's working, breathing, and living anywhere in her vicinity made her stomach churn. Sitting across from Con, she barely choked down a meager portion of the baked beans with johnnycakes Maisey had taught her to cook over the campfire. She'd made suppers when married to Ian, but not over open flames.

Con cleared his plate without commenting on her lack of appetite. He stood and stretched. "I'm for bed early tonight."

She nodded. "I don't blame you. I'm weary myself."

"I wasn't this tired after climbing California Hill."

Bry remembered the long ascent in vivid detail. "I wish we hadn't abandoned our stove."

"We had to. You know that. Otherwise, we might have lost the mules on the climb to Windlass, or in coming down. Don't concern yourself over a stove, Bry. I'll have another freighted by wagon. As it was, even with their load lightened, the mules complained the whole way up the hill, and then stampeded to water in Ash Hollow."

"You're right, of course." But somehow leaving the stove behind had seemed so final. She wasn't much for cooking, but a stove provided more than a hot meal. It warmed a house in winter plus heated water for bathing and washing. She couldn't get used to the constant dirt on the trail, which formed mud when the spring rains fell or hazy clouds when they didn't. The dust penetrated everywhere. She found it in her clothing and high-topped boots — even in the pores of her skin. Like the other women in the train, she looked forward to a chance to do the wash.

Bry covered the beans, gathered the tin dishes, and scoured them with sand before rinsing them clean. She hung her dishtowel to dry over a waist-high clump of sagebrush and smiled at the snoring from Con's tent. Too keyed up to follow his example, she made her way to Maisey's camp.

Maisey sat on an upturned crate across the fire from Avery.

Beside her, Phoebe spooned beans into her mouth with a chunk of cornpone clutched in her fist. "You're welcome to join us—and your brother too, of course."

"That's a kind invitation, but we've already taken supper."

"Then perhaps a slice of dried apple pie?"

Bry summoned a smile. "Thank you, no."

A small crease formed between Maisey's eyes. "A little tea?"

"Really, I'm fine. I thought you might have finished supper and want company." Bry stepped backward. "I shouldn't intrude."

Maisey shook her head in gentle reprimand. "You could never do that."

Avery smiled. "If you'd care to sit, please do so."

Little Phoebe gnawed on her cornpone and watched her with such gravity Bry couldn't help but laugh. "All right. You've persuaded me." She perched on an overturned crate near Maisey, who had risen and stood poised to help her. "But please, sit down and finish your supper."

"All right, if you're sure there's nothing I can offer you." Maisey sank back onto her crate and picked up her plate. Phoebe crowded against her mother's skirts and opened her mouth for another bite of beans.

Bry smiled but then noticed that Avery balanced his plate on his knees and leaned far down to eat. Quick sympathy sprang within her. It had to be difficult to do everything one-handed. Until now, he'd made it look easy. He lifted his head, and widened his eyes but didn't point out her rudeness in staring.

"I—I've forgotten my manners. Please forgive me." She averted her gaze at once. The cookfire's flames couldn't be hotter than her face.

"Where's your brother?" Maisey spoke into the silence.

"Riding with the ancient kings of Tara, for all I know. He's asleep." Her attempt at humor sounded strained to her own ears. She stole a glance at Avery.

He'd set his half-emptied plate aside and now stood. "As I will be soon."

Maisey jumped to her feet. "But you haven't finished your supper!"

"I don't want it."

Guilt flooded Bry. If only she hadn't stared at him. She must have made him self-conscious. She bit her lip, loath to apologize and possibly cause him further discomfort.

"Goodnight." Avery spoke in a clipped tone, but his parting glance included Bry.

Maisey waited until the wagon flap closed behind him before turning to her. "I'm so ashamed. It's not like Avery to be rude. What must you think?"

"No, this is my fault." Bry kept her voice low. "I embarrassed him by watching him eat."

Unshed tears stood in Maisey's eyes. "It's natural to be curious. Avery knows that, and I'm sure he doesn't blame you. Your reaction may have reminded him of when, well of—"

Understanding dawned. "You mean..." Bry hesitated, "... of when he was injured?"

The tears tipped onto Maisey's cheeks, and she brushed them away. "He can't seem to leave it behind. He doesn't always say when memories come, but I can tell they torment him. Sometimes in his dreams, he relives the day it happened."

"I'm so sorry."

Maisey brushed away her tears. "I'm certain he'll recover, given time."

"I don't know how a person can get over an event so cruel."

Phoebe ran to the crate where Avery had sat. Her chubby fingers grabbed an uneaten portion of cornpone and lifted the prize to her mouth. The plate wobbled and tumbled to the ground, spilling its contents. Phoebe's eyes widened, then her face screwed up, and she let out a wail. Maisey's sigh sounded tired.

Bry jumped up. "Let me." After upsetting the entire family, calming Phoebe was the least she could do. She caught the child's squirming body into her arms, but then Phoebe quieted and laid her head against Bry's chest.

Maisey smiled approval. "She's taken to you."

Holding Phoebe close, Bry sat down with the overturned plate at her feet.

Phoebe gazed up at her in wonder. With gentle fingers, she touched the droplets that fell to Bry's cheeks.

Bry hiccoughed on tears and laughter.

"Why, whatever's wrong?" Maisey asked.

"I must be . . . overwrought tonight. My little brother . . . was just Phoebe's size . . . when he died with Mam. Sometimes she reminds me of Liam."

"Oh, you poor lamb. Your brother and mother, too? I knew something was wrong tonight. Are you missing them?"

Bry let out a shaky breath. "I do, off and on, but it all happened long ago. It shouldn't affect me so."

Maisey extricated her daughter from Bry's arms and spoke above Phoebe's golden curls. "Grief doesn't mind its manners, Bry, but comes and goes at its own will."

Bry scrubbed the tears from her cheeks. " I shouldn't have given way to my grief, not in light of your own difficulties."

"Nonsense. I consider you a friend, and friends share their troubles."

She smiled. "I think of you the same way."

"So then, tell me, what happened to make you miss your mother?"

Bry clasped her hands together. "Con said something amiss."

Maisey shifted Phoebe in her arms. "Do you want to talk about it?"

"It's not important." Burdening Maisey further tonight would be unthinkable. In light of the Wilcox's troubles, her upset over Thad now seemed petty. What had he done, really, but mistake her interest in him? *And take her for the wrong kind of woman.*

She pushed the discomfiting thought away. She could accept Con's choice of a ranch hand, so long as Thad kept well away from her.

Bry woke to stabbing pain and barely managed to stifle a moan. Flexing her foot, she massaged her calf muscle until the pain eased. At least as her body grew used to the rigors of the trail, the cramps came less often. The light filtering through the wagon bonnet was still faint, so she nestled down into the feather tick and composed herself for a few minutes more sleep.

Muffled thuds like the beating of hooves crowded the edge of hearing. Her mouth went dry, and she sat up, straining to hear above her ragged breathing. Could Indians be stealing the livestock?

She eased to her feet, swung a shawl across her shoulders, and closed her hand over the stock of the rifle beside the bed. Con had taught her to shoot, but she had no confidence in her ability to hit anything. Hopefully, she wouldn't need to fire.

Two steps took her to the rear of the wagon, and with nerveless fingers she fumbled to untie the pickle string. At last it gave, and she widened the opening to peer out with rifle poised.

The wagon camp slept beneath a pewter sky. Nothing stirred but a strand of hair the wind whipped against her cheek.

Bry stepped out of the wagon and went down the rear steps into the grass. The dark shape of Con's tent hunched a few paces away, but she wouldn't wake him unless it became necessary. Perhaps she had only dreamed of hoofbeats.

Where was the sentry? She looked past the silent mounds that were oxen slumbering and caught the gleam of a rifle across the wagon circle. Tension drained from her. All was well.

The thump of distant hoofbeats reached her.

Bry jerked toward the sound. On the open prairie, a lone Indian leaned over a jet-black horse galloping in a circle. She opened her mouth to call for Con, but no sound came. She raised the rifle to her shoulder and tried to steady it with shaking hands. Why didn't the guard shout the alarm? He should have noticed something wrong by now. As clouds raced across the moon, the running horse disappeared into shadow. It emerged with the Indian gone from its back.

Bry gaped. Had she lost her mind? But then she spotted the man hanging low from the horse's side.

How could he cling there without falling off? He pulled to his knees on the horse's back, maneuvering with such grace he seemed to dance.

Bry lowered the rifle. Not only was the Indian out of range, but he seemed familiar. He was too far away to tell for certain, but she could swear…

The horse turned, and the rider jumped to his feet, balancing on the running creature with knees bent and arms extended. Bry closed her gaping mouth. Such a feat did not seem possible. She must be dreaming, after all.

The Indian dropped into a seated position. He must have seen Bry, for he slowed his horse and rode toward camp. About to call out, she stopped herself when she caught sight of the one-armed sentry, his rifle shouldered, watching the rider. Avery would not adopt that casual posture for the approach of an Indian.

The rider had to be Nick. A few minutes later he reached the wagons. Avery backed to allow him inside the wagon circle, then chained the opening he'd made.

Nick started toward Bry, the moonlight shining across his face.

To keep from waking her brother, she walked toward Nick. "That was beautiful. I've never seen such riding."

He reined his horse to a stop. "Thank you. I don't find much chance to practice, but I woke early this morning, and Avery didn't mind letting me out."

"I wonder that you're willing to leave the safety of camp."

"Duty often requires it of me. I don't fear the wilderness, Mrs. Brennan. It has nurtured me all my life."

The tilt of his head made her suddenly aware she stood barefooted and with her hair pulling out of its plait. She wore only her shift but thankfully had covered herself with a shawl.

Mumbling something, she backed away.

Nick vaulted from the horse and landed on his feet with ease. "Sorry if I disturbed your night's rest."

Remembering the reason for the other apology he'd given her, Bry couldn't meet his eyes. "Where did you learn to ride like that?" she asked to cover her embarrassment.

"Among my mother's people, the Cheyenne."

"Did you live with them?"

"Once." The terse word gave away nothing.

She didn't blame him for his reluctance. Why should he tell her anything about himself? And yet she longed to know more about him. That fact pulled her up short. "I should go."

"Wait." His voice stopped her, and she turned.

He closed the distance between them. "When my father died and I was still a boy, my mother took me to live with her people." He spoke just above a whisper. "My mother's brother, Nahkohe, took me in hand and taught me the things I would need to know as a man—how to ride, hunt, and even how to treat a wife. He imagined I would fit into the tribe."

"Didn't that happen?"

"No." The word throbbed in the air. He turned his head, looking away toward the river.

She saw the dark stain of a bruise on his jaw. Thad must have done that. Quick sympathy sprang through her, and the urge to touch him took possession of her, but she curled her hands into fists instead. The silence between them lengthened. Bry bit her lip, loath to leave. "Your horse handles well."

"I've trained Tavo since he was a colt."

"Tavo? Is that a Cheyenne name?"

"Yes. It means 'black horse.'"

"Tavo." She tested the name on her tongue. "That's beautiful."

The dark horse flicked his ears and brought his head up from grazing.

Bry laughed. "Look, he knows we're talking about him."

"Tavo likes women's voices. My mother and sister spoiled

him."

"You have a sister?" As soon as the words left her mouth, she wished to recall them. "I—I'm sorry. It was forward of me to ask."

"My sister is called Monevata, which means Rising Bird. She lives with our mother's people."

"But you don't." What madness had taken hold of her? She seemed unable to control her tongue. If he'd wanted to talk about his family or his living arrangements, he'd already have done so. She drew a steadying breath. "I know what it means to feel like you don't belong." She followed his gaze to where silver light cut across the Platte River in a path to the full moon, which hung low in the sky.

He turned toward her. "It's almost morning. When the camp wakes, you shouldn't be found alone with me."

"No." He was right, but somehow, she couldn't quite break the invisible tie that bound her to him.

He stepped closer and tilted her face. His thumb stroked her cheek, and her knees went weak.

"I should go." But she remained with him.

"Yes." His head bent, and his mouth followed his breath to brush hers in a soft caress. Her lips tingled, warming against his, and her heartbeat quickened. Long-buried longings stirred within her. She pressed closer in his arms and yielded to his kiss. What had started as simple exploration deepened into unbridled passion. Bry clung to him, swept by the power of the force that joined them.

He groaned low in his throat. "Yes."

Bry pressed the back of her hand to her mouth and pulled in air. "This can't happen."

A look of pain crossed his face. He stepped away from her and turned away.

CHAPTER ELEVEN

"W ELL, WELL. S O THAT'S HOW THE wind blows." Avery's low voice greeted Nick.

He could just make out Avery seated on his wagon tongue, a rifle beside him as he took his turn at sentry duty. "That particular wind might turn into a *hevovetäso.*"

"And what, pray tell, is a hay-vo-we-tess?"

"A whirlwind."

Avery's laugh, although quiet, sounded loud in the stillness. "Love can feel like that."

Annoyance pushed Nick into speech. "Nothing can come of it."

"What makes you say that?" Avery's tone held compassion.

Nick reminded himself to keep his voice down. "How can you even ask that question? You see what I am, what she is."

"I saw plenty just now."

"That was a—mistake. If her brother saw me, he'd attack me. Even if I won against him, I'd still lose."

Avery let out a low whistle. "It's like that, is it?"

"You saw his reaction the other day. He'll never let his sister marry someone like me. And even if he would, plenty of other people wouldn't want to let it happen."

"What about you?"

Yes, what about me? He shrugged. "I don't matter."

"You're wrong about that, my friend. I saw horrible things in the war. Enough to teach me that every life counts, or at least it should." He stood and faced Nick. "You have to take hold of what you want."

"Even if it means bringing pain to someone you care about?"

"Let her choose whether the joy is worth the sorrow."

"Did you allow your own wife that privilege?" Nick regretted the words at once. He'd gone too far, and he knew it.

"What's that supposed to mean?" Avery's tone took on a decided sharpness.

"Never mind."

"No, now you've started, finish your thought."

Nick chose his words with care. "It seems to me that a person with an injury such as yours might be better off living in town. The frontier demands a lot out of a man."

"I can do this." Avery emphasized every word.

"Why do you want to? You have nothing to prove."

"You're wrong about that." Avery paced back and forth, but then came to rest before Nick. "I won't let you turn this on me. We were talking about you."

"Me? I'll always have to prove myself."

"I'm not sure that claim holds merit."

"What do you know about my life?"

"Maybe more than you guess. People don't look me in the eye either."

Nick's breath hissed between his teeth. He didn't have to ask what Avery meant. He'd seen enough cruelty against anyone who looked different to know.

"I'm half a man in some people's eyes." Avery went on. "But I'm not willing to let what others think keep me back. I suggest you do the same."

A welcome current lifted tendrils that had escaped Bry's pins. She set down the wooden pails she carried and adjusted the ties beneath her neck so her bonnet fell backward off her head. She shook her hair free and closed her eyes as the breeze combed her tresses. How she loved the cool before evening. At such a time, going to the river to haul water didn't count as a chore.

"Wait a moment and I'll come with you." Maisey called from behind her. Normally, Bry would have welcomed company, but after long days of riding in the heat, she felt raw in body and soul. Waiting for Maisey, she looked back to the Wilcox's camp.

Thad watched her from beside Maisey's cooking fire. He gave her a glinting look before turning again to Avery and Maisey. What were they talking about with such intensity? Thad moved on to the next wagon camp, where he went into a huddle with Marsh Davis.

Uneasiness stirred in Bry's stomach. *Something must be wrong.*

Maisey joined her, and together they followed the faint trail that led to the river. They met Natty Davis on the path.

"Good afternoon." Maisey nodded at the girl. "Thanks again for watching Phoebe the other day."

"She was no trouble." The girl's sweet smile lifted Bry's spirits. "Ma says I can watch her whenever you want."

Maisey's expression lightened. "I'm thankful for that. Mornings are hardest, so if your Ma can spare you then, I'd appreciate your help."

"She'll let me, I'm sure." Beaming, Natty passed them and hurried down the trail without spilling water from her buckets.

Bry laughed. "She's thrilled to bits."

"That makes two of us."

Bry sobered. "Should you ever need me to take Phoebe off your hands, I'm more than willing."

Maisey's eyes brightened with moisture. She averted her gaze, blinking. "That's kind of you."

"Nonsense. I want the chance to hold that little darling again, and I'm sure Con wouldn't mind, either."

The path crested a small rise before going down to the bank, where the gurgling of water met them. Wind rippled the swollen surface of the Platte and birds trilled in the grasses growing right up to its edges.

Maisey stepped onto a large flat stone that jutted into the river and bent to fill her buckets.

"What news did Mr. Taylor bring?" Bry couldn't resist asking.

Maisey straightened with her buckets not yet filled. "I meant to tell you. It's Mrs. Wallers. She's taken a turn for the worse."

"But they took out her septic tooth."

"Maybe not soon enough. She kept her misery to herself longer than she should have, afraid to have it pulled."

"Mr. Wallers lagged behind and brought his wagon into camp late the last two nights to spare her the worst of their wagon's jostling. Now she can't tolerate even that. Tomorrow we'll lay by for her sake, but it may be too late." Maisey brushed the back of her hand over her eyes. She filled her buckets and stepped off the rock.

"But she was going to visit her sister." Bry didn't know Mrs. Wallers especially well, but the woman had been kind when she and Con arrived in camp. Since then, the Wallers's had exchanged greetings and a word or two whenever they met. They'd even traded desserts once. Elmira Wallers made a delicious bread pudding. Bry frowned. It didn't seem possible that she might never hear the woman's throaty laugh again.

"Pray for her, Bry, and then leave her to God."

Balanced on the flat rock, Bry found looking into the flowing water dizzying. She dropped to her knees and squeezed her eyes shut. Might as well pray while in this position. She wasn't any good at speaking with the Almighty, but she had to do something. *God, you can't let Mrs. Wallers die. Mr. Wallers needs her, and her sister is expecting her.*

"Bry," Maisey whispered.

She opened her eyes. A stag, poised to step, stood on the opposite bank of the river. Scenting the air with nostrils flared, the stag stared back at her for a breathless moment. An ache pulsed through Bry at the creature's wild beauty. The poetry of the moment rendered her speechless.

Children's chatter wafted from the direction of camp, and the deer bounded away.

"Wasn't he magnificent?" Maisey whispered the words on a note of awe.

"Oh yes."

"Of course, Avery would want to shoot him."

"Con would too." Bry dipped one of her buckets and watched the clear water swirl into it. "There's a lot to be said for venison on the table, I suppose." Bright droplets sprayed as she raised the bucket and plunked it onto the flat rock. Water ran down its wooden sides into a small puddle at her feet. "Still, I'm glad our stag got away." She lowered the second bucket into the silken flow.

Maisey sighed "I'm sorry Mrs. Wallers is so ill. It's selfish to say this, but I'm glad for a chance to do laundry and wash the dirt from my hair. It feels so stiff and gritty."

"Don't fault yourself." Bry hoisted her buckets. "You're just being practical. Besides, Mrs. Wallers may not die."

"It seems likely."

"I don't know. Maybe God sent that deer while I was praying for Mrs. Wallers as a sign of His intentions."

"Whatever those might be. I hope she recovers, but if she doesn't we can comfort ourselves in the knowledge that heaven is a nobler place. I'd like to take Mr. Wallers supper and see if I can help somehow. Will you—"

"Watch Phoebe?" Bry grinned. "If I must."

Nick stabbed his shovel into the earth, dusted off his hands and picked up his hat.

Wallers knelt on the other side of the shallow grave Nick had filled, rocking as he sobbed. His wife had succumbed in the night. Members of the wagon train clustered behind the new grave, their heads bent in prayer. All but Bry, who stared at Wallers with tears glistening. Nick resisted the urge to go to her. Neither her brother nor Thad Taylor would allow him to comfort her.

"For all flesh is as grass, and all the glory of man as the flower of grass." Brett read from the Bible, his voice rising and falling. "The grass withereth, and the flower thereof falleth away."

Con put his arm around Bry, and she turned her face to his shoulder.

Nick bent his head in prayer.

"But the word of the Lord endureth forever." Brett closed his Bible with a thump. "Elmira Louise Wallers, may you rest in peace."

The rushing of the river, ever present, waxed loud. Maisey laid a wildflower posy on the grave and touched Wallers's shoulder. She returned to her husband's side, and the two moved off toward the encampment. Others did the same. The crowd thinned until only Nick remained with the man still weeping over his wife's grave. A shift in his posture told Nick that Wallers knew he stood nearby. Eventually the man stopped weeping, and Nick stepped forward to help him rise.

Squinting his reddened blue eyes, Wallers and clasped Nick's hand. His skin shone pale against Nick's. "Thank you for staying with me."

"It wasn't anything." He pulled the man to his feet and steadied him with a hand to his elbow.

"You're wrong about that." Wallers swung about to peer at him. "It meant a lot, and I'm grateful."

"You're welcome."

Wallers' face puckered. "My wife was all the family I had left. We couldn't bear children, but loving a good woman was enough for me." He drew a shaky breath. "Now she's gone, I have no one."

Nick put an arm around the grieving man's shoulders. "Let's go back to camp." Wallers cast a lingering glance at the grave. "The Missus would want me to take care of myself." He squared his shoulders and turned away.

Nick kept pace beside him along the trail toward camp. Bry walked toward them before they reached it. Wearing a high-necked blue dress and with her hair up, she looked fresh and sweet. The wind whipped a few dark locks across her face, stirring the memory of her hair slipping through his fingers. Nick murmured something as they met, but her attention was mostly for the bereaved man by his side.

"Maisey sent me to fetch you, Mr. Wallers. It's time to eat." She fell into step alongside him and described the fare in a soothing voice. Nick held back and let them go without him. He had no taste for joining in the muted laughter. He had never understood how people could so quickly exchange the sorrow they displayed at a graveside.

About to skirt the camp to reach his tent, Nick checked. He'd seen . . . yes, there . . . a black horse galloping from the west, a rider bent over its back. It would take a while for the rider to reach them.

The grass swished behind him, and Brett appeared at his side.

Nick repressed his start. He'd been so caught up in watching the distant rider, he had nearly missed Brett's approach.

Narrowing his eyes to steely slits, the wagon master watched the rider approach. "Who can that be, all by himself?"

Nick squinted into the distance. "He's wearing a Union uniform."

"Fort Sedgwick is two days' travel yet. What's a soldier doing so far east?"

"Good question. Let's hope there's no trouble ahead."

"Did you say something about trouble?" Thad Taylor joined them beside Brett.

"Now, let's not jump to conclusions. We don't know anything yet." But Brett's creased brow gave away his suspicions.

The horse and rider vanished into a dip in the trail but swung into view at the next rise. The hoofbeats drummed louder every moment. The soldier pulled up a small distance from them and waved an arm.

"What's he doing?" Thad asked.

Brett nodded toward Nick. "Let's go find out what he wants." Thad started out with them, but Brett turned on him. "I don't recall sending you an invitation to the party. Wait here."

Thad frowned, but when they set off again, didn't follow. Nick managed not to grin. He really shouldn't rejoice, but if anyone needed a set-down, it was Thad Taylor.

Bry turned Mr. Wallers over to Maisey and looked around for Con. She bit her lip. Thad stood alone at the edge of camp, watching Nick and the wagon master walk toward a man on horseback. How odd. Whatever the disturbance, it would draw attention. She'd better catch Thad now, while he was alone, and no one would notice. Her stomach tightened at the thought, but she stiffened her spine. Her skirts swished in the grass as she walked toward him. If anyone saw her seek Thad's company, there'd be talk, but she couldn't let herself care about that. Certain things needed to be said, and the sooner the better.

Thad looked around as she neared. "Mrs. Brennan." He lifted his bowler hat and his eyebrows. "You surprise me."

She nodded in greeting, cautioning herself not to react to his obvious gloating. No point in getting his back up from the start. "I guess that makes us even."

His smile slipped.

"My brother tells me he hired a ranch hand."

A teasing light glinted in his eyes. "I'm touched you'd mark the occasion."

Anger flared through her, but she tamped it down. "What are you up to?"

"Nothing, darlin', that you won't want."

She stared at him. *Has the man entirely lost his mind?* "You're dreaming again."

"You don't say?" He chuckled. "I wouldn't mind waking up next to you."

"You'll never have the chance." Bry tossed her head. "Why not accept that? Con can find someone else to work the ranch."

"There's only one problem." His smile vanished altogether. "You don't really want me gone."

"I most certainly do."

"Why come to me then?" He arched a brow. "You could have

gone to your brother instead. But you haven't told him anything about me, now have you?"

Bry took a step backward. "Leave Con out of this."

"That's fine by me." His hand clamped her wrist. "What happened the other night can be our secret."

"Let go of me." She kept her voice low and resisted pulling away. Struggling to free herself would cause a spectacle that Con was sure to hear about.

From the slow smile that spread across his face, Thad understood her predicament and relished her discomfort. He pulled her nearer. "When you scowl at me like that, it makes me want to kiss you."

"Stop it." Bry fought panic. Anyone—maybe Nick—might look their way.

He released her. "All right, at least for now. But we're not finished by a long shot."

She backed away, rubbing her wrist. "Stay away from me, or I'll tell my brother." She spun on her heels and fled. Blinking away tears, she admitted the truth. Trying to change his mind about hiring on with Con had been short-sighted.

By confronting him, she'd turned herself into a more challenging target

CHAPTER TWELVE

NICK WALKED WITH BRETT ON THE lighter trail worn by human and animal feet that ran alongside the deeper ruts made by wagons.

Sitting straight in the saddle above a lathered and heaving Morgan, the soldier Nick had spotted held up a hand. "Don't come any closer. There could be death on me. We have Indian activity near Fort Laramie and cholera among the settlers waiting at Sedgwick for clearance to travel west. Doc Wellesley's taking care of the sick, but he needs more laudanum."

Brett squinted against the sun. "That's a common problem these days, but I guess you know that."

The soldier nodded. "That I do. The war drained us dry. I'm headed east to beg laudanum from Fort McPherson. Name's Private Ward Jackson. Folks call me Jackson."

"I'm Brett Colter, and this here's my guide, Nick Laramie. Let's hope they have what you need at McPherson and that the fever doesn't touch our train."

Jackson gave a curt nod. "Sure you want to go on?"

Brett whistled. "It's that bad?"

Nick had seen his share of cholera and could picture the despair at Fort Sedgwick. You could never tell when the sickness would strike or who it would take.

Brett tilted his head "There's trouble at Laramie, you say?"

The soldier shifted in the saddle. "Red Cloud's got himself stirred up over Bozeman's new road."

"I knew that much. That's why I planned to take my train the long way to Fort Hall and into Montana Territory from the south." Brett narrowed his eyes. "Will the soldiers even let us past Sedgwick?"

Jackson opened his canteen, swilled water, and swiped an arm across his mouth before answering. "You'd need to make it there alive first. I don't mind telling you, the hair on the back of my neck stood on end all the way from the fort."

Brett folded his arms across his chest. "Did you see anything?"

"No, but I felt eyes watching me." Jackson glanced sideways at Nick then back to Brett. "There are varmints out there, and I don't mean the four-legged kind."

Nick frowned. The soldier meant Indians, of course. He made them sound like beasts.

"You should be safe from here to McPherson." Brett's voice cut through Nick's irritation. "Leastways, we didn't notice anything out of the ordinary between here and there."

Jackson took off his cavalry hat and scratched his head. "Beggin' your pardon, but that don't mean nothing. These days one man can get through just fine while the next gets killed. Same goes for wagon trains. If you want the truth, you folks would be better off turning back."

Brett shook his head. "We'll take our chances but camp shy of Sedgwick all the same."

Jackson snorted. "Do that and you could end up with an arrow in your back. But I reckon it's your call whether to die of cholera or a tomahawk."

Nick walked beside Brett toward the tables where some of the women still served food. He had a lot on his mind after talking with Jackson. Brett wouldn't want to turn the wagon train around, but maybe he should. Over the years Nick had witnessed many deaths on the trails west. Some couldn't be helped, but others were caused by ignorance or carelessness. Rifles went off accidentally. Children fell under wagons. Men drowned when overloaded wagons tipped over at river fords. Women's skirts blew into cooking fires during high winds and set them ablaze. He had no doubt that the wagon train would see more deaths before it reached Alder Gulch. Gazing into the lingering crowd, he wondered who among them wouldn't survive the journey. He pulled his thoughts from their path and went to stand before Bry.

She offered them wedges of potato pie. "I'm sorry it's gone cold." The dullness in her eyes betrayed that something besides cold potato pie troubled her, but then they'd just buried Mrs. Wallers. He took a portion from her with a smile, glad when her brow smoothed and a faint smile lifted her lips.

Her shy smile riveted Nick, but he tore himself away and sat on an overturned crate near Brett. Most everyone had eaten, except a few stragglers like them. As Bry had mentioned, the potato pie had gone cold, but it filled his belly all the same.

Brett bent over his food with appetite but eventually looked up. "I need you to find us a camping place near the fort but outside its gates."

Nick hid his dismay. After helping dig Mrs. Wallers' grave and attending her emotional burial, he'd rather have rested a while before riding out. "All right."

"I know it's a bother," Brett conceded. "But once we know what's ahead, we can figure out how to slip past Sedgwick."

"You intend to bypass the army?" Nick couldn't hide his surprise.

Brett's eyes glinted. "Let's just say I'll do whatever it takes to reach Montana Territory in one piece. I'd rather miss the fort altogether, to tell you the truth. I've seen what cholera can do."

Nick mopped up the last of his beans with a bite of soda biscuit. "The day's half gone. I should head out. I doubt I'll return tonight, but I'll try and meet you on the trail early."

"All right. Stay away from other people as much as you can. We can't have you coming down sick."

Nick stood, ready to be on his way now that leaving was inevitable.

"And Nick?"

He waited for the wagon master to speak.

"Be careful."

Nick smiled. "You can count on it." He couldn't resist a last glance at Bry, lifting her hands from soapy dishwater to mop her brow. He set his jaw, determined to abide by his word and keep her safe. She seemed to feel his gaze, for she glanced up and their gazes meshed. He tipped his hat before turning away.

At Nick's whistle, Tavo lifted his head and pranced toward him with tail held high. Nick bridled and saddled his horse, then tied on saddlebags. He mounted and turned westward, putting Tavo through his paces until his black hooves flashed out in a full gallop. The noonday sun beat across Nick's shoulders, but a slight breeze took the edge off the springtime heat.

The trail followed the Platte on one side and mile after mile of green prairie on the other. The wind sighed through the grasses while a flock of bluebirds undulated in a dark cloud across the sky. The journey could have been pleasant if not for the vigilance required. Maybe Jackson hadn't been the best choice of messenger to ride between the forts. He seemed excessively concerned about danger, perhaps more than warranted. Still, Nick would do well to take the man seriously. Ignoring any warning about this part of the trail, in particular, wasn't wise.

Nick steered clear of the newly-built town of Julesburg but returned to the trail near the charred remains of the first Julesburg. It had been burned during raids by the Cheyenne, Lakota, and Arapaho in retaliation for the massacre at Sand Creek. Looking over the charred remains of the town, a lump clogged his throat. *When would the killing end?*

He halted Tavo at the banks of the Platte where the current pulled at grasses bowing from the banks. He'd thought to guide the wagon train to the Upper California Crossing, and then westward along the river's north bank. However, in the distance, he could make out the camp with a row of bodies lined up and waiting for burial. He would have to backtrack and find a site farther from the fort. He didn't like being so close to hostilities, but it would be better to facer flesh-and-blood opponents than a sickness that crept up on a body unseen.

He rode across the plains and veered back to the trail east of the new Julesburg. He had no illusions about stopping here. Many of the settlers he'd known at the old town were now dead, and residents of the new town would fire at him first and ask questions second.

He led Tavo to a low bank of the Platte and slid to the ground. After hours in the saddle with few rests, he needed to stretch his legs. Tavo waded into the water and lowered his head to drink. Nick scanned the area. With the view clear in all directions, this was a good spot for the wagon train to camp.

An arrow glinted, embedded in the grass at his feet. Nick glanced about but detected no one near. He crouched to examine the arrow. Sinew lashed the flint tip to a red-stained shaft fletched with gray eagle feathers. Balancing the arrow in his hand, he scanned the edge of the meadow where sparse cottonwoods branched above the gleaming water. His fingers found three familiar circles ribbing the dogwood shaft—Kicking Horse's mark. He sucked in a breath. How long ago had his stepbrother lost an arrow here?

He straightened and whistled for his horse, who was tearing at grasses. Tavo whinnied and trotted over, but then turned a baleful-looking eye in his direction. Nick smiled and patted his neck. "Don't worry. I'll let you graze, but not yet."

He sprang onto his horse's back and turned Tavo's head eastward. He'd promised to meet the wagon train early, so he should travel at least partway back. Clouds gathered in the sky, and a storm broke. He rode on with rain dripping off his hat brim. The trail soon slicked into mud. To save Tavo's hooves from the damage too much moisture could cause them, he pulled aside and pitched his tent on a bank above the swelling river.

He laid down in his bedroll, still thinking about the buffalo arrow he'd found. No good would come of mentioning it to Brett. Judging by its weathered condition, Kicking Horse must have lost the arrow months ago. Finding wasn't proof that his step-brother or any of his mother's people were in the area tonight.

With his decision made, he closed his eyes to sleep, but uneasiness brought a hollow feeling to his gut.

Nick spent a rough night in partial wakefulness due to the rain lashing his tent and his natural wariness while in a hostile setting. He woke to find the storm cleared. Fitful light filtered through the shredded clouds to wash the sky with colors. He set out, keeping Tavo to a walk on the slippery track.

The sun and wind took the sheen off the mud. When the puddles finally dried, he urged his horse into a canter. He stopped to stretch his legs and allow Tavo to drink from the river, then returned to the trail. He pulled up, straining his ears. West of him hooves thudded, harnesses jingled, and wagons rattled. He sent Tavo into a gallop. After he rounded a bend, the wagon train came into sight.

Brett waved from the back of his buckskin quarter horse and rode ahead to meet him. "Am I glad to see you. How's the trail?"

Nick wheeled Tavo and fell into step beside the wagon master. "Passable."

A jackrabbit bounded from the brush and crossed in front of the horses. Tavo shuddered and tensed, ready to bolt. Nick restrained his horse with a taut rein and soothed him with a gentle word.

Brett's horse shied and danced. "Whoa!" The wagon master gave a sharp cry. "Honestly, I don't know which is worse, critters running out to scare the horses or prairie dogs leaving holes for them to step in." His buckskin snorted but settled down, and they started off again. "Did you find a good place to camp?"

"Yes. We'll have to stop away from the fort, just past Devil's Dive."

"That's farther away than I'd like."

"There's cholera at California Crossing or we could have stayed there."

"I suspected as much. Did you see anything out of the

ordinary?"

"Nothing." It was, in a manner of speaking, the truth. A Cheyenne hunter losing a buffalo arrow on the prairie wasn't uncommon. That he'd found it near a site of open conflict or that it belonged to his stepbrother didn't have to matter.

Brett nodded. "Jackson seemed a mite jittery to me. His nerves probably had him imagining things. Still, doubling the watch tonight won't hurt."

"There's a herd of buffalo between here and Devil's Dive."

"I'm partial to buffalo steak. Normally I'd be all for a hunt, but in these parts, we shouldn't risk a delay." Brett took off his hat and mopped his brow with his kerchief. "Unless, of course, the soldiers make us cool our heels. Then we'd have time to cure meat."

They rode through miles of waving grasses, falling into a comfortable silence. The mud had hardened to the texture of mortar by the time they stopped to water the livestock and eat the noon meal. Nick sat on a sun-warmed boulder gnawing on jerked venison. He glimpsed Bry in brown calico, her skirts swaying as she brought a plate of food to her brother.

"I'll ask again. You want something besides jerky?" Brett's voice intruded into his thoughts.

Nick pulled his gaze from Bry. "Sure, thanks." He accepted a plate of cold beans and several pieces of the fried bread called bannocks from Brett.

Brett filled his own plate and plunked down in the sun beside him.

Nick tore into a bannock and chewed. Bry's laugh drifted to him, and his gaze strayed back to her.

"A man can want things that maybe he shouldn't," Brett's voice intruded.

Nick met the wagon master's gaze. "True."

Brett grunted. Applying himself to his food, he said nothing more. A bee buzzed past. Oxen lowed. A child whined.

"Reckon you saw what was left of Julesburg."

"I did."

Brett shook his head. "A man's not safe in his bed. Things were a sight easier before the soldiers started coming to the forts with nothing to do once the war ended. Now, look at the hornet's nest they've stirred."

"I can't see a way forward without more bloodshed."

Brett paused with his tin cup partway to his lips. "If that happens, I'd as soon that it doesn't involve us."

CHAPTER THIRTEEN

GUNSHOTS WRENCHED BRY FROM SLEEP. SHE sat up, blinking to focus in the faint light. A scream split the air. Many hooves beat the ground, shaking it so badly that vibrations went through the wagon. Bry pushed herself from bed and stood with a sick feeling crawling through her stomach. Her hands shook as she loosened the pickle string that held the canvas at the rear of the wagon together. She looked out and gasped.

A solid wall of moving flesh pounded in a black tide across the plain. Unless the herd could be diverted, it would reach the encampment. She squinted into the near distance and pulled in a shaky breath. Could she really see horsemen wearing feathered headdresses riding back and forth through the dust cloud behind the charging buffalo? Bry hauled air into her lungs. They seemed to be deliberately driving the herd into camp.

"Stampede!" The wagon master shouted the alarm and ran to catch his horse.

Parker Jones, Brett's mule skinner, reined in the prancing horse he rode. *"Indians!"*

Horses reared, mules kicked, and oxen bawled as the livestock crashed into the chained wagons that corralled them. Women and children screamed. Men shouted.

Con emerged from his tent and turned his head toward her. "Bry, hide under the wagon!" He ran toward the wagon circle.

"Phoebe!" Maisey's shrill cry raised the hair on Bry's arms.

Bry heaved in a breath. "God, please keep Phoebe safe."

Maisey whirled into sight, her clothing disheveled. Beside her, Natty peered into the wagon circle. From the panic on their faces, Bry had no doubt what had happened.

"I'm sorry, Mrs. Wilcox. She was with me one instant and gone the next."

"That doesn't matter, Natty." Maisey spoke in a sharp voice. "We have to find her."

The Wilcoxes rose before anyone else to hitch their team, which would be the reason for Natty watching Phoebe at this hour. Bry's heart went out to the troubled girl. "Children that age can run off in a blink." She offered Natty the comfort Maisey was too upset to offer. An image of Liam running down the road returned to haunt her.

"Oh, where can she be?" Maisey's voice broke.

Bry caught Natty by the shoulders. "Where were you when Phoebe ran off?"

"Not far from here. She went that way." She turned and pointed into the wagon circle where their terrified livestock were bolting. "There she is."

At first Bry could make out only dust, but a breeze shifted it to reveal a golden-haired little girl surrounded by plunging beasts.

Natty didn't hesitate but climbed over the chained wagon wheels and flung herself after Phoebe.

"Come back!" Maisey started after her.

"I'll get Con's rifle." Bry turned back to her wagon.

"Good idea." Maisey spoke over her shoulder. "Hurry." She darted after Natty, and a wall of churning dust shut behind her.

Bry charged into her wagon and took up her brother's rifle. He'd shown her how to fire it once, but she wasn't all that sure about doing so. She shouldn't rush into a stampede without protection, though. She hurried down the steps and, hampered by her skirts, climbed over the chained wagon wheels.

Dust stung her eyes. Tears rolled down her cheeks. She blinked to clear her eyes. A stampeding ox thundered toward her. She couldn't move her legs, let alone raise her brother's rifle. She breathed a prayer and waited to meet her Maker. The bellowing beast bore down on her but veered at the last moment.

Bry's legs turned to rubber. Blackness pressed her vision, and she willed herself not to faint. She'd lost sight of Maisey, and with her sense of direction gone, had no idea which way to run. A rampaging horse bumped her, and she pitched to the ground. She tried to pull in air but couldn't. Where the rifle had fallen, she didn't know. Another ox huffed and foamed as it pounded toward her. With no time to escape, Bry closed her eyes. She gulped in air at last and opened her mouth to scream. The ox churned the dust, so near that its breath warming the air she breathed. Massive hooves lifted from the ground and thudded as they came down on the other side of her. The rear hooves narrowly missed her face.

Breathing heavily, she pushed to her knees then staggered to her feet.

A strong arm clamped her waist. Her rescuer swung her upward and held her sideways before him on his horse's bare back. "You're safe now," a husky voice said.

"Help Maisey, *please*." She turned her head and looked into Nick's dark eyes. "Phoebe's in trouble."

Gunshots shattered the silence. Men from the wagon camp rode between the bellowing buffalo and the wagons, waving their hats and shouting. Roaring and snorting, the panicked herd split to flow around the camp. War whoops cut through the din. Someone shrieked, followed by more shooting.

"I got him!" the wagon master's voice called out.

"The cowards are running off." Parker's voice came back.

A wagon splintered apart, and a bawling ox bolted through the breech. Another wagon went down. Eyes rolling, chests heaving, and spraying lather, the horses and mules funneled with the oxen through the opening.

Dust hung in the air so thick Bry could see little. She felt Nick start. He wheeled his horse and sent it forward.

Out of the shroud, Maisey came into view, sitting in the trammeled circle the livestock had left behind. She cradled Phoebe to her chest while silent tears coursed down her cheeks. Natty lay nearby. She must have fallen with her arms stretched out, reaching for Phoebe. She lay in that position, bloodied and still.

Nick's horse had barely stopped when he slid to the ground and knelt beside Natty. Bry followed more slowly, stricken by the sight of death. Natty's eyes stared at the sky, and her chest no longer rose and fell.

A mourning dove cooed in a willow behind Bry, standing at Natty's grave. Two more holes awaited others who had fallen during the stampede. Thankfully, none of them belonged to Phoebe, who had escaped with only scrapes and bruises. Wilt Chandler had been a boy of eighteen with his life ahead of him when a buffalo broke apart the wagon he'd been hiding under. His mother stood by his side, watching his face intently as if she expected him to wake. Wilt's father rubbed his wife's back and worked his jaw. Drew Lansky had died an agonizing death after taking an arrow. His new wife stood over him, wringing her hands and weeping.

Ginny Davis placed a bouquet of wildflowers on her daughter's motionless chest. Dressed in her best gown of green calico and white lace, Natty lay in a coffin Brett and Nick had made from the remains of one of the broken wagons. Ginny smoothed her daughter's bright hair with a gentle hand and a tender smile, then bent to kiss her forehead. With Natty's eyelashes lying in tawny crescents against her cheeks, if not for her ashen skin, she might have been asleep. Bry swallowed against a lump in her throat. Mam and Liam had looked the same before they'd taken them away from her. Bry heaved a shaking breath. *Why God? Tell me why these things have to happen.*

The green prairie rolled away as far as the eye could see, silent as God. Con's arm encircled her, and she leaned against him.

With tears sliding down her cheeks, Ginny gazed at her daughter a final time. She stepped backward, while Marsh and their other children moved to her side. Marsh took Ginny's hand, and together they watched Nick and Parker Jones lift the coffin lid into place, shutting Natty out of sight forever.

Nick struck the first hammer blow, and Ginny winced as if the nail pierced her flesh. Nick looked at her in question, but she shrank against her husband.

Marsh nodded to Nick. "Get on with it."

The ping of metal on metal quieted the song of the dove. Nick and Parker lowered Natty's coffin into the grave they'd dug to receive it. The first shovelful of dirt rattled onto the casket. Ginny fell to her knees, her lips moving in fervent prayer.

Bry twisted her hands together. Why should Ginny's face glow instead of darkening with anger against the God who had stolen her child? Why hadn't the Almighty spared a sweet girl like Natty?

Why hadn't he saved Liam and Mam?

The question knocked the wind from Bry. There seemed no rhyme or reason to dying, almost as if . . . as if God hated them all. Her audacious thoughts brought her back to childhood with Mam chiding her. *Bryanna! Mind your manners.*

Remembering Mam's special name for her eased some of the tightness in her chest.

Con slid his hand under Bry's elbow, but she drew away from him. Was her brother caught up in memories of Mam and Liam, too? Like so many who lived in the disease-ridden slums of Manhattan, they'd died of cholera.

Marsh helped Ginny rise and pulled her closer. She rested her head against his shoulder. The merciless wind whipped Ginny's skirts as she and her husband stood looking down at their daughter's grave.

Parker finished mounding dirt over the coffin while Nick drove a crude cross into the earth. Early sunlight caught the inscription Brett had whittled into the rough plank. *Natalie Ruth Davis, 1851—1865, heaven's angel.*

"Going on with cholera at the fort and the Indians rising is plain crazy." Marsh Davis stood square as he faced the wagon master at the edge of the wagon camp. Others in the wagon train pressed into a circle around them, and a few murmured their agreement. Nick stepped closer to the wagon master, ready to defend him if necessary.

Marsh fisted his hands at his sides. "We should have turned back before this. If you'd had the sense to turn back—" He swallowed, the cords of his neck tensing. "Natty didn't have to die."

"Marsh, you're grieving." Despite the gentleness of Brett's tone, Nick sensed his uneasiness. "It's natural to be angry at such a time."

"This is more than that, Brett. I've lost faith in you. If, against all reason, you insist on continuing, how many more will you sacrifice?"

Several in the crowd raised their voices to back him up, but others protested in the wagon master's favor.

Brett held up a hand, and the crowd quieted. "Marsh, I'll put your discourteous words down to sorrow. However, I must speak up for myself. The renegades who stampeded that herd bear the blame for your daughter's death, not me. You'll understand that someday, I hope."

"All I see is a man bent on reaching the gold camps, no matter what the cost."

"I reckon he's right." One of the wagon leaders moved to stand behind Marsh. Muttering, Marsh's other supporters joined him.

"Turn back if you want." Parker stepped forward on Brett's other side. "But don't accuse our wagon master while you do it." Those who favored Brett lifted their voices in agreement.

"Not you nor anyone else can judge what's in another's heart." Brett spoke above the crowd. "Most in this wagon train are set on mining for gold. If I turn back, they'll try to reach Montana Territory by some other means. That might not turn out well. I have a duty to see them through."

Marsh's nostril's flared. "When they're scalped in their sleep, they won't thank you none." His followers called out noisy agreement.

Nick pictured his rifle, which he'd stowed in Brett's wagon this morning. Hopefully he wouldn't need a weapon, but he didn't like the turn the situation had taken. Brett tried to shout to be heard, but the crowd drowned him out. A rifle shot rang out, and a glance revealed Parker lowering his gun, having shot into the air. The mule skinner spoke into the silence. "Let our wagon master have his say."

Brett frowned. "I'll tell you this and be done with it. If I worried about death from arrows, camp fever, and everything else that could go wrong, we'd never have left Independence in the first place."

Marsh's forehead creased. "That's fine for you to say, but I have a family to look after. I refuse to risk their lives for the sake of gold fever."

"You must do as you see fit, the same as me." Brett shrugged. "The wagon train will continue with or without you."

Marsh glared at him. "Come morning, I'm headed back to Missouri."

Parker whistled. "That'll take a month and a half."

"Better wasted time than a war hatchet in the chest." Marsh turned toward those gathered behind him. "Well? Who's coming with me?"

Bry slowed down when she reached the Wilcox camp. "I came as soon as I heard."

Maisey was sitting on a crate beside the unlit cook fire, twisting her hands in her lap. "I couldn't wake her from her nap." She whimpered. "I'm scared to death."

Avery stood behind his wife, a helpless expression on his face.

He nodded to her. "Phoebe will be all right." He spoke the words forcefully, as if willing them to be true.

Maisey shook her head. "We don't know that yet."

Avery gripped Maisey's shoulder. "She's in good hands, darling." He glanced at Bry. "Doc Mather thinks she must have hit her head during the stampede."

Maisey's face crumpled. "How could this happen? She seemed fine."

"The doctor is keeping watch over her." Avery spoke in a calming voice.

Bry restrained her own reaction to Phoebe's plight, unwilling to burden the Wilcoxes with her fears. She restrained the reassurances that pressed her lips. How could she give them when only God knew what would happen? After Natty's death, losing Phoebe would be hard to bear. "I'm sure he'll do his best." She could offer that much comfort at least. "Meanwhile you must look after yourself. I'll send Con over with supper later."

Avery gave her a faint smile. "That's kind of you." He squeezed Maisey's shoulder. "Why not lie down a while? Phoebe will need her mother rested when she wakes."

Bry said goodbye to them and returned to her camp. She threw herself into cooking the best supper her meager skills allowed. Her cooking had improved of late. She'd already started bread, and there was plenty of buffalo meat. One outcome of the stampede had been plenty of fresh meat.

Con returned to camp while she was rolling out pastry. He looked into the pot in which she'd boiled the filling. "That smells good."

"I'm taking advantage of the chance to make a dried apple pie, although I wish we'd laid by for a better reason."

"We leave bright and early tomorrow, minus nine wagons."

She raised her eyebrows. "That many are turning back with Mr. Davis?"

"I'm afraid so. We won't, of course, and neither will more than twenty others."

She nodded.

"I wouldn't stay on with the train if I didn't think it best. You know that, don't you?"

She put down her rolling pin. "I trust you, Con."

His forehead smoothed. "I'll do my best to keep you safe, I promise."

Bry paused on the wagon steps and waited for Nick, striding across the wagon circle in the dusk, to reach her. She'd been about to retire early, giving up on saying goodnight to Con. The day had started with the burial and ended with Marsh challenging Brett, rousing strong emotions that left her weary. She'd left her brother at Avery's fireside discussing the fact that nine wagon owners had opted to turn back, leaving the other twenty-one to go on without them.

Nick stopped at the foot of the steps and gazed up at her with his brow puckered. "Where's Con?"

"He took supper to the Wilcox camp and hasn't returned yet."

"Thank you." Nick turned away, but then swung back. "Will you and your brother go on to Montana?" He blurted out the question.

"Why wouldn't we? Con's ranch is in Montana."

Nick's forehead smoothed. He gave a brief nod. "We'll see you there safely."

She smiled at his brisk tone when he'd already given away that he cared. Warmth went through her at the fact. "Thank you."

Nick returned her smile before starting back toward the wagon master's camp. He moved with easy grace, making it easy to understand how he rode a horse with such agility. A sigh escaped her, and she lingered until he vanished behind Brett's wagon.

Bry stretched out on her feathered tick but tossed and turned, kept awake by rain pattering against the wagon bonnet. Even without the storm, remembering the way Nick had looked at her earlier would have kept sleep at bay. She pressed a hand to her stomach to quiet the odd sensation of pain mixed with joy that came whenever her thoughts dwelt on Nick. That happened more often of late. She had only to recall the kiss they'd stolen in the early morning, and her thoughts carried her into his arms again.

A gust shook the bonnet, and she rolled onto her side with a sigh. She couldn't seem to free herself of the man, and now even the desire to do so faded. She couldn't afford to let that happen. Ian had seemed loving while courting her, but after they married had turned into someone else. You couldn't tell with people. She wasn't about to risk what remained of her stability on another love that could go wrong. No, thank you. She would reject any further advances from Nick and ignore her yearning to accept them.

Shifting to her back, she opened her eyes in pitch darkness. "God, if you care about me at all, help me stay strong. And when Nick rides ahead of the train, please keep him safe." Since she was rejecting the man, it seemed only fair to petition the Almighty on his behalf.

She turned to her side and finally drifted into sleep. Blue jays squawked, waking her. Groaning, she sat up and pushed her hair out of her eyes. Morning light filtered through the bonnet. The rain had stopped, but travel would be muddy. If it didn't rain again, the wind might dry the trail by afternoon. She stood and drew her shawl about her against the cold. It would be warmer then too.

"Have you had your beauty sleep?" Con's voice sounded entirely too cheery at such an hour. "Care for breakfast?"

"I didn't mean to oversleep and leave all the chores to you."

He laughed. "I'm teasing, Sis. 'Twas a bad night with the rain and all. Come and eat."

She pulled on her wool traveling costume, bound her hair with a blue ribbon at the nape, and went out to join Con by the fire. He offered her a bowl of oatmeal. "This will warm you from the inside."

"You don't look any the worse for spending the night in your tent." She spoke her thoughts aloud. "Did you stay dry?"

"Mostly." He flashed a smile. "Don't worry about me. I've learned to sleep anywhere."

The sudden image of her brother slumbering beside her on the dirt floor of the tiny tenement they'd shared with their aunt, uncle, and cousins imposed itself. "I suppose you have."

He frowned. "Why the gloomy face?"

"'Tis nothing."

He gave her an appraising look. "Then you won't mind smiling for me."

She scowled at him. "What a plague you are! I'll smile when I decide to and no sooner." Drat him, but her lips curved upward anyway.

His grin broke out. "That's better."

She'd slept far too long. Wagons were already gathering in a small knot along the trail. Some faced westward while others pointed the opposite direction. She swallowed her oatmeal in a rush while Con harnessed and hitched the mules to the wagon. Together, they broke camp, but she would have precious little time to say goodbye to those who would leave them today.

She found Ginny outside the Davis wagon. "It won't be the same without you." Bry would miss seeing Ginny bent over her cooking fire and hearing her call to Natty and her other children not to run ahead on the trail.

Ginny offered her a faint smile. "I'll always have fond memories of you and the other women."

Brett Colter approached Marsh, who stood beside his hitched oxen holding his bullwhip. "God speed to you."

Marsh turned to the wagon master. "Good bye, Mr. Colter."

Brett dipped his head. "Safe journeys."

Neither man offered to shake.

Bry watched the wagon master stride away. "I hope you don't mind going back like this." Mr. Davis had a strong mind, and Ginny might not have had any say in the matter.

"I'm not unwilling. Truth to tell, I'd rather return home to Indiana."

Bry could almost envy the woman the home she wished for when she herself had none.

Ginny moved closer and spoke near Bry's ear. "I hope you won't think ill of my husband. He—" Her face contorted and for a moment it seemed she couldn't go on. She heaved in a breath. "He favored Natty."

Bry gave her a quick embrace, tears misting her own eyes. "I'll never forget your sweet daughter."

Ginny nodded. "She was a blessing to us."

"Get up." Marsh flicked his whip into the ground beside his team of oxen.

Ginny squeezed Bry's arm. "I'll pray that you reach your brother's ranch safely." She hurried off to walk beside her husband while he drove the oxen from the side.

With a hollow feeling in her stomach, Bry watched them go.

Con's arm slid around her shoulders. "Come away."

A part of her yearned to go with Ginny and the others. She'd never say so to Con, but from the look of sympathy on his face, her brother must guess her feelings. She let him lead her toward their wagon and the future that awaited her in Montana Territory.

CHAPTER FOURTEEN

"Whoa!" The command, shouted in panic, carried to Nick above the seesaw braying of mules. He swiveled in the saddle to look behind him, already suspecting what he'd see.

A mule team had bolted out of line, sending the wagon it hauled careening. A woman's screams pierced the air, and Maisey Wilcox's pale face looked back from the wagon box. Avery rode astride the left wheel mule, the customary position for handling a team. Listing sideways in the saddle, he seemed ready to fall but righted himself. The jerk line he'd held dragged on the ground, leaving him with no way to control his team. The mules turned back onto the path, headed toward Devil's Dive, the notorious drop they'd navigated the day before.

Nick heeled his horse, then urged Tavo into a gallop.

Hooves pounded behind him. A glance over his shoulder showed Con following. The mules huffed and brayed, raising dust. Tavo laid his ears back and, sides heaving, closed the gap. The stallion drew even with the left lead mule. Nick sprang upward and into a crouch on Tavo's back, then lifted to his feet in a loose-kneed stance. He'd done this a thousand times. No use dwelling on what might happen if he fell beneath the pounding hooves. Nick gauged the distance, then sprang through the air. He landed square on the mule's back, but slipped sideways and grabbed the harness. The runaway creature bucked and brayed but couldn't fight more than that while strapped in harness.

"Hang on, Mrs. Wilcox." Con called to the woman being tossed around in the wagon. He rode up beside the right lead mule opposite the one Nick rode. Con leaned out, trying to grab its headstall.

Nick crawled forward along his mule's rocking back. He reached for the line where it passed through the metal terrets on the collar. The ground slipped by with dizzying speed. Forcing his gaze upward offered no comfort, with Devil's Dive careening into view dead ahead. Avery's white face turned toward Nick with a look of panic. Gratitude went through Nick for the fact that neither of them had fallen from their mules' back.

"Hurry!" Con sounded panicked. He'd failed to catch hold of the mule.

Nick didn't need goading. He'd seen horses roll down impossibly steep ravines just for play. He had no reason to assume these mules wouldn't go over the edge, full tilt. If they did, the wagon would break apart, and he didn't want to think about what would happen to Mrs. Wilcox. Both he and Avery would be thrown and possibly trampled. Grasping the line, Nick swung his legs down and sat upright. The mule brayed and tossed its head. "Whoa!" Adding his own cry to Avery's, Nick hauled on the line.

The left mules checked their speed a little, slowing the entire team, but time ran out. The edge of the drop rushed closer, and Nick tensed for a leap. The ground would slam him hard, but if he could roll, he might save himself.

Gunshots kicked the air, and the mules veered to run along the edge. Nick's backward glance revealed Con brandishing his revolver while racing his horse between the mules and the drop-off. Avery's face, in the quick glimpse Nick saw of it, looked pinched from strain, but, by some miracle, he'd managed to hold on. "Gee!" Nick yelled, yanking the jerk rein to guide the team away from the edge.

The lathering mules showed the whites of their eyes but slowed and turned. The wagon bounced along behind the terrified draft animals. Nick circled onto the trail behind the rest of the wagons, and then drew the mules to a halt. They stood chuffing with heads lowered and sides heaving. Con let out a whoop, but Nick remained silent and held the jerk line taut. He wouldn't put it past the ornery creatures to bolt all over again.

"Are you hurt, Mrs. Wilcox?" Leather creaked as Con dismounted. He reached up to help Maisey down from the wagon.

"Only some bruises, I think." She answered him in a shaky voice. "Thank goodness Phoebe is riding in Doc Mather's wagon. What about Mr. Wilcox?"

Nick slid to the ground and went to Avery, who clutched the mule's collar in a death grip. "You all right?"

Avery shook hair out of his eyes. "I reckon so."

Nick restrained the urge to help him dismount. A man had his pride.

Avery flexed his good hand. "My wife and I might lie at the bottom of the ravine except for you both. I'm obliged."

Nick smiled. "I'm glad it worked."

Mrs. Wilcox flung herself against her husband's chest with a cry, and he buried his face in her hair, which had come down sometime during her wild ride. As the two swayed together, Nick's chest constricted. What would it be like to have someone care that much about him? He didn't dare let himself think of Bry. To give the embracing couple privacy, he turned his back on them and walked toward Con. "Thanks for your help back there." He watched Con for his reaction.

"I did what was needful." Con spoke haltingly, not meeting his eyes.

Nick nodded and turned away.

"I've never seen anyone ride the way you did, Laramie," Con went on. "People would pay to watch. Where did you train to perform such feats?"

He shrugged. "I learned to ride among my mother's people."

"I've heard stories of the Cheyenne's prowess on horseback. I didn't quite believe them until now."

"Look at those mules!" Avery advanced on the chastened creatures.

Con laughed. "They wore themselves out for certain."

The mules stood in harness with heads bowed in an attitude of utter dejection. Nick put his hands on his hips. "I could almost feel sorry for them if they weren't such a nuisance. You'll be lucky if they'll stir themselves to pull your wagon into camp."

Avery's lips lifted in a faint smile. "A miner needs his mules, I've heard, but if I had it to do again, I'd buy a team of oxen instead."

"I don't blame you." Con poked around the outside of the wagon. "Looks like you have a broken axle."

Avery let out a cuss word, then glanced back to his blushing wife. "Sorry to offend your ears, sweetheart."

"I'll help with the repair," Con volunteered.

"I'd better tell Brett to hold on." Nick whistled for his horse. Tavo appeared on the crest of a hill.

"Mrs. Wilcox will ride back with you," Avery said.

She shook her head. "Thank you kindly, but I'll stay here."

Avery smiled at her. "You'll be safer and more comfortable in the train."

Mrs. Wilcox folded her arms. "I'll be happier beside my husband where I belong."

Nick gathered his horse's reins and waited for the final decision without comment. He knew better than to intrude in a discussion between a husband and wife.

Avery shook his head. "You won't have much to occupy you while we fix the wagon."

"Don't send me away. Please."

"You're as obstinate as one of those mules." Avery scolded her, but softly.

"I thought I'd lost you." Her voice wobbled dangerously close to weeping.

Avery's expression softened, and he stroked his wife's face. "Have it your way, sweetheart."

Nick tipped his hat to the woman who obviously knew her own mind, then vaulted onto Tavo's back. He caught up to Brett astride his horse beside his wagon.

"Are the Wilcoxes all right?" Brett asked. Behind Brett, Parker straddled one of the heeler mules, ready to guide the team.

"They're shaken but none the worse," Nick answered. "An axle broke on their wagon, though. They need time to replace it."

Brett whistled. "I hate to say this, but I think it's in the best interests of the train to go on to the next camp. We're in a dangerous location and need to settle in before dark."

"You're not going to leave them behind, are you?" Nick had seen this sort of thing before. Sometimes wagon masters laid by when misfortune struck, but not always. The good of all members of the train weighed more heavily with them than the welfare of a single family. And of course, certain members of the wagon train were in an all-fired hurry to reach Montana's gold camps.

"They can catch up to us. The spot you scouted isn't far, right?"

Nick didn't like the wagon master's decision, but it was Brett's call. He pointed into the distance. "On the other side of that bend you'll find a meadow by the river." He frowned as an unpleasant thought occurred to him. If the wagon train left Con behind, Bry could wind up stranded while waiting for her brother to return to their wagon.

Kilkenny shifted beneath Bry, and she placed a hand on the mare's neck. She could see her brother crouched beside the Wilcox wagon a little way back. Something must have gone wrong to keep Con from returning, but he'd better start back soon. With the livestock hitched after the train had nooned on the banks of the Platte, no one could want to delay starting up again. The wagon train would move on and leave them behind.

"Wagons ho!" the cry rang out, confirming her suspicions. The Conestogas in the forefront rumbled into motion.

Bry shot a helpless glance at her brother's team before touching her heels to her horse's flanks. She hoped the mules would show their usual obstinance and refuse to budge while the other wagons trundled by. If they went anywhere at all, they might follow along with the train. She couldn't worry about the mules, though. She needed to tell Con and the Wilcoxes that the train was leaving them behind.

She urged Kilkenny into a gallop, and the mare stretched her legs as if grateful for the chance to run. The hot wind buffeted Bry's cheeks and whipped her hair into her eyes. Clawing it away, she pressed forward. The mare's hooves ate up the ground.

Movement at the corner of her eye drew her attention. Warriors on painted ponies emerged from the crouching shadows along the river. Bry let out a whimper. Hooves thudded behind her. Shouts went up from the wagons. Indian riders rushed toward Con and the Wilcoxes. The breath clogged in her throat. She'd never reach them in time.

One of the riders split off from the rest and headed straight for Bry. The hair on the back of her neck bristled. Whooping, the warrior bore down on her. Bry wheeled Kilkenny and spurred her toward the wagons.

Hooves thudded behind her. She wanted to weep. They would murder her too. The hair on her nape bristled with the certainty that an arrow or a tomahawk would find her any second.

The warrior reached her and leaned out, catching Kilkenny's bridle. The mare whinnied and tossed her head but drew up. The warrior yanked the reins from Bry's grasp. He watched her with bright interest from astride his spotted war pony, his face striped with red paint. A scar ran like tears down his cheek. Other Indians came up behind him. Nick neared also. She had to warn him. "Don't come near!" Fear heating her veins, she slid from Kilkenny's back. She'd never escape. If they were going to kill her, let it happen quickly rather than by the lingering tortures only whispered about. She stumbled away, running for all she was worth. From the sound of hooves, the warriors followed.

The ground caved from beneath her foot. She pitched forward and went down. Bry scrambled to her feet and held her hands like a shield before her.

The painted pony slid to a halt close by. The warrior on its back leaned over her with the feathers of his war bonnet fanning out. He reached for Bry, quick as a snake's tongue, and gripped her arms.

Bry screamed, the sound tearing from her soul. The warrior hauled her upward. He held her before him, his arm an iron band about her middle. She breathed in the odors of sweat and grease.

"No!" The bellow came from nearby.

The warrior turned his pony, bringing Nick and his racing horse into her view. He'd come after her. The other warriors broke past, riding toward Nick. Bry's captor shouted, and the warriors turned back to flank him on either side. It wasn't hard to guess that he was the leader of the band. The fringed shirt and air of authority he wore matched the obvious rank proclaimed by the many feathers trailing from his bonnet. Why had he prevented the warriors from attacking Nick?

Bry hauled in a painful breath. "Leave me," she yelled to Nick. Her captor shouted in a language she couldn't understand and tightened his arm about her. She struggled to breathe. Black dots swept over her vision. The world spun away. She felt herself sag.

"You're hurting her." Nick's voice summoned her from the edge of fainting.

The arm around Bry eased. She dragged in air and waited for her head to clear before pulling upright. She stared at Nick in wonder. Why had this warrior who commanded so many listened to him?

"You speak like a white man." Bry's captor spoke so abruptly that she started. "Have you forgotten our mother's tongue?"

The savage manhandling her was Nick's brother?

"I speak the woman's language for her sake." Nick nodded his dark head in Bry's direction.

"What is she to you?" The warrior demanded. He added a phrase in his own dialect.

Nick shook his head. "No. She travels with her brother. If you take her, Kicking Horse, searchers will come."

"We travel by paths the white man does not follow." The arm around Bry's waist tightened. "I have claimed her."

Nick's jaw firmed. "A white woman cannot belong to a

Cheyenne."

"This one does." Kicking Horse spoke in a commanding voice without turning his head. The warriors at his sides trained their bows on Nick. "If you love your life, dismount now."

Bry's heart pounded in her throat as she watched Nick's jaw tighten. The tension stretched to a breaking point. "Please do it," she begged him.

Nick hesitated, then dismounted. He stood in a defiant stance while one of the warriors took his horse's reins. "You're making a mistake, I tell you. She's bad medicine."

Kicking Horse shook his tomahawk. "Leave me, Wolf Walking, before I forget our mother's love for you."

Con registered the passage of time and looked up from the broken axle. The wagon train was moving. He'd better ride back and see to his mules. From the look of things, the Wilcoxes would still need help after he settled Bry into the night's camp. Avery had thrown himself into repairing the axle. Or at least he was trying. Some tasks required the use of both arms. Con had been able to assist a little, but the man's confounded pride stood in the way. Mrs. Wilcox hovered near her husband and occasionally offered to help. Avery snapped at her to leave him alone, perhaps more forcefully than he might have done under different circumstances. His wife hadn't taken his response very well, and they'd gotten into something of a dither.

Con stood and dusted dirt from his hands. "Sorry, but I'd better go. I'll come back tonight."

Avery extricated himself from beneath the wagon and extended his hand to Con. "Thanks for staying behind with us this long."

Con nodded, and then glanced at Mrs. Wilcox. "Why not come along with me? You'd be safer with the train, and my sister would welcome your company."

Something thudded. A gurgling sound came from Avery. Con turned his head. Mrs. Wilcox screamed.

Avery's eyes had gone wide. His fingers closed around an arrow shaft protruding from his throat. He swayed, then toppled to the ground. Mrs. Wilcox caught at her falling husband and went down with him.

Con dove beneath the wagon while arrows zinged. War whoops punched the air. Hoofbeats shook the ground. Con came up on the far side and peered out past the bonnet.

"Help me! He's dying." Mrs. Wilcox cradled her writhing husband, who was rasping in strangled breaths.

Con pulled his Colt revolver and called to the distraught woman. "Crawl to me. You're in danger."

Her face twisted. "Don't ask me to leave my husband."

He held out a hand to her. "He would want you to save yourself."

Avery's struggles stopped. He lay staring at the sky, his chest no longer moving.

"No!" Mrs. Wilcox wailed. Tears swamped her eyes, and her shoulders shook.

Con braced himself to go after her. Crouching low, he left the shelter of the wagon.

A bow twanged.

Con spun backward and hit the ground in the tall grass behind him. With an arrow embedded in his flesh, warm liquid coated his fingers. Fighting off lightheadedness, he felt his wounded shoulder. He gritted his teeth and broke off the shaft, panting to manage the pain.

He patted the grass around him, but his gun eluded him. It must have flown from his hand when he fell. It couldn't be far. He crawled through the grass, searching frantically. His hand closed over the smooth wooden grip of his revolver.

Mrs. Wilcox shrieked.

Con pushed to his knees, ready to take aim.

Blackness swarmed over him.

Kicking Horse closed in on the crippled wagon, his arm clamped around Bry. She darted her gaze through the warriors ahead of them. Con seemed to have vanished. The riders shifted, and she picked out Maisey on her knees weeping, her head bowed. Bry spotted the man lying on the ground beside Maisey, and a sick feeling clutched her stomach.

Movement caught her eye--Con stealing out from behind the wagon, headed toward Maisey.

One of the warriors pulled back his bow. An arrow glinted through the air. Her brother went down.

Bry whimpered.

Kicking Horse chided her in his own tongue, and his arm around her middle momentarily cut off her breath. Head reeling, she gasped in air.

Please, God. Don't let Con be dead.

Maisey lifted her head, and the breeze swept back her hair, fallen from its pins, as the warriors approached. The ones in the front rode around her, while the others went on to pillage the wagon. Bry tried to find Maisey in the confusion, but all she could see were bobbing headdresses and the thrashing legs of war ponies.

One of the warriors pulled Maisey onto a horse and tied her hands while she sagged in the saddle.

Kicking Horse wheeled his war pony and rode toward the river, taking Bry with him.

CHAPTER FIFTEEN

NICK RAN TOWARD THE CRIPPLED WAGON in the distance, his heart heavy with despair. Without a horse, he had no hope of reaching it in time to help Bry and the others. He dreaded to think what might happen. With Kicking Horse about to kidnap Bry, any delay increased the chances he'd succeed,

"What happened to your horse?" Parker's voice penetrated Nick's gloom.

On the crest of the rise behind him, Parker sat on the wagon master's Morgan horse. Nick started toward him. "You're a sight for sore eyes, but why aren't you with the train?"

"Brett took over the mules and sent me to check on things." Parker rode to meet him. "He's softer than he lets on."

"I'm glad of that. I could use a ride. A Cheyenne band took my horse. They made off with Mrs. Brennan and are attacking the Wilcox wagon."

"Climb on."

Nick mounted behind Parker, who wasted no time heading for the Wilcox wagon. His stomach churned as the Morgan brought them nearer. The wagon and the area around it were too still. The Cheyenne had gone, leaving no sign of life behind them. He tried to hold onto hope, but he'd seen too many ambushes to doubt what they would find.

At the sight of Avery's mangled body, Nick sucked in a painful breath.

Parker reined in the Morgan. "Poor cuss."

Nick dismounted and bent over the crippled man who had become his friend. "I'm sorry, Avery." He closed Avery's eyes and turned away with a lump in his throat.

Martin Wallers came around the wagon, leading his horse through the tumbled crates, broken dishes, and other items taken from inside the wagon and strewn about. "The heathen have done their horrid work. They're gone now, and the two women with them."

Nick put a hand to the back of his neck. "Has anyone found Conner Walsh?"

"No sign." Wallers pushed back his bowler hat, and a graying lock of hair sprang onto his forehead. "Are you sure he was here?"

Nick nodded. "He was helping Avery with his axle."

"They must have taken him, too."

Nick didn't argue that he thought they probably hadn't. Defeating a man in combat brought more honor for a Cheyenne warrior than conquering a woman or child. Besides, women and children more readily accepted captivity than men. "We should look a little harder." He didn't want to make the suggestion with everything in him crying out to go after Bry. Her brother might be lying wounded nearby, though. They couldn't leave without making a concentrated effort to find him.

"Yes, of course." Parker's saddle creaked, and he dropped to the ground.

Wallers gave a firm nod.

"Let's hope he's not lying dead." Parker moved past the spot where Avery had bled and died. "I don't care to come across another massacred body."

Walking a little apart from the other men who had ridden back from the train to help, they fanned out in order to cover the area well.

"There's blood here." Nick shouted the alert, then followed the crimson trail while the others caught up to him. His foot bumped against something hard in a stand of tall grass. He reached down and retrieved a Colt revolver. He stared at the weapon, trying to recall if he'd seen it in Con's hands.

"He's over here." Parker's voice rang out. He bent down, vanishing behind the grass. "They shot him, but he's still alive!"

Nick reached the stricken man along with the others.

Parker, bent over Con, looked up. "He's lost a lot of blood."

"We have to remove the arrow right away, or he'll bleed to death." Nick drew his knife from its sheath.

"Hold on there." Timothy Dales, normally a quieter member of the train, spoke. "Shouldn't we take him to camp where the doctor can see to him?"

"There's no time for that." Nick wondered if they would try to prevent him from making an effort to save Con. "The arrow tip is designed to keep blood flowing through the wound." He could have added that he'd seen such an arrow bring a buffalo down often enough, but he rarely mentioned his life among his mother's people to settlers. Wallers' face took on as pale a hue as Con's. None of the men looked particularly stalwart, with the exception of Parker. "Hold him down." Ignoring their discomfort, Nick gave the order in a brisk voice. "He might jerk if he wakes and cause the knife to slip."

Parker pinned Con's shoulders. The others hesitated, but then moved in to hold down his legs. Nick made short work of removing the arrow and ended as Con woke with a scream.

Nick whipped the kerchief from his neck and pressed it to the wound. "Sorry I had to do that."

Con made no reply, having fainted again. He lay pale and still, his chest barely rising and falling.

"God knows if he'll live." Nick spoke his thought out loud.

Wallers cleared his throat. "We'd better get him to the doctor before long."

"Moving him might kill him." Parker grunted. "But I guess we don't have a choice."

Nick tensed. Staying put might be better for Con, but they'd fall so far behind the wagon train that they might never catch up. Even if someone persuaded Brett to lay by for a couple of days, that would be too short a time to make a difference. They'd have to take the chance. "Ride ahead, Parker. We should alert Brett to the presence of Cheyenne warriors in the area and ask to bring back a wagon for the wounded man."

Parker shook his head. "After what just happened here, I doubt he'll want to risk anyone else."

Nick squinted against the sun, which had lowered in the sky. "We'll have to take Con by travois, then."

"A *what?*" Parker's eyes narrowed, then widened. "Oh, you mean a drag sled."

Nick squinted toward the lowering sun. "We'd better hurry while we have light. We can cut down a couple of saplings for poles and use what's left of the wagon to make ties and a sling to carry Con."

Nick and the others set about fashioning the travois from the wagon wood. He worked all the more quickly whenever Bry entered his thoughts. She would thank him for looking after her brother, but he yearned to take one of the horses and ride after her. However, that could result in his being hung as a horse thief. He'd been too close to the rope a time or two already. He should ask Brett to release him from his employment and to loan him a horse to go after Bry.

Meanwhile, he prayed that his step-brother would protect his prisoner. He frowned at the possibility that Kicking Horse would keep her safe from the other warriors but not from himself.

Nick wouldn't put anything past the son of his father's murderer.

"I intend to go after the women." Nick looked across the fire at the wagon master, waiting for his response.

Brett poured coffee from a blackened pot into a tin cup. Some of the liquid splashed out of the pot to sizzle on one of the stones sheltering the fire. "I was planning on sending a rider—you possibly—to let the general at the fort know what happened." He held out the cup to Nick. "Instead of abandoning the wagon train on a death mission, why not let the soldiers go after the women?"

Nick sipped the steaming brew. "You know as well as I do how that could turn out for the Cheyenne."

Brett scowled. "After what Long Knife did to your father, why do you care?"

He recoiled inwardly at the name of Kicking Horse's sire, the man who had killed his father and kidnapped his mother. Nick had lost both parents that day. His mother had refused to give her reasons for marrying her husband's murderer, but Nick suspected that Long Knife had forced her by some means. Long Knife and Kicking Horse had taught Nick what it meant to suffer. He'd been thankful when his mother's death had at last freed him from any obligation to remain. An image of dark eyes swimming with tears passed before him. Rising Bird, had clung to his saddle the day he'd ridden away. "Please, Wolf Walking, don't leave me."

Pushing away the memory of his half-sister's grief, Nick moved closer to the fire. If only things could have gone differently. Turning his back on his sister had broken his heart. Sometimes all you could do was avoid a bad situation. Now, here he was, arguing with Brett about returning to his mother's people, something he'd never expected to do.

Brett shook his head. "All I know is that I need to deliver this train to Montana Territory. You signed on to help me, remember?"

"I haven't forgotten that, but sending me after the women could prevent bloodshed."

"I can't wait for you and chance another attack."

"You could move closer to the fort. From the sound of matters, delaying might save the train rather than harm it."

Brett's scowl gave his opinion of that idea. "And risk cholera?"

"That might be safer than bypassing Sedgwick to blaze your own trail."

Brett watched him in the firelight. "You've got your mind made up to go after that woman, don't you? That's what this is really about."

Nick reminded himself that he didn't have to tell Brett

anything. "I'd like to leave with your blessing."

"All I can give you is my understanding. If I were a younger man—" Brett threw a stick into the fire, then glanced up. "Do you love her?"

"That's my business."

"You tell yourself that, but even thinking that way of a white woman can stir a heap of trouble. If that brother of hers finds out that you touched her in any way, he'll make that business of yours his own."

Brett's words struck Nick to the heart. "I won't lay a hand on her, but I can't abandon her. I'm surprised you can."

"When folks decide to travel west, what happens to them along the way is their lookout. I but I can't afford to dally." The wagon master glanced beyond Nick to Parker, who walked into the circle of firelight. "How's Con doing?"

The mule skinner smiled, revealing gapped front teeth. "I reckon the Almighty's watchin' over that one. Doc Amos says that if the arrow had been any closer to his heart, he'd have died."

"They tell me you saved him." Brett nodded to Nick. "He'd have bled to death without you. Using a travois to carry him was quick thinking."

Nick glanced away, unused to praise. "Will he live?"

"Doc can't say. He's comfortable, anyway. Doc wants to put him in the tick bed in the back of your wagon. He can't lay him in his own with Phoebe there."

"He'll need to recover quickly." Brett squared his shoulders. "After tomorrow, we move out."

Parker frowned. "One day's rest isn't enough time."

"It's all I can give." Brett flung out the dregs of his coffee. "Where's Con's wagon?"

"Thad brought it along and took care of his livestock to boot."

"Good. Find someone to drive it when we leave."

"Thad should be willing." Parker moved off.

Brett turned back to Nick. "I'd ask you to leave the Widow Brennan for the soldiers to find, but I'd be wasting my breath."

"I'll catch up to the train."

"You'll have a hard time finding me off the trail."

"I can do it."

Brett grunted. "I reckon you could, if they don't tomahawk you. I don't like you riding off alone."

"I'll have a better chance on my own."

"If you don't wind up dead."

"You know I'm right. After the massacre at Sand Creek, any white man who falls into the hands of the Cheyenne won't live long." Reports of Colonel Chivington's brutality at Sand Creek had seared Nick's mind. The Cheyenne who had survived the carnage wouldn't forget the suffering of the family members they lost that day.

"What guarantee do you have that Kicking Horse won't treat you the same as a white man?"

"None."

Brett whistled, low. "I wish I had your gumption. Your father was the same. All right, then."

"There's just one thing."

"Oh?"

"I need to borrow a horse. The Cheyenne took Tavo."

"Well then, you'll have to ride Buck."

Nick stared at him. "But that horse is half-broken."

"Keep him, as far as I'm concerned. You're the only one who could ride him anyway."

Nick grimaced at the memory. "I managed to stay on, if you call that riding."

"He's the one I can spare." Brett shrugged. "Take him or leave him."

Bry jerked awake to the thudding of hooves. The ground sped past beneath Kilkenny, whom she'd been allowed to ride. She clutched the saddle, thankful she hadn't fallen. Her body ached from remaining in the saddle late into the night. She'd held a rope, fastened under her horse's jaw, while her captor led Kilkenny. A little way ahead, Maisey rode Tavo, led by the warrior who had claimed her.

Cool air touched Bry's face, damp like tears. Water murmured over rocks somewhere ahead, insects chirped, and a distant night bird lifted its lonely song. The upheaval that had brought her to this pass seemed but a ripple in a pond, soon forgotten. The world she'd known would go on without her.

With the shock so raw, she hardly knew what she felt. Her mind whirled whenever she tried to make sense of things. Her breath hitched at the thought that her quick-tempered brother might have landed himself in one fight too many. *No! Con can't be dead.* Tears blurred her eyes, and she squeezed them closed with a shuddering sigh. Mourning her brother seemed wrong, an admission that he was gone forever. Con had always been larger than life, and his death didn't seem possible.

The scent of water permeated the air, growing stronger until they finally splashed across a stream. The tortuous journey continued, and she drifted in and out of a stupor. In the dead of night, they stopped at last.

Kicking Horse's rough hands gripped her waist and pulled her from Kilkenny's back. She slid down the mare's side but had to grasp the saddle to remain standing. Her entire body ached from the long ride, and her tongue felt thick and dry.

Kicking Horse turned away. She swayed on her feet but managed to remain upright despite her dizziness.

The warrior who had captured Maisey said something in his language and extended his water skin to her.

An arm dragged Bry backward at the waist, and she turned her head in sudden fear. Holding her against him, Kicking Horse tipped a water bag to her mouth. She gulped down the gamey contents until he snatched it away. Her stomach churned, and she leaned forward to retch.

With a spate of words, Kicking Horse pulled her behind him to the stream they had crossed. He motioned to the surface, then to the front of her dress. "Wash yourself."

Bry scanned the trees that lined the banks and cast deep shadows in the moonlight. She repressed the urge to bolt into their concealment. Giving in to panic might bring about Maisey's death in addition to her own. Bry leaned down and cleansed her face, then tore a strip of lace from her riding costume and used it to clean her garment. She rinsed the lace and let it fall from her fingers onto the bank when Kicking Horse glanced away, then cupped her palms to drink. The water tasted sweet, and she quenched her thirst.

She hoped the night's journey would end here so they would be closer to anyone who tried to find them. However, she wasn't sure what would befall her when the war party stopped. They continued on, leaving the question for another time. The ground rose steadily toward a bluff that reared its black head against the starry sky.

They hurried down a trail that climbed into the rocky fastness.

How Kilkenny kept her footing while climbing over crags, she didn't know. Bry made the mistake of looking down at the moonlit landscape far below. The dizzying height churned her stomach.

A chill wind and the ripple of water announced that a large river, probably the Platte, lay below. Without warning, the warriors turned their horses down the steep slope. Her captor followed, leading Kilkenny. Bry clutched the saddle, her heart pounding. Her horse reached the river, which ran deep in this place. Kilkenny forded it behind her captor's pony, swimming almost at once.

Please God, look after Maisey and me. Bry breathed the prayer. She might be out of practice in speaking to the Almighty, but it seemed high time to start. Kilkenny reached the opposite shore and much to Bry's relief, gained a foothold. The mare heaved out of the water, raining silver drops in the moonlight.

It seemed obvious to Bry that they'd traveled a route meant to throw off rescuers. They emerged from the river and separated into squads that rode in different directions, creating multiple trails that would confuse their true direction for anyone with the temerity to track them.

They entered a valley where a winding stream glinted, and flowers opened their cups in anticipation of the sun. Underbrush tangled beneath ancient trees in wild glory, and birds opened their throats to proclaim a new day.

The war party stopped at last, and sentinels moved into position to guard the camp. Bry dismounted quickly to prevent Kicking Horse from dragging her from the saddle. He sought her out and caught hold of her wrist. "You come here." He dragged her with him.

Bry turned her head to look for Maisey and found her being hauled in a similar fashion. Bry's captor stopped and called out. Several warriors started toward them, tomahawks in hand. Kicking Horse released her wrist. "Lie down."

Bry tried to convince herself that they wouldn't have brought her this far to kill her. She sent up a silent prayer and prostrated herself beside Maisey, braced for whatever happened.

CHAPTER SIXTEEN

NICK HEADED EAST, OR AT LEAST he tried going that direction. Buck had other ideas. No sooner had Nick settled into the saddle than the palomino took off southward. Taking control before a rider could was an old trick, although the stallion no doubt thought he'd invented it. He'd grown fond of Brett, and parting with the wagon master had been more of a wrench than Nick had expected, or he would have been more on guard. After a brief battle of wills, he brought the unruly horse to heel.

Once conquered, Buck submitted to his rider's wishes like a well-trained mount, but Nick knew the horse's docility for a ruse. He remained vigilant, watching for Buck's ears to flatten backward, signaling an intent to rebel.

The incident had cost Nick time. He'd left with morning light barely touching the sky, while now dawn blossomed at the horizon. A cool wind blew, but the sun would soon rise and burn off the clouds to warm the day.

Bry must be awake at this hour. He could picture her, still flushed with sleep while hauling water, gathering firewood, or otherwise carrying out a slave's duties.

The Cheyenne treated their slaves well when they adopted them, but he wanted so much more for Bry than a life of servitude. If only he had the means and the right to give her something better, he wouldn't hesitate. Avery had challenged him to cast aside his reservations. He wished he could believe that would be best for her, but the most he could hope to offer her was a chance at freedom.

Kicking Horse might have other plans for her than slavery. The thought spurred Nick onward.

Attuned to the tension in the animal beneath him, Nick

intercepted Buck's occasional forays away from the trail and pointed the horse toward the site of yesterday's massacre.

All lay in silence, as if the birds of the air knew to avoid this place. He passed the crippled wagon with his throat thickening. He'd arrived too late to help Avery. Bringing Mrs. Wilcox and Bry to safety seemed the least he could do to respect the memory of the man who had befriended him.

He turned Buck toward the river and drew up on the bank, gauging the river's speed and depth. The level had fallen since early spring, exposing rocks and rapids. The crossing would be a challenge on a docile horse. He nerved himself and pushed the palomino forward.

Buck halted at the edge, refusing to wade into the flowing water.

Nick sighed. This would be a long ride.

Bry longed to comfort Maisey, who pressed against her side, trembling. She had no way of knowing, while guarded by three warriors with tomahawks ready, whether taking her friend's hand would bring blades down upon them both. Faced with imminent death, Bry discovered a hunger for prayer for the second time that night. The choice seemed clear—lift her heart to God or descend into despair so dark it could swallow her sanity. Sleep, under the circumstances, kept its distance.

"You come." A hand shook her shoulder. "Catch horses."

Bry sat up, blinking in the light. "You want me to catch the horses?" she repeated her captor's words, trying to make sense of them.

"White man's horses run away from the Cheyenne. You come."

"All right." She stood stiffly. Hopefully, they wouldn't want her to catch the Wilcox mules as well.

Kilkenny walked to her sweetly enough, but Tavo shied away

when she tried to approach him. The desire to free him shook her with its intensity, but if she did Kicking Horse might be angry with her. She spoke to the horse in soft tones, pleased when he pricked his ears forward attentively. It took a little time, but she brought him in as well. The Wilcox mules took even longer to catch.

Maisey was sitting on the ground where she'd left her, eating buffalo meat and crackers. Bry's stomach clamored for food, but she had to choke down the portion their guards gave her. They moved off a bit, preoccupied with making ropes and repacking their plunder, which gave her a chance to talk with Maisey.

"They killed Avery." Maisey spoke in a bleak tone.

"I'm so sorry." The words felt inadequate, but they were all the comfort she could give. She released a shuddering breath. "I think they killed Con too."

Maisey leaned her head against Bry's shoulder. "He didn't deserve what they did to him."

Bry blinked away tears brought on by her friend's simple gesture.

Maisey hiccupped on a sob. "I won't be there when Phoebe wakes up."

"Doc Mather's wife will comfort her."

"But it won't be me. Oh, what's to become of us?"

Bry pulled in a breath. "I wish I knew."

Nick reined Buck in on the creek bank. Something white had caught his eye. He dismounted and picked up a bit of lace. He'd noticed the same rose pattern on Bry's riding garment. The little creek burbled in its bed while he considered what it meant.

Had Bry left this scrap as a sign for him to follow? From what he knew of her, it seemed likely. She must be keeping her wits about her. He had a notion that life had not treated her well. Despite that, he'd seen her put her hands on her hips and toss her head on more than one occasion. While the gesture might annoy him if he ever found himself on the other side of an argument with her, he appreciated her unbowed spirit.

He wasn't surprised Kicking Horse had brought her by this route, but it was good to have confirmation of the direction they had taken. It saved him time he could put to better use. He investigated the area for other clues and found tracks leading to a faint trail that climbed a bluff. Kicking Horse must have chosen the seldom used path, which no wagon could negotiate, to avoid being followed. Quick sympathy went through him at the terror the women must have felt while traveling this route.

The thought of traversing such a precarious path on a half-wild stallion gave him pause. One missed step and a horse could plummet into the gorge, carrying its rider to certain death. If only he had Tavo, he wouldn't hesitate. Buck was another matter.

Somewhere on the other side of the river waited the two women, and their plight would not leave his thoughts. What must they feel, torn from everything familiar?

Whatever happened, he must make the attempt to reach them.

One of the guards tied a collar made from animal skin around Bry's neck. To this he knotted a long cord. Across her front, he slipped a quillwork band attached to cords he wound around her upper arms. By means of these cords, he guided her the small distance from the camp and along a trail through the heavy timber.

Maisey followed, walking in front of another guard.

The ancient cottonwoods above Bry lifted their branches high as if in praise to God. Shattered beams filtered through the leaves to paint patterns at her feet. A stream ran beside the path then wandered away like an orphaned waif lost in the woods.

The beauty of the scene would normally have prompted a rise in her spirits, but now it mocked the ugliness of her circumstances.

To be reined like a mule erased her very humanity. She had no idea where the guards were taking them, but her mind clamored with horrifying suggestions.

They turned off the path into a small clearing where two stakes thrust starkly upward from the ground. A pile of smaller pegs waited between them. Bry's guard shoved her to the forest floor and gestured a warning that she should not attempt to rise. He tied the cord attached to her collar around one of the stakes. After stretching out her arm, he drove a peg into the ground and fastened her wrist to it with more cording. He repeated this process until he had secured her hands and feet, then stood back.

Bry turned her head and met Maisey's eyes. The other guard had restrained her friend in a similar fashion.

The two warriors exchanged a few words, and one of them laughed.

Bry's heart thudded in her chest. What did their captors plan to do?

The warriors spoke again, their speech carrying from the path. They continued talking as they moved away. Finally, the voices faded.

Bry summoned her voice. "Are you all right?"

"I wish they'd killed me along with Avery." Maisey spat out the bitter words.

"Don't say that."

"Why not? Dying would be better than living as a captive of my husband's murderers."

Bry could sympathize with her friend's sentiment, but she refused to surrender. If she could help it, Maisey wouldn't either. She cast about for something soothing to say. "That would leave Phoebe without a mother. I know it's hard, but try not to take on so." It wasn't much but all she could manage while in need of comfort herself.

"It's hard to hope when you're trussed like a holiday turkey. I can't even scratch an itch."

Satisfying an itch was the least of their worries, but Bry

refrained from stating the fact. She'd rather that Maisey focus on small annoyances rather than on their greater peril. If a bear or other animal attacked, they would have no way to defend themselves. If the guards didn't return to free them, they could die of neglect. She had never felt so vulnerable. "We should take this opportunity to devise a plan to escape."

"If we tried, they'd hunt us down and kill us," Maisey wailed. "Oh, why did any of this have to happen?"

Bry stared at the leaves swaying overhead, now stained with mauve in the first blush of sunset. Maisey's question burned within her also. *Why?* Phoebe and Avery hadn't deserved to die any more than Con should have taken an arrow. How could a good God allow such horrible acts? Mam and Liam would be alive today if the Almighty had acted on their behalf. Why hadn't He prevented her family from being trapped in the slum? He might have kept her from marrying a man who would abuse her. Why would He allow them to be staked to the ground, vulnerable to any predator that cared to rip their throats out?

"We should pray." Maisey spoke haltingly, as if she didn't believe her own words.

"Why do you hesitate?" Bry asked, unwilling to reconcile her friend's present weakness with the strength she'd shown until now.

"Seems like God might be mad at me."

"That's ridiculous," Bry chided. "I've never known anyone more heaven-bound than you."

"I don't want to talk about heaven right now," Maisey snapped.

Surprise rippled through Bry, but she restrained the urge to question her friend. When it came to matters of faith, Bry was still learning where she herself stood. The hollow ache in her stomach revealed an uncomfortable truth. Maisey's steadfast trust in God had been an anchor to which Bry had unknowingly clung. Now she felt cut adrift, spinning out of control in a wild current.

Staring into the shadows of a moon-washed night, Bry strained to hear above the rustling leaves of the giant cottonwood overhead. The spaces between Maisey's replies had lengthened, then stopped altogether. How could she sleep in such a state?

Bry started at every sound. When a stone turned in the stream, she knew it. A whippoorwill that flew into the tree above her did not go unnoticed. The night bird opened its throat in a lonely cry that matched her soul's yearning for release. She'd heard that the birds served as an omen of death in Indian lore. While she might once have laughed away the superstition, at present shaking it off seemed harder. She couldn't save herself from disaster but remained alert until the night frayed at the edges like a worn-out garment unraveling toward dawn.

The voices of the guards dragged Bry from sleep. Shivering in the morning chill, she turned her head and found Maisey looking her way. "Good morning." Maisey greeted her with a smile and spoke in a stronger tone than the one she'd used the night before. "Did you pass the night well?"

"No, but it's over now. You slept."

Maisey's smile faltered. "I dreamed about Avery dying." She shuddered.

"Don't think on it."

"I can't seem to help it. The memory returns again and again. It takes me over so completely that I fear it will drive me insane."

The guards arrived and untied them with swift skill. Bry sat up, stretched her stiff muscles, and rubbed her wrists.

The warrior who had freed her paused while wrapping the cords that had bound her. He glanced pointedly at her. "Mo'ehno'hame."

Bry recognized the word the Cheyenne used for horses and sighed but nodded her understanding. It had become her duty, apparently, to chase down the horses and mules who wanted nothing to do with the thieves who had stolen them. After the night she'd spent, the chore seemed arduous. Maisey had somehow escaped this task, perhaps to keep her and Maisey separated during the times they went about unrestrained. Bry couldn't imagine trying to run with sentinels watching over the livestock, however.

The horses were growing used to the routine and came to her more readily this morning. The mules were another story. She persevered and accomplished the task anyway, but it cost her the chance at breakfast and earned her a frown from Kicking Horse for the late start the delay gave them.

The sun glared down on her uncovered head while they rode endlessly through dry landscapes of burning sand, sagebrush, and cactus. With no friendly stream to offer relief, they continued through the scorching heat.

"Mahpe!" She called the word she'd heard the warriors use for water in a voice that croaked from her parched throat.

Kicking Horse didn't respond but urged his horse faster.

Bry listed in the saddle but jerked upright, narrowly avoiding a tumble. Thirst pressed her to the point of torture, and she closed her eyes in an agony of despair. Images of cooling drinks flowed across her mind, offered then quickly withdrawn. The prospect of death, so fearful in the night, now became a release from torment.

The sun advanced in its course across the bleached sky and hung in full swelter above the horizon. The trail entered a valley where green grass grew and a river glimmered. A brook made its way down the hillside nearest them to join the larger waterway. Bry wanted to weep. The vision seemed a dream, one she could not fathom. Kicking Horse dismounted and lifted her from the saddle. He laid her in the shallow bed of the brook. Upstream from her, Maisey's captor lowered her into the water.

Bry didn't have the energy to drink, but the silken water cooled her heated skin and called her back from the brink of insensibility. Her strength returned, and she lapped at the water until she could sit up and carry greedy handfuls to her mouth.

Kicking Horse had remained behind while the others continued on. Without the paint he'd worn in battle, he seemed younger. His mouth slashed a straight line above a strong chin, and hollows shadowed his face beneath his high cheekbones. She didn't want to think well of him, but he had helped her at a time of need. She offered him a fleeting smile. "Thank you."

He nodded. "You will see I can be kind."

Bry shrank from his lustful stare. She tried unsuccessfully to climb back onto her horse.

He lifted her, still dripping, into his arms. "When we reach our village, you will become my wife."

CHAPTER SEVENTEEN

THE WARRIORS RAISED THEIR VOICES IN whooping cries that penetrated the fog surrounding Bry. Exhaustion from the long ride had bowed her head, but she made the effort to look up. Running a thick tongue over her cracked lips, she squinted into the afternoon glare.

Tepees made of animal skins, unadorned or painted with horses or other symbols, pointed skyward. On the outskirts of the village, laughing children played with hoops but abandoned their game to run with glad cries toward the approaching riders. Two old men who had sat together watching the children at play now stood. Women carrying water bags, netted fish, and baskets of food turned with expectant faces.

A woman stood transfixed at the near edge of camp. A water bag slipped from her grasp and hit the ground as water sloshed and spilled. Her glossy hair fell from a middle part in two long braids to her waist. Shells dangled at her ears and wrapped her throat. A quill vest tied with laces covered her chest. She started forward, the fringe of her dress swaying, and her steps picked up speed until she was running.

The man who had captured Maisey stopped his pony when he reached the woman. She stopped short of him, peering with her dark eyes at Maisey. The woman tilted her head and spoke to the man, her words flowing like music despite her strident tone.

He answered in an irritated voice, and the woman stepped back. She swept a glance over Bry, then said something to Kicking Horse. The children came up behind the woman and, with dark eyes, stared at Bry and Maisey. After a moment's silence, the tallest boy called out in a mocking voice, and the others joined in with laughter. Bry didn't understand their words, but the message was unmistakable. Other women and the old men who had watched the children turned wary expressions toward Bry. She sat taller in the saddle, not willing to let the children see how their unkindness wilted her like a flower denied rain. Her stomach ached, and a sudden yearning pierced her. She longed to sit at her mother's knee, as she'd done long ago in Ireland.

Kicking Horse scolded the children, and they fell back. He dismounted from his pony, the feathers of his war bonnet floating in the breeze. Bry slid from the saddle and looked for Maisey. Her friend stood cowering against the horse she'd ridden, skittering a bewildered glance about. Bry went to her.

Kicking Horse greeted the woman who had argued with Maisey's captor. They spoke to one another in a rapid-fire exchange, but then in softer tones, seemed to reach some sort of agreement.

The woman turned her gaze on Bry and Maisey. "I am called Vay-kay-soto-aha-est-see, Rising Bird in your language." Her husky voice pulsed below the high-pitched chatter and laughter as the returning warriors received their welcome.

Bry stared at her. "You speak English?"

"My mother taught me."

"This is my sister," Kicking Horse explained. "She will take you into her tepee and care for you."

Bry sent the woman an uncertain look that was met by a smile. "Thank you."

Rising Bird's face softened. "What are your names?" Her glance took in Maisey as well as Bry.

One look at her friend's alarmed expression convinced Bry to answer for them both. "I'm Bry, and this is Maisey."

Rising Bird repeated their names, then pointed to Maisey's captor. "My husband Ahanu—He Laugh."

Ahanu's scowl did not seem very mirthful to Bry.

Rising Bird nodded to the leader. "O-hoh-tay-hah-me—Kicking Horse."

Kicking Horse grunted at the sound of his name. He walked off toward the war ponies, and Ahanu followed.

"Come and rest," Rising Bird invited. She led them through the village to one of the tepees painted with running horses and gestured toward the circular opening in its side.

Bry stepped inside with Maisey close behind. She blinked to help her eyes adjust to the dim interior and eventually made out a bed of skins on the bench along the wall and a fire circle in the middle of the tepee.

"Sit." Rising Bird waved a hand toward the bench.

Maisey obeyed at once, looking like an orphaned child. She'd lost her bonnet, and her hair fell in a tangle to her waist. One of her sleeves had a tear at the shoulder, and the hem of her skirt hung filthy and ragged. Bry sat beside her friend, taken by the desire to shield her from further suffering.

Rising Bird brought them a water bag to drink from then fetched dried meat. She sat beside them while they ate. Emboldened by the woman's quiet presence, Bry asked the question uppermost in her thoughts. "What will happen to us?"

"I don't know." Rising Bird frowned. "My brother does not listen. White women are bad medicine. Soldiers will come."

Bry's heartbeat picked up its pace. "Then let us go."

Rising Bird stared at her. "That is not for me to decide. The soldiers killed my brother's wife at Sand Creek. He says that you will replace her."

Bry's face heated. "I would not make a good wife for such an important man as your brother. I know nothing of your ways and would pine every day to return to my people."

Rising Bird considered her words, but a woman called into the tepee before she could reply. Rising Bird rose in a graceful movement and went to her. After a rapid conversation, she returned with a bundle of beaded skins in her arms. "From Namid, my husband's sister." She thrust the bundle toward Bry with a glance at Maisey.

Outside the tepee, a drumbeat started up, soon underscored by chanting voices. Rising Bird looked out from the entrance, then turned back with her eyes gleaming. "Ahanu is already dancing, and I will too. We will be gone a long time. Stay here."

"Wait!" Bry called, emboldened by curiosity. "You spoke only of me. What's to become of Maisey?"

Rising Bird's glance slid away. "She belongs to Ahanu." She slipped through the opening, but her whispered words lingered in Bry's mind.

She divided the clothing with Maisey, the skins soft in her hands. She would rather not change from her own garments, but they had become tattered and provided less protection from the elements than these would.

She slipped out of her dress and discarded it in favor of the fringed and beaded buckskin one. The garment hung to mid-calf, which felt a little strange. It left her high-laced boots and knitted stockings immodestly exposed, but the shorter length brought a freedom of movement she'd never known.

Rising Bird had left several water bags and packets of dried meat on the bench. Bry frowned at them, struck by a suspicion.

"She wants us to escape." Maisey spoke Bry's thought out loud.

Nick reined in his horse, listening. A distant drum pulsed like a beating heart beneath the rattle of gourds and scratching of bone instruments. He had little doubt what he would find upon reaching the encampment. Avery's scalp, decorated with fur and beads, would be stretched across a hoop and circled by dancers. By this means the Tsistsistas, as his mother's people called themselves, celebrated victory while honoring a fallen enemy, now assigned to protect the warrior who had slain him.

Resisting the impulse to race across the prairie and search for Bry in the village, he turned aside. He had pushed his horse and himself too hard, and they both needed rest. Nick tilted his water skin and took long gulps while Buck drank from the river. In the fading light, the surface of the North Platte gleamed in shades of brown and blue.

The emotions churning within Nick—anger, sorrow, fear—were old companions. Confronting Kicking Horse was the last thing he wanted, but it had been forced upon him. "I don't know how to walk this path, God." His whisper stirred the air. "I need help."

A gust whistled down the river like a breath from the Almighty, fanned his face, and fell away. The blast had revived him, and with more heart, he pushed his horse into motion. The stop had done Buck good, and they reached the village swiftly.

He hesitated at the edge of the firelight, not certain of his reception. These were his mother's people, but he had rejected them by leaving.

Strong Bear looked back at him from the crowd gathered around the dancers. His former friend's start gave away that he'd recognized him.

Nick lifted a hand in greeting.

Strong Bear didn't return his smile. He spoke to the warriors beside him. Heads turned. Dark eyes gleamed.

Nick swallowed his disappointment at his old friend's rejection. He would find no help from that quarter. He scanned the crowd for other familiar faces, and his stomach tightened. Kicking Horse stood beside Ahanu, a wolfish look on his face that reminded Nick of the expression his step-brother had worn after raiding the ranches along the Little Blue. Terrible as those attacks had been, atrocities by the soldiers against the Cheyenne had since rivaled them. Nick wanted nothing to do with senseless bloodshed, no matter which side caused it.

He dismounted and, with reluctant footsteps, walked toward Kicking Horse. A blow struck his back, and he fell forward.

Nick broke his fall with his hands, pain jarring his wrists. Rocks scraped his palms. He rolled to the side an instant before Strong Bear flung himself over the place he had vacated.

Nick shoved to his feet. Several of Strong Bear's friends caught him from behind. "Why do you greet me as an enemy?" Nick challenged in Cheyenne.

"You do not belong among us." Strong Bear growled.

"Have you forgotten my mother was one of you?"

"It doesn't matter who your mother was." Strong Bear drove his fist into Nick's stomach. Nick grunted and would have doubled over, but his captors kept him upright.

"And so, Wolf Walking cowers like a trapped coyote." Strong Bear spat out, rage twisting his face. He hauled back his fist again.

"Don't!" A woman cried in a voice Nick recognized.

With an ache in his heart that hurt worse than the pain in his stomach, he lifted his head and found her standing beside Strong Bear. It had been over ten years since he'd seen his sister. Little more than a child when he'd left, she had grown into a beautiful woman. Her almond eyes shone, a lamp that revealed her inward beauty. Glossy hair sprang above her well-shaped brow. He caught his breath at how closely she resembled their mother.

"*Please.*" Rising Bird's forehead puckered. "Don't hurt my brother."

"This dog is not your brother." Strong Bear's fist thudded into Nick's eye, snapping his head back.

Rising Bird screamed.

The drum stopped beating.

"What is this?" Kicking Horse strode toward them across the grass. "Strong Bear, you fight without honor."

Strong Bear scowled. "This cut-hair deserves none."

Kicking Horse's nostrils flared. "Let him go."

At their war chief's low command, those restraining Nick released him.

The drum started beating again.

"Thank you." Nick cupped his eye with his palm.

"Why have you come?" Kicking Horse snapped. "I thought you wanted to live as the white man's brother."

That wasn't what he'd said, nor was such a thing possible, but there was no point in arguing when he'd come to negotiate. "The two women you took—the soldiers will search until they find them."

"We have taken others, and the soldiers did not follow."

"The soldiers no longer fear the Tsistsistas in the way they once did. Let me take the women to the fort, so the soldiers will not come."

"Don't listen to his lies," Strong Bear growled. "He loves those who killed my sister and your wife."

"Silence." Kicking Horse scowled at the man, then turned toward Nick. "My sister loves you, Wolf Walking. For her sake, I will not take your life for daring to ride here. Now leave us."

"I will go." Nick agreed but stood his ground. "Only let me take the women."

Kicking Horse shook his head. "One belongs to me, the other to Ahanu."

Rising Bird stepped forward and turned pleading eyes on Kicking Horse. "If you wish to please your sister, give me one kindness. Let my brother sleep this night in my tepee."

Kicking Horse frowned, and the scar Nick had given him carved a line into his cheek. "This is not wise."

"I beg this of you. Wolf Walking is precious to me, and I may never see him again."

"One night only, and he must surrender his rifle to Ahanu."

"Why do you let her persuade you?" Strong Bear asked.

"I have made my choice." Kicking Horse scowled at Strong Bear. "You will not interfere."

Namid ran from the shadows beside the tepees and into the firelight. "The captive women—they are gone!"

The Cheyenne's wild music made Bry uneasy, but it hid her thrashing while she crawled through the sage and bunch grass behind Maisey. She put her knee down on something prickly and sucked in a breath but continued on. Scratches from barbs and even the rattle of snakes paled beside the specter of recapture.

The grass lengthened to waist-high, not tall enough to completely hide a person. Maisey lurched to her feet and fled hunched over. Bry did the same, her breath rasping in her throat as she caught up to her friend. Their flight felt strangely similar to when she'd hidden in the fields around her family's farm while playing tag with her brothers. She'd giggled then. Tears dampened her face now.

Bry glanced toward the village. The dancers seemed so near and their chanting so eerie that goosebumps raised on her arms. When the music halted, she couldn't bring herself to look again, despite the curiosity that burned within her. Running in this position made her dizzy. Her face flamed with heat, and perspiration broke out on her brow. Her side cramped, forcing her to slow. The water skin she carried across one shoulder slapped her side annoyingly, making her want to drop it. She didn't dare leave a sign of their passing, however. If they managed by some miracle to escape, she would need the water it held.

Darkness crouched at the edges of daylight, waiting to spring over the grassland. A short distance ahead, the Platte gleamed in the breathless time before the sky streaked with red and the sun plummeted to earth.

An uproar from the Cheyenne village rose above the rushing of the river. The hair at the back of Bry's neck bristled. Maisey swung toward the village. "Oh no, hurry." She dug her nails into Bry's arm, her eyes glazed. "They're coming after us."

"Stop it!" Bry gave her a shake. "You can't panic. We have to think."

"That won't help." Sorrow chased fear across Maisey's face, but then her expression cleared. "We need to pray."

Bry stared at her. It was good to see her friend's faith recovering, but she shook her head. "There's no time." Bry started off again.

"All right then." Maisey called from behind her. "I'll pray for us both."

"We need to find a place to hide." Bry turned back to hurry her friend along.

Maisey yelped and pitched forward.

"Are you all right?" Bry went to her.

"I rammed into a rock hidden in the grass." Maisey rolled onto her side, moaning. "My foot feels like it's broken."

Warriors on horseback galloped from the village in all directions, darker shadows against the darkening plain.

Bry grasped Maisey's arm. "Come on. *Get up!*"

"What's the use?" Maisey gasped out the question. "They're going to kill us."

"Don't say that!" Bry hoisted her friend upright. "You have to try."

Maisey moaned. "Go on without me."

"I'm not leaving you." Bry moved in to brace her on one side. "Lean on me."

"You are a stubborn woman." Maisey hobbled in the direction of the river. After a few steps, Maisey walked more steadily. She pulled away and picked up speed. "Over there." Maisey started toward a stand of trees lining the bank.

"No, wait," Bry called softly. "That would be the first place they'd look." With the water cutting deeply, they couldn't ford the river. Bry scanned the area and pointed. "Do you see the cave in the bluff above the waterline?"

Maisey shook her head, then nodded. "I'm scared, Bry." She all but sobbed the words between gasps. "I can hear them coming."

Bry hurried after her friend, who rushed ahead.

Maisey reached the cave and peered inside. "It's snug, but two can fit."

Bry hesitated. The cave was smaller than she'd realized. Although hard to spot, it could become a death trap if any of their pursuers found them. What else could they do, though, with time running out? Even if they could ford the river, they'd never outrun warriors on horseback. With hoofbeats pounding the air, she faced the horrible truth. They had little hope of saving themselves.

"Why aren't you coming inside?" Maisey called from within the cave. "They'll see you."

Bry shed her hesitation and wedged herself beside Maisey. It helped to squeeze her eyes shut so she wouldn't see the narrow space entombing them, but a whimper escaped her anyway.

Maisey's hand covered hers. "Tell me what's wrong," she whispered.

"I hate confining spaces." As a small child, she'd once climbed into Mam's clothing trunk. The lid had slammed shut, and she hadn't been able to open it and free herself. She'd cowered inside, crying, until Con raised the lid and sang out that he'd found her. Since then, she'd been unable to abide tight spots.

Maisey's hand closed over hers. "I'm sorry."

Bry strained to hear any sound from their pursuers, but the cave muffled the pounding of horse's hooves. "Maisey?"

The hand covering hers gave a squeeze.

Bry swallowed against tears. "I'll pray, too."

They bowed their heads, and their foreheads touched. Bry lifted a silent prayer. *God, I'm not sure why you took Mam and Liam. Maybe I didn't pray hard enough. Well, I'm praying now. Please don't let Maisey suffer anymore. And if you can see your way to looking after me too, I'd thank you.*

A feeling akin to peace washed over her. In its comfort, she opened her eyes.

Kicking Horse glared at Bry from the mouth of their refuge. He turned his head and shouted something in the Cheyenne tongue, then reached in and grabbed her arm.

Bry wanted to weep. They'd left Rising Bird's tepee with such high hopes.

"You come." He yanked her from the cave.

Their hands parted, and Maisey cried out.

Bry stood in silent disgrace as her captor collared her and tied a slave halter around her. More warriors dismounted and rushed to the cave entrance, Ahanu among them. Bry barely saw any of them, except for one man. Nick Laramie's gaze collided with hers. Relief washed through her, leaving her weak. *Nick had come to save them.*

Or had he? Nick looked so much like one of the Cheyenne warriors that her stomach clinched in protest. What did she really know about him except that she couldn't stop thinking about him? The first sight of Nick had excited fear in her. Perhaps that impression had been right, after all. Could she have let fascination blind her?

Ahanu pulled Maisey into the open and secured her with a halter. He climbed back onto his pony and rode off at a walk, bringing Maisey along by the cords of her halter and collar.

Kicking Horse prodded Bry, and she stumbled to his horse. He barked something in Nick's direction and rode off while she struggled to keep up.

Why had Nick joined the Cheyenne after telling her that he'd left them forever? She didn't want to believe that he'd lied to her. Had he traveled with the wagon train in order to turn on it? She'd heard of such happenings. Nick had chosen the campsite the Indians stampeded the buffalo herd through, and he'd stopped Avery's runaway mules in the place where Kicking Horse had attacked. If Nick had betrayed them, he had caused the deaths of Phoebe, Avery, and Con.

Despite herself, she'd instinctively trusted Nick. She should have guarded her emotions better. Hadn't she learned anything from Ian? After a man won your heart, he turned on you.

CHAPTER EIGHTEEN

NICK RESISTED THE TEMPTATION TO TRY to overpower Kicking Horse and make off with Bry. It was too risky, and Bry might get hurt. Besides, his sister loved his stepbrother, although Nick had never felt a kinship with him. And he had Maisey to consider. She'd been through enough. He couldn't possibly save Bry and abandon her. Nick dismounted and trailed through the village behind Bry and Kicking Horse, equally trapped as the prisoners he had come to free. He couldn't leave Bry and Maisey, nor at the moment could he save them.

Kicking Horse had resented his presence among those searching for the women, but he'd had to risk it. Prisoners who attempted escape might be put to death when recaptured. What he would do in that event, he didn't know, but if he didn't act quickly, a terrible fate could await them.

Night's curtain had descended by the time Nick dismounted a small distance from the figures circling by firelight. He'd seen the scalp dance go on for days, but with only one victim to honor, this one would probably end sooner. The drum throbbed, and medicine men's voices rose and fell in a hypnotic rhythm. The maidens circled one of Kicking Horse's wives, who lifted high the scalp pole as she stepped and bobbed on the south side of the fire. The young men lined up across from them, while the medicine men beat the drums and the married men's voices rose and fell in a hypnotic cadence.

Nick dismounted and moved into the shadows as close as he dared to Kicking Horse's tepee. Bry stood with her head bowed before his stepbrother, pacing before her with his hands fisted. "You women will suffer for making a fool of Ahanu and me," he snarled in English. "Tomorrow morning your punishment will begin. I will start by letting the women and children beat you." Nick tensed. ready to defend her should his stepbrother show signs of physical violence.

Ahanu rose at the edge of the village and started across the path. Maisey sat behind him, tied by a collar rope to a stake with her hands and feet bound. Ahanu strode into his tepee, followed by Rising Bird. Their voices murmured, then rose in obvious disagreement. Nick couldn't hear their words but guessed his sister didn't like the idea of Maisey belonging to Ahanu any more than he did. Owning a slave raised his sister's status, but Ahanu might have certain intentions toward Maisey.

Kicking Horse gave a command to several warriors who had searched for the prisoners with him, then vanished into his tepee. Two warriors took hold of Bry and half-carried her toward Maisey. They bound her hands and feet while a third drove a stake into the ground. Nick's heart bled for both women, but he restrained the urge to fight for them. Doing so would only result in his own death while leaving them in captivity.

Their task completed, the warriors moved off toward the dance.

Tears streamed down Bry's pale cheeks, and she looked utterly broken. Nick's heart ached to save her and Maisey from the humiliation that would face them in the morning.

Bry sat weeping, and no wonder, after what Kicking Horse had threatened. Nick gritted his teeth, restraining the urge to comfort her. He turned aside, determined to find the one man with more authority than Kicking Horse.

The old chief sat, not among those watching the dancers, but at his fireside. Viho's wrinkled face broke into a smile. "You have returned to us, Wolf Walking. Welcome home."

"Thank you." Nick lowered himself onto the bench across from him. "I want to return the white women to their people. I ask that you help me."

Viho gazed into the fire, the seams in his face deepening. "You ask a difficult thing."

"Not one too hard for a chief like you."

Viho frowned. "That might have been true once. Why do you want to take them?"

Nick hadn't expected this question. He considered the best answer to give. What could he say that would sway the chief? "I want to free my mother's people from the curse they bring. The women are bad medicine for the Tsistsistas."

The old chief pierced him with a bright glance, and took on an expression that chased the years from his face. Nick remembered the man as he had been—tall and noble but fearsome, yet beloved by the children in the village. "I believe you. Things have changed between our people and the white man. They came, and we were glad to share what we had with them, but they only took more. When they began to destroy the buffalo we need for food, we fought back. I am not sure our war chief cares to please the white man anymore."

"It is because of all you say that I make my request. The white men are like the sands of the desert. No one can count them, and still they keep coming. The Tsistsistas must learn to live in friendship with them or perish. Keeping the white women will not bring peace."

"There is wisdom in what you say. I will ponder what to do. You will remember that a chief does not command of the Tsistsistas in the way of the white man. I can only add my voice to your request before Kicking Horse and Ahanu. Tell me, Wolf Walking, what you are willing to pay for the women. Would you give up your horse and rifle? Do you have any money?"

Surrendering his rifle would feel a lot like letting go of his father, who had owned it before him. And Kicking Horse had already taken one horse from him. It hardly seemed fair to give him another. In the old chief's view, however, Kicking Horse had won Tavo as spoils of battle. On the other hand, what choice did he have?

The old chief watched Nick's face without speaking, then

nodded his approval before Nick could speak. The old chief had always been able to figure him out. Nick needed to say the words anyway. "To free the women, I would give up everything I own."

Bry stirred and lifted her head. Light painted the sky at daybreak with a glory that stood in stark contrast to the torments of her soul. With the morning chill raising goosebumps, an aching stomach, and gritty eyes after a restless night, she found it hard to rejoice in the beauty of nature. She had hoped, when Con brought her West, for more than suffering upon suffering. All the pathways of her life had narrowed into this one sunrise as a prisoner of the Cheyenne. Would she see another?

The drumbeat throbbed in the air, as it had when she'd fallen asleep the night before, but more quietly. She turned her head and found Maisey sitting up with a bewildered expression on her face. "What's to become of us?"

Bry frowned. "I don't know."

"I'm cold—so cold."

"Try not to think about your discomfort."

"I can't help it." Maisey's voice broke.

Why God, does sweet Maisey have to suffer? Bry raised her question to the silent heavens.

The warriors who had restrained her last night reappeared. They untied and haltered Bry and Maisey, then led them inside Kicking Horse's tepee.

Bry's pulse jumped at the sight of Kicking Horse seated on a bench, with Ahanu across from him. Smoke from the fire between them wafted skyward through the gap where the support poles crossed. Kicking Horse met Bry's gaze with a glittering look. With nostrils flared, he barked a command. Several warriors left the tepee.

Bry had no idea what Kicking Horse had said, but the

knowledge that his anger had not cooled churned her stomach.

"You will pay with your life for running off." Kicking Horse delivered their death sentence with a smug look on his face. Maisey whimpered, but Bry made no sound. Her life, which had seemed intolerable a few short hours ago, now became precious. She would cling to it if she could. "I beg you for mercy." She rasped the words barely above a whisper, but Kicking Horse's scowl told her he had heard them. She went on with her hope fading. "Being separated from our people and seeing those we love slain before our eyes fevered our minds."

Kicking Horse slashed his hand in a cutting gesture. "Enough! Plead no longer. Ahanu and I have decided your punishment. Rather than merely having the women and children beat you, we will make you targets in a war game. Each of you will be tied to an unbroken horse we'll turn loose. Our warriors will follow, shooting at you. Pray for an arrow to take you quickly. If your horse escapes, it will carry you wherever it goes until you die."

Bry moved with a strange detachment toward the horses, which pulled at their ropes, showed the whites of their eyes, and stomped the ground in a frenzy. She felt almost separate from her body, as if she might view her death from afar. Maisey, beside her, prayed openly. A group of women and children had gathered, and Bry knew a moment's thankfulness that Kicking Horse had not carried out his threat to have them pummel her to a slow death. The horrid fate he planned for her would be torture enough to endure before she passed beyond his ability to hurt her. She had not turned her head to look at Kicking Horse beyond an initial glance. He and Ahanu sat in the saddle among the warriors waiting for the sport to begin. Nick was nowhere in sight.

The sun beat down, warming the day. Few clouds hid the sky, and wildflowers woven into the grasses opened their faces to bask.

A sense of peace at odds with the situation flooded Bry, as if God Himself soothed her spirit. Holding her head high, she went forward to meet her doom. Her brow prickled with perspiration. The soft thud of her footfalls mingled with her rasping breaths and Maisey's quiet prayers. The scent of trammeled grass rose, sweet and sharp.

Warriors holding the horses they would ride watched their approach. Regret flickered across the face of the guard standing ready to hoist her onto the horse's back, or so she imagined. Whatever had caused his expression, it vanished as she reached him. He lifted her.

A voice called out in ringing tones.

The guard turned with Bry in his arms. The warrior about to lift Maisey straightened and peered toward the crowd. The mob of women parted for a wizened man who strode between them with Nick beside him. The old man held himself with such authority, and the others deferred to him so quickly, that he could only be their chief.

The old man and Nick stopped before Kicking Horse and Ahanu. The chief gestured toward Bry and Maisey and gave some sort of pronouncement.

Lowered abruptly to the ground, Bry stood on shaking legs and waited for her fate.

Nick took a seat beside Viho in Kicking Horse's tepee and met his stepbrother's glare head-on.

"What is this, Viho?" Kicking Horse scoffed. "Do you bring this one to challenge me? What has he said to make you speak for him?"

"I am not so old that I cannot speak for myself. You must not kill these women. Free them, or you will bring disaster on us all."

"Old Chief, I respect your wisdom." Kicking Horse spoke the mild words in a tone that grated. "However, these women have brought shame to me and Ahanu. Will you ask us to overlook this insult?"

"A wise man does not allow emotion to sway his decisions. Can you not see that you brought this shame upon yourselves by raiding the white man's wagons? Wolf Walking tells me that they will not overlook an offense to their women. If soldiers destroy the village because of your shame, you will not be able to hold up your head. I have heard the whispers. Some among us do not wish to follow you as war chief because your attacks on the white man have put us in peril." Viho looked to Ahanu, seated beside Kicking Horse. "You fought with your woman over your slave. Don't look surprised that I know this when you were not quiet. You must not bring sorrow to your tepee or to the Tsistsistas. The captives are bad medicine. Accept the payment Wolf Walking is prepared to make for them and be rid of them."

Kicking Horse's jaw firmed, and he took on the hostile expression of a man who had been struck. "I like nothing you say, Old Chief, but I will listen for my mother's sake. She taught me to honor you."

"That is more than your father ever did. Long Knife died because of his foolhardy nature. He should never have gone on that raid. You have given me hope that you will not repeat his mistakes."

"What will he pay for the captives?" Kicking Horse spoke without shifting his gaze to Nick.

"He can tell you that." Old Chief smiled fleetingly. "I have decided to add a well-trained pony for each of you to his offer."

Nick cleared his throat. "I will give all that I have of value. Keep my rifle, Ahanu. My horse I give to you, Kicking Horse."

Ahanu gave a nod. "I am happy to accept your rifle."

"I won't take anything from you but your life!" Kicking Horse bellowed. "Let us fight with knives, Wolf Walking. Kill me, and you can take the woman I own. But I will not lose."

"Come now, Kicking Horse," Old Chief intervened. "The horse is lively but of a good blood. What good will come of making your sister weep?"

Kicking Horse's jaw worked, and the veins on his neck stood out. He remained silent a long time, but nodded at last. "Take the women and go quickly, before I change my mind."

CHAPTER NINETEEN

Bry stood on a rock with water hurtling below her feet. She barely remembered the journey to the river with Nick and Maisey except as a trial of endurance. She wouldn't ask Nick to slow their pace, however, not with the fear of pursuit crawling down her spine. Her mind could not take in what had happened. To be liberated from certain death counted as a miracle by her reckoning. Nick had paid dearly to free them, and she would always feel grateful to him.

He had said little since parting from his sister. Did he wish events had gone differently, and that he hadn't been saddled with two mouths to feed besides his own? It seemed a fair objection, but one she didn't care to know he would make. She'd lost her perspective since she'd first met the man, and kissing him had only confused matters further. She pulled herself up short with a small shake of her head. The question of how they would survive without a rifle or horse remained a far more important puzzle than how she felt about Nick.

She breathed in the moisture-laden air lifting off the river. The beauty of the river soothed her tired mind. Sunlight danced in eddies, glowed in frothing rapids, and lit the grass on the opposite bank in vibrant hues of green.

Nick's gaze searched her out.

Bry looked away, her emotions raw.

"We can't cross here." Nick spoke in a brisk voice. "We'll have to follow the banks to a ford west of here."

Maisey came up from the water. Having scrubbed her cheeks pink, she would look fresh and young if her eyes hadn't held a bruised look. "Thank you for what you did back there." She gave

Nick a strained smile. "You saved our lives."

"We're in your debt." Bry stepped down from the rock and went to stand beside Maisey. "You saved us from a hideous death. I shudder to think what might have happened if you hadn't helped us."

Nick shrugged. "I had to do it. I couldn't live with myself otherwise. Now, if you ladies are ready, we should move on." He led them along the North Platte westward. Bry's heart lightened at the fact that no one pursued them. Only this morning she had cursed the sunrise, feeling that her life had ended. Whatever else the future held, she would look back on this day as a new beginning.

They stopped to rest at a river crossing. Nick moved a little way upstream while Bry and Maisey took refuge from the heat in the shade of a cottonwood spreading its branches above the water. Chatting about small matters like the type of berry a flowering vine would yield, the best way to raise bread dough, and their favorite songs comforted Bry. Nick returned with lengths of bark stripped from a tree. He smiled in response to her questioning look. She watched his hands move deftly, with a skill he must have learned from his mother, to work the bark into rope. "What are you making?" she asked.

"Rope to weave into a fishnet." His smile died, and he shot a glance behind her.

A chill walked down Bry's neck. Expecting the worst, she turned her head.

Rising Bird rode toward them along the thin trail that followed the river, leading three horses.

Nick went to greet her. "My sister, what have you done?"

"I bring gifts for you."

Nick's eyebrows shot upward. Bry recognized Tavo among the horses. The other two were Indian ponies.

"Will you return my horse to me? What will Kicking Horse say?"

"Nothing." Rising Bird lifted her head defiantly. "My brother gave these horses to me. They no longer belong to him."

Nick shook his head. "I hope you will not have trouble because of this."

Rising Bird slid from her horse's back. "I have brought you blankets and food also." She included Bry and Maisey in a sweeping gesture.

Bry found her tongue. "Thank you." Maisey smiled. "Those blankets will come in handy."

Rising Bird's forehead puckered. "I am sorry for what you have suffered among my people." She turned back to Nick. "I brought a fishnet for you." The two walked along the bank, away from Bry and Maisey and lowered their voices. What bittersweet words passed between them as they parted without knowing if they would see one another again?

When Rising Bird said goodbye, Bry embraced her with a full heart. "I will miss you."

"I wish we could have been sisters, but you are not for Kicking Horse." Rising Bird's dark eyes flicked to her brother.

Nick took his sister into his arms. "If you ever have trouble too great to bear, send for me. I'm going back to our mother's little cabin above the Missouri."

Rising Bird smoothed the side of his face. "Travel well, my brother."

Bry eyed the dark clouds piled in the sky. The day that had started sunny now turned gray. "Those clouds promise rain." She pointed, hoping she was wrong.

"I would rather not get drenched." Maisey voiced sharp alarm.

Nick cast a glance at the sky. "Looks like a summer storm brewing. We should move farther into the trees."

Rain pelted Bry while she and Maisey helped Nick build a lean-to from woven branches. Bry ducked beneath it with Maisey while Nick retrieved the blankets Rising Bird had given them. Brightly colored in a block design of the type traded at the forts, the wool blanket warmed her despite its dampness. Nick crouched on her other side, sheltering her with his warmth.

Maisey clutched her blanket about her and huddled against Bry. Her shivering seemed more intense than conditions seemed to warrant.

Bry laid the back of her hand on her friend's forehead. "You're burning up with fever."

"I don't feel well." Maisey's teeth chattered.

"You should sit in the middle away from the rain." Bry glanced at Nick.

He left the shelter, and after Bry and Maisey shifted over, entered on Maisey's other side.

"What can we do for her fever?" Bry asked him.

"Nothing until the rain stops. That might not be morning." Nick met her eyes over Maisey's head. "Sleep if you can."

"I doubt that will be possible." Exhaustion tugged at her lids, however. She leaned against the tree trunk behind her and closed her eyes to soothe them.

The rustling of leaves recalled her from sleep. She opened her eyes to find Maisey sipping from a tin cup with Nick looking on. "This is too hot." She blew on the steaming red liquid. "And it tastes like bark."

"It *is* bark."

Bry sat up.

Nick glanced at her. "You're awake."

"We were trying to keep from disturbing you." Maisey made a face at her cup.

Bry rubbed a kink in her neck. "The wind in the trees did that."

Nick nodded. "It hasn't died down much. The rain stopped in the night."

He must have stayed awake to know that. Why? Had sleep eluded him or had he watched over them while they slumbered? The thought of being protected by Nick sent warmth through her.

Bry looked away, hiding her face. "How are you feeling?" She asked Maisey.

"Chilled and a bit strange." Maisey shook her head. "I'm not sure I can drink this."

Bry looked to Nick. "What have you given her to drink?"

"Tea steeped from white willow bark. It helps with fever." He smiled at Maisey. "At least it does once swallowed."

Maisey sighed and lifted the cup. "All right."

Bry spotted a curl of smoke rising from between stones near the river bank. "I'm surprised you could start a fire." Sun and wind had dried the grasses, but most of the timber remained damp.

Nick shrugged. "Finding dry wood is not so difficult once you know where to look." He pointed upward.

She tilted her head and peered at the dead branches that bristled from the tree trunk beneath the living ones. "I wouldn't have thought to search there."

"Finished!" Maisey lowered the cup.

Nick took it from her. "Are you well enough to ride?"

"Yes." Maisey spoke without hesitation.

Bry frowned. "Are you certain?" She understood her friend's eagerness to continue their journey. She wouldn't rest easy until they had put more distance between themselves and Kicking Horse. She wasn't entirely convinced Maisey should ride with a fever, though.

"I'll be all right." Maisey's smile fell flat.

The Indian pony Bry had named Fiona carried her into the sunlight. The warmth sent up steam from her clothing. Nick went ahead on Tavo while Maisey swayed in her pony's saddle between them.

The trail they followed climbed into hilly terrain dotted with stands of timber that grew ever thicker the farther west they traveled. Nick reined in at the top of a hill and waited for them to crest it. Bry caught her breath at the view that stretched a long way across grassy hills to the distant mountains. "Where are we?"

Nick scanned the hills. "In Crow territory." From his tone, they were not a friendly tribe. "Let's move off the trail and look for a place to camp. We've gone far enough for one day."

One glance at Maisey's pale face made Bry agree with him. If he hadn't called a halt, she'd have done so for Maisey's sake. Nick took the lead, guiding them cross-country through gulches cut by cascading streams and beneath pine and cottonwood trees. They entered a sheltered valley ringed by bluffs. Eagles wheeled above a stream that curved through the grass. Nick dismounted and reached up to help Maisey. She sagged into his arms, and he lifted her down. He steadied her on her feet, but she held onto him, swaying.

Bry lowered herself from Fiona's back and went to her friend at once. "What's wrong?"

Maisey passed her tongue over her cracked lips. "I'm dizzy. I think I didn't drink enough water today."

Nick left Bry supporting Maisey and rummaged in the saddle bag for Maisey's water skin. "Here. Drink this, but not too fast."

Maisey tilted her head and drank greedy gulps.

Nick touched Bry's arm. "Stay with her. I'll turn the horses out."

Bry helped Maisey into the shade beside the stream and bathed her brow. Nick returned with a cautious expression. "I think we should move away from this spot. It's too near the best way in."

Supporting Maisey between them, they moved deeper into the grassy valley and stopped beside a weeping willow with tresses flowing to the ground. Nick left Bry and Maisey to rest within the circle of its branches. Through this living screen, Bry could see him netting fish for their supper. She wrapped Maisey with a blanket and watched over her while she slept. The branches hung down all around them, shutting green light into the enclosure. Every so often a breeze rustled the leaves and wafted their sun-warmed scent to Bry. The hushing sound mingled with the gurgle of the stream and the cry of birds in a gentle melody. Bry yawned and laid down beside Maisey.

The drumming of hooves jolted her awake. Her heart pounded. Lifting onto her elbow, she peered out through the leafy veil. An Indian, with his forelock cropped and ruffling in the breeze and the remainder of his hair braided on both sides, entered the small valley in front of a band of warriors. Beside him rode another brave, darker than the first, his hair bound in a topknot. Both wore quill collars at their necks, large white shells dangled from their ears, and erect feathers fanned at the back of their heads. These must be warriors from the Crow tribe Nick had mentioned. They looked so fierce that she didn't blame him for wanting to keep out of their way.

Where was Nick anyway? She turned her head but found him nowhere in sight. He must have heard the newcomers arrive and hidden himself.

A quick check informed Bry that Maisey had not wakened. She hoped her friend would remain asleep and miss the excitement, and that nothing would come of the Crow occupying the valley with them. She studied the approach of what turned out to be a small group of warriors. Intent on watering their horses and themselves, they didn't venture near.

A hand touched her shoulder.

Bry pressed the back of her hand to her mouth, barely stopping her scream.

Nick whispered in her ear. "It's me."

She nodded.

Nick removed his hand, but he didn't withdraw the arm he'd placed around her.

She leaned into him, not caring whether she shouldn't.

A couple of the warriors, deep in a discussion, walked toward their hiding place.

Bry held her breath.

The Indians passed by their shelter, still absorbed in their conversation.

What had Nick done with the horses? The question made Bry's mouth go dry. She would have to wonder, because she didn't dare speak out loud.

The two Indians who had strayed returned to the band at the

stream. When their water skins and horses were filled, they departed the valley.

Bry sank against Nick, weak with relief. His arm tightened reassuringly. She lifted her face, ready to whisper the question that had troubled her. He glanced down in the same moment, and their gazes meshed. Bry forgot whatever she'd been about to say. He stroked her cheek, his eyes soft. Bry couldn't look away. He lowered his head and touched his lips to hers. She sank into his kiss, lost in a thousand delights.

"Where am I?" Maisey called out in a frightened voice.

Nick released Bry, and she pulled away, not certain whether to be thankful for the interruption or not.

CHAPTER TWENTY

BRY FEARED THAT MAISEY MIGHT JOIN her husband in death, but her delirium and fever finally passed. Her illness had confined them to the valley for several tense days. Nick remained vigilant for any sign of the Crow. When they could continue their journey, they traveled away from the main road between Yellowstone country to the east and the mining towns along Alder Gulch. The countryside grew lovelier the higher they climbed, with ponderosa pine giving way to the lodgepole variety, and larch supplanting cottonwood. Sagebrush, bunch grass, and prickly pear fell away, replaced by a landscape where lush undergrowth and tall trees sprouted from rich soil. Mountains floated above the swelling hills. Birds opened their throats in the brush and treetops or took to the sky, their wings glinting in the sun. Flowers bloomed in an avalanche of color—lilies, blue flag, wild rose among the ones Bry recognized. She breathed the scented air deep into her lungs. It hardly seemed possible that a week ago she had dwelt in misery as a slave. Now, thanks to Nick, she was free.

She had forgotten herself in his arms under that willow tree. Her horse strayed toward a shrub bursting with wild roses, but Bry pulled her back on task. It was just as well that Maisey had interrupted them. Since that day, her gaze tangled with Nick's at unexpected moments, and her breath caught in her throat. She'd have to remain on guard to avoid another mistake.

In a wide part of the trail, she urged Fiona forward to ride with Maisey. "How are you holding up?"

"Much better, thanks."

"I'm glad to hear it. When we reach Virginia City, I'm hoping the sheriff will put us on a stagecoach to the Bitterroot Valley. With any luck, one of the stops will be within hailing distance of Con's ranch. "The thought should have cheered Bry but instead started a hollow ache in her stomach. She'd have to part from Nick, a thing logic urged her to do but her heart resisted.

They rounded a bend and came upon two men in rough mining garb on horseback alongside the road.

Nick stiffened his back and slowed his horse.

"Well, what have we here?" asked the miner wearing a red plaid shirt.

"Why it's an Injun and two squaws," answered the man in work clothes sewn from jean cloth. His eyes widened. "Wait a minute. Jacob, do you see what I see? Those women are white."

Jacob rode into the trail. "Best stop right there."

His companion joined him in blocking the way. "Yes, better tell us what you're up to with those women."

Bry stared at them in dismay. One moment they had been riding along in harmony and the next they were facing two hostile men who seemed more than ready for a fight. "Gentlemen," she cried when she recovered her wits. "You must not harm our rescuer. We were taken captive by the Cheyenne, and this man freed us at great personal cost."

"It's true." Maisey spoke in tones that brooked no argument. "We owe him our lives."

The jean-clad man blinked, but his companion's expression hardened. "There's no call for an Injun to mess about with white women." He looked sideways to his companion. "Ain't that right?"

"'Course it is." The man in the plaid shirt stroked a rust-colored beard. "I say we hang him."

Nick flung himself low on the side of Tavo's saddle and plunged his horse toward the miner. Nick's fingers curved around the gun barrel, preventing it from completing its upward arc. The weapon slipped from the man's grasp into Nick's hand. The miner's huffing breath and widened eyes signaled his surprise. Nick sped out of reach. He wheeled Tavo around while returning to the saddle, but not fast enough.

The miner in the red shirt leveled his pistol at Nick. A gunshot blasted, and the ball slammed Nick's shoulder with merciless force while Tavo screamed. Nick sagged in the saddle, fighting lightheadedness. The women's screams penetrated the blackness that assailed him, goading him to stay awake. He had to keep the women from falling into these ruffian's hands. He drove Tavo back toward Jacob, whose horse must have reared when the gun went off. The man had fallen from the saddle and now scrambled to his feet. Mustering the last of his strength, Nick jumped down from Tavo and launched himself at Jacob. Another gunshot punched the air. Jacob hauled back a fist. Nick moved swiftly, twisting his arm behind him in a wrestling move he'd learned from Kicking Horse. He positioned the man in front of him and held the gun to his head while eyeing his partner. "Drop it."

Like a predatory animal searching for a prey's weakness, the man in the red shirt divided his attention between Nick and Jacob. Nick repeated his demand more forcefully.

"Do it, Weland." Jacob's voice shook. "I don't want to get shot today, if it's all the same to you."

Glaring at Nick, Weland laid his gun on the ground.

Nick's head swam and his shoulder burned with agony, but he held firm. "Now back away."

Weland obeyed more slowly than when he'd relinquished the pistol. Nick hurried Jacob forward. He claimed the gun and tucked it in his belt, gritting his teeth to prevent himself from crying out from the fire in his shoulder. With his head reeling, he pushed Jacob away and staggered back. "Mount your horse."

Jacob captured his horse, which danced with skittishness, and jumped into the saddle.

"Ride east and out of my sight." Nick clicked the gun lever for emphasis.

Jacob slapped the rump of his horse. "Hee-yaw!" The horse

bolted, and Weland followed in short order. The pair sped away until they were out of firing range, then slowed and looked back. After exchanging glares, they continued east and vanished into the distance.

Nick knew better than to trust them to stay away. "We need to move out of sight in a hurry."

"But you're wounded." Bry stared at his shoulder, her face pale.

"There's no help for it." Nick pressed his bandana to his wound to stem the bleeding. "I have to ride." He led them off the trail and over the hills, knowing the miners would stick to the trails. They crested a rise and descended out of sight from the trail. He stuck to paths forged by animals, faint and sometimes precarious but usually reliable in the pursuit of water. He wasn't disappointed when they came to a stream cutting through one of the gorges. Pines sent out a heady fragrance in the heat. He dismounted at the stream, but his knees buckled, and he crumpled to the ground.

"Nick!" Bry rushed to him, and Maisey joined her. The two women propped him on either side, and Nick stumbled to his feet. He recovered his balance then pulled away.

"You're too weak." Bry followed him.

Nick nodded, having come to the same conclusion. He let the women help him sit on the stream bank. Bry cleansed his wound and Maisey went back to Tavo looking for bandages in his saddlebag. He gritted his teeth while Bry prodded his wound. She lifted her head, very near. "It looks like the ball passed through."

"I'll live a while yet, God willing."

Their gazes caught. Despite the dirt streaking her face and worry shadowing her eyes, she had never looked more beautiful. "Mind you do." She told him in a husky voice.

Bry jerked awake and sat up straight. She should never have nodded off like that, not with Nick fighting for his life. Watching over him while he slipped in and out of a fever had taken a toll. She pulled back his bandage and winced. The wound had putrefied, despite her every attempt to keep it clean.

They had moved deeper into the gulch a little distance uphill and behind a group of tumbled boulders. Anyone entering the gulch below their hiding place would not see them. She wouldn't put it past the two miners they'd met to arm themselves and search for Nick out of spite. She doubted their interference on behalf of white women had anything to do with gallantry. The two had persecuted Nick despite the protests she and Maisey had raised, a fact that proclaimed them bullies. Bry gusted a sigh. She'd hoped to end this ordeal in Virginia City. Gone was her hope that the sheriff would send Maisey and her to the Bitterroot Valley by stagecoach. They would have to avoid the town. If the two miners returned, they could accuse Nick of all sorts of crimes. He'd taken their guns, for one thing, and that might count against him as stealing.

Nick inhaled several gasping breaths. She bent over him, watching his chest rise and fall until he settled into more peaceful sleep.

"Bry." Maisey's whisper stirred the air near her ear. "You should rest."

She didn't budge, unable to make herself leave Nick's side.

"Come on." Maisey laid a hand on her shoulder. "If you don't watch out, you'll get too sick to care for him."

Bry nodded, surrendering to common sense. She stood, stiff from sitting in one position for so long. Earlier, Maisey had cooked a stew from buffalo jerky and the wild greens Nick had taught them to gather. Her portion had congealed into an unappetizing mess, but she'd gulped it down. She had to keep her strength up or she would never reach Con's ranch. Would she find both her brothers there?

Nick pulled himself out of a state of waking slumber and opened his eyes to find Bry looking down at him. Her lips trembled, and tears shimmered in her eyes.

"Crying?" He reached up and stroked a bright droplet from her cheek. "What's wrong?"

She shook her head and clasped his hand. For a moment, he thought she might kiss it. "You worried me for certain."

Her raw emotion shook him to the core. How could he resist surrendering to his feelings when she gazed at him like that? And yet he must. He pushed to sit up, but a headache slammed him, and he sank back again. "I need water."

Maisey hovered over him and lowered a water skin within his reach. "I'm glad you're awake, Mr. Laramie."

He squinted with the effort of remembering what had laid him low. "My wound—it festered."

"That's right." She gave a brief nod.

Maisey moved back and Bry came into view again. "You've had a fever, which seems to have broken." "We've done our best to give you water, but you could drink only a little at a time."

"Thank you." The cork in the neck of the water skin gave beneath his fingers. Long gulps soothed his throat. He passed his arm across his mouth. Pain flared in his shoulder, and he grimaced. "How long have I been out?"

Maisey relieved him of the water skin. "You slept for a night and most of the day."

Bry leaned forward and touched his clammy brow, his mother's gesture in his childhood. He'd never expected to feel such a touch again. Her hand withdrew, but he yearned to recapture it. She smiled. "Your fever is gone. The herbs must have helped."

He stared at her. "Herbs?"

Bry lifted her eyebrows. "You are not the only one who knows how to heal with plants, Mr. Laramie. I found an herb I know growing on the banks of the stream. Ribwort, my mother called it in Ireland. Plantain is another name for it. Mam used it to stop bleeding and draw poisons from our scrapes."

"I'm grateful it worked. You may have saved my life."

Bry's lips curved in a soft smile. "I've paid you back a bit, maybe."

Nick couldn't decide which affected him more—her tears or smiles. He tried to sit up, succeeded this time, and scanned the sky. Cloud wisps broke its vastness, and its blue deepened as light washed from the sky. "We should leave in the morning."

Bry's forehead puckered. "Will you be strong enough to ride then?"

"I have to be. Staying in one place is risky." Although he doubted Weland and Jacob would make an effort to track him, experience had taught him to take nothing for granted. "We'll have to keep well away from towns."

"I thought as much." Disappointment showed in Bry's face, telling its own story. She had suffered a great deal and must crave comfort. "We're about a week away from your brother's ranch." He did his best to soften the blow. His own words had the power to wound him, he discovered after uttering them. Once he had safely delivered her to her brother's ranch, he would say goodbye to her forever. It had to be this way, but tearing out his own heart might hurt less.

Maisey gave a soft moan.

He swept a glance over her troubled face. "Are you wondering what's to become of you?"

"You'd be welcome to stay with us, I'm sure." Bry spoke into the silence that grew between them. "I thought you would know."

"I appreciate that, but I need to find Phoebe at once."

"I'm sure Rob would willingly search for her while you recover your strength. You've been through an ordeal and must rest."

"Would your brother do that for me?"

Bry smiled at her. "I can't imagine that he'd say no."

"All right, but I wouldn't want to be beholden for very long."

Nick could understand her sentiment, but a widow faced few prospects in the West. Maisey's situation resembled his own in some ways. Sidelined from what others called normal life, she had to survive. That might mean ultimately returning to any family she might have or staying with Bry longer than she hoped. She could also remarry, a distinct possibility in the female-deprived West, where mourning often surrendered to more practical matters.

Nick wouldn't find it difficult to fall asleep again, but he propped himself against the boulder behind him, determined to remain awake. The rock felt solid at his back, radiating the sun's warmth. A golden eagle wheeled above the gulch, catching fire in the sunset. A white-tailed creature with brindled fur vanished into the underbrush, a jackrabbit escaping its predator. Nick smiled, although the eagle had lost a meal. Bry brought him smoked fish from the supplies Rising Bird had given them, and he chewed while wondering about his sister. Had Rising Bird told Kicking Horse and Ahanu what she'd done with the horses, and if so, how had they responded? Nick probably shouldn't have accepted her gift, but Bry and Maisey's needs had weighed on him.

He didn't understand why God had placed these two women in his charge, but he would lay down his life to protect them.

Nick woke to the murmur of voices. He crouched beside the boulder, listening intently. The voices carried from a little distance away, and he had only heard them on one occasion, but he recognized them. He couldn't hear their words, but the tones they used reeked with hostility. Weland and Jacob had thrown caution aside, apparently, in order to argue with one another.

Nick cast a glance behind him. Bry and Maisey had bedded down in a flat place hidden by a large rock. Hopefully, they would stay put. He strapped on his gun and crept along the boulder, waiting to spring.

The voices moved nearer, rising in pitch. Nick could pick out words here and there. "Filthy Injun." — *"Your* fault." — "She's mine." He pulled his gun, hoping not to need it.

Scuffling sounded behind him, faint but detectable. Bry peered around the boulder.

He jerked his head in warning.

She withdrew.

Nick strained to make out the two men's conversation but caught only phrases until they moved within range.

"If we find them, I have dibs on the black-haired Bridget." The voice belonged to Jacob.

"I fancy the gray-eyed one. Reminds me of a soiled dove I was fond of in St. Louis." He chuckled. "Almost got myself killed over that one."

Nick gritted his teeth, their motives in 'protecting' the women now clear.

The miners scanned the ground near the mouth of the gulch. "Look at all those tracks! They're going every which way." Jacob scratched his head. "How's a body supposed to know which one to follow?"

Nick smirked, glad he'd had the energy to scramble their tracks before they'd entered the gulch.

"You don't. That's the whole point, in case you wondered. It's an old Injun trick to throw off pursuit."

"Well, what do you think, Weland? Which way should we head?"

"My gut says they went this way."

Footsteps crunched as the miners strode into the gulch. Nick risked a glance. Both men carried rifles. He gripped his gun tighter. How were the women holding up to this?

"You sure?" Jacob asked. "No one would go through here. The gulch is too narrow, and it would be no fun climbing those rocks."

"That's what you're supposed to say," Weland scoffed, but the footfalls halted. "I don't see any tracks climbing out."

"Maybe they're hiding up there." Jacob sounded spooked.

"Don't be an idiot. They came this way more'n a day ago."

"But you shot him. Maybe he holed up afterwards."

"You might have a point." The crunching started again and climbed toward the boulders.

Nick peered around the rock. Jacob's red plaid shirt stood out like a flag as he and Weland scrambled over boulders. Nick pulled out of sight, bumping his shoulder against the rough rock. A hiss of pain escaped him.

"What was that?" Jacob's shout echoed through the gorge.

"Pipe down, will you? How do you expect me to hear anything but your voice?"

"It sounded like a snake."

"Shut up and let me listen."

Nick held his breath. The silence stretched to breaking point.

"Nope." Weland crowed at last. "I don't hear nothing."

"It's gone now."

"Then you don't need to worry. Come on."

Nick risked another glimpse. Racing up the gorge, the miners stumbled over loose rocks, every footstep bringing them closer. Jacob fell and let out a string of oaths.

Nick cocked the pistol, bracing himself to lean out and fire.

"Careful!" Jacob's cry of alarm jolted along Nick's spine.

"Have you lost your mind?" Weland asked in a tone that implied he knew the answer.

An uncanny high-pitched rattle lifted the hair at the back of Nick's neck.

"Snakes! The rocks must be full of them." The footsteps retreated and faded altogether.

He waited until their voices faded before calling to the women. "You can come out now."

Bry and Maisey rounded the boulder that had sheltered them from view.

"Have you moved the horses?" He asked the question uppermost in his mind.

Bry shook her head. "They're still where you left them—out of sight, farther back in the gulch near the headwaters of the stream."

"How did we miss the nest?" Maisey shuddered.

"We climbed here near nightfall. That's when snakes go into their holes." Nick pocketed the gun. "They're most active in the early morning."

"You mean—now?" Maisey looked all about.

"I suppose we have today's visitors to thank for pointing out the rattlesnakes." Bry spoke on a wry note.

Nick smiled. "That's so."

Maisey moved nearer to Bry. "How will we pass the nest to leave?"

"Maybe we should wait until dark again." Bry sent Nick a questioning look.

He nodded. "That would help us avoid any type of snake we might stumble across. Weland and Jacob will most likely have given up and gone back to the road by then."

Bry folded her arms. "Good riddance to the pair of them."

CHAPTER TWENTY-ONE

BRY REINED IN BESIDE NICK AND Maisey and surveyed the scene before her. Daylight splintered into beams that fell like a blessing across the mountains, while sparrows, bobolinks, and wrens warbled sweet melodies. The Bitterroot River curved, very blue, through the soft grass that filled its namesake valley. The breeze lifting her hair mingled the sharp scent of water with the aroma of rich soil.

Con had spoken of this valley with the enthusiasm it deserved. How easy to feel that her sufferings would not touch her here. She hoped with her whole heart to find her brother had returned alive to this special place. Her reluctance to learn his fate had vanished, replaced by anticipation. She would rather know the truth. If Con had passed beyond the mortal veil, denying the truth would not recall him from death. However, if by some miracle her brother lived, her heartache could end. Today would always and forever be a waymark in her life. Whatever she learned, the torment of wondering her brother's fate would be laid to rest.

Con hadn't told her the precise location of his ranch, but he'd mentioned their cousin who lived in the town of Liberty. Finding the ranch would require a visit to Sean, or Shane as he now called himself. Con had said a trifle disapprovingly that their cousin had changed his name to sound more American. Bry hadn't argued the point, but she didn't agree that wanting to fit in with your chosen people betrayed your former country. She'd heard of other immigrants changing their names, especially those with hard-to-pronounce spellings. Sometimes it could mean the difference between finding work to feed your family and going hungry.

They entered the small town of Liberty, which Shane and his

wife, America, had founded and named after their young daughter. Bry swallowed. After losing Liam and then Phoebe, the thought of meeting Shane's four-year-old daughter and younger son, Seth, brought a lump to her throat.

Maisey, beside Bry on her pony, sighed. "That view is really something."

"I've never seen a valley more beautiful." Bry nodded. "Living here seems too good for me."

Nick, on her other side, turned toward her. "Don't speak that way of yourself."

With his forehead creased and weariness in his bearing, he seemed burdened with care. Her heart went out to him. The journey had brought Maisey and her home, but Nick had nothing to look forward to but a wanderer's existence. He might stay with them for a fleeting time before moving off to somewhere else.

How impossible to think that he would leave her.

The strength of the emotions welling within her stole her breath. Nick's gaze caught hers, and she couldn't look away. It seemed that the closer they came to parting, the more their glances clung.

A lone rider on his way home to Liberty gave them directions to where Shane lived, although they wouldn't have had to search long in the small town. Shane had built his house on the outskirts, closest to the school, which made it easy to locate. Twin casement windows in the front of the log home gazed over a large meadow dotted with wildflowers. They path led to the home's entrance, faced away from the schoolhouse and sideways to the road. A wooden gate below an arch squeaked in protest but swung open to allow them inside the picket fence surrounding the home. A tap at the door went unanswered. Bry swallowed her disappointment. To finally arrive, only to find no one home made her want to weep.

"What should we do?" Maisey asked in a bewildered tone.

Bry shook her head, at a loss.

Nick touched her arm. "Wait here in case someone comes, and I'll ask around."

After the two miners had attacked Nick outside Virginia City, Bry didn't like the idea of him approaching strangers. "I'll go with you."

He shook his head. "I'd rather you stay here. It's plain you women need rest."

Bry glanced at Maisey, then nodded her agreement. Arriving at her cousin's place had brought home her exhaustion. The long journey to reach this front door had drained every ounce of energy from her. She suspected that her trials as a captive had marked her more deeply than she knew.

Nick went through the gate and strode along the path toward the road.

"You there," a feminine voice hailed from the direction of the schoolhouse. "Are you looking for Reverend Hayes?"

Nick turned and removed his hat. "Good afternoon, Ma'am. Yes, we are."

"We?"

" Reverend Hayes's cousin and her friend have traveled a good distance to visit him. Do you know where either he or his wife are?"

"I guess I should." The woman laughed. "I'm Mrs. Hayes. I was walking back from a neighbor's house when I heard your voices and saw the horses."

Surrendering to curiosity, Bry started toward Nick. A woman with her blonde hair partially hidden by a bonnet and wearing a calico dress in a brown floral pattern over a tan background came into view. On her hip, she carried a tousle-haired boy, and a little girl with curly hair, fair like her mother's, hid behind her skirt.

"Pleased to meet you. I'm Nicholas Laramie." He looked toward Bry and Maisey as they came through the gate. "And this is Reverend Hayes's cousin, Mrs. Bryanna Brennan, and her friend, Mrs. Maisey Wilcox."

"My husband's cousin!" The woman turned her head toward Bry, and her golden hazel eyes widened. "Why are you dressed in those clothes?"

Bry, about to greet Shane's wife, lost the path of her thoughts.

Shane started toward her. "The women were prisoners of the Cheyenne until I freed them."

America Hayes gave Bry a sympathetic look. "I'm sorry that you came to such a pass, but you're safe with us now."

Bry shook America's hand. "That means a lot. This is my friend, Maisey Wilcox."

America smiled at Maisey. "Welcome. You and Bry must stay with us as long as you like." She turned to Nick. "Thank you, Mr. Laramie, for your kindness to these women."

"He suffered a gunshot wound on our behalf." Bry voiced her foremost concern. "Is there a doctor who can examine him?"

America's eyes widened. "Goodness, yes. I'll ask the neighbor to send for Doc Bailey. Reverend Hayes went to help dig a root cellar, and I'm not sure when he'll return. You must come inside and sit down."

"Really, I'm all right." Nick held the gate open. "The wound pains me but is starting to heal."

America raised her eyebrows. "Having the doctor see to your injury wouldn't hurt."

Bry smiled to herself. This strong-minded woman seemed just right for Shane.

Nick followed behind them to the door. "I have no money to pay for medical care."

America paused with her hand on the knob. "Don't let that concern you. Doc Bailey lets folks work off his fees, but if that failed, I'm sure my husband would want to take care of the cost. We must have the doctor examine the ladies after their ordeal."

America led the way inside her home. A pad of stones made do for an entryway, with wooden floors beyond. More stones formed a chimney for the small fireplace in the parlor. Wallpaper embellished with birds and flowers covered the walls behind modest furniture that looked comfortable. They followed their hostess into the kitchen, where wooden shelves laden with dishes and food stuffs climbed the walls. An oak table stood in the middle of the room with matching chairs around it. "Please, seat yourself."

America waved her hand toward the chairs and peeled her children from her person. She bent to her daughter. "Liberty, take Seth and play with him in the other room while I make something to eat."

Liberty stared at Bry with luminous blue eyes and crept closer until she touched Bry's knee. Bry pulled in a breath. The small gesture reminded her of Liam. She blinked away moisture and smiled at Liberty. An answering smile flitted across Liberty's face, then she took her little brother's hand and went through the doorway to the parlor.

Maisey's face puckered and tears swam in her eyes. No wonder, since Phoebe was approximately the same age as Liberty. Bry stepped closer to her friend in silent support.

Maisey seemed to master herself with an effort and sank into one of the chairs around the table. "It's wonderful to sit on something other than a rock or log."

"I can imagine. Will you take tea?" America asked in a brisk voice. "This occasion calls for a bit of luxury, don't you think?"

"That sounds lovely." Bry sat across from Maisey with a sigh.

America opened the cast iron stove and added wood to the fire burning inside. "Reverend Hayes will be pleased to see you, Bry, and Rob as well."

"Rob made it to Con's ranch, then?" Excitement lifted Bry's voice.

America smiled. "He came to visit soon after arriving. The ranch is a day's journey across the valley, so we don't see as much of him as we'd like."

"Con and I were on our way to his ranch when . . . we were separated." She couldn't wait another minute before asking the question that pressed her mind. "Tell me, will I find him there?"

"I really don't know. It's been a month since we last saw Rob. He did say he was expecting Con and you." America pulled a tin of tea down from a shelf. "You can find out tomorrow if you like. I'm sure Reverend Hayes will show you the way. Meanwhile, I intend to make sure you're well fed, scrubbed, and clothed. You'll sleep in a soft bed tonight."

Bry pressed her lips together. America's generosity was almost more than she could bear. "I hope we won't intrude."

"You could never do that." America frowned, then smiled. "You're family."

"You're lucky to be alive, young man." In the Hayes' parlor with the children banished, Doc Bailey pulled the bandage tight over Nick's wound. "If the bullet had come any closer to that artery, you'd have bled to death."

"It must not have been my time to die." The thought gave Nick pause. He sometimes questioned the value of his existence, but God appeared to think differently. He would ponder that during the lonely days in his parents' cabin.

"Want my advice?" The doctor snapped his medical bag shut. "Stay out of situations where bullets fly, or you'll occupy an early grave."

"I'll bear that in mind." Nick pulled on his shirt and started on the buttons.

"You've lost a lot of blood. Have you felt any dizziness? Confusion? Shortness of breath?"

"More in the beginning." He'd hidden his symptoms to avoid worrying his companions.

The doctor nodded. "I wouldn't advise riding off in a hurry. Give yourself a chance to regain your strength."

"Reverend Hayes might not want me as a house guest for long."

Doc Bailey gave him a piercing look. "You don't know him very well, do you? He'd give you his own bed rather than turn you out."

"Mrs. Hayes said you allow your patients to work off their fees." Nick followed him to the door. "I'm willing to do so for mine and also for the ladies."

"I wouldn't dream of charging." Doc Bailey opened the front

door and looked back. "Mrs. Hayes told me what you did for those poor souls."

"Have they suffered any harm?"

"I can't divulge medical details, but I will say that some injuries can't be seen." He shook his head. "Say goodbye for me to the Reverend and his Missus. If I do it, I'll be here another hour talking, and my wife would like to see me tonight."

Nick shook his hand. "I will."

Doc Bailey nodded and shut the door behind him.

Nick looked into the kitchen, ready to deliver the doctor's message, only to be intercepted by Mrs. Hayes. "Sorry, but you can't come in right now." She swept a glance over him. "Perhaps later?" Steam rose from the metal washtub in the corner, and a folding screen papered with twining roses leaned against one wall, that when set up would protect the privacy of the bathers.

He went back to the paw-footed sofa. The oil lamp on the small table beside him glowed with warm light that didn't reach the edges of the room. The clock on the wooden mantle ticked away the time. Scenes flickered across his mind—Bry watching him with her forehead puckered, riding ahead with the wind tugging her hair, leaning down to him as he helped her from the saddle. He shifted, dispelling the memories. If he didn't harden his heart to the woman, parting from her would hurt worse than his bullet wound.

Boots thumped on the path outside, and the knob rattled.

Nick stood.

The door swung open, and a man that must be Shane stood in the entrance. Light from his lantern pooled at his feet and sent his shadow racing along the wall. Of medium height and with a compact frame covered by denim work clothes, the man carried himself well and would make a tough opponent. Fighting appeared to be the last thing on his mind, for he broke into a smile. "My wife sent me to retrieve you from the parlor, Mr. Laramie. I'm Reverend Hayes, Shane to you."

Nick shook the hand Shane extended. "Thank you, and please call me Nick."

"I've set up a bed for you in the school teacher's cabin. We lost our teacher to wedlock and have yet to find a replacement."

Nick followed him into the night. They tramped past the darkened hulk of the schoolhouse toward a light shining through the trees behind it. A short path led them to a cabin. The door squeaked, and they went inside. Shane lit the lantern suspended on a rope above the table while Nick studied his surroundings. The small cabin seemed luxurious after having no roof over his head for weeks on end. A wooden board, wash tub, and shelves along one wall served as a kitchen. In one corner, a ladder climbed to a darkened loft.

"There's a change of clothing." Shane pointed to a stack of folded denim, a cloth he must favor, on the bed. "You're welcome to keep them."

"Thank you."

Shane lowered himself into one of the wooden chairs at the table. "You're from the Cheyenne tribe, are you?"

Nick sat across from him. "My mother was. She married a French trapper."

"That explains the origin of your name." Shane leaned against his backrest. "How did you become acquainted with my cousin?"

"I guided her wagon train."

"She speaks well of you."

"I'm glad to hear it."

Shane went to the door. "I'd better help my wife settle our other guests. I can let you know when the wash tub is free if you like."

"I'd be obliged." Nick saw him out. He went inside the cabin and sat at the table. He was glad for Bry's sake that her cousin had taken her in, but he couldn't get used the having the duty of watching over her taken from him. He couldn't get over the strange feeling that a part of him had been cut away.

His usefulness to Bry had come to an end. He shouldn't linger at her cousin's house, no matter how gracious the invitation.

Shane came back to let him know that the bath water was free.

After his bath and wearing clean clothes, Nick returned to the cabin with the wind sashaying the leaves in the trees behind the schoolhouse. Shane accompanied him, carrying a lantern to light the way.

At a dip in the trail, Shane lifted the lantern, making the shadows jump. "I wanted to ask you something. My cousin is worried about her brother Con. Do you know what's happened to him?"

"Not entirely." Nick avoided a root that could trip him. "I saw him shot, then took him to the wagon train. I don't know whether he lived."

"I hope to find him alive and well tomorrow."

"I'll ride along with you."

"Are you certain? An injury such as yours needs rest. I suspect you haven't had much chance for that. If I may say so, it seems like a strong wind would knock you over. Why not stay until you're stronger?"

Nick shook his head. "Thanks all the same, but I'll see the ladies through to their destination."

"I can understand that, I suppose, but don't feel like you can't change your mind."

"Thank you. I appreciate the offer."

Inside the cabin, Shane lit the hanging lantern, then bade Nick a goodnight. Left to the silence blanketing the little cabin, Nick took off his boots, more than ready to climb into bed. Sleep eluded him, however.

Remaining here, while tempting, would only remind him of what he couldn't have. Mrs. Hayes claiming Bry, had brought to mind his own loneliness. His parents were gone, but whenever he stayed at the cabin where they had lived together, he felt himself part of a family. He'd be better off in the cabin on the cliff above the Missouri, hundreds of miles away, where he belonged.

Having decided his course, he allowed sleep to take him at last.

A knock intruded into an uneasy dream that had him fighting Kicking Horse to the death. He dragged on his trousers and opened the door.

"Good morning," Shane greeted him. "How did you sleep?"

"Well enough. I'll be ready in a moment."

"We're in the kitchen."

The aromas of fried bacon and coffee drifted to Nick as he entered the kitchen. America Hayes stood at the stove, flipping pancakes. Bry, wearing blue gingham and Maisey in green calico, rushed about to bring platters laden with pancakes, bacon, and eggs to the table.

"Looks like we're in time for breakfast." Shane clapped his back. "Sit down, and I'll pour you some coffee."

Nick stared at him. "At the table?"

"Where else?" Shane chuckled, but then sobered. "I'd be honored to share my table with you."

America Hayes gave her husband an approving glance. "Yes, join us, please. Sit anywhere."

Nick lowered himself onto the woven seat of a ladderback chair.

Shane took down two coffee mugs from a kitchen shelf. "Sugar or cream?" He laughed. "Don't look so surprised. We bought a milk cow not long after settling here. Milking Daphne is a burden and keeping the milk fresh a challenge, but we sell off or give away what we don't need. Sometimes we barter for eggs and such. How do you take your coffee?"

"Black."

Shane plunked two mugs on the table. He straddled the chair next to Nick and folded his arms across its back. "Being Irish, I know what it is to suffer from the ignorance of others. Our Lord did as well."

Nick considered this idea. "Do you mean when they crucified Him?"

"Well yes, but before then too. When Jesus sat down to eat with sinners, the hypocritical teachers of the law questioned it. Do you know what he said to them?"

Nick cast back to his mother reading the Bible passage to him as a child, but he couldn't remember the details. "What?"

"That He was called to sinners, not to those righteous in their own eyes. Each of us has gone astray, but God caused the punishment for our sins to be cast on His Son. Through repentance, not by our own actions, we avail ourselves of His salvation. Those who pretend they are better than others have lost sight of that fact, if they ever knew it."

Shane's words were a balm but hard to fathom after Nick had spent much of his life learning at the hands of others how inferior he was. Changing his thinking would take some doing.

CHAPTER TWENTY-TWO

BRY HAD EXPECTED SOMETHING SMALLER, BUT her brother had built a ranch house large enough to shelter his entire family. Her throat tightened with the realization that Con had meant to do exactly that. If only Da were alive to see it, he'd be proud. The rectangular building rose two stories in height. Green shutters graced the casement windows, and white paint covered the clapboard siding. Pillars supported the balcony above the front porch. No one stood there now, but she could picture Con looking down over the railing. She hung back, so taken with the image that it almost seemed she could wish him here to greet her. The others went up the steps, and Shane knocked on the door.

She clasped a hand to her stomach as if that could quiet its churning. Nick turned his head, and their gazes meshed. She walked up the steps and came to rest by his side. Footsteps padded toward the door, the glass knob turned, and Rob looked out. He stood in stockinged feet and wore trousers of tan canvas and a red shirt with a tab collar. With his red hair rumpled and one side of his face, he must have woken from a nap. "Bry?" He stared at her from deep blue eyes.

She rushed to her brother, whose bear hug lifted her off her feet. "What are you doing?" She laughed. "Put me down, you oaf!"

He set her on her feet and held her at arms' length. "I thought never to see you again."

She frowned. Why would he think that unless he knew of her kidnapping? And if so, could that mean . . . "Did Con find his way here?" The question burst from her on a wave of hope.

"He never came."

"But you said—" The wind went out of her. How had Rob

heard about her kidnapping, if not from Con?

"Rob?" A blond-haired man clad in blue and wearing waders strode from the barn. He halted below the porch steps with his gaze fixed on Bry. "How did you escape? We'd all but given you up for dead."

Bry stared at Thad Taylor, the last person she expected to come across. "What are you doing here?"

He smiled. "Your brother hired me on to work for him, as you'll recall."

"But why did you come without him?"

"I carried a message from Con notifying Rob that he was recuperating at Fort Sedgwick."

Bry closed her eyes. Con was alive! Giddy with relief, she swayed on her feet. A hand closed bracingly over her elbow. She opened her eyes and looked into Nick's concerned face.

"Step away from that woman," Thad growled.

"There's no call to attack him." Shane protested in a sharp voice.

"Rescuer? He's one of the savages who stole her."

"Stop this!" Bry glared at Thad, reminded all over again why she detested him. "Mr. Laramie is my friend."

"And mine." Maisey spoke in a quiet voice that nonetheless carried. "Say nothing against him in my presence."

Thad's face turned red, but he restrained whatever he'd been about to say.

"Why don't we go inside to discuss this?" Rob suggested. "You must all be tired and famished."

Her brother's glance hadn't included Nick, but Bry latched onto his arm and pulled him inside with her. She gasped at the beauty of the entryway, where a graceful flight of stairs curved to the second floor. Sleek paneling, red carpeting, and a gold chandelier dripping with prisms declared her brother's wealth.

"It's stunning," Maisey breathed.

Rob smiled at her. "The house took me that way too." He led them through a door and into a parlor wallpapered in a beige fleur-de-lis pattern and scattered with chairs and sofas upholstered in leather and blue velvet. "Have a seat. Thad, go and make tea and coffee, will you?"

Thad scowled but went off.

Bry hid her amusement at her brother's masterful removal of Thad, but then Rob had always been good at managing people.

Maisey took a seat on a velvet sofa edged with carved mahogany. Bry sat beside her. Shane stepped forward to greet Rob properly, and Nick sat in a leather chair. The window covered in white lace behind him contrasted with his dark masculinity. Bry pulled her attention from Nick with an effort and focused on what Rob was saying to her.

"If Con delays coming home much longer, I'll go after him myself."

Bry pulled in a breath. "I'd rather not have to worry about two brothers at once, but I know better than to expect anything else from the pair of you."

"You're one to scold." He arched his brows. "I feared the worst for you. Are you all right, then?"

"Neither Mrs. Wilcox nor I have had lasting damage, except to our reputations." Not that she'd had much of hers left after Jeffrey Wainwright's contribution.

"I'll flatten anyone who speaks ill against you in my hearing," Rob declared. "None of what happened was your fault."

"Dear Rob, always ready to defend me."

"Who will look out for you, Mrs. Wilcox?" Rob asked. "Do you have any family near?"

"They're all in the East," Maisey answered. "They didn't approve of my marriage and, well—I have no one to return to."

"You must stay with us." Rob glanced at Bry. "As my sister's guest, of course."

"I've already invited her." Bry smiled at Maisey, then turned back to her brother. "Mr. Laramie is recovering from a gunshot wound inflicted while he defended us from rough men."

Rob studied the carpet and made no reply.

"He's welcome to stay with us." Shane perched on an

upholstered chair. "I told him so this morning."

"You're asking for trouble." Thad came in carrying a blue willow tea tray with a matching pot and cups. "My wagon train learned that the hard way."

Nick's head came up, and his jaw tensed, but he said nothing to defend himself against Thad's insinuation.

"He gave up everything he owned to free my cousin and Mrs. Wilcox." Shane contradicted him with an edge to his voice. "I count him a friend."

"Thank you." Nick nodded to Shane, then stared at his hat, which he turned in his hands. "Unfortunately, I can't accept your invitation."

Nick didn't elaborate, and Bry refused to argue with him in front of her brother or Thad. It didn't seem possible after all they had been through that Nick would no longer be part of her life. "Where will you go?"

"I haven't seen my cabin in too long." Still examining his wretched hat, he spoke with little inflection, as if leaving her meant nothing to him. "It's time to lay in food for the winter."

"In early summer?" Bry, taken by the desire to weep, could barely swallow her tea.

"Don't let us keep you," Rob intervened, "since you're anxious to be on your way."

Bry glared at her brother. "You can't mean that."

"He's traveled all day with an injury to bring your sister safely to you." Shane's voice cut across Bry's protest. "I shouldn't have to mention this, but he deserves the offer of lodging for the night."

Rob's face took on the mischievous look he wore whenever he was up to something. "That's no trouble—if he wants to bed down in the barn."

An audible gasp came from Maisey.

"If you're short on beds, give him mine." Shane snapped.

"That won't be necessary." Nick stood. "I know when I've outstayed my welcome. Ladies." He nodded to Bry and Maisey in turn, put his mangled hat on his head, and strode from the room.

Bry scrambled to her feet and followed him.

"Let him go." Thad called after her.

She caught up with Nick on the porch. "Wait! You can't just leave like this."

He turned back to her. "It's for the best."

"Please." Moisture started to her eyes. "Don't do this."

"Sweet Bry." Nick cupped her cheek with his hand. "Save your tears for someone else."

She shook her head, unable to speak without weeping.

He stepped backward, his gaze burning into hers.

Bry stared at him with all the longing she had denied.

"Better move along." Thad growled from the doorway behind her. "You'll find your horse saddled in the barn."

With a last lingering look, Nick turned on his heel and walked away from her.

Bry returned to the parlor and discovered that the atmosphere had grown considerably colder. Shane had risen and was looking out one of the windows with his back to everyone else. Maisey sat with her hands folded demurely in her lap but a frown on her face. Above his coffee cup, Rob watched Bry's friend with sad eyes. Growing up, Rob had always set himself to please others, especially members of the female persuasion. He'd changed of late, but Maisey's disapproval must disturb his composure. If Bry wanted to be uncharitable, she would say it wounded his pride. She sat down again with a sigh. Rob wasn't normally rude, but Thad seemed a bad influence on her brothers.

Thad swaggered in and took the chair nearest Bry. A silent wave of despair crashed through her. Would she never be rid of the man? When Rob offered to show Bry to her room, she jumped at the chance to escape. Maisey sprang to her feet at once, obviously eager to retire as well.

Shane remained in the parlor with Thad while her brother lit the way down the second-floor corridor with an oil lamp. Rob opened a door and stood back to allow them into a room. Bry examined the chamber in bemusement while Rob lit a lamp on a side table. She wouldn't have guessed Con would paint walls such a delicate shade of pink or choose bed curtains and bedding festooned with cabbage roses.

Rob turned to Maisey. "My sister is next to you. I hope you pass a comfortable night. Breakfast at eight?"

She smiled. "Thank you."

In Bry's room, several oil paintings depicting forest scenes adorned the walls, suspended by slender chains from the picture rail below the cove ceiling. Bed hangings in shades of brown and cream hung from the canopied bed and at the windows. A quilt in similar hues covered the bed. Bry went to the window, searching the gathering dusk for any sign of Nick in the distance. She found none. Rob touched her shoulder and wished her sweet dreams, but she couldn't bring herself to respond. It would take some doing to forgive her brother for turning Nick away.

The door shut softly behind him.

Bry rested her forehead on the cool pane and released a shuddering breath. The depth of her sorrow told her what she'd refused to admit. Despite her best intentions, she had fallen in love with Nick.

Bry waited until after breakfast to emerge from her room. Even if she had been hungry, she couldn't have faced Thad. He'd weaseled into her life with neither of her brothers noticing. Thad desired her, but as a woman to conquer, not someone to love. She couldn't in her wildest dreams picture him giving up anything he cherished for her, as Nick had done.

She found Maisey alone in the parlor, reading a battered copy of *Uncle Tom's Cabin.* "You look comfortable."

Maisey set the book aside. "I'm glad you're awake finally, but you've missed breakfast."

Bry waved a hand. "I needed sleep more than food." She perched on the sofa beside her friend. "Where is everyone?"

"Reverend Hayes has already gone. He said to tell you goodbye. Your brother and Mr. Taylor went looking for wolves troubling the cattle."

"That's just as well." Bry spoke without thinking, but then remembered her manners. "I mean—"

"I feel much the same." Maisey smiled impishly. "I'm grateful for the peace and quiet."

"I don't appreciate the way Rob treated Nick."

"That was unfortunate, but perhaps your brother had his reasons."

Bry couldn't emulate Maisey's graciousness, so she did the next best thing and said nothing.

Maisey stretched and stifled a yawn. "Shall we scout out some tea? I could do with a cup myself."

The sparse kitchen reminded Bry more of Con than the pink bedroom. Maisey opened the firebox door in the cast iron stove. "Oh, good. A few coals are still burning. Your brother made breakfast, but I don't mind cooking to earn my keep." She pulled kindling from the firewood bin and set to work reviving the fire.

Bry filled the kettle and located a tin of English Breakfast tea and sugar-biscuits in the open cupboard. More searching through the shelves below the counter turned up the tea service they had used the previous day.

Bry assembled the tray and once they'd prepared the tea, carried it into the dining room. She'd taken an aversion to the parlor where memories of Nick might rise up to haunt her. Besides, a large window in this room overlooked the river. An oriental carpet padded Bry's footsteps. She set the tea tray down on the long oak table and sank into one of the ladder-back chairs ringing it. A gold and crystal oil chandelier dangled above the table, and a border of green and gold branches twined around the ceiling cove. "It hardly seems possible that Con accumulated all this wealth, never mind that he has done so by mining in the back of beyond."

"That doesn't surprise me at all, having met your brother." Maisey poured tea and extended a cup and saucer to her."

"America tells me he's stolen the hearts of her children also. I'm so glad he's alive to see them grow up."

"Phoebe is fond of him." Maisey bit her lip and looked away.

"I'll ask Rob to look for her soon." The last thing she wanted at the moment was to talk to her brother, but she would do it for Maisey's sake.

The corners of Maisey's mouth turned downward, and her eyes went dull. "She turned four yesterday."

How that fact must have stirred Maisey's heartache, but she'd never once let on. Bry sought a way to comfort her friend, but she could make no sense of the tragedy. It didn't seem fair that God had allowed Con to live but hadn't intervened for Maisey. Avery was dead and Phoebe could well be also. Why would God, whom she'd been taught was just, do such a thing? "I'm sorry."

Maisey dashed away tears. "Sometimes I think I can't go on without my family."

"If I could carry your burden, I would."

"Sweet Bry." A faint smile touched Maisey's lips. "Only God can do that."

"How does your faith remain strong in the face of all you've suffered?"

Maisey's eyes lit. "What else can I do but cling to my Savior?"

"Why should you when God allows harm to innocent people?" The question burst from the depths of Bry's soul.

Maisey arched her brows. "I don't think we can blame God for evil. There's another source for that."

"But God is all powerful—"

"Which makes it easy to lay everything that happens at His door. Think about it, Bry. If God's will was always done, we wouldn't have to pray for it."

"But why does evil exist at all?"

"That's not God's doing. We have free will, and we live in a fallen world." She offered Bry a gentle smile. "I think that's the whole truth of it."

CHAPTER TWENTY-THREE

THE CHANDELIER BATHED THE TABLE IN a warm glow, and the curtains drawn across the window shut out the night. The clink of cutlery against porcelain, quiet voices, and the murmur of the river in the background bought an ambiance that stood in marked contrast to Bry's inner turmoil. She cut into the tender steak Maisey had cooked to perfection but barely noticed its flavor. Being anywhere near Thad had her on edge. She avoided his glances and gave short answers to the questions he asked. Rob received similar treatment, although for different reasons. He had wounded her and hurt Nick by siding with Thad, and she couldn't seem to leave behind the pain his betrayal had caused. Brothers weren't supposed to break your heart, but both of hers had conspired with Thad to do so.

Maisey turned to her. "You're quiet tonight."

"Feeling ill?" Rob asked.

"No, I'm not sick." Bry laid her fork down, her appetite gone. Was it too soon to excuse herself?

"We should fetch the doctor for you anyway." Rob drank water from his glass. "You don't seem yourself at all."

"There's no need. Doc Bailey has already examined me."

Rob leaned back in his chair and watched her, his blue eyes lighting with speculation. "And?"

Heat rush into Bry's face. It would escape Rob that asking about her physical examination in front of Thad might embarrass her. She could forgive her brother that much, knowing he had never been one for tact. "I am well." She didn't reveal everything the doctor had said. If Thad knew that Doc Bailey thought her nerves were strained and had told her to avoid alarms, he would use the information against her somehow.

She could feel Thad's gaze on her without turning her head.

"You need a diversion." His wheedling tone grated on her nerves. "Ride with me tomorrow, and I'll show you the range."

She sighed. "That wouldn't be proper."

"Out West we don't stand on convention."

"I appreciate that Mr. Taylor." She leveled a glare at him. "But I don't want to go with you."

"I can come too, as a chaperone." Rob turned his head toward Maisey. "Perhaps Mrs. Wilcox would like to come along."

"I, for one, don't want to see a horse anytime soon." Bry snapped at him, losing her patience. "I've spent weeks in the saddle."

Rob winced a little around the eyes. "I didn't mean to upset you."

"I'm afraid I don't want to go riding, either." Maisey spoke into the silence. "Perhaps another time?"

Thad gave Bry a beguiling smile. "We could walk down by the river tomorrow evening around sunset."

"You should," Rob urged. "It's cooling when the wind blows off the water."

Bry stared at her brother in exasperation. He seemed to champion everything Thad said and did. Deciding to change tactics, she summoned a smile for Thad. "Thank you, but I've had my share of the outdoors for a while. I'd rather stay inside. My brother seems taken with the idea. I'm sure you could persuade him to accompany you."

Maisey stifled a sound behind her hand, and a fit of coughing momentarily overwhelmed her.

Rob laughed outright. "I'd make a poor substitute in your place."

Irritation shot through Bry. Rob's remark betrayed that he understood and approved Thad's intent. "I'm sorry, brother of mine, but I'll thank you to let me pick my own walking partners."

Rob shook his head. "If you only would."

"If I want none, that is my decision, I should think." She rounded on Thad. "What sort of nonsense have you put in my brother's head?"

Thad's nostrils flared. The only answer he gave her was an assessing look. Bry's temper broke on the realization that she had stepped wrong with him again. She should never have issued a new challenge.

"Bry—" Maisey's forehead puckered. She opened her mouth to speak, but then closed it again. "Please excuse me. I have a headache." She fled.

"You will apologize for your rudeness!" Rob thundered.

Bry jumped to her feet. "Don't you dare lecture me after the way you treated Nick."

"So, that's what this is really about?"

She tossed her head. "I have no idea why you would say that."

Rob sighed. "Never mind, Bry. It's plain that you're in love with the wrong man."

"How I do or don't feel about Nick Laramie is no one's business but my own. What does it matter anyway? He's gone down the road, thanks to you." She choked out her last words.

Rob looked away from her.

Thad smirked.

Bry ran from the room, never stopping until slammed into her bedroom. Chest heaving, she leaned against the closed door behind her. Tears streamed down her cheeks. She tilted her head back against the door panel, closed her eyes, and abandoned herself to sorrow. So long as Thad lived here and kept her brother in his pocket, there could only be more scenes. Nothing would change when Con returned either. He thought as highly of Thad's opinion as Rob and had an equal penchant for intruding into her affairs. It broke her heart to admit it, but she couldn't stay here. Yet, where else could she go? Shane and America would take her in, but it would be unfair to burden them. She would have to work. Perhaps she could find a position in a nearby established town like Hell Gate or Deer Lodge.

A tap came at the door behind her. She scrubbed the tears from her cheeks with her palms. "Who is it?"

"It's me."

Maisey. Bry had forgotten to take her friend into consideration. Maisey seemed to be settling in well. Maybe she wouldn't mind Bry living elsewhere. Con might need a cook, and he wasn't likely to mind little Phoebe running about the place, if it came to that. She opened the door. "Come in."

Maisey had taken her hair down but hadn't yet changed for bed. She placed the oil lamp she carried on a table. "I heard you come upstairs, and I wanted to say I'm sorry."

"You? Whatever for? I'm the one who should apologize."

"I could tell you were being pushed into an uncomfortable position, and I should have stood by you instead of rushing off."

"Nevertheless, I must ask your forgiveness for making you uncomfortable. I hate upsetting you."

"Of course I forgive you. It's hard to fault you when I would have lost my own temper in the same situation. It's just that I can't bear to see you arguing with your brother when I'd give anything to see mine again."

"I didn't realize. Please, take a seat."

Maisey sat in the rosewood slipper chair by the window and folded her hands in her lap.

If only she had pinned up her brown hair rather than allowing it to cascade in waves about her, she would look prim and proper.

Bry sank into the chair on the other side of the window across the small table where the lamp glowed. "You said something before about your family not approving of Avery."

"My parents didn't want me to marry him, even tried to prevent it by forcing me into an engagement with a wealthy man. I eloped with Avery instead. We didn't have a lot of money, but I would do it again."

"Didn't you go to your parents afterward and try to make peace?"

Maisey nodded. "Yes, but they're set in their ways. My family will never overlook that I disgraced myself and shamed them by running off with someone beneath my station. My parents disowned me and told me never to return. They don't want anything more to do with me."

"I'm sorry, Maisey. Maybe they'll have a change of heart."

The look of despair on Maisey's face answered that idea. "Your friendship means a lot to me. Thank you for giving me a small place in your family."

The breath clogged in Bry's throat. She couldn't face herself in the mirror if she left Maisey behind. Before they could leave, she needed to ask Rob to search for Phoebe. That would be more difficult after her fight with Rob, but she'd do it tomorrow.

The chorus of "Oh! Susanna" carried from the kitchen in Maisey's sweet soprano. Bry paused with her hand on the stair rail and shook her head in wonderment. How could Maisey, who had suffered incredible loss, find the lightness of heart to sing? The lively melody chased away the gloom that had haunted Bry through the night. Running away would have been easier, but she wasn't entirely sad that she had chosen to stay a little longer.

A heavenly aroma wafted to her from the kitchen. At Bry's greeting, Maisey broke off her song. "Good morning. The men have gone outside."

That was just as well, Bry decided, because she didn't know what to say to Rob anymore. She could find words for Thad all too easily. After talking with Maisey last night, she wanted to guard her tongue a little better.

Maisey, her sleeves rolled up, swished a dish in soapy water. "Did you sleep well?"

"Not really." Bry nodded toward the faucets above the sink. "I didn't notice them before. How is the water supplied?"

Maisey smiled. "I had the same question. Your brother told me that a windmill pump brings water through the pipes."

"I'm beyond being surprised by anything around here. You look right at home, by the way."

Maisey laughed. "I should. I've done plenty of dishes in my life."

Bry pulled a cotton dishtowel from the wooden rack in one corner and picked up a plate to dry. "Thanks for what you said about your family last night. I needed to hear it. I'm going to try harder with Rob."

"I'm glad." Maisey rested her hands on the edge of the sink and glanced sideways at her. "If you want my advice on what to do about Mr. Taylor—"

"I'd welcome it." Bry faced the dry plate outward behind the plate rail in the wall rack.

"All right." She hesitated as if choosing her words. "I've noticed that responding when he goads you gives him the ability to control your emotions and reactions."

"You're right, I suppose. I suspect control is what he's after."

"Don't let him succeed."

"If only my brother would see the man clearly, I wouldn't have to stand up to him." Bry whipped the dishtowel across another plate.

"Give him time. He may come to share your opinion."

Maisey didn't seem to like Thad any more than she did.

"You must be hungry. Once I finish the dishes, I'll put on the kettle, fry an egg or two, and slice the raisin bread I made this morning."

"Is that what smells so good?" Bry breathed deeply.

Maisey's face flushed. "I hope you like it."

"If it tastes anything like it smells, I'm bound to. Thank you, Maisey, for letting me impose on your kindness. I'll rise earlier from now on, so I can lend a hand with breakfast."

"All right, but don't worry about it overmuch. I enjoy cooking."

Bry kept Maisey company and lent a hand at cooking. She left Maisey humming while preparing a dried apple pie for dessert and wandered into the sitting room. A less formal room than the parlor, it boasted maroon walls, several rocking chairs grouped around a table, and a blue velvet fainting couch that would make a comfortable place to read. Dust lay everywhere, however. Bry sighed. Since coming here, she had learned the futility of trying to keep pace with the dust that blew in from the dirt road. She restrained the urge to go in search of a dust cloth. Tomorrow would be soon enough to tackle the problem. She wouldn't begrudge herself a moment to rest.

After cracking open the windows to let in a flow of cooler air, she went to the bookcase to choose a book. She decided on the three volumes in the Great Expectations series by Charles Dickens and settled down to read. Caught up in the story, Bry lost track of time.

Maisey looked in on her. "You seem comfortable."

Bry glanced up. "Sorry, I meant to come back and help with dishes."

"It's all right. They're done now, and dinner's all set to cook when we're ready." Maisey's forehead puckered. "I wonder—have you asked Rob to look for Phoebe yet?"

"I will when he comes in today, I promise."

"Thank you." Maisey gave her a wan smile. "I think I'll lie down for a bit."

Bry closed her book. "Are you all right?"

"I'm still tired from…everything, I suppose."

"If you want to stay in bed, I can cook dinner alone."

Maisey shook her head. "I'm sure I'll be rested by then."

After Maisey went upstairs, Bry settled down with her book again. The sun shifted position, forcing her to close the window, which trapped the cooler air she'd let into the room. She also pulled the curtains against the heat. She returned to the fainting couch and lost herself in the story once more.

"You look particularly lovely at this moment." Thad spoke from the doorway.

Bry started, wrenched from the fictional world she had entered. She closed her book but kept her place with her finger.

Mindful of Maisey's advice, she refrained from issuing a challenge over his intrusion. Nor did she state that his compliments were unwelcome. Telling him so would only make him praise her more. What time was it? She consulted the clock on top of the bookshelf. "Good afternoon, Mr. Taylor. I didn't expect you back so soon. It's only three. Did my brother come in with you?" She searched the entryway behind him, but Rob was nowhere in sight.

"He wanted to watch over a cow about to birth."

Bry frowned. "If he doesn't come back by supper, please ride out and relieve him. I have something important to discuss with him." She didn't want to wait another day to ask Rob to look for Phoebe.

Thad scanned her face with narrowed eyes but didn't ask her to explain. He nodded toward the book in her hand. "What are you reading?"

She shrugged. "Something I found in the bookcase to pass the time." Sharing the story with him would feel too personal.

Thad peered at the book. "That's a novel, isn't it?"

"What's wrong with that?" Struck by the realization that she had allowed him, yet again, to draw her, Bry pressed her lips together and resolved to say no more.

"My parents taught me better than to read lies in book form."

Bry stared at him in amazement. "How can anyone think of novels like that?" She could remember her father reading from his well-worn copies of the *Leatherstocking Tales* in her childhood. She'd cut her teeth on the rousing adventures of Natty Bumppo, the frontiersman who went by such romantic names as Deerslayer, Pathfinder, and Hawkeye. When the Wainwrights had culled their bookshelves, they had passed unwanted titles to the servants. Many of the books had not been read, but merely displayed for effect. Within their pages, she had escaped the drudgery of her life, if only for a time.

Thad's eyes gleamed. "You're bound to have all sorts of mischief in your head from reading."

She set her book aside and stood up, feeling at a disadvantage while lying on the fainting couch. "I'm sorry you take such a narrow-minded view. Don't let me trouble you with my presence." She swept past him.

Thad caught up to her in the entryway and pulled her to him. "Not so fast, *Irish*."

Jeffrey had called her the same name in exactly that tone. Come to think of it, there wasn't that much difference between the pair of them. Thad's high-handed attitude reminded her of Ian when he'd been drinking. If she spoke back to him, he would backhand her. She'd learned that keeping her mouth shut hurt less. Well, not today. "I'll thank you to let go of me." She enunciated each word.

"Spending time with the savages hasn't improved your manners any." Thad slid his hand over her mouth and whispered near her ear. "It's time I taught you some." He thrust her before him through the doorway and along the corridor. Maisey no longer worked in the kitchen. Bry hoped, as Thad dragged her toward the back door, that her friend was close enough to hear.

Could this really be happening to her again? She seemed to attract the wrong sort of man altogether. Sick to death of being mistreated, Bry drove her foot down on Thad's instep and twisted in his arms. She had to get away or at least make enough noise to alert Maisey. Her soft slipper made no impact on Thad, and his bear hug stifled her efforts to escape. He jerked open the back door and pushed her through it. Stepping sideways, he hauled her with him into the timber. The wind-tousled trees sent shadows crawling over her. Thad dragged her up a hill and over the side. He finally took his hand from her mouth but replaced it with his lips.

His assault on her mouth ground her teeth against her lips. Utterly disgusted, Bry struggled in his arms.

He lifted his head, his breathing not quite even. "I've wanted to do that for a long time."

Bry's palm itched to slap him, but his embrace trapped her hands between them. "Don't think I won't tell my brother," she spat.

"Do that, and I'd have to kill him."

"You don't mean that."

"Try me." Thad released her.

Bry rubbed her arm across her mouth to erase the feel of his kiss. If she told Rob what Thad had done, things might get out of hand. Rob was no fighter. He'd survived growing up in the slum due to a combination of Con's protection and his own sharp wits. He would be no match for Thad in a fight.

He stepped back with a knowing look on his face. "You liked it anyway. Don't pretend you didn't."

She tossed her head and gave him a withering look. "If you believe that, you're a bigger fool than I thought."

A slow smile spread across his face. "Begging for more?" He started forward.

Bry broke and ran. His laughter followed her into the forest. Dappled shade swayed beneath her feet, making her steps uncertain. She slowed and looked back. Relief shook her. He hadn't followed. She stumbled in the direction of the house. Returning to it seemed to take longer than leaving it. She halted beside a snag broken by some long-ago accident and strained to hear the river's rushing, but it no longer lifted its voice. The only sounds were the sobbing of a mourning dove and the thud of her heartbeat in her ears. She took a different tack that led into an unfamiliar canyon. Her stomach clenched, but she wrapped her arms around herself and took a deep breath to ward off panic.

She struck out with renewed determination. After what seemed endless wandering, she leaned a hand against the smooth-scoured wood of the broken tree from before. It had cost her a lot of energy to wind up in the place she'd left behind. Which way had she been traveling when she'd reached the snag before? A glimmer of memory stirred, and with her hope renewed, she set off again.

The sun slipped downward and dangled above the horizon, ready to drop. Gazing into the near distance, Bry wanted to weep. The same broken snag thrust into the sky with sunset blazing behind it.

CHAPTER TWENTY-FOUR

MOONLIGHT SILVERED THE TIPS OF THE grass in the small meadow where Bry kept watch on a fallen log. Coyotes set up a racket that made her skin crawl, and she tightened her grip on the pointed branch she held. It wasn't much of a weapon but might protect her in a pinch.

Rob would be searching for her, but she hadn't made it easy for him. The hope of finding her way back to the ranch had no doubt carried her far afield. Would Thad tell her brother anything to help him find her? It seemed unlikely. She knew very little about Thad except that he delighted in taunting her. Had he been serious about killing Rob? She didn't know. Losing Liam had been bad enough. She would do or say nothing that could take another brother from her.

The coyotes howled again, but from farther away. Some of Bry's tension drained from her. An owl hooted in a nearby pine, and she started. She released a shuddering breath and waited for her heart to stop racing. She needed to calm down, or by morning she'd have turned into a deranged woman, jumping at every sound. A gust of wind ruffled the meadow grasses and made her shiver. It would be less windy in the trees, but she couldn't persuade herself to shift.

She would rather spend the night in the open where she could see a predator approaching than in the forest closeness where she could not. The gingham dress that America had given her was too light to afford much protection from the elements. Her slippers had likewise proved inadequate for tramping through a forest. She had picked wild strawberries while following the stream into the meadow, but her stomach growled for more substantial sustenance.

What she wouldn't give for a slice of Maisey's dried apple pie, eaten in the warmth and safety of the dining room.

The moon, nearly full, climbed in the sky and shed its light across the wild lands. Creatures that had been hidden now sprang into relief. A jackrabbit watched her with glowing eyes before bounding into the safety of a thicket. In one of the trees, a bird slept with its head tucked. Movement at the edge of the clearing resolved into a foraging buck and doe.

The wind picked up, and the temperature dropped. Bry stood, ready to seek shelter at last. The deer lifted their heads and froze in place, staring into the distance. Bry's skin crawled. They weren't facing her. A bird call pierced the air, raising the hair on Bry's nape. The sleeping bird stirred, gave the same warning cry, and flew out of the tree. The buck and doe bounded away. Bry started for the trees, her fear of the shadows paling beside the skin-prickling fear of whatever was coming in the night.

The clop of hooves was the first sound she recognized, followed by the murmur of voices. She halted in confusion. If Rob and some of their neighbors were searching for her, she should call out. It might be outlaws or Indians, though. She couldn't take a chance. Her hesitation broken, she hurried to find a hiding place.

The voices grew louder, speaking a language Bry recognized. One of the voices stood out in particular. She shrank into the shadows, trembling. The riders came into view, following the stream as she had done. Feathered headdresses shone blue and the reins glinted in the moonlight. One of the ponies snorted, and the first of the Indians pulled level with her, so close that Bry didn't dare to breathe.

What was Kicking Horse doing so far from his village?

Nick stood on the edge of the cliff and looked down at the Missouri flowing between its banks in bright currents. Here and there eddies swirled, whirlpools ready to suck a swimmer down, even one as strong as his father had been. Long Knife had counted on that when he'd thrown his rival into the river. Nick would have jumped in after his father, but his mother had restrained him. She'd told him afterward that she couldn't have borne losing him too. She'd believed Long Knife when he'd claimed it had been an accident, but Nick knew what he'd seen.

He turned away from the river. There was no point in dwelling on what he couldn't change. He had paid his respects to his father, whom the river had refused to give up. His mother lay far from here among her people, parted from him in death as she had been in life.

Strange, but the cabin was smaller than Nick remembered. Why its size had never bothered him before he didn't know, but it did now. He would always treasure the memories it stirred for him, but he couldn't settle into it this time. Restlessness plagued him, dragging him out of bed at night and leading him down paths he'd explored only in childhood. The sense of his family that lingered in this place wasn't enough for him any longer.

The worn path behind the cabin climbed the hill where his family had picked wild blueberries. Had they remained, it might have eventually held their graves. The ground contained one body, however. Anyone who chanced upon the flat stone that marked the grave would not understand its meaning. Only he knew that the white wolf lay beneath it.

The time had come to say goodbye.

Nick knelt beside the stone and bowed his head. " God, I can't carry this burden anymore. Help me to belong somewhere."

The sun beat down, a hawk whistled, a bee buzzed past. The breeze whispered in his ear. He lifted his head, determined to offer his services to the preacher who had welcomed him at his table. That would bring him within a day's ride of Bry. Did he trust himself to stay away from her? He ought to leave her alone. She was bound to marry, and probably sooner than later. That would be hard to endure, but not knowing how she fared was no easier.

He admitted the truth to himself. So long as Bry lived and

breathed, he needed to be near her, whatever it cost him.

Bry woke to bird cries, the whistling of chickadees and cheeping of sparrows among them. She sat up, woozy-headed and blinking away sleep. The sky had lightened toward morning. She lay on her back in the forest sediments and watched the fading stars beyond the treetops. How small she felt in all creation, and how weak. Could God really see her? With so many others to consider, why would He trouble to look after her? The Almighty hadn't stopped Ian's fists or Jeffrey's assault. Nor had He prevented Mam and Liam from dying or Con from being shot in front of her. The stars blurred behind her tears. Mam wouldn't have approved of these thoughts. "Please help my brother find me." She whispered the prayer.

She'd given up hope of finding her way out of the woods. Her efforts had carried her in the wrong direction. She should have paid better attention to what Nick had said about finding her way in the woods. She'd heard that a lost person should remain in one place, and now she understood why. Wandering about, trying to find her way back, had exhausted her and allowed no time for matters of survival. Nick had taught her a few things about living in the woods. She didn't have his skill, but she could put together a lean-to that would shade her by day and hide her at night. Hopefully, she wouldn't need one for long. Nick had shown her how to make fire from a bow drill, a rock with a hole, and a tinder bundle. Smoke curling into the air might help her brother find her, but after seeing Kicking Horse and his band ride through, she hesitated to light a fire.

Sunbeams burst from behind the hills, gold like the precious metal that had lured Con to this place. They gilded the sky, a symbol of hope that pushed back the darkness. Bry stood and stretched, ready to face the day's challenges. She foraged juneberries to ease her hunger pangs, then gathered fallen branches and brush for the lean-to. She moved away from the meadow to build her shelter, although she didn't abandon the open spaces entirely. It seemed logical that her brother might follow the stream as both she and the band of Cheyenne had done. Absorbed in weaving together her shelter, she didn't at first notice the thud of hooves in the meadow. She lifted her head, listening intently. No sound of voices carried to her, making it impossible to tell if Kicking Horse had returned. She crept through the trees to peer out from behind a bush at the edge of the meadow.

Rob, red hair springing from beneath his bowler, sat astride his Morgan horse. "I don't like the signs of Indians I'm seeing." Rob glanced about. "I could swear we're being watched."

Bry held back when she saw Thad riding a black horse beside Rob. If the man taunted her, she might not be able to hold her tongue, even for her brother's sake. Nick had taught her more than how to survive, apparently. Whether or not she ever saw him again, she would always thank him for reminding her that she mattered. When had she strayed from the spirited woman she had been?

"I doubt she'll have come this far afield, anyway." Thad's gaze passed over Bry's hiding place. "We should probably search closer to the house."

"Wait . . ." Bry called, but her voice came out a whisper.

Rob turned his horse, and the two men started off without looking back.

Bry ran out behind them. "Don't leave me!" Her cry was stronger this time.

Rob wheeled his horse around. "Bry? Are you all right?"

"I'm better now you've found me."

Rob broke into a grin. "Did you think I wouldn't?" He rode back to her and swung down from his horse. "You scared us, I don't mind telling you."

Bry threw herself into her brother's arms with tears running down her cheeks.

He held onto her. "Thank the Lord you're safe."

Over her brother's shoulder, Bry met Thad's gaze. He strode

toward her. "Whatever made you wander off like that?"

She caught her breath. He was laughing at her, daring her to tell on him, certain she wouldn't. Ian had done the same thing. She pulled away from Rob to face Thad. "You know why."

Thad's eyes widened, but he otherwise gave no reaction. "I'm not sure what you mean. If I knew the answer, I wouldn't have asked the question."

He spoke in such a reasonable tone that if she hadn't known the truth, she would have believed him. "That's a lie."

"You're overwrought, Mrs. Brennan."

"Of course, I am. Who wouldn't be?" She wanted to stamp her foot for emphasis, but behaving like that might make her seem unbalanced.

"Come on, Bry." Rob touched her arm. "The sooner we take you home, the better."

She held back. "I didn't go walking alone if that's what Thad told you."

Rob's nostrils flared, and he divided a glance between them. "What are you saying? Did something happen I should know about?"

Thad's eyes glittered, and he laid a hand over the gun strapped at his side.

The steam went out of Bry. "Only a moment's nonsense. I'll never let it happen again." She lingered over her last sentence, watching Thad's face change.

"You'll want to look after yourself better in the future." Thad's smile didn't reach his eyes. "You're not in Boston anymore."

She started. How did he know where she'd lived? Was he acquainted in some way with Jeffrey Wainwright? If so, he might know the reason she'd been dismissed from service. She reined in her imagination. More likely, Con or Rob had mentioned Boston in conversation. She didn't like that idea much better. "Thank you for your concern on my behalf, Mr. Taylor. I'm sorry to have worried you, Rob."

"I'm sure to have lost ten year's growth, but none of that

matters. Climb on my horse, and we'll head home."

Bry eyed the large animal. "He's bigger than I'm used to."

"You can always join me on mine." The look Thad gave her belied his innocent tone.

She shook her head. "That would mistreat your horse. A Morgan is stronger."

He removed his hand from his gun and gave her a winsome smile. "You are a wise woman."

CHAPTER TWENTY-FIVE

BRY DRESSED IN A HURRY, EAGER to catch Rob alone. Her ordeal had driven thoughts of Phoebe's plight from her mind, but she would delay no longer in enlisting her brother's help.

Rob was collaring the Morgans when she entered the barn. He looked over his shoulder. "You're up early."

"I need to talk to you."

His brows shot upward. "Is something wrong?"

"Well yes, but don't look so worried. It's nothing to do with you."

Rob completed his task and stepped away from the horses. "Tell me, then."

"Maisey and her four-year-old daughter were separated when she was kidnapped."

"That's terrible. Does Maisey have any idea where to find her?"

"Phoebe was in the doctor's care. She went on in the train. We hope she's still with Doc Mather and his wife."

"It seems likely." Rob's face took on a tender look. "Shall I find out for her? I can ask at the forts, to start."

"I thought you might."

"Of course." Rob gave a swift nod. Why hasn't Maisey mentioned this?"

"I told her I would, but I've been . . . preoccupied lately."

"Any idea where the doctor might have gone?"

"None."

"That's helpful."

"He might have left word for Maisey at one of the forts, in case she was freed."

"It's somewhere to start, anyway." Rob turned back to the

horses.

Bry hurried to the house with a lighter step than when she'd left it. She hurried to the kitchen to tell Maisey the good news. She found her friend hovering over the cast-iron frying pan, where bacon sizzled. "Rob's promised to search for Phoebe."

Maisey sat down on the kitchen stool and dissolved into tears.

Bry touched her shoulder before taking over at the stove. "He'll find out where she is, I'm sure of it."

"Look at me." Maisey dried her eyes with a dish towel. "Here I am crying when I should celebrate."

"I'm sorry it took me so long to ask him about Phoebe. We've been at odds with one another over one thing or another since I arrived, which made it hard."

"I'm only grateful for your help."

Bry moved bacon to the draining rack above a platter beside the stove. "About Rob – he can be rough around the edges, but he has a soft heart."

Maisey nodded. "I'm learning that."

The Bitterroot River wallowed between its banks while Tavo lipped the water, his sides heaving. Nick could see Conner Walsh's ranch from here. Bry would be inside, avoiding the last of the day's heat. What was she doing at this moment? He could picture her with her head bowed, reading a book with rapt attention. Perhaps she was taking tea with Maisey. The image of steam swirling from her cup to bathe her face tantalized him. What would the two talk about? He had no idea.

Had Con returned home to his sister? What a reunion that would have been. Con had made Nick's life uncomfortable, but he couldn't blame a man for wanting to safeguard his sister. He would try to view Rob's annoying hostility in the same light.

He hoped Thad had moved on but doubted it. He seemed the

type to latch on until forced to leave. Nick's jaw tightened with regret at leaving with Thad still at the ranch. If the man had caused any trouble for Bry at all, he'd hear from him.

Tavo lifted his head and shifted as if anxious to continue the journey, but Nick placed a quieting hand on his horse's neck. He wasn't ready to put distance between himself and the woman he loved. Bry's nearness tempted him to do something rash, like knock on the ranch house door and ask for her. That would only cause trouble between Bry and her brother.

Someone stood in one of the upstairs windows. He couldn't make out the person from here, but his heart thudded faster. The unknown figure lingered before abandoning the station.

Nick signaled to Tavo and left the riverbank behind. It might not have been Bry, but his emotions slammed him anyway. He loved her beyond bounds. That alone was reason to move down the trail without factoring in her brother's reaction to a visit from him. He made camp for the night. Tomorrow would be soon enough to show up on the Hayes's doorstep. He lay in his bedroll watching the stars, listening to a night bird's whistle, and thinking of Bry. He had come back because he couldn't stay away, but he was no closer to knowing what to do about his feelings for her.

He rode into Liberty early in the day and found Shane coming out of his barn. He grinned at Nick. "Why hello there. I'd given up on seeing you again."

Nick dismounted and shook his hand. "If your offer still stands, I'd like to take you up on it. I'm willing to work in exchange for my keep. My father taught me to hunt and trap, and I'm happy to supply food for the table. I can help with chores too."

Shane nodded. "You're welcome on your own account, but that's wonderful. You can have the school teacher's cabin for a few months. How long do you expect to remain with us?"

"I don't--" Nick's mind raced with convincing replies, but he couldn't seem to choose one. "I'm not entirely certain, to tell you the truth."

Shane's gaze pierced his. "What is it that you want, Nick? This doesn't have anything to do with my cousin, does it?"

"I can't say it doesn't." He kicked a rock and watched it land. "That's not all there is to it, though."

Shane studied him a moment "It's going to be hot today." He turned back into the building he'd left. "Let's water your horse and give him a bag of oats, shall we?"

"Thank you." Nick followed him beneath the shade of the barn roof. It would take a while to feel less awkward, but the preacher's warm greeting moved him closer to that mark. He couldn't bring himself to voice his hopes to Shane, but maybe someday he would come to think of Liberty as his hometown.

That happened sooner than he'd expected. Within weeks he fell into a comfortable routine, going out around dawn every couple of days to hunt, check his fish weir, and gather food from the wild. Shane sometimes asked him to go along to distribute the bounty he brought in to the neighbors or help with some project or other. Most of the townsfolk eyed him with suspicion at first, but with Shane speaking well of him, their attitudes started to change.

Liberty and Seth had shown no hesitation in flinging themselves at him when he crouched to speak to them. He flinched a little when that happened but managed to mask the pain to his wound. Their mother noticed, apparently, for she cautioned the children to have a care. They restrained themselves for a day or two, but after that whenever he visited, they barreled into him. He'd recovered enough to withstand the assault, and the ache in his shoulder paled beside the children's affection.

He walked into the Hayes's home through the back door near time for Sunday dinner, a meal he always took with the family. The aroma of roasted pheasant filled the kitchen. The children greeted him with their usual onslaught, and he made a fuss of them in return. He turned Seth over and held him upside down while the little boy squealed with joy. Liberty gave him a captivating smile and offered him a wilting wildflower, saying that she had picked it for him. He took it from her pudgy fingers with all the care he might have given a precious jewel and tucked it into the buttonhole at his collar.

Shane looked on with an amused expression. "You've stolen my children's hearts, and no mistake."

Nick laughed. "It's mutual."

"You do realize that your fate is sealed, don't you?"

"Oh?" Nick gave Seth a final turn hanging upside down. "And what is that?"

Shane exchanged a glance with his wife, who smiled and went back to pouring water from a white porcelain pitcher into glasses. "We've decided to follow our children's sensible example and adopt you."

Nick straightened while the children clung to his legs, giggling. "I'm honored." He forced the words past the emotion choking him. He'd found a place to belong.

The cool air of early morning poured through the window in Bry's room, billowing the chintz curtains. She pulled aside the soft fabric and breathed in the moisture-laden air. A summer storm had passed in the night, freshening the grass and cleansing the cottonwoods lining the river. She'd slept through the rain, weary from putting up huckleberry jam and preparing food for today's journey with Maisey.

Rob went into the barn, probably to hitch the horses to the wagon that would carry them to Liberty. They would spend the night at their cousin's home, then attend the monthly Sunday meeting the next day. It would be interesting to hear Shane preach, something she would never have guessed he'd do. That was the way of it, though. Hardship forced a person's back against the wall, and when every effort failed, it was either rely on your Maker or perish. She'd had to learn that lesson herself.

Shane had been a rough youth while coming of age in Manhattan's Five Points slum. She'd felt sorry for her cousin, whose parents had died in the potato famine. He'd escaped starvation in Ireland, only to be raised by Uncle Seamus, who had demonstrated that he cared more for the bottle than the nephew in his charge. He had drunk away most of the money he'd earned and cuffed Shane whenever he'd protested. It was a wonder her cousin had survived his upbringing at all.

Growing up in a slum crammed full of immigrants, with its filth and crime, had been hard for Bry, but at least her family had loved her. Con had tried to bring Shane home to live with them, but with so many mouths already to feed, her parents had refused. Shane must shoulder the burden of his own care. She had disagreed with their decision, but she understood why they had made it. They'd had little enough to eat themselves, plus younger boys than Shane had to support themselves by their wits.

She shook off her thoughts. Today should be a lighthearted day, not one filled with shadows from the past. Her cousin had turned out well, and her own life had improved also. She would never have the kind of love her parents had held for one another. That possibility had ridden away with Nick. She could make a good life for herself regardless. Establishing roots in her new homeland was a step in that direction.

In the kitchen, Maisey greeted her with a smile, and the aromas of bacon and coffee beckoned. She poured coffee for them both. "Are you all packed?"

"Yes." Bry accepted her cup with a smile. "Rob told me last night that he wants to leave after breakfast."

"I'm looking forward to seeing America and her precious children again." On the last words, a wistful note crept into Maisey's voice.

Bry hoped that Rob would find Phoebe alive. Meanwhile, she would do her best to distract Maisey. "Did you hear the storm last night?"

"The rain lashing my window woke me, but I didn't mind. I like storms, and we needed relief after all the heat."

"Maybe it will make the trip cooler." Bry took a cautious sip of coffee, fearful of burning her tongue.

"That would be nice. " Maisey picked up a knife and sliced one of the potatoes.

"I don't know about you, but I've given up on having milk-white skin."

Maisey nodded. "That's for women who live in the East."

Bry turned a strip of bacon with a long-handled fork. "Would you ever go back?"

Maisey lifted her shoulder. "I'm here now."

"I know what you mean. You have to give up a lot to live in the West, but in my view, it's worth it. Where else could you find such freedom?"

Rob looked in at the door. "Is breakfast almost ready? We need to leave soon."

"Not quite. Now out of the kitchen!" Bry shooed him away. Rob ducked out of the doorway, laughing.

A smile lit Maisey's face. "It's good to see you and Rob at ease with one another."

"Being lost in the woods changed my mind about a lot of things." Bry removed the cooked bacon from the sizzling grease and added the final batch. "My brother has a desire to travel. It pains me to say this, but once Con returns, we may not keep Rob very long. I want to enjoy having him around while I can."

A small furrow appeared between Maisey's brows, but she went on slicing without replying. Bry watched her, wondering what she was thinking. Maisey had loved Avery deeply and wouldn't look elsewhere for a long while, but she and Rob showed a preference for one another. If they were to marry one day, Maisey would become her sister.

Bry laughed. "Listen to me, pretending to know what my brother will do. Rob might as easily stay on to help with the ranch and keep our family together. We've had little chance of that for a long time."

"I hope he will want to stay." Maisey finished slicing potatoes and reached for a bunch of the wild onions they'd discovered while picking huckleberries. "There's nothing more important than family."

"That's true, although when the fever to go westward grabs hold, people don't usually stop to consider what they're leaving behind. It's only later that they realize. Con vanished for years. He eventually returned to his family, but by then he'd missed the final years of our father's life." Bry shook her head. "We both did."

"I'm sorry to learn that. I'd give anything to make peace with my parents."

"Maybe you should try." Bry lifted the last of the bacon from the pan.

Maisey stepped in to add the potatoes to the pan. "They closed the door to that in no uncertain terms." Bitterness crept into her voice.

"People say things in anger that they later come to regret. They've had time to reconsider. Why not give them the chance to change their minds?"

Maisey picked up a wooden spoon and stirred the potatoes. "I'll give it some thought."

Bry finished her coffee, which had grown tepid. She had parted with her own father on good terms, but after her yearning to leave Five Points became a reality, she hadn't looked back. She hoped Maisey wouldn't make a similar mistake.

Despite Rob's intention to leave early, an emergency with one of the cattle delayed their departure. Thad almost remained behind to look after it, but he and Rob decided that wouldn't be necessary, much to Bry's dismay.

The men sat in companionable silence most of the way, exchanging few words except when they joined in the women's conversation. Maisey and Bry drank dippers of water, wore bonnets as protection from the sun, and moved into the shade whenever they stopped. Night fell before they reached Liberty. Thad lit a lantern and suspended it outside the wagon box. It swayed in time to the creak of the wagon, sending shadows jumping. Bry found the lantern's glow comforting. After a day spent in the heat, she and Maisey fell silent as well. Bry sighed. They had enough food and drink for comfort, should a mishap prevent them from reaching her cousin's house, but she would welcome a chance to wash and a safe place to sleep.

The schoolhouse receded in darkness, but the Hayes's windows glowed with warm light. Shane emerged from the house, carrying a lantern. America appeared in the doorway without the children, who must be in bed. Rob helped Maisey down from the wagon, while Thad lifted his arms to Bry with a smug look on his face. Bry turned away from him and poised herself to climb to the ground on her own.

"Have a care!" Shane put down his lantern and sprang forward.

A figure moved along the path behind the schoolhouse. Leaving the shadow beneath the trees, the man stepped into the moonlight.

Bry drew in a sharp breath.

"What is *he* doing here?" Rob asked.

Shane lifted Bry down from the wagon. "Mr. Laramie is our guest."

Thad scowled. "You'll regret that."

"I'll thank you to keep your opinions to yourself." Shane's voice cut like steel.

Bry barely heard any of them. She'd thought Nick gone from her life, but here he was, walking toward her.

"It's good to see you again, ladies." Nick smiled at Bry and Maisey then nodded to Thad and Rob. "Good evening, gentlemen."

Bry stared at the man before her. "You came back."

He gave her a rueful look. "My cabin was too lonely, as it turned out."

"I'm glad to find you here." Maisey smiled.

"Come inside, why don't you?" America waved a hand toward the door. "There's no need to stand about in the dark when we have perfectly good chairs inside."

"Go ahead, Rob." Shane gestured with his head. "I can care for the horses."

"I'll help you," Nick volunteered, but he didn't move away from Bry. "Sweet dreams." "Won't you come in, too?" America asked him.

"Thanks all the same, but it's late." He gave Bry a last, lingering look.

Remembering to breathe, she followed America into the house. Why had Nick refused to join them? Questions pressed her mind. Why had he come back to Liberty? She could almost persuade herself that he wanted to be closer to her.

Nick drove the wagon into the barn and parked it beside Shane's. He unhitched the horses by the light of the lantern the preacher held aloft. Shane joined him as he led the Morgans to the watering trough. The lantern attached to the wagon box cast a golden circle, matching the glow from the one Shane propped on an overturned barrel. With the ceiling out of sight in the darkness and the horses feeding in their stalls, the quiet barn soothed Nick. He'd fondly imagined he could remain composed around Bry, but the longing to hold her shook him to the core.

Maybe staying here wasn't going to work after all. Where else could he go? His parents' cabin dwelt in silence. The wagon masters who had been like friends had traveled far away. He felt cast adrift, drowning in a whirlpool.

He led one of the Morgans into a stall and picked up the curry comb. The other one followed Shane into the next stall.

"What happened back there?" The question came from behind the wooden stall divider between them.

"What do you mean?" Nick asked the question, although he might know the answer.

"Why turn down a perfectly good invitation to be with the woman you love?"

"Are my feelings that obvious?"

"Of course, but then so are hers."

Nick had no right to feel the hope that leaped within him. He put the curry comb aside and reached for a body brush.

"Why don't you want to be around her?"

"It's not that—at least not directly." Nick stopped talking while deciding how much to reveal. Shane was a preacher he admired, but he wasn't ready to talk about the reasons he could never marry Bry. He chose a simpler explanation. "It would only upset her brother or spark a fight with Mr. Taylor."

Shane made a sound suspiciously like stifled laughter. "I take your point, but there's more than good manners involved. What do *you* want, Nick?"

Shane had asked that before, and Nick gave the same answer now. "I don't know."

"You may tell yourself that, but I doubt you really believe it. Deep down, you know exactly what you want."

Nick concentrated on the rhythmic motion of brushing the horse.

"I know first-hand what it's like to deny yourself the love you need," Shane went on. "I told myself I was doing it for noble reasons, but do you know what? It smelled an awful lot like fear."

Nick exchanged the body brush for a hoof pick. "You don't understand what it's like to be half-Cheyenne."

"Fair enough, but I know what it is to be Irish and unwelcome. Don't let the opinions of others guide you. You may need to overcome more obstacles, but there's no reason you shouldn't have the best of life."

Nick said nothing more. He appreciated the preacher's perspective, but opinions did matter. They kept you from fitting in.

CHAPTER TWENTY-SIX

BRY DRAGGED HER ATTENTION BACK TO Shane's sermon with no clue what he was talking about. It didn't help that Thad had seated himself rather smugly by her side, placed there by her brother's maneuvering, or that Nick kept watching them from across the room. The next time she talked to Rob alone, she'd let him know exactly what she thought of his matchmaking. Meanwhile, she had to put up with Thad's nearness. Even if she'd been willing to endure the stares that moving away from him might cause, she would do nothing to disrupt the service.

The town of Liberty didn't have a formal church yet, so Shane held Sunday meetings in the schoolhouse. The building was adequate, if not lovely. Built in a rectangle, it had an entryway lined with long benches and rows of hooks that must come in handy for hanging school bags, jackets, and scarfs. In the main room, desks lined up in neat rows waited for students. The church-goers climbed the stairs to the second floor, built by the townsfolk for gatherings. Shane's pulpit stood at the end of an aisle between two rows of benches.

Bry pulled her attention back to her cousin and did her best to pay attention. Fortunately, Shane turned out to be a compelling speaker, and he'd chosen an interesting topic. He came out from behind the pulpit and paced before the congregation. "In Biblical times, three men were cast into an oven so hot the heat killed the guards who threw them in." He paused as several ladies gasped. "They had displeased the king by refusing to bow down and worship his god." Shane bowed his head amid silence throbbing with anticipation. Some of the listeners leaned forward in their seats. Shane lifted his head. "The men fasted and called upon the one true God, hoping He would deliver them. Whether or not that happened, they resolved to worship only Him." He moved back behind the pulpit. "Their faith received its reward when they emerged from the furnace alive." He smiled. "The king saw a fourth man with the appearance of an angel in the furnace. God had delivered them."

Bry leaned against her seat back, thankful the men had survived their long ordeal. She understood the helplessness they must have felt. Discussing a fiery furnace seemed appropriate with the weather already heating up outside. The men in the story had shown a faith much like Maisey's. They had trusted in God who, by their own admission, might not deliver them. She was beginning to understand why. God had not thrown them into the furnace any more than He had caused the stampede that took Natty's life or the attack that killed Avery and harmed Con. Those acts sprang from the heart of evil, and God was not evil.

The congregation rose for *Amazing Grace*. Bry glanced sideways at Thad, who sang the hymn in an angelic voice and with every appearance of enthusiasm. She hadn't thought him capable of finer feeling. He turned toward her slightly and smiled as their eyes met. Bry looked away, and her gaze collided with Nick's. She lost her place in the hymn. What would Nick think about her sitting next to Thad as if they were a couple?

The service ended none too soon for Bry. The congregation moved into a room with a kitchen at one end where a potluck waited. The feasting began. Bry filled her plate with baked beans, fried chicken, potato cakes, and a salad composed of cultivated lettuce, wild greens, and other delicacies. The congregation had positioned a table for the preacher and his family on the balcony. A tarp strung from the eaves and propped by poles provided shade. Shane and America were already there, talking with Rob and Maisey, who sat across from them. Bry claimed the place next to Liberty, who perched on several large books in the chair beside her mother. The engaging child's chatter prevented Bry from having to sit in awkward silence next to Thad, who had taken a seat on her other side. When would the man comprehend that she wanted nothing to do with him?

Maybe he already knew. Thad rejoiced in overcoming her objections, especially when using force. He professed to care about her but seemed only to want a victory. She would not wish this feeling of being hunted on another woman, but she hoped he would find something to occupy him elsewhere. She didn't understand much about love, but she knew enough to say that Thad's pursuit of her had nothing to do with that tender emotion.

She went back to the kitchen for a slice of dried apple pie and spotted Nick on the chair against the wall. Why sit alone like that when he could share the preacher's table? At least in part, he brought his loneliness on himself. He flicked a glance at her and then away. A sick feeling churned her stomach. She had her answer. She returned to her table and tried to pick up the thread of conversation, but it was hopeless. Nick was avoiding her. Why? Had he come to the wrong conclusions about her and Thad? She looked up to discover Shane watching her.

Shane frowned. "You haven't touched that piece of pie."

"I can't eat it after all. Do you want it?"

"It would be a shame to let it go to waste."

She passed the dessert to him.

America smiled at her. "I couldn't finish everything I took either."

"There was a lot of food," Maisey agreed.

"A walk might help." Thad gave her a smile that made her skin crawl. "We can take a stroll after it cools a bit."

Bry stopped herself from snapping that she didn't want to go anywhere with him. The heat, combined with her upset over Nick, had her on edge. "I doubt I'll want to stir." She kept her protest mild.

The entire household went down for a nap to sleep off the effects of the potluck. Shane and America took Seth and Liberty into their own bed and divided their children's rooms among their guests. While Maisey slumbered in the bed she'd used before, Bry lay on a cot, resisting the urge to sleep. The house quieted, and she crept through the kitchen to the back door. It creaked open. She held her breath, but no one came to investigate. Bry pulled the door shut behind her and set off toward the little cabin behind the schoolhouse. Calling on a bachelor in his quarters could compromise her reputation, but after watching Nick ride away from her once, she had no intention of leaving without having a word with him. Did he care for her or not? She couldn't go on wondering. If, as she suspected, he believed a romance existed between herself and Thad, she needed to set him straight.

Nick didn't answer her knock, and she stood on the porch wondering what to do.

Footsteps came from the path to the schoolhouse, and Nick appeared beneath the cottonwoods. She went down the porch steps and rushed to meet him.

Nick stopped before they reached one another. "What are you doing here?"

Bry clasped her arms around herself, cool in the shade beneath the trees. "We're going back soon, and I don't want to miss the chance to ask you something."

Surprise registered on his face, then a mask came down, hiding his feelings. "What do you want?"

Now that the moment had arrived, Bry hesitated to speak. What if he rejected her? She drew an unsteady breath. Painful or not, she needed to know the truth. "Why wouldn't you sit at Shane's table today? He invited you."

"It was better that way."

She couldn't read his expression. "Were you avoiding me?" She might find out the truth by telling him how she felt, but she couldn't bring herself to say the words. With his head tilted politely and a neutral expression on his face, he seemed remote. Had she misread him entirely?

Tears trembled on her eyelashes. "I shouldn't have come." She stepped away from him.

A look of sorrow spasmed his face. "Wait, don't go."

Tongue-tied, she watched him close the gap between them.

"Bry." His voice shook with emotion. He cupped her face with one hand and caressed her cheek with the other. "I'm so sorry."

She stared at him with the world collapsing around her. She stumbled backward and ran from him.

She looked back to find Nick standing where she had left him. He turned away. She hurried to the house, let herself in the back door, and crept to her room. Curled on her cot, she breathed in and breathed out. She couldn't think, could only feel.

Nick didn't love her.

How much time passed, Bry didn't know, only that shadows crept across the floorboards. She heaved a breath and stood. America might come looking for her if she didn't emerge. She bathed her face at the wash stand, squared her shoulders, and left her refuge She would have to join the merriment to avoid casting a cloud over the happy gathering. Nick would stay away from the house to spare them both, of that she was certain. She wouldn't have to endure the torment of his presence, knowing what a fool she had made of herself.

America looked up from a cup of tea at the table. She scanned Bry's face, and her brow puckered.

The quick concern in her eyes made Bry feel like weeping. Her sadness felt too raw to share, and she couldn't make small talk right now. That left escape as her best option. "Please excuse me. I want to check on Kilkenny. She was a bit nervous with the other horses about."

America's lips parted, but then closed again. She nodded. "I'll make a fresh pot when you return."

Bry dove for the back door before she lost control. She walked toward the barn, hoping to hide there, but Shane's whistle carried from inside. She veered toward the schoolhouse and turned toward the rear door. It was too hot to stay in the open, and she didn't want to risk Thad spotting her. The last thing she needed was an argument.

Thad stepped out from the shadows beneath the trees and stood before her on the path.

She stared at him, startled to see him on the heels of her thought.

His gaze traveled her face. "You seem a mite restless today."

Had he watched her leave the house? If so, what had he seen? She took hold of herself. Thad would have confronted Nick if he'd noticed them together. He was bluffing.

She summoned a smile, determined to prevent him from discovering her state of mind. "I came out for a walk, but it's too hot."

"All by yourself? I'd have escorted you if you'd let me know."

"I didn't want to disturb you."

"I wouldn't have minded." He gave her a charming smile. "I'd sacrifice sleep to spend time with you."

She doubted that but kept her opinion to herself. "I should go. If you'll pardon me . . ." She brushed past him.

"Not so fast." He caught her by the elbow.

"Let go of me." Her voice trembled with anger.

He laughed. "Not so polite now, are we? I like you better full of sass anyway."

"That's neither here nor there, Mr. Taylor." She kept her temper in check, but her voice rose in volume. "Release me at once."

He trapped her in his arms.

"Stop this instant!" She twisted, struggling against his strength.

His laugh rang out. "Admit it, Irish. You want to kiss me again."

"I never did in the first place." She turned her head sideways to avoid his lips. "If you think otherwise, you are mistaken."

He cupped the back of her head, and his face hovered above hers. "Let's put it to the test, shall we?"

"Let her go." Nick's voice commanded. "She doesn't want your attentions."

Thad loosened his hold, and Bry turned around. Nick hastened down the path from his cabin.

"Can you give us some privacy?" Thad rapped out the question. "We're having a spat." He broke into a rueful smile that might have convinced Bry if she hadn't known the truth.

Nick checked his stride while emotions warred across his face.

"That's not true." Bry jerked her arm out of Thad's grasp.

"Step away from her." Nick growled, low.

Thad's gun appeared in his hand. "I let you stop me once before, but not this time."

Bry swallowed her fear. She had to say something to prevent Thad from using his weapon. "Mr. Taylor, I believe you are unwell."

His high-pitched laugh seemed to confirm her theory. "I'm just fine, Mrs. Brennan, but thanks for your concern." He shifted her behind him and leveled his gun.

"What are you doing?" She clawed at his gun arm. "You can't shoot Nick." Thad's six-shooter went off, and the ball ricocheted about. He shook her off, and she sprawled in the path. "You call him Nick, while I'm Mr. Taylor? That's cause to be rid of you both."

"Put away your gun." Shane emerged from the barn. "There's no need for violence."

"Keep your distance, preacher." Thad leveled his gun at Shane. "You wouldn't want to get hurt."

"Have you no conscience?" Bry stood to her feet. "Would you be so brazen as to harm a man of the cloth?"

"Do you think I care anything about that?"

"I doubt your mother would be pleased." She tried a new tack. The Taylors had money and privilege, but that must have been a bad combination for Thad.

"Leave my mother out of this." Thad pointed the gun at Nick again, and Bry gauged the distance she would have to jump. Thad grunted. "You die first, Injun."

Bry hurled herself toward Thad's gun arm, Nick dropped and rolled into Thad's legs, and another figure leaped from behind. The gun went off, and a man screamed. Blood spattered Bry. She panted in air. Blackness crowded her vision. *Nick can't be dead.*

She woke in strong arms with Nick's face hovering above hers. "Bry? Are you all right?"

"You're alive." She grasped his arm and pulled to sit up. She searched frantically for his gunshot wound but found none. Then who had been shot? She caught sight of a sickening pool of blood soaking the dirt where she had collided with Thad and the other person. "What happened?"

Nick kept an arm around her. "They've taken Thad's body away. He'll never bother you again."

Footsteps crunched on the path. "How's my sister?" Rob asked.

"I'm all right." She stood with Nick's help and hugged her brother. "Thad gave me a fright."

"He terrified all of us," Rob assured her. "When he threw you to the ground, it took ten years off my life. I thought he was going to shoot you before I could reach him."

"You were the one who jumped on him when I did?"

"That was another horrifying moment. Whatever possessed you to put yourself at risk like that?"

"I couldn't let him shoot Nick." She blurted out the truth.

Rob divided a glance between them. "I see." He extended his hand to Nick. "Thank you for what you did for my sister."

"Of course."

Rob held Bry's elbow protectively as he escorted her toward the house. "I was wrong about Thad, I'm afraid. Can you forgive me for thrusting him upon you?"

"It created trouble for me, but the worst of it was being at odds with you. I can forgive you, but I hope you've learned your lesson."

He put his hand over his heart. "Don't worry. I have."

Bry pulled in a relieved breath. She loved her brother, but he wasn't any good as a matchmaker.

Nick kept to his cabin and out of Bry's way. The house had remained silent the day after Thad's death, but then voices and even laughter once more. By Doc Bailey's account, Thad had died almost at once after being pierced by his own bullet. Nick hated that Bry had been present. He worried that after latching onto Thad's gun arm, she might blame herself for his death.

He flipped a johnnycake, part of his supper, and tried to pull his thoughts from Bry. She was due to leave tomorrow, as Shane had stopped by this morning to make certain he knew. Having given him advice about Bry that day in the barn, Shane had said nothing more on the subject, but Nick could feel him thinking. He wished he could make the preacher understand what a bothersome time Bry would have as his wife.

A rap sounded at his door. "Just a minute!" he called while slipping the johnnycake onto a plate and removing the pan from the burner. He opened the door. Rob Walsh stood on his porch wearing work clothes and a bowler hat. He looked somewhat sheepish.

Nick hid his surprise. "Good evening." He opened the door and stepped back. "Care to come in?"

"Thank you." Rob followed him into the cabin and glanced around. "Looks like you're comfortable."

Nick smiled. "Thanks to the Reverend and Mrs. Hayes. It's temporary, though. I'll need to move to a cabin of my own soon." He gestured toward one of the chairs at the table. "Have a seat?"

Rob nodded and sat down with his bowler balanced on his knee. Nick joined him at the table, not entirely at ease. Rob's attitude toward him had shifted in recent days, but to be sought out by him seemed odd. Nick waited for him to speak.

"We're leaving in the morning. I wanted to talk to you beforehand." Rob ran a finger along his collar, as if it was tight. "Now that Thad is gone, we're in need of a new ranch worker. I'd like to take you on. Besides your wage, you'd have your own cabin plus meals at the house."

"I'm honored you would think of me." Nick weighed the idea. The position sounded tempting, but it would require him to leave the town where he'd begun to put down roots. He'd also be too close to Bry for comfort. "Your brother would rather hire someone else."

"He sent me ahead to run the place, and he'll abide by my decisions." Rob stood, clutching his hat. "Thank you again for protecting my sister."

"I was glad to do it."

"She speaks highly of you."

What had she said about him? Vanity prompted him to ask, but he ignored it. "I feel the same about her."

Rob smiled. "That's wonderful."

"It is?" Surprise lilted Nick's voice.

"I'll be honest. I've made mistakes where Bry is concerned, and I'm trying to make amends. My sister has taken a shine to you, and she needs a husband. I wouldn't stand in the way."

Nick went still. Settling down with a job, a home, and best of all, the woman he loved sounded too good for belief, but it was more than he should hope for.

"Think about it tonight and let me know in the morning."

Nick shook his head. "Thanks for the offer, but I can't put Bry in that position. Besides, Con didn't take to me. He'd resent coming home to find me at the ranch."

Rob gave him a measuring look. "I might have misjudged you."

CHAPTER TWENTY-SEVEN

BRY HEAVED A SIGH, THANKFUL THE solemn journey home had ended at last. The trip should have been easier now that Thad wasn't present to make innuendos or intercept her glances. She had no reason to mourn for him, but she couldn't rejoice in the death of another person. She'd never know the evil that had twisted Thad's thinking, but when he'd sung beside her in church, she'd glimpsed a better side of him. How sad that, had he given it rein, he would probably be alive today.

Rob swung her down from the wagon and reached up to help Maisey. Bry went into the silent house. Everything was as they'd left it, which meant that Con had not returned while they were gone. She paused in front of a framed picture of him in the sitting room. When would her brother come home? Rob carried the crate of leftover supplies into the kitchen and their valises at the foot of the stairs, then drove off for the barn.

Maisey headed into the kitchen, and Bry went around opening windows, letting in the rushing sound of the river. Twilight was poised to bring in the night, and any breeze that came up would drive out the heat the shut-up house had collected. There was no need to cook supper. They had eaten well on the journey, thanks to America's kindness in supplying them a basket filled with corned beef, soda biscuits, pickles, and lemon pie. They had only to unpack and bathe before it would be time to retire. After spending several nights on a cot, Bry welcomed the chance to sleep in a real bed.

The crate that had held the jerky, crackers, and dried fruit they'd forsaken in favor of America's meal stood empty on the kitchen counter. Maisey was nowhere in sight, but she must have put away the leftover supplies. She'd also lit a fire in the oven and put pots of water on to heat. Looking forward to washing away the grime of travel once the wash water warmed, Bry went up to her room. The window drew her at once. The sky had caught fire where the sun blazed at the horizon, and long shadows swept across the land. After emptying the trunk that had held her clothing, she went down to check the wash water.

Rob came in through the back door, sat on a stool, and untied his boot laces. He wore a leather vest and trousers of jean cloth. With his hair flaming in the last of the daylight slanting through the window behind him, he looked masculine and capable but also poetic.

"Do you want coffee?" She beckoned toward the pot.

"Don't trouble yourself, Bry. It's been a long day, and you're bound to be weary."

"I'll confess to that."

He pulled off a boot. "How are you doing otherwise?"

She shook her head. "I keep thinking about what happened."

"This has been hard on you."

"I met Mr. Taylor's parents in the wagon train. They would grieve if they knew about their son."

"We should try to notify them."

She nodded. "I can't imagine what they will suffer, knowing he brought about his own death."

He pulled off his other boot. "I was hoping we'd find Con here."

"Me too."

"I was planning to search for him if he wasn't here when we returned. Now I think I should look for Phoebe."

"Find Maisey's daughter first, but then you might have to go after Con. I hate the idea, though. It's a bad time to travel. Now that the War Between the States is over, soldiers have poured into the forts. They needed another enemy to fight, so they're going after the Indians."

"That would seem to make the trails safer."

"Maybe someday it will, but right now it's stirring trouble with the tribes. I'd hate for something to happen to you." She didn't add that he wasn't a fighter like Con.

"Don't worry about me, Bry. I can't leave the ranch for long without someone else to look after the cattle, not to mention you and Maisey. The cattle don't require much care on the open range, but when they do, it's important to be present. I wish Nick had taken Thad's job."

"You offered it to him?"

He came to her, standing beside the sink. "Forget about Nick, Bry. I told him I wouldn't stand in the way of a marriage between you. He turned me down flat."

She stared at her brother in horror. "I can't believe you would humiliate me so completely."

"What do you mean? I was only trying to help. I could tell that you were taken with him."

"I hope you didn't say that to him."

He winced. "I may have said something similar."

She touched her heated cheeks. "I can never face him again."

"Don't take it like that." He patted her arm clumsily.

"How else is there to take it? You, brother of mine"—she poked him in the chest—"were going to stop playing matchmaker."

His eyebrows lifted. "I never promised such a thing."

Bry cast back in memory. Now that she thought about it, she might have mistaken his meaning. That was beside the point. "I don't care what you didn't say. You shouldn't have done it."

"Well, I wouldn't have, not if I'd known how it would turn out."

"Stay out of my business. You always mess things up." Bry stormed out of the kitchen and up the stairs, then slammed her bedroom door for emphasis. She sank into the slipper chair by the window. Tears pressed her eyes and spilled down her cheeks.

When she'd woken in Nick's arms, he'd seemed to care, and this morning he had come by the kitchen and wished her a safe journey. Construing an interest in her, however, must have been wishful thinking. If she'd needed any further proof that Nick didn't love her, Rob had provided it.

Bry dashed away tears and went to answer the quiet knock at her bedroom door.

Maisey stood in the corridor with an oil lamp hanging from one arm while she balanced a wash pitcher and basin. She'd taken off her bonnet, and her hair had slipped its pins. Faint smudges beneath her eyes betrayed her weariness. "I thought you'd want wash water."

"Thank you." Bry relieved Maisey of her burden. She placed the pitcher on the lower shelf of the wash stand and set the basin in the circular cutout designed to hold it. Candles flickered in holders that branched out from twin spindles that rose from the stand and suspended a mirror between them. Bry's reflection betrayed her swollen eyes and tear-stained face. "I guess it's obvious I've been crying."

"I heard you."

"Rob and I had an argument."

"You're both tired from the journey, I expect."

Bry sighed heavily. "My brother means well, I know he does, but he makes my life harder."

Maisey nodded. "I've noticed that he's not aware of the sort of thing women understand."

"Then he should stop meddling in my life."

"Give your brother time, and I think he'll sort that out for himself." Maisey gave her a quick hug. "Things will look better in the morning."

Bry nodded for her friend's sake, but she doubted that.

Tavo's hooves kicked up dust, sending motes spinning in the fading light that fell through the barn's high windows. Nick led the stallion into a stall. A grizzly bear had been seen in the area of late, and leaving him out for the night would be foolish. Nick latched the stall while Tavo nudged him for attention. He rubbed his horse's neck, and Tavo lowered his head invitingly. Nick laughed and scratched the favorite spot behind the stallion's ears. Nearly losing Tavo had given Nick a greater appreciation of his mother's last gift to him.

Shane, wearing his slouch hat and leading his Morgan, appeared in the open doorway. A birthing had gone wrong, taking him away all day. Shane's horse clomped beside him to the watering trough against one wall.

Nick started toward him. "How's the baby?"

"Gone." Shane shook his head. "Doc Bailey says the mother almost followed the child to the grave. Her husband was overwrought, to say the least. Thank the Lord she pulled through." He removed his hat and wiped his brow with a red bandanna. "I need to talk to you."

"What about?"

"I could use your help with a problem, if you're willing."

"Of course."

Shane smiled. "Maybe you should wait to answer."

"All right, but I'm more than happy to ease your burden while I'm here."

"Thank you. Before I tell you what I want, I need to know why you turned down a job at the Walsh ranch."

"You knew about that?" Nick had said nothing in the two weeks since Rob had made the offer.

Shane nodded. "Rob told me before he left. Did you refuse the job for personal reasons?"

"I'm thinking of moving on."

Shane studied him. "Are you certain that's what you want? You could build a cabin on our land."

"Thank you, but I've taken advantage of your good graces long enough."

"You wouldn't be imposing. I know you'd work hard for your

keep, and to be honest, I could use another man's help around here. With you near, I feel better about leaving my family when duties take me away from home. I hope you'll decide to stay on."

"I appreciate the invitation. What did you want help with?"

"Would it be too awkward for you to stay at Con's ranch for a couple of days? Rob doesn't want to leave the women alone after all the horse thieving and the sighting of what appears to be a band of renegades. Rob wants to look into the whereabouts of Maisey's young daughter, and he needs to hire a few ranch hands to drive cattle to the miners in Bannack, Virginia City, and Helena. That likely means traveling to Corvallis or even Hell Gate. I promised him I'd look after the ranch, but I'm having a hard time breaking away long enough to do it."

"Is my going a good idea? I'm sure it's not proper for a bachelor to sleep under the same roof as two widows."

"You could stay in the cabin Thad used, and you wouldn't have those widows to yourself. My wife plans to visit and bring the children. I'd ride along to escort the wagon to the ranch. I've heard that a strange tribe has moved into the area. There have been no raids, but better safe than sorry. Rob would ride back with you in time for next month's Sunday meeting."

Nick would rather look after Bry himself than rely on someone else to protect her. "When do we leave?"

Bry lifted the pitchfork and tossed hay into one of the feeding troughs then paused to wipe the perspiration from her brow. She'd taken on filling the watering and feeding troughs for the livestock to spare Rob the chore. The past couple of days had been especially hot, not cooling down much at night. The wind that normally followed the river channel and breathed into the ranch house had died down, offering no relief.

From outside the open barn doors came the beating of hooves and creak of a wagon. That must be Shane, come to help with the ranch while Rob searched for Phoebe and went to Hell Gate to find someone to take over Thad's duties. The thought of a strange man around the place gave her the fidgets—but she should welcome someone to help her brother and take over the chores she was now doing. Her reaction wasn't entirely logical, but she couldn't seem to help herself. Thad's ill treatment must have marked her more deeply than she'd known.

She went to the door to watch for Shane's wagon. Rain hadn't fallen for a while now, and a tail of dust followed the wagon traveling the road to the ranch house. The man handling the horses' lines wore Shane's slouch hat. She squinted. Another man rode ahead of the team. Something in the way he held himself reminded her of . . .

Why had Nick come? Had he changed his mind about taking the job?

The ranch house door opened and Maisey crossed the porch. She went down the stairs, obviously ready to greet the newcomers. Bry shrank back in the doorway, then retreated into the barn and pitched hay more vigorously than before. With any luck, she could avoid going in until supper time. Then she'd only have a meal to make it through before she could take refuge in her bedroom. She would miss out on a longer visit with her cousin, but she wasn't ready to face Nick after what her brother had told him. The fact that Nick knew how she felt about him and didn't return her feelings added humiliation to hurt.

A horse and rider trotted past the doorway—Rob, coming in from the range. He must have seen Shane arrive. She could hear his voice in conversation with Maisey and Nick. America chimed in, and the children's laughter rang out. The urge to join in came over her, and she began to feel foolish for hiding. If she delayed any longer, her rudeness would be plain. Pretending she hadn't heard the wagon wouldn't be honest. Besides, Rob was likely to come looking for her. Surrendering to the inevitable, she braced herself to leave the barn.

The back door opened silently, sending a bar of light across the plank floor. Bry turned her head. An Indian stood in the doorway, framed by the light behind him. With his back to the sun, she couldn't make out his features, but his feathered bonnet looked familiar. She jerked, recognizing Kicking Horse. He raised a knife as if to hurl it at her. "Scream, and I will kill you."

From the vicious look on his face, she believed him. He could have saved his breath. With fear clogging her throat, she couldn't have made a sound. Two warriors slipped into the barn and stood on either side of their leader with drawn bows aimed at her.

Bry stared at Kicking Horse in disbelief. Why had he come after her? Nick had paid the price to free her.

He strode toward her, moving into the light from the high windows. He seemed wilder than before, even desperate, with a predatory look on his face that chilled her blood.

She took an involuntary step backward, but then forced herself to remain still. She didn't want an arrow to pierce her. Whatever else happened, she refused to die within reach of her family.

Kicking Horse twisted her around and pinned her arms, then pulled her against him with his knife at her throat. Bry trembled. The blade pressing her skin felt sharp. "You belong to me, not to him." He snarled the words near her ear.

Outside the barn, the children's excited voices threaded through the happy tones of the adults. A sick feeling churned Bry's stomach. Her family was so near. What if Kicking Horse meant to harm them? Even now, the rest of his band could be creeping up on her family and Nick. She couldn't bear it if anything happened to them.

"I haven't had a chance to scrub the cabin yet, but I'll give it a once-over after we water the horses." Rob's voice came from close at hand. "I appreciate that." Nick responded above the clop of hooves. Bows ready, the warriors left Kicking Horse's side and flanked the barn entrance. Bry hauled in air. Her brother and the man she loved would be shot before her eyes. Warning them might come at the cost of her own life, but she screamed anyway.

Rob called out a warning.

Bowstrings twanged and arrows zinged. Kicking Horse's blade bit into Bry's flesh.

CHAPTER TWENTY-EIGHT

WARM BLOOD TRICKLED DOWN BRY'S NECK, but the knife withdrew. Kicking Horse twisted her hair until she gasped. "Such a scalp as yours"—he murmured near her ear—"would look beautiful on my belt." With his knife arm raised for a throw, he maneuvered her backward toward the exit.

Running feet pounded the ground outside the barn opening.

The Indians launched more arrows from the entrance.

A gunshot boomed, followed by a heavy thud. One of the warriors lay on the barn floor in a spreading pool of blood.

Bry's stomach churned, and she fought the urge to vomit.

The second warrior notched a new arrow in his bow. The sharp click of a gun came from outside the barn. The Indian backed away from the entrance.

Kicking Horse pulled her along faster. The bright daylight outside made her blink. From inside the barn came Rob's voice, telling the warrior to lay down his bow. Three horses waited behind the barn, near the wall. Two were Indian ponies. The third was a dun of a larger breed. Bry stared at the third horse, a dun with the same star on its forehead as Kilkenny. She gasped and might have gone to her horse, but her captor hauled her onto the smallest pony instead.

"Don't try to run, or I'll kill you." He took the reins of her horse and rushed to mount Kilkenny.

The temptation to disobey Kicking Horse and ignore his threat gripped Bry. Escape seemed simple. She had only to slip from her horse and step back inside. He wouldn't follow her with Rob in the barn. She tensed, ready to slide from her horse and run for her life. The knife in his hand gleamed wickedly, and she subsided. As war chief of his tribe, Kicking Horse would have no trouble with his aim.

Nick peered around the corner of the barn.

Bry couldn't help her start of surprise. "Where are you taking me?" she asked Kicking Horse to distract him.

He scowled at her without answering, put his knife in his teeth, and gripped Kilkenny's saddle. Nick cocked his gun, the metallic click filling the silence.

Nick crept around the corner of the barn. Bry sat on an Indian pony with blood staining her neck and running into the collar of her dress. With Kicking Horse taking a hunting knife from between his teeth, Nick could imagine what had caused her wound. He steadied his hand and pulled back the trigger.

Kicking Horse stiffened and brought back his throwing arm.

"Drop your weapon." Nick kept his aim steady while resisting the urge to look at Bry. Whatever her condition, he could help her best in this moment by keeping his attention trained on Kicking Horse.

Kicking Horse's face took on a calculating expression. He threw the knife.

Bry screamed. Nick hurtled sideways, his gun discharging. The knife spun in an arc and stuck, point down, behind where he'd stood. Kicking Horse jumped off his horse and rammed into Nick. The impact carried them both down and jolted the gun from Nick's hand. They rolled into the horses. The pony Bry rode squealed and pawed the ground.

"Get off!" he shouted to Bry, but then Kicking Horse claimed his attention, and he didn't know if she had. He gained his feet together with his stepbrother. A quick glance showed his gun nowhere in sight. He faced off with his stepbrother, the knife between them. Nick circled the blade while watching Kicking

Horse.

"I knew it would come to this one day, Wolf Walking." Kicking Horse ground out the bitter words. "You've always hated me."

"That's not true. I hated Long Knife for what he did to my parents. That had nothing to do with you."

"Why should I listen? My father warned me against your lies. I will make you pay for speaking ill of him." His voice broke.

"You can't expect me to respect my father's murderer, the man who gave my mother the baby that killed her in childbirth."

"Such things happen. It was the wish of Ma'heo'o to take mother and child."

"Do not blame the Great Father for what Long Knife did. If he hadn't stolen my mother, she would still live."

Kicking Horse dug his toe into the ground and sprayed dirt upwards. Nick jerked his head sideways to avoid being blinded, but the move cost time. Kicking Horse came up grasping the knife hilt. Nick dove after him and clamped his hand over his stepbrother's. Kicking Horse pushed his free hand into Nick's face. Nick repaid him in kind as they fought for the knife.

Bry steadied herself against the rough wall. She should call to Rob and tell him Nick needed help. She went to the doorway and looked inside the barn. Rob and the warrior he had captured were gone. The man who had been shot lay motionless where he had fallen, death glazing his eyes. She couldn't have walked past him for anything. Turning back, she skirted the barn toward the corner.

Nick stood up and pulled Kicking Horse with him. He held the knife to his stepbrother's throat. "I could take your life."

Kicking Horse spat on him. "Go ahead. Kill me. But you will never take away my father's honor."

Bry couldn't stand by and watch a man knifed to death, even a man who had threatened to do that very thing to her. She wanted to call to Nick, but her voice stuck in her throat. The world spun, and she put a hand on the wall to steady herself.

Nick released his stepbrother. "My sister loves you. I will spare your life, but you must stop making trouble. Why try to steal the woman I bought from you?"

"Old Chief should not have made me sell her, and my sister shamed me in front of the village when she gave you back the horse I won."

"Is that what this is about? Your pride?"

Kicking Horse's head lifted, and he fixed a penetrating gaze on Nick. "Give my captive to me."

"Bry is my woman. I'll never give her up. You freely sold her, and I paid the price you asked. My sister did nothing wrong. Go home, Kicking Horse, and treat her with kindness."

Kicking Horse strode to the horses and climbed on the calmer of the two ponies. He glared at Nick from its back. "You are dead to me." He rode straight at Nick. The pony lifted onto its hind legs and pawed the air. Nick threw himself to the side, narrowly avoiding the flailing hooves. The horse came down, and Kicking Horse leaned forward, snatching the knife from Nick while he was off-balance.

Bry edged toward the corner of the barn.

Kicking Horse's pony plunged her direction.

Rob came around the corner with his rifle raised. The bolt clicked.

Kicking Horse wheeled the pony around. He started toward the river, taking his mount on a weaving course.

The rifle boomed. The bullet pinged off a rock and ricocheted further. The bolt engaged again.

"Stop!" Bry called. "There's been enough bloodshed."

Rob lowered his rifle. "Are you all right?"

"Mostly." Her head had cleared, but she couldn't stop shaking.

"Your neck is bleeding. What did that *coiriúil* do to you?"

In his anger, her brother had slipped into their native tongue to call Kicking Horse a criminal. She touched her throat, and her fingers came away sticky with blood. "The wound doesn't feel deep. I'm fairly certain Kicking Horse didn't intend to cut me. His hand jerked when I screamed."

"He shouldn't have held a knife to your throat." Rob glared after the fleeing figure. "How is it that you know this fiend?"

"He's the one who took me prisoner."

Rob's eyes widened, and his jaw tensed. "I shouldn't have let him get so far away." He shouldered his rifle and started for Kilkenny with purposeful steps.

"You don't want to go after him." Bry shivered at the thought of what could happen to her brother. "He's probably on the way to join the rest of his followers. I saw his band ride by when I was lost in the woods."

Rob halted in his tracks. "I wonder why he showed up with only two warriors."

"That's something I'd like to ask our prisoner." Nick looked past Rob to Bry. "Did you see where my gun went?"

Bry nodded. "It landed in that blackberry thicket."

"It figures."

Rob turned to Bry. "Let's get you inside and take care of that cut."

"Yes, but first put Kilkenny in the barn." She went to her horse. "She's been through a fright."

Rob gazed at her with a look of wonder. "You're a strong-minded woman."

"Thank you. That's what Da used to call Mam."

Her brother gave her a faint smile and led both horses toward the front of the barn.

"I would do it myself"—she informed him to ease her guilt for ordering him around—"but I don't want to look at that dead body again."

"I'm sorry you had to see that, Bry."

Nick strode to her with his gun newly returned to its holster and several scratches on his hands. "Let me look at your throat."

She lifted her chin, and he probed her wound with gentle

fingers.

"You're right. It's not serious., " His breath fanned her skin as he spoke. "You may get away without a scar." He took off his bandanna, shook out the dust, and wrapped it around her neck.

"Either way, I'll count my blessings. Kicking Horse didn't make off with me and none of the people I love died." She sucked in a breath. Her last words had revealed too much.

"Bry—" His gaze held such intensity she couldn't look away. He lowered his head, and his mouth hovered above hers. She caught her breath. Nick straightened and scanned in the direction of the river. "We should go inside. Kicking Horse might come back with more of his followers."

She nodded and let herself lean on his strength. Rob came out of the barn and walked beside them. No sooner had they thumped onto the porch than the front door burst open. Maisey drew them inside in a rush. She stared at Bry's neck, but then hurriedly dropped the bar into place and shot the bolt. "We're in the parlor. I'll fetch the medicine kit." She spoke in a rush and hurried out.

Bry entered the parlor, and America stood up from one of the leather chairs. "Thank the Lord you're safe. I've been praying ever since you screamed." With the children asleep on the couch across from her, she spoke quietly. "What happened?" She touched her own throat.

Bry fingered Nick's bandanna. "It's nothing that wash water and a bandage can't improve."

"I'll heat a pan of water." America hurried into the short corridor that opened to the kitchen.

Bry turned to Rob. "Where is Shane?"

Rob glanced at Nick. "He's giving medical attention to the prisoner in the root cellar."

Nick's jaw tightened. "I'll go and have a word with the captive."

Maisey appeared in the doorway, carrying a tin box. "The trap door to the root cellar is in the kitchen."

Nick strode from the room with an air of purpose.

"You can find me in the entryway, keeping watch." Rob took

himself and his rifle off.

"Sit down, and I'll take a look at your neck." Maisey opened the satchel that contained the ranch's medicine kit. Bry winced as she pried Nick's bandanna from her congealing wound. Maisey looked up at Bry with an encouraging smile. "Thank goodness it wasn't worse. When I think what could have happened—"

"I feel much the same." Bry let out her breath on a sigh. "I'm delighted not to become a captive of the Indians all over again. I just wish I knew how Kicking Horse found me."

"Is that the same Indian who kidnapped you before?" Shane stood in the doorway from the kitchen corridor.

She nodded. "I'm sure he's one of the renegade band that has moved into the area. I'm beginning to fear I'll never be free of him."

CHAPTER TWENTY-NINE

BRY STARTLED AWAKE AND JERKED TO a sitting position, her heart racing. Lightning flared in the night sky behind her bedroom curtains. She sagged against her pillow and waited for her breathing to calm. Images from her dream spun through her mind—coyotes on the hunt, grotesque figures gyrating around a fire, and her mother's voice shouting warnings. She banished them but lay awake, jumping at every sound. Those scraping noises could be cottonwood branches rubbing together or bowstrings bending. Did rain rattle the panes or the hand of an intruder eager to break in? That creak on the stair might come from house timbers settling or a stealthy footstep. She pulled the covers over her head, resorting to a childhood tactic to banish the monsters that preyed on her imagination.

Sleep wound its arms around her and drew her to itself. Bry resisted, unwilling to give up her watchfulness, but surrendered at last.

Soft light edged the curtains by the time she woke. She padded across the carpet and looked out. The barn stood sentinel on a rise above the banks of the Bitterroot, the gray light deepening its red to mahogany. Mists hid the river but curled into the air to mark its course. Kicking Horse had disappeared into the pine trees on the other side. She scanned for any sign he intended to return with his band. She found none and turned from the window with a sigh. Allowing yesterday's attack to fill her mind would rob her of peace.

She attended to her grooming and put on her favorite dress to cheer her. She'd sewn it from fabric with blue and brown stripes that Rob had purchased for her at Fort Owen. She paused on the stairs with her hand on the rail. Nick stood watch at one of two tall windows in the entryway. With his hair rumpled and stubble shadowing his face, he looked appealingly masculine. Catching herself staring, she averted her gaze.

"Did you pass the night well?" The burr that edged his voice gave away his tiredness.

"For the most part. What about you? Have you slept?"

He smiled. "I will soon."

"Thank you for protecting me from Kicking Horse. If he had made off with me again—" She shuddered. "Confronting your brother can't have been easy for you."

His jaw tightened. "That was less of a hardship than you might suspect."

She nodded, having overheard his exchange with Kicking Horse.

He looked out the window again, and she went into the kitchen. The root cellar door was chained and padlocked, the only indication that anything unusual had happened. The coffee pot steamed on the stove, and the aroma of bacon filled the air. Maisey stood watching pancakes frying in a skillet.

"Good morning," Bry summoned as much enthusiasm as she could.

Maisey glanced at her. "Sit down, and I'll bring you a cup of coffee."

"Thank you." Her friend's kindness took the edge off her nerves. "But I should help you with breakfast."

"You can crack the eggs." Maisey waved at the basket Rob had brought home from the neighbor who kept them supplied with butter, milk, and eggs in exchange for regular cuts of beef. "I was planning on scrambling them, unless you want to cook them differently."

"That's fine." Bry took down a bowl from one of the shelves, selected a wooden spoon from the crock filled with utensils, and perched on a stool at the counter. She tapped the first egg and emptied it into the bowl.

Maisey slid a cup of coffee onto the counter at Bry's elbow, then opened the warming oven and slid more pancakes onto the plate inside. She poured batter from the pitcher into the bacon grease in one of the pans and picked up the spatula to turn the pancakes cooking in the other.

America appeared in the doorway. "I'd have come down sooner, but Liberty needed me more than usual this morning. She's always been sensitive to my emotions, and I'll admit to being tense." She stepped into the kitchen. "What do you want me to do?"

"You could set the table." Maisey smiled. "Then let everyone know that breakfast will be ready soon."

"Gladly." America went to the shelf that held china. "How many are there? Let's see —we make five with Nick, and you have three to feed. That comes to—"

"Eight plates," Bry announced.

Maisey gave a slight shake of her head. "Nine. We should feed the Indian Rob captured."

"Of course." America smiled at her. "It's kind of you to think of that."

"What will become of him?" Maisey asked.

Shane looked in at the open doorway. "I couldn't help overhearing. Rob plans to take the prisoner to the sheriff in Hell Gate for questioning."

"I hope they can find the renegades and drive them from the valley," Bry murmured. "I would hate for anyone else to go through what I did."

"Rob has decided to wait on his cattle drive." Shane leveled a glance on her. "You and Mrs. Wilcox must come home with us until this threat passes."

"What about my horse?" She didn't want to turn Kilkenny out on the range where Kicking Horse could claim her again.

"Bring her along. There's room in the barn."

America looked up from counting out plates. "That's an excellent idea, Shane. I confess that under the circumstances I'd rather not stay in a place with such far-flung neighbors."

"I can't fault you for that." Bry touched the bandage at her throat. "I feel nervous about remaining here myself. I wish I knew how Kicking Horse found out where I was."

"He may have followed Nick to us."

Of course. It made sense that Kicking Horse would have recognized Nick on the road. She doubted he'd traveled all this way to recapture her. No. His aim had been to take her from Nick. She beat the eggs with more force than necessary, struck by the irony of Nick calling her his woman when he didn't want her either.

Riding beside Bry felt familiar to Nick, except this time instead of a deerskin dress she wore an elegant riding costume with a split skirt. He approved of the outfit. The few women in his life whom he'd seen riding side-saddle had looked none too safe. His mother had found the sight amusing and wondered out loud why a woman would risk her neck to look ridiculous. Cheyenne women, as she had said, were so much more sensible in such matters.

The curve of Bry's cheek and the way her hair swept away from her forehead into her bonnet distracted Nick. He longed to free the dark ripples to flow down her back. Almost kissing her behind the barn had been a natural response to the danger they'd survived, proof that living close to Bry would not work. He'd thought he could keep his distance, but circumstances kept throwing them together. It was only a matter of time before he surrendered to temptation. That wouldn't be fair to her.

He dropped back. Rob nodded to him from the wagon box where he guided his team of Morgans. Maisey sat beside him on the seat. With Rob's bowler perched on his head and Maisey engaging him in conversation, they might have been any couple on an outing, if not for the renegade tied up behind them. Last night the prisoner had stared at him in mute hostility and told him nothing. He did the same now with his chin even more jutted.

Shane brought up the rear, driving the Conestoga wagon that

had brought his wife to Montana. America and the children were hidden behind the wagon bonnet, but he could hear their voices. Shane smiled at Nick, his slouch hat shadowing his eyes. "It would be a fine day for a drive if we didn't have to watch for unexpected company."

"There's been no sign of anyone so far."

"That's welcome news, but I won't rest easy until we reach home. The town of Liberty doesn't possess a jail, but we can guard the prisoner in the schoolhouse overnight."

"I'll stand the first watch," Nick volunteered. "I'd like the chance to talk to him again. Maybe I can persuade him that working with the sheriff would be in his best interests."

"I wish you every success. Hopefully, we can stop these renegades without bloodshed."

They'd left the ranch early and reached the Hayes's house by supper time. Maisey and America started supper while Bry and Rob took care of the horses. Shane settled Nick to watch the prisoner in the schoolhouse meeting room.

"Do you wonder what will become of you?" Nick asked in Cheyenne after Shane left them.

With his hair loose and feathers fanning behind his head, the prisoner sat on the chair they had tied him to with quiet dignity. He stared at Nick, worry plain on his face, but gave no answer.

"What is your name? Surely telling me that much will do no harm."

The silence lengthened between them. Sighing, Nick lowered himself to a ladder-back chair, ready to pass a long evening.

"I am called after the wild wind that blows where it will. You cannot hold me." Bitterness and a certain arrogance laced the prisoner's voice.

"Minninnewah, why do you ride with Kicking Horse when he ignores the wishes of Old Chief, your safety, and even his own promises?"

A flicker of doubt chased across Minninnewah's face, but then it hardened. "Old Chief lives in the past. He is an old man who loves to smoke the pipe of peace while our people die. He doesn't understand what we need now that the white man has come."

"Kicking Horse knows even less what to do. He won't save you. Remain with him, and you will go to your fathers too soon."

Minninnewah scowled, but the emotions warring with one another on his face told Nick he had made progress. Nick leaned back in his seat. "We will take you to the sheriff."

"I will kill you." Minninnewah thrashed about, fighting his restraints and nearly toppling his chair. His efforts slowed and finally stopped.

Nick stood and circled the prisoner's chair. "That would be unfortunate, since I can speak your words in the sheriff's tongue." He stopped in front of Minninnewah, but the prisoner would not meet his eyes. Nick returned to his chair. "If you want my help, let me know."

Minninnewah bowed his head. He refused to touch the food Shane brought for him, but sullenly darted glances about as if searching for an escape. Nick remained vigilant throughout his watch, an effort that wore on him. When Shane returned to sit with the prisoner through the night, Nick sought the bed in his cabin with gratitude.

He rose at dawn, ready to leave for Hell Gate. After helping Rob hitch the wagon, he persuaded their captive to climb into it. Hopefully, he would help them find the renegades before Kicking Horse's discontent could escalate into bloodshed.

Bry looked up from reading Jane Eyre at America's gasp. In the hour after supper they had gathered in the living room to read in companionable silence while the children played with a stuffed tiger and a small wooden rocking horse at their feet.

America shook the letter in her hand. "We have a schoolteacher."

"Oh?" Shane smiled at his wife and turned a page in his worn Bible.

"Miss Emma Duncan has accepted our offer and will arrive forthwith." Her smile faded. "We'll need the schoolteacher's cabin sooner than expected."

Shane frowned. "I suppose it's too late to write and let her know not to come so soon?"

"I hate to ask when we said she could move in early."

"That was before Nick came to stay with us."

"I know, but still—"

"Don't worry about it, Sweetheart." Shane smiled at her. "We'll figure something else out."

Bry brightened. "Maybe the neighbors will let Nick stay with them until he builds a cabin for himself. They have the room and seemed to take a shine to him. That is, if Nick plans to stay in Liberty. Has he said anything to you about his future?"

"We've spoken about it. I'm not certain he's made up his mind. " Shane spoke with constraint.

Bry wondered what her cousin wasn't saying. She laid her book aside, having lost the story thread.

America frowned. "I hope he can do that soon."

Shane marked his page in his Bible. "I'll raise the subject when he returns."

America folded the letter and slipped it back into its envelope. "We should go to the fort soon."

"Oh?" Shane raised his eyebrows. "Do we need to buy something?"

She shook her head. "No, not really, but the local tribes gather there."

"That's true." Shane watched her face.

"I think we should reach out to the local tribe." She leaned forward. "The schoolhouse won't be in use on Saturdays. We could teach the Flathead children then. We could help them and at the same time avoid trouble with the Indians."

"How noble." Maisey put down the copy of *Godey's Magazine*

and Lady's Book that she'd been leafing through. "I'd love to help with something like that."

Bry stared at her friend. Why would Maisey want to nurture these children when Indians had stolen her from her own?

Shane gave a nod. "It could work out, provided the townsfolk don't reject the tribe."

"They would take their lead from us, don't you think? This might be a way to stop bloodshed before it starts."

Shane smiled at her. "I love your enthusiasm. Let's bring it to prayer before making a decision."

Maisey stood up. "Is everyone ready for blackberry crumble?"

"Yes!" The children shouted. Their mother shushed them, but with a smile.

"I'll help serve." Bry went into the kitchen behind Maisey.

The patter of tiny feet followed them.

"No running in the house," Shane called.

Bry put on the tea kettle and took down plates. Maisey cut the dessert with a pie server. America came to steep the tea, and Shane guided the children outside to wash their hands at the pump.

"It's good to know that you're interested in helping with the Flathead children." America returned to their previous conversation. "I hope it works out that you can."

"Why do you want to?" Bry asked Maisey the question bothering her. "You have no reason to love the Indians."

"This isn't the same tribe who wronged me." Maisey shrugged. "Even if it was, I wouldn't want revenge."

"Why not?" Bry's own resentment rang in her voice.

Maisey paused with the pie server in her hand. "I haven't forgotten my sufferings, but the right to retribution belongs to God, not me. Leaving their fate in God's hands allows me peace of mind."

"You've made a good choice." America finished pouring tea and set the pot down on a tray. "Hatred breeds hate. It can imprison a person."

Bry sipped her tea and pondered the matter of forgiveness. She'd heard it mentioned in church a time or two, but it had never caught her attention in exactly this way. She carried a forkful of blackberry crumble to her mouth, its sweetness at odds with the bitterness welling within her soul. She'd been shouldering a burden Maisey had released to God, and the difference between their recoveries couldn't be clearer.

Nick could see the crossroads waiting for him beneath the wide sky. One turning would take him to the town of Liberty to be near Bry. Another led past Con's ranch onto the long road to the cabin above the Missouri. He drew Tavo up, and Rob's wagon rattled to a stop beside him. The sun beat down. A meadowlark trilled in the bushes that lined the road. He'd made his choice. Now he needed to carry it through. There was no point in delaying. He forced himself to say the words that would separate him from Bry forever. "I won't be going on with you."

"What do you mean?" Rob asked. "Aren't you returning to Shane's house?"

"It's time for me to leave."

Rob tilted his head. "I thought you belonged with us now."

That was all he'd ever wanted—to belong. It lay within his grasp. All he had to do was change his mind. Nick pushed away the temptation. He couldn't go on chasing an illusion. "I wanted so badly for my life to be different, but I need to stop pretending."

Rob shook his head. "What about my sister? I'm convinced that she loves you, and I thought you'd had a change of heart about her. It seemed that way when you defended her the other day."

He wasn't convinced Bry loved him, despite what her brother said. Yes, she had clung to him after he'd saved her, but that was only natural. She'd had a shock. Hadn't she kept her distance after that? "She'll forget about me and go on with her life. Somewhere there's a man who can teach her what it means to be truly loved." He didn't want to think about Bry in someone else's arms, and he couldn't imagine not being there to make sure she was safe. He would have to trust God and her family to watch over her. Otherwise, he could never bring himself to leave.

"I thought that might have been you. Don't you love her?"

Nick watched the lark flit from one serviceberry bush to another. "How I feel doesn't matter." He loved Bry to distraction, but he wouldn't admit that to her brother. If Rob was right about her feelings, that was all the more reason to leave. Staying near the woman he loved might cause her to share his lonely fate.

Rob shook his head. "I don't understand you, and that's a fact. For what it's worth, I don't want you to go."

"I wish it hadn't turned out this way."

Rob's forehead creased. "Allow me to apologize for being wrong about you."

"Thank you for saying that."

Rob shrugged. "I don't suppose it changes your mind, but it needed to be said. Go if you must, but come and say goodbye to everyone."

"Slipping quietly out of their lives will hurt less."

Rob snorted. "If you believe that, I have a fairytale castle to sell you."

"It's what I always do. I don't know anything else."

Rob cocked a brow. "Maybe you should learn something different."

"I'll write to Shane and America thanking them for their hospitality. Please give your sister and Maisey my best regards."

Rob narrowed his eyes. "I have half a mind to tell you to deliver your own messages. Ever ask yourself what you're running from?"

Nick opened his mouth but closed it again. He looked away, avoiding Rob's gaze.

"Go on with you then, and safe journeys. If you ever want to come back, look us up." Rob took up the lines and called to the horses.

Nick watched the wagon out of sight, then turned his horse in the direction he didn't want to go.

CHAPTER THIRTY

BRY PULLED THE MOBCAP FROM HER head and let herself out onto the schoolhouse balcony. After scrubbing the floor in preparation for Sunday meeting, she needed a rest before returning to the house. She scanned the dirt road that cut through forests and grasslands on its way to Liberty, but it yielded no sign of Nick and Rob. With the day wearing on toward supper, they would arrive soon. She shouldn't watch for Nick but couldn't help herself. Maybe she would always look for him. Questions vexed her in idle moments, as now. Had he turned down Rob's job offer to avoid her? Why had he lowered his head as if to kiss her behind the barn, only to withdraw? Was she right in assuming he didn't love her? She sighed. The answers always eluded her.

Geese arrowed across the sky, winging toward the river. She breathed in then out.

Volunteering to clean the schoolhouse had given her the privacy she needed to grapple with her thoughts and feelings. She'd felt especially in need of time alone since last night. Learning the depth of Maisey's forgiveness had caused her to examine the very roots of her being. She'd been taught in church to be merciful to others, and that vengeance belonged to the Lord. She had made the attempt but couldn't say she had fully released herself from the men who had wronged her.

Identifying hard feelings against those who had inflicted violence on her wasn't difficult. Ian, Jeffrey Wainwright, and Kicking Horse sprang to mind. She'd also held onto wounded feelings brought about by Rob's missteps and Nick's abandonment. She'd allowed bitterness to eat at her, making her into a shell of the vibrant woman she had been. It had even caused her to doubt God's love.

Well, no more. She refused to go on letting this secret pain destroy her. Curling her fingers around the railing, she closed her eyes and spoke to God alone.

The door behind her opened a short while later. "Here you are." Maisey said. "Supper is ready. Are you all right?"

Bry dashed away tears.

A wagon trundled along, coming from the direction of the crossroads. The driver's bowler hat identified him as Rob, but he was alone. "What's happened to Nick?"

Maisey came to stand beside her. "Maybe he's been delayed by the sheriff to communicate with that Indian. He does speak Cheyenne."

"I hope that's all." Bry found it hard not to fret.

"Why don't we go find out?"

They let themselves out of the schoolhouse and entered the barn behind the wagon.

"Whoa!" Rob called. The wagon shuddered to a halt. He gave Bry a long look before jumping down, then took off his hat and walked toward them.

Bry hurried to meet her brother. "I'm glad you're back."

He embraced her. "Me too."

Maisey joined them. "Welcome."

He smiled. "Thank you. It wasn't a pleasant task, and I'm glad it's over."

Maisey frowned. "What happened at Hell Gate?"

"The sheriff decided to keep the renegade for questioning. Maybe he can get more out of him than we did. I asked after Doc Mather and found out he and his wife live there. They're away for a wedding, but the sheriff said he'd deliver a message when they return."

Maisey gasped. "Did he—did the sheriff say—"

"He mentioned seeing a young girl in their care but didn't know her name."

Maisey pressed her hands to her cheeks and released a

shuddering breath.

"I'm sure it must have been your Phoebe." Rob rested his hand on her shoulder. "We should know before long."

She put her hand over Rob's. "Thank you. I hope to hold Phoebe in my arms soon."

"I'm sure you will." Bry smiled encouragingly at her friend. "You've done well, Rob."

His ears turned pink. "I'm glad to help."

Where's Nick?" Bry could no longer hold back her curiosity.

"He decided to go home."

Rob spoke gently, but his words slammed into her all the same.

"Why would he do that?" Maisey asked. "He seemed adjusted to living here."

"He wouldn't say exactly. It was most annoying, if you want to know, but I couldn't force the man to explain himself."

Bry stared at her brother, taken aback by his emotional reaction. The last time he'd spoken to her of Nick, he'd told her to forget him. Now he seemed genuinely sorry Nick had gone. Tears pricked her eyes, and she grasped at a straw. "Did he say whether he's coming back?"

"I wouldn't count on it, Bry."

She wrapped her arms around herself and tried to believe that Nick was really gone. His actions clarified matters between them. *Or did they?* Nick's absence was as mysterious as his presence had been. What was the point in wondering? Whether or not he loved her made little difference to the fact that he was gone.

Nick turned aside from the path and looked out over the Bitterroot River, running in a deep channel between narrow banks. Dusk crouched at the edge of day, ready to spring. He led Tavo down a hillock onto the bank. Three herons flapped down the river and out of sight around the bend. The water dashed and frothed against dark rocks in the shallows near shore. The stallion lowered his head to drink, his ears flicking at a fly. Nick went upstream to fill his own need for water and replenish his water bags.

He turned Tavo out to graze in a small clearing then sat on a fallen log. He pulled strips of jerky and the last of his pemmican from his saddlebags. From the cottonwoods across the river, a horned owl hooted in advance of nightfall, and a distant fox wailed in search of a mate.

Once he had satisfied his hunger, Nick followed the river bank in search of a willow tree. There was time before dark to set up a fish trap in one of the streams that emptied into the river. Making little sound, he traveled under cover to avoid giving away his position should Kicking Horse or any of his band be near. He climbed into a willow hanging its tresses down to the water and scanned the area before cutting the branches he would need.

Gaps between the trees on the opposite bank showed him an Indian camp that must have been there a little while, judging by the branches driven into the ground around the fire to make backrests and the presence of lean-to shelters. He clung to the willow trunk, straining his ears, and caught the murmur of voices. These grew louder, and he picked out the sound of Kicking Horse's voice.

Nick shifted to ensure he was concealed, and not a moment too soon. Kicking Horse walked down to the river on the opposite shore with Strong Bear beside him. Strong Bear bent to fill his water bag while Kicking Horse waited on the bank. "Now, what did you want to tell me?"

Strong Bear straightened with bright droplets running from the bead fringe of his water bag. "I know where the white women are."

"Why do you say this?"

"I saw them standing on a balcony like the ones at the forts."

"Where?"

"In the white village where the crazy preacher lives."

Nick frowned. He had to be referring to the town of Liberty and Shane.

Kicking Horse strode back and forth on the bank. "Why did you not capture them?"

"A man in a wagon drove up. With other buildings nearby, I didn't know how many people might hear if they screamed. I had just taken horses from a neighbor, and I thought their owners might be after me."

"Enough!" Kicking Horse backhanded him, and Strong Bear spun backwards to sprawl at his feet. Kicking Horse stood over him, nostrils flaring. "Your excuses hurt my ears."

Nick had never seen his stepbrother so fervent. His passion bordered on lunacy. Sorrow washed through him. Clearly, Kicking Horse hovered on the brink of madness. Insanity might explain Long Knife's actions, as well.

Strong Bear touched a hand to his bleeding lip. "I tell you where the white women are, and this is how you repay me?"

Kicking Horse had gone back to pacing but now stopped. "I am sorry, Strong Bear. Your words made me doubt your courage."

Strong Bear jutted out his chest. "I am not afraid of the white man."

"That is good to say, but words are only words. You will have another chance to prove yourself in the morning." He pulled Strong Bear to his feet. "Come with me to tell the others to ready themselves for battle. Tomorrow we will ride to the white village and take many scalps."

Nick pointed his horse in the direction his heart led. He had to reach the Hayes house soon to protect Bry and the other innocent people from falling prey to Kicking Horse's sick rampage. He couldn't see the trail beneath Tavo's hooves but trusted his horse's night vision better than his own. He'd waited for Kicking Horse and Strong Bear to vanish into the trees before dropping out of the willow. Night had fallen shortly after he'd taken to the trail. The moon moved behind cloud cover, deepening the darkness. Creatures of the night stirred all around him. At times, he picked out the scream of badgers, an owl's hoot, and the grunt of a bear.

The irony of being forced by circumstance to return to the people he had left behind did not escape him. This had happened before, when he'd gone to the Cheyenne village. God Himself seemed to be standing in his way. His father had read to him from the Bible in childhood, and one of the passages came to mind now. In the story, an angel of the Lord stood in the road to prevent a donkey carrying a man called Balaam from passing. Balaam beat his poor donkey, trying to make it go. No matter what path they took, the donkey stopped whenever the angel appeared. Finally, God opened Balaam's eyes to see the angel. Nick felt something like Balaam tonight. Every road he took away from Bry led back to her. The donkey he had been beating was his own ability to isolate himself from others, but it wouldn't carry him anymore.

He'd deceived himself to think that he could stay away from Bry at such a time. Going back until the danger was over made better sense. After that, he'd find somewhere else to live. Whatever else he did, he couldn't return to the cabin. Perhaps one day he could bear walking the paths of childhood again. Right now, they only reminded him of all he had lost.

The crossroads gleamed in the faint light cast by moonbeams. The larks that had earlier darted among the serviceberries had all gone to sleep. When next they woke their song would herald a day of bloodshed.

He rode past the hulks of the school and barn. The Hayes house stood in darkness. He dismounted and pounded the front door. "It's me, Nick, with urgent news."

The door swung inward, and Shane stood in the opening, holding an oil lamp high. He stood back. "Come in."

Nick obeyed, and Shane shot the bolt.

"I'm glad to see you again." Rob climbed down the ladder from the loft. "What brought you back?"

"I found Kicking Horse's camp and overheard him planning to

attack the town in the morning. He knows that Bry and Maisey are here."

Rob looked from Nick to Shane. "What do we do?"

America's voice, soothing her children, came from another room. He must have woken them.

Bry looked out from behind a partially-open door. Nick tried not to stare at her but couldn't help himself. With a long braid over one shoulder and her eyes wide, she looked so vulnerable that his desire to protect her increased. Their eyes met for a long moment, but then she withdrew without greeting him.

Shane led the way into the kitchen and plunked the lamp down on the table. "I'll warn the town before daybreak. Someone should ride to the fort and let Major Owen know. It's not a proper fort, but if anyone can round up help, he can."

"I'll go." Nick knew he could ride fast the longest. "I'll need a fresh horse, though."

Shane glanced at Rob. "Keep an eye on the place while I'm gone."

America entered the room, wrapped in a shawl. She went to her husband's side.

Shane put his arm around his wife and drew her close. "There's Indian trouble. I have to warn the others, but I'll come back soon. Go to the schoolhouse. It's easier to defend, and a person can see into the distance from the balcony. Stay safe, my darling. " He kissed the top of her head. "May the Lord watch over us all."

CHAPTER THIRTY-ONE

BRY LEANED AGAINST THE BEDROOM DOOR and closed her eyes. Nick had come back, but she couldn't risk the disappointment of hoping he would stay.

"What's going on?" Maisey asked.

"Nick says that the renegades plan to attack the town in the morning."

"Oh, no. How will we defend ourselves?"

Bry shook her head. "No one would have to if I'd turn myself over to them."

"Don't talk like that." Maisey came to stand before her.

"It would spare the lives of others."

Maisey took her by the shoulders. "Do you honestly think those who love you would prefer that?"

Bry dashed away tears. "Sweet Maisey, what would I do without you?"

Bry left Maisey to finish dressing and went to her own room to change into a plain dress of blue gingham. Afterwards she followed the voices to the kitchen. Rob glanced at Bry as she entered, but Nick seemed prepared to ignore her. She took a chair at the table, but everyone else remained standing. Shane kissed America goodbye and disappeared through the door to the rest of the house. He came back with a gun belt strapped about his hips. Bry stepped aside as Shane and Nick strode to the front door.

Maisey emerged in time to see them go. "I can't believe this is happening."

A determined look replaced the bewildered expression on America's face. "Let's get started. We have work to do. Go, everyone, and gather the belongings you'll want in the schoolhouse. Make it quick but remember that anything left here might be destroyed."

Bry thrust clothing and grooming supplies in her suitcase, then returned to the kitchen. She helped America pack crates of food, ammunition, and other supplies for Rob to carry. The children wouldn't go back to sleep. Liberty clung to her mother's skirts, and Seth kept whining. Bry picked Seth up and bounced him. That mollified the little boy only briefly, and she looked forward to giving him over to his mother. Meanwhile, Maisey bundled some of the children's clothes and toys into pillowcases.

With their tasks completed, they made their way in darkness to the schoolhouse. Bry climbed the stairs to the meeting room, where America hoped to put Liberty and Seth down again. The children didn't want to sleep, although they obviously needed to. The meeting room, located in the center of the building, had no windows to give views that might later frighten the children. Rob carried in two rocking chairs from the gathering room, and America laid out bedding. Bry took Seth off his mother's hands and cradled him while crooning "Einini," a lullaby she remembered her mother singing to her. "Little birds, little birds, sleep, sleep. Little birds, little birds, sleep, sleep," she sang in Gaelic. Seth nestled against her, sucking his thumb. Liberty drew near and watched her with tired eyes. Bry stopped rocking and held out her free arm to the little girl. Liberty smiled and climbed onto her lap. America stood watching for a moment, then slipped from the room.

It took a little doing, but Bry finally coaxed the children back to sleep. She laid them on their beds and tiptoed from the room.

Unlike the quiet atmosphere in the meeting room, the gathering place hummed with activity. America and Maisey were in the kitchen putting away food, for all the world as if preparing for a potluck after Sunday meeting. Maybe it helped them to keep busy.

Rob alone remained motionless, having positioned himself behind an overturned table on the balcony. From this vantage point, he kept watch with two rifles beside him.

She went out and crouched at his side. "Have you seen anything?"

He shook his head. "Not yet."

She released her breath. If only Nick's warning had been a false alarm. They would know soon enough. The sky had lightened to pearl gray, gleaming between the darkened tree branches, and the clamor of birds greeted the new morning. "I hope Shane comes back soon."

Rob glanced sideways at her. "I don't like how long it's taking him."

"Knowing Shane, he won't come back until he's warned every last soul in these parts."

Rob's lips lifted in a smile. "You know our cousin well, but he won't leave his family to go through this without him, not if he can help it."

"I want you to show me how to shoot a gun." The request came easy, which surprised her, considering how odious she found the idea. She'd never liked guns. They were noisy, and they could kill a person.

Rob gave her a quizzical look but nodded. "It's a skill to have, I suppose, but I'd rather you didn't feel the need to acquire it. If it comes down to trouble today, you can reload for me. All I ask is that you stay inside." He nodded to the rifles lying within reach. "One is mine, and the other belongs to Shane. If something prevents him from making it back in time, I'll shoot his rifle when mine runs out of ammunition. I'll show you how to load them."

Bry paid close attention, happy to learn the task wasn't difficult.

Hooves thudded the ground below.

Bry stiffened.

Rob tensed, then smiled. "It's only Shane. He's brought people to help defend the schoolhouse. Go down and let them in, but be quick about it. I have a bad feeling that something's about to happen."

Bry hurried down the stairs and threw open the door before

Shane could knock. He rushed inside, followed by a small crowd of armed men and frightened-looking women. Bry recognized many of the faces. She barred the door and followed them upstairs.

Shane and those who had accompanied him had arrived in time to keep from being caught in the open, but they had little chance to orient themselves. Shane did the best he could, assigning guard posts and making sure everyone had a supply of ammunition. Will Buckthorn, their closest neighbor, joined Rob behind the table. Bry spotted his wife, Hettie, in the kitchen with America.

The men stood beside the windows with their rifles in hand. The women had gone to the pot-bellied stove, where they warmed themselves and their children. Fear showed itself in their skittish glances. Babies wailed. The younger children fussed and turned their faces against their mothers' skirts. Those old enough to understand what was happening stood with eyes wide. The older boys and several of the women joined the men at the windows, ready to reload their rifles.

Shane was embracing America in the gathering room. "Rob just saw something," Bry told him. Now that the Indians might be coming, she didn't feel so comfortable with her brother on the balcony. She had seen arrows fly before, and one of them could wind up behind his table.

Shane went out and crouched beside Rob. Bry crowded the window near the balcony with America and Maisey. She scanned the countryside. Noticing nothing unusual, she let out a sigh of relief. Rob must have been mistaken. A flicker of movement caught her eye. She pulled in a breath. "Do you see them? They're traveling beneath the trees, away from the road."

America recovered first. "We shouldn't stand pressed against the window."

"You are right, of course." Maisey stepped away. "I'm afraid curiosity bested me."

Maisey and America returned to the kitchen, but Bry couldn't pry herself away from the window. She shifted to the side but continued to peer out through the glass. The renegades advanced on the property slowly and with obvious stealth, which made it clear that they didn't know the reception they would receive.

Bry watched the advancing warriors with the same helplessness that had gripped her when the buffalo herd had stampeded the wagons. There was nothing she could do to stop the wave of destruction threatening to engulf them. The warriors left the concealment of the trees and rode across the grassland toward the schoolhouse.

Bry's mouth went dry. The sight of the painted faces beneath their war bonnets and the wicked-looking tomahawks, lances, and bows they carried would strike fear into the bravest of hearts. Feathers streamed from the manes and tails of ponies marked with symbols similar to those on the warrior's faces. Arrows bristled from beaded quivers. A few had acquired rifles, Kicking Horse among them. He rode in the lead, a red zigzag crossing a band of yellow on his forehead and the black shape of a hand covering the lower part of his face. She sucked in a breath. Kicking Horse had frightened her with a knife. He seemed even more terrifying with a rifle.

The Indians came within range, but those in the schoolhouse held their fire. Bry laid a hand over her churning stomach. The Indians crept closer.

"Fire!" Shane shouted.

Shots rang out. Indians fell from their horses and stained the grass with their blood.

A bloodcurdling cry shook the air, and the renegades surged forward.

Seth wailed, and America hurried to the sanctuary. Many of the women scurried behind her.

"There's more of them coming from behind the schoolteacher's cabin." Marcus Colby, one of the people she recognized from Sunday meeting, called from his position near the kitchen window.

The renegades circled the schoolhouse, their battle cries raising prickles on Bry's skin. She shrank away from the window, having seen enough to know that those in the schoolhouse were outnumbered.

Bry pushed the hair out of her eyes and loaded another round of shells in a rifle. Her existence had dwindled to this single task, over and over again. Annie Bodmer sat next to her on the floor, her fingers flying as she loaded a rifle. Her husband, Jedidiah, was a bear of a man with a shy smile whom Shane had stationed at a side window.

Glass shattered downstairs, someone shrieked, and gunshots popped. Shane rushed past and pounded down the stairs. Bry's gaze met Annie's in wordless communication. Annie pressed her lips together and loaded faster, and Bry gave renewed attention to the rifle before her.

Before Shane had banished her from the window, she'd glimpsed bodies strewing the grass, but several of those defending the schoolhouse had also fallen. Twice they'd fought off intruders coming through busted-out windows. How long would it be before one of them broke through?

The moans and wails coming from downstairs made it hard to concentrate. From the snippets Bry and Annie had overheard, one person was dead, and another seemed ready to succumb. Maisey had administered aid to the wounded from their meager supplies. Bry didn't envy her the job, but Maisey would give it all the sympathy inherent in her nature.

"Help is here," Rob sang out. "A group of men went after the renegades, and not a moment too soon."

Bry's shoulders sagged with relief.

Shane looked out the window next to the balcony. "Some of the Indians are turning tail. Why are the rest still fighting?"

"It's hard to say." Will called from the balcony. "They can't possibly win against the mob carrying rifles that's riding down the road. Most have figured that out, but some are hard-headed, I guess."

Bry finished loading a rifle but no one brought another.

"I think they're surrendering." Excitement lifted Shane's voice.

Rob peered over the table to the scene below. "What is Nick doing?"

Bry ran to the window. Shane shifted for her, despite his earlier insistence that she keep back. Nick was riding out from the group of men beside a man with a graying beard.

"That's Major Owen from the fort." Shane gestured toward them. "He must have put together a group of volunteers to help us."

Several guards with rifles drawn flanked Nick and Major Owen. They rode toward Kicking Horse, who had thrown down his rifle and now waited with his head high. As Nick and the Major neared, Kicking Horse pulled his knife and let it fly.

The two guards fired their rifles.

Nick fell from his horse. Bry's scream tore the air.

Nick dropped down on the side of his horse. Kicking Horse's knife whistled through the air. If he hadn't moved, the blade would have embedded in his flesh. A woman screamed. Rifles blasted. Something thudded to the ground, and a cry went up from the renegades. The horse Major Owen had loaned Nick for the return journey shuddered and stomped. Nick pulled back into the saddle.

Kicking Horse lay staring at the sky with such a blank expression that Nick would have taken him for dead had his bleeding not shown that his heart still pumped.

Major Owen fired three shots into the air. "Calm yourselves. I don't want any more of you to die."

Nick repeated the Indian agent's words in Cheyenne, and the rest of the warriors quieted. He dismounted and ran to his stepbrother's broken body. What he could see of the damage

Kicking Horse had sustained did not look good. Major Owen dismounted and bent over Kicking Horse. He looked up with an expression that confirmed Nick's conclusion. They couldn't save his stepbrother.

He tried anyway, taking off his bandanna and holding it to the stomach wound.

Kicking Horse roused from his stupor and said something so quietly that Nick had to lean down to hear.

"Have you come to mock me while I die?"

Nick frowned. He had never been able to convince his stepbrother that he didn't hate him, and it looked like he never would. "I've come to help you if I can, to ease your journey from this world."

Kicking Horse's weak laughter turned into coughing. "Will you keep them from trapping my spirit in the earth?"

Nick recognized his stepbrother's mocking challenge as a request. He fought an inner battle, but then made his decision. "I will do as you ask for my sister's sake." As the words left his mouth, he knew them for a lie. "I'll do it for your sake as well." He told the whole truth.

Kicking Horse's face convulsed in what might have been grief. He grasped Nick by the shirt with surprising strength and pulled him down to speak near his ear. "I would have killed you."

Nick covered Kicking Horse's hand with his own. "Go to our fathers in peace, my brother. I forgive you." He spoke the necessary words stiffly, but he said them.

The strain in his stepbrother's face eased. His hold slackened, and he fell back with a long sigh. His chest no longer rose and fell, and the blood stopped flowing from his wounds.

Maisey pulled back the parlor curtains as a phaeton pulled by two dappled white horses wheeled to a stop in the drive leading to the barn. "We have a visitor!"

America poked her head around the door from the kitchen. "Who can it be?" She hurried to the window. "I'm sure I don't know anyone who would drive such a fancy carriage. There's a woman with him."

Bry came through the doorway and joined them. "My goodness, but it's Doc Mather."

Maisey's heart leaped. "So it is." She craned to see. "Is there— do you see—"

"The woman is holding a child." Bry's voice lilted.

Maisey's head reeled, and she put a hand on the windowsill for balance. "Phoebe." The name wrenched from her lips. Maisey could see that the woman held her daughter. She ran to the door and jerked it open.

Maisey stopped before going through the gate. What would Phoebe feel when she saw her? She was too young to understand that she hadn't abandoned her on purpose. Her daughter might reject her.

"What are you waiting for?" Bry opened the gate for her.

America touched her back. "It will be all right."

Maisey set her fears aside and went toward the Marthers, who were walking toward them. Mrs. Mather wore a woebegone expression and cradled Phoebe facing toward her. Doc Mather walked while turned toward his wife as if to shield her. They met on the path from the barn. "We came when we heard you were free. We've taken care of your daughter all this time." Doc Mather announced in a somber voice.

"I'm obliged to you." Maisey's voice sounded rusty.

Phoebe turned her head with a squeal and squirmed at once. Mrs. Mather glanced at her husband then put Phoebe down.

Maisey held out her arms and gathered the sweet weight of her child when she hurtled against her. She kissed Phoebe's soft cheeks and her blonde curls. Phoebe stared at her with a look of wonder and brought a pudgy hand up to stroke her tearful face. "Ma?"

Maisey kissed her daughter's fingers, laughing. "I'm right

here, Phoebe. We're together again." She stood up, holding tight to her child, and Phoebe nestled against her neck.

Mrs. Mather watched her with sorrow in her eyes. "We've grown fond of Phoebe."

Doc Mather touched his wife's elbow. "But we know we have to give her back."

"Thank you." Maisey smiled at them both. "You're welcome to visit her whenever you like."

Mrs. Mather brightened.

"Thank you, my dear." Doc Mather beamed at her. "We'd like that. Our family has been split by distance, and it would be nice to think we had a sort of granddaughter near."

"Won't you come in?" America invited them with a smile. "You'll have a lot to talk about."

Nick returned on the horse Shane had loaned him, pulling the travois that had carried his brother's body to its final resting place. Shane looked up from mucking out a stall in the barn, nodded, and leaned on his shovel. "You're home in time for supper. Shall we set a plate for you?"

"I'd like that, if it's no trouble."

Shane smiled. "We'd make a place for you regardless. You'll need a bed, I suppose."

"I'd appreciate one."

"It's the least we can do. We're grateful for what you did to save us. If you hadn't ridden to the fort, things would have happened differently." Shane leaned his shovel against the wall. "I'll let my wife know. I think we can put you up in the cabin a while longer."

"Thank you." Nick led his horse toward the watering trough. "I'll only stay the night."

Shane looked back from the open doorway. "Are you sure?"

"I left my brother high in a tree where his body won't be

disturbed. Now I have a journey to make. My sister loved Kicking Horse and will grieve."

"I'm sorry about what happened, Nick."

He nodded. "Kicking Horse died as he lived, always at war. I wish he hadn't waged it against me."

Shane grimaced. "I saw him throw a knife at you."

"He aimed his hatred at me, but mine was for his father, Long Knife. Kicking Horse should never have become my stepbrother. Why did my father have to die? He didn't do anything to deserve it except marry the woman Long Knife wanted."

"Is that what stood between you?"

"Yes. After Long Knife took my mother into his tepee, he poisoned Kicking Horse's mind against me. Long Knife hated me because I knew what he had done. I saw him drown my father, but no one believed me, not even my mother."

"How wretched."

"Long Knife stole both my parents from me, and he separated me from my sister."

Shane looked down at the horse drinking from the watering trough. "You have a clear choice."

"Oh?" Nick asked, bracing himself for what the preacher might say.

Shane pinned Nick with his gaze. "You can cling to your outrage and suffer the consequences of bitterness or release yourself through forgiveness to live in freedom."

The horse lifted his head from the watering trough. Nick took the reins and began walking him. The preacher made sense, but he shook his head. "I don't know how to forgive."

Shane kept pace with him. "None of us does. God had to show us how. When Jesus was dying on the cross, He asked His Heavenly Father to forgive his tormentors."

"I don't know how He could manage that."

"It took love."

"I've never felt that tender emotion for Long Knife."

"Love isn't an emotion, although it can call many of them

forth."

Nick grappled with this concept, which was new to him. He didn't want to ask the next question, but his curiosity demanded it. "Well then, if love isn't an emotion, what is it?"

Shane smiled. "What is love? Finer minds than mine have argued that riddle. I'll defer to the Bible's definition. It tells us that love is patient and kind. It's not given to jealousy, boasting, or pride. It doesn't demand its own way, nor is it rude or irritable. Love doesn't keep a record of wrongs. It hates wrongdoing and rejoices in the truth. Love bears all things. It believes, hopes, and endures always. Love never dies. All of that is summed up in one simple statement. 'God is love.'"

Nick couldn't fathom everything Shane said, but he recognized its truth. He kept moving, and Sparky clopped along beside him.

"You will notice that all of love's traits inspire decisions, not feelings," Shane went on. "Kindness comes from compassion, humility causes a person to forsake pride, and so on. Love shows itself in actions."

Nick winced inwardly. He'd kept an account of Long Knife's sins, focused on himself and ignored others, and given up on his love for Bry. No wonder she had run from him that day outside his cabin. He'd rejected her first by refusing to sit with her at the preacher's table during the potluck. "I have a lot to learn."

"We all do. Learning to love others well takes a lifetime."

Shane left, and Nick led his horse to a stall for grooming. He applied the curry comb to a patch of dried mud, soon absorbed in the simple task. A scuffling sound alerted him, and he lifted his head in quick alarm, but then relaxed. "Hello, Bry."

"Shane said you were out here." She stopped outside the stall. "I wanted to tell you that I'm sorry about what happened to your brother."

Nick returned to grooming Sparky. "You had no reason to love him."

"I can't rejoice in another person's death, regardless of what he did to me, and I know Kicking Horse mattered to you."

"We weren't on the best of terms." His voice came out gruff.

"He was still your brother."

He tugged on a knot in Sparky's mane. "Thanks for your sympathy, but Kicking Horse never acted like a brother to me."

"That's all the more tragic."

Nick exchanged the curry comb for a body brush without replying. He couldn't even picture what a real family relationship with Kicking Horse would have been like.

"Shane said you are only here until tomorrow morning."

"I need to go to Rising Bird."

"Will you tell your sister something for me?"

Nick glanced at her in surprise. "Yes."

"Will you please—" She seemed unable to go on for a moment. "Let her know that I don't hold what her brother did against him."

"She will take comfort from your words."

"I'm glad. I needed to say them for my sake as well as hers." She glanced at him. "Do you plan to return?"

He made his decision. "Yes."

"How soon?"

He looked up in surprise. "I'm not sure, but I doubt I'll stay away long."

Her face had gone red. "Would you be willing to ask after Con at Fort Sedgwick?"

"I'd be happy to do that, Bry."

"Thank you. Maybe now we can find out what's happened to him."

CHAPTER THIRTY-TWO

BRY OPENED HER EYES AND GASPED as a face pushed up against hers. The next instant she laughed and pulled little Seth into her embrace. "How did you get in here?"

Seth's eyes danced, but he smiled beatifically. His charm was not unlike his father's. A glance revealed Maisey's vacant bed. The door, which must not have latched securely, stood ajar.

Bry pulled Seth onto the bed and tickled him. He collapsed in giggles, and she tugged him close to kiss his curls. How like Liam he felt in her arms. Tears pricked her eyes as the old sorrow stirred, but another emotion won through—joy. She could never forget Liam, but how could she grieve with such a precious child as Seth in her arms?

America tapped on the door. "So sorry, but is my son in there?" A hint of panic colored her voice." I seem to have misplaced him."

"He's here," Bry hastened to reassure her.

"May I come in?"

"Please do."

The door swung inward, and America rushed in, looking a trifle distraught. She gathered her son in her arms and held him tightly. He snuggled his head under her chin.

Bry smiled at the touching scene. "He scared me half out of my mind, if you want to know. I woke with his face two inches from mine."

"Ah, yes. That trick. I'm sorry he woke you."

America shut the door after she came into the room, for which Bry was thankful for modesty's sake. She laughed. "Don't be. It's a memory I'll cherish. Besides, I meant to get up earlier to help you prepare for Sunday meeting."

"Everything is done, but we do have the out-of-town folks to look after. The ones who live farthest away are easy guests. They usually sleep in the gathering room and use the schoolhouse kitchen, but I always check to make sure they have everything they need."

"I admire your calm when you're about to be descended upon."

America rubbed Seth's back. "It's part and parcel of being a preacher's wife. I adore my husband, and I love my life. Caring for others is a privilege, not a hardship."

"I envy you."

"Why do you say that?"

Bry clasped her knees. "You sail through life as if nothing bad has ever happened to you. I wish I could be as happy."

America sank into the rocking chair beside the bed with a smile touching her lips. "You'll be relieved to know that I'm far from perfect. I've made plenty of mistakes. One of the worst was when I ran away from the man I loved."

"You did that?"

"Oh, yes." America frowned. "I almost didn't marry Shane."

"Even though you love him?"

"I refused *because* I love him."

"But why would you think like that?" She shouldn't have asked such a personal question. Bry's face heated.

"I know it's hard to understand, but my decision made sense to me at the time. You see, I didn't feel worthy of my husband's love." She hesitated. "I suspect Nick is traveling the same road I did, but for different reasons. You never know, he may sort himself out yet. Lifting prayer on his behalf wouldn't hurt." America stood and shifted Seth to her hip. "I should go and let you dress."

Bry heaved a shaky sigh. "Thank you for what you said."

America smiled. "Will you allow me a piece of advice?"

Bry nodded.

"Don't leave your happiness in anyone's hands but God's."

Nick reined in Tavo and gazed at his sister with a sense of homecoming. She bent over a fish trap at the edge of the river, the fringe of her dress swaying with her movements. Her hair hung in braids on either side of her head, and the sun gleamed on her bronze skin. Smiling, Nick watched her toss fish into a basket. She emptied one trap and squatted beside the next. She reminded him of their mother, who had been partial to the catfish in the Missouri. She had taught him both her skill and respect for nature.

Rising Bird must have seen him, for she straightened and stood watching him with all the grace of a doe. He nudged Tavo forward, and Rising Bird ran to meet him. "You came back!"

He leaped down from his horse to embrace his sister. She smelled of sunshine and river water.

Laughing, she pushed out of his arms. "I am happy to see you again."

"You don't ask why I have come. Perhaps you know the reason."

Her eyes grew sad. "Some of Kicking Horse's followers returned to the village. They told me what happened."

"I wish he hadn't died."

Her face took on the cautious look it always wore when he referred to their stepbrother.

How much grief had his anger caused her?

She looked up at him. "I thought I might never see you again."

"I haven't been fair to you. Please forgive me."

She looked away from him. "I understood."

"It caused you pain, and for that I'm sorry."

She tugged his hand. "Come to my tepee, my brother. Tonight, we will have plenty of fish."

Ahanu was less happy to see him than Rising Bird had been. He frowned but allowed Nick to stay. Rising Bird stuffed the fish with herbs and smeared clay thickly over their scales. These she put into the embers of her fire, along with clay-wrapped vegetables, and covered the clay bundles with ashes and glowing coals. After the fish cooked, they peeled off the clay, which also removed the skin and scales, leaving only the tender flesh. They sat on the benches in Rising Bird's tepee and, whenever they ran out, took more food from the embers until they could eat no more.

Nick answered Rising Bird's many questions about his travels and activities since she'd seen him last.

"What happened to the white women?" she asked. "I heard that Kicking Horse died trying to recapture them."

Kicking Horse had died trying to kill him, but if she didn't know that, he wouldn't inform her. "They are safe and well."

"I didn't agree with what Kicking Horse did, trying to take the women back after you paid their price." Ahanu scowled. "He wanted me to go with him, but I refused."

"You made a wise choice." Nick nodded approval. "It may have spared your life."

Ahanu's nostrils flared. "The young men in the village are like dogs who taste blood and lust for more. They refuse to listen to Old Chief when he calls for peace. Not even the Council of Chiefs could stop them from calling for more raids."

"That will lead to no good." Sorrow smote Nick as he pictured the destruction that would bring upon his mother's people. "If you ever need help, come to me."

"I would not have thought it necessary before the massacre at Sand Creek," Ahanu said. "Now I'm not so sure. Let us hope that this trouble passes, and peace comes."

"I will pray that it does."

"If not, we will come to you." Rising Bird's eyes gleamed as a smile spread across her face. "We have happy news, my brother. I carry Ahanu's child at last."

Nick smiled. "Now, that is something to celebrate."

"You must come back sometimes, my brother, and see your nephew grow up."

"I will," Nick promised. How close he had come to missing this blessing. He wouldn't make that mistake again. Looking back, he could hardly understand why he had believed he couldn't live in either of his parents' worlds when he could belong to both.

On the morning of Nick's departure, Ahanu extended Nick's rifle in both hands. "Accept this gift from me."

Nick looked at him in surprise. "That rifle was my payment for the slave I bought from you."

Ahanu nodded but pushed the rifle toward him. "And now I give it back to you."

Nick lifted the familiar weight of his father's Henry rifle. "Does it not please you?"

Ahanu shrugged. "Why should I pay for bullets when I can make as many arrows as I need for free?"

Nick smiled. "You have a point."

Ahanu lifted his head in a proud gesture. "I choose the old ways, Wolf Walking, and to live in friendship."

Bry dried her hands on a dishtowel while admiring the neat jars of blackberry jam with wax seals cooling on the kitchen counter. "Now that's a pretty sight."

"It's worth a few scratches." Maisey rubbed a welt on her arm.

"We'll have biscuits in the morning so we can sample the fruit of our labors."

Everyone in the household had been fed, the dishes were done, and Bry had finished wiping down the counters. Bry sighed. After a day spent cooking and making jam, she was as overheated as the kitchen.

"That was heartfelt," America observed with a smile. "Shall we join the men? It's cooler outside." She picked up a tray filled with tall glasses of vinegar lemonade, and Maisey hurried to open the back door for her.

Shaded in the afternoon, the back porch provided the coolest place to wait out the heat. Bry sat on a ladder-back chair beside Rob, who was holding a sleepy Phoebe. Bry lifted one of the glasses from the tray America extended to her and took a long drink of the refreshing beverage. Maisey, on her other side, waved a fan she'd folded from a scrap of paper. Some of the air she stirred cooled Bry's face as well.

"My legs ache," America said. "I'm not complaining, though. It's nice to go back to normal."

"I was just thinking that we should return to the ranch." Rob lifted his voice so all could hear.

"There's no rush," Shane assured him.

"We're enjoying your company," America added.

"It's mutual, but there's no need to abandon the ranch now that the renegades are gone."

Maisey's fan stopped moving. "I should let you know that I won't be going with you."

Bry had been drinking from her glass but now set it down with a small thump. "What do you mean?"

"Shane and America have invited me to stay with them and work with the Indians.

"We've decided to open a Saturday school for the Flathead children," America said in a rush.

Maisey's eyes shone. "I'm going to teach them."

"How can you when you don't speak their language?" Bry asked.

"A member of the tribe has agreed to translate for me while I work on learning the language."

Bry didn't like the idea. "What about Phoebe?"

America waved a hand. "She'll be no trouble to have around. Liberty adores her, and they play well together."

"That's wonderful." Bry hoped it went well for Maisey but had her doubts. Working with Indian children had caused a horrifying massacre at the Whitman mission. After a number of Cayuse children had died from measles, the tribe had blamed the missionaries. That had been almost twenty years ago, but the episode had so shocked people living in Boston that while working for the Wainwrights, she'd heard it brought up as a reason to stay in the East and avoid the Western pioneer nonsense.

"We'll miss you." Rob's voice held regret.

"I can't thank you enough for taking me in and finding my daughter."

Rob smiled at her above Phoebe's blonde head. "That was my privilege."

Bry decided to make the best of things. "You must come to visit when you can."

"You're welcome anytime." Despite his smile, Rob's eyes were sad.

Bry and Rob left for the ranch the next day. They lingered so long in saying goodbye that they would arrive late in the day, possibly after nightfall. The idea of coming back to a dark house put Bry on edge. The renegade threat had passed, but Rob seemed more vigilant than usual. He appeared sunk in gloom for reasons she could guess, and the day crept by with little conversation to lighten the journey.

The worst of the heat cooled in the breathless hour before full dark. The wind forgot to blow. The moon hung, pale and apologetic, above the horizon, and the stars hid until the black of night should reveal them. The horses clopped along the road in the half-light, the creak and sway of the wagon lulling Bry. Rob remained silent beside her. She wasn't sure her brother knew what he wanted in life, but she could tell he'd had a strong reaction to leaving Maisey behind. For her part, Maisey seemed not to have awakened to the prospect of acquiring another husband. Perhaps she never would.

Maisey was the sort who would plant roots wherever she landed, but she hadn't dug in deeply at the ranch. Neither had Bry, for that matter, but she knew the reason for that. "I don't expect Con to be waiting at home." She spoke her thought out loud.

"I've been troubled about him a lot lately."

"Could Thad have lied to us when he said Con was alive and

recovering at Fort Sedgwick?" She asked the question that most troubled her. "Thad lied in so many other ways. That might have been one more."

"Anything's possible, I suppose."

"I asked Nick to stop at the fort and inquire after Con." Bry spoke gently, not certain how Rob would receive this news.

"I hope he learns something. If not, I think I should search for our brother. Too bad that I'll have to give up the cattle drive. The ranch is Con's dream, and I wanted to make a success of it for his sake."

She repressed her fear that she would lose both brothers. "I think you should go on the cattle drive."

"What about you? I'll not leave you alone on the ranch. You're one of the reasons I didn't leave before this."

"Shane would always take me in again."

"He and America have been kindness itself. Another thought would be to find a reliable manager."

Remembering his poor judgment over Thad, she spoke quickly. "I like your first idea best."

"I'd have to pick up supplies for the trip, ask Shane to take you in again, and make arrangements for the cattle. Lorne would probably look after them."

"Lorne?"

"I guess you've never met our nearest neighbor." Rob's forehead pleated. "I'm not so sure living on the ranch is right for you, Bry. It isolates you too much."

"You should worry about Con before you start in on me."

Rob gave her an arch look. "You're telling me I'm a mother hen."

"Con needs looking after."

"And you don't?"

"The ranch is fine for me. I like the quiet."

He called to one of the horses, which displayed interest in a patch of grass growing alongside the road. "A lonely ranch is no place for a woman in the prime of life. You should find a husband

and settle down to have a family."

She laughed. "Dear Rob, always looking to pair me off. You're worse than Con."

"I thought it would be Nick for you."

Bry recognized the question in Rob's statement, but she didn't answer it. Certain things were none of a brother's business.

They made the broad turning and rattled toward the ranch house. Bry didn't like coming back to the darkened building at nightfall, but she and Rob had lingered too long before setting off this morning. She cringed at the memory of what had happened here. If Nick and Rob hadn't rescued her, she might even now be a prisoner.

"Steady goes it," Rob said in a soothing voice. "Kicking Horse can't hurt you anymore."

She drew a shaky breath. Knowing that Kicking Horse was dead didn't make the memories any less horrible.

"Whoa!" Rob called to the horses, and the wagon shuddered to a stop. He jumped down and lifted his arms to Bry. She let him help her from the wagon. Rob lit a lantern and started toward the house. She walked beside him, jumping at shadows. He unlocked the door, and it swung inward under his hand. The uncertain light wavered across the entry walls. How soulless the house seemed, devoid of life. Had it only been a short while since they'd left? It seemed longer.

"Come now." Rob took her hand.

Bry started up the stairs beside him. The upper corridor reposed in shadow. Bry peered into her dim surroundings while Rob pushed open her bedroom door. "Inside with you."

A glance showed her that no intruder lurked within the chamber.

"Lock yourself in while I check the house over. I doubt I'll find any intruders, but it will ease your mind."

She nodded. "I guess I can use a mother hen now and again."

The ranch came into view, and Nick urged Tavo a little faster. He was anxious to return to Bry, although he wished he could bring her better news about Con. He couldn't imagine how it would feel to learn something similar about his sister. Whatever happened between them, she would need support, and he intended to give it.

He had to turn aside to water his horse before reaching his destination. He chafed at the delay but allowed Tavo to wade into the water and drink. Nick watched the opposite shore, still looking for Kicking Horse even though he knew he would never see his brother again. Birds sang in the willows; their voices joined in a cheerful chorus. A fish jumped and fell back, sending out bright rings in the water. When Tavo stopped drinking and lifted his head, Nick took up the remainder of his journey at once.

After his second knock, Bry came to the door. He didn't delude himself that her parted lips and expectant expression were for anything other than news of her brother. Her rumpled hair and puffy eyes betrayed that she must have risen from a nap. "I'm sorry to disturb you," he told her.

She gave a slight shake of her head. "Don't worry about that. Do you have word of Con?"

"I do." He glanced about. "Where's Rob? He'll want to know too."

"He's outside somewhere. Come in, will you, and tell me what's become of my brother."

He stepped past her into the entryway. She shut the door and laid a trembling hand on his arm. "Was Con at Fort Sedgwick?"

He covered her hand with his. "Once, but no more."

Her eyes widened, and her face took on a look of strain. "What do you mean?"

"It doesn't look good, I'm afraid. Con was worried about you and in a rush to leave the fort. His condition was so grave that the doctor warned him to stay put. Con ignored the advice and rode off anyway."

"He could be alive."

"Yes, it's possible, but he's vanished. No one remembers seeing him, and if he'd followed you to the Cheyenne village, my sister would have heard of it. He left the fort months ago, and no one seems to have seen him since."

Her fingers curled into his arm. "Con can't be dead," she murmured. Her face went white, and she sagged against him. He lifted her into his arms and carried her to the parlor couch. After loosening her collar, he went into the kitchen and returned with a glass of water and damp cloth. He set the water aside and ran the cloth over her face and neck. Her eyelids fluttered, and her eyes opened.

"Did I faint?" she asked in a weak voice.

"I believe you did. How do you feel?"

"I'm all right." She tried to push up.

He steadied her. "Take it slow."

Her hair had come loose from its pins and now tumbled around her. She gazed at him with such innocent trust that the urge to protect her overwhelmed him.

The front door opened and boots thumped the floorboards. Nick turned his head, ready to greet Rob.

"What are you doing to my sister?" Rob bellowed from the doorway.

Nick released her and stood up. He'd almost forgotten how the settlers viewed him. Somehow, he'd expected Rob to be different.

"Nothing." Bry shook the hair out of her face with a toss of her head. "I fainted."

Rob went to his sister. "Are you all right?"

"Yes, but I had a shock. Nick told me that Con has gone missing."

Rob looked at Nick. "Sorry I overreacted. What happened to Con?"

Nick couldn't hide his surprise at Rob's apology. "He disappeared after leaving the fort to search for Bry."

"That settles it." Rob declared. "I'm going after my brother."

CHAPTER THIRTY-THREE

NICK WOKE IN DARKNESS AND WENT still, listening for what might have disturbed him. Coyotes howled and yipped nearby. A pack of coyotes could bring down grown cattle, but they were more likely to kill calves in the spring. He went outside with his rifle and fired shots into the air. That should scare the predators off long enough for him to go to Sunday meeting. He wouldn't stay away long, but he would see Bry there, and what he had to say to her was long overdue. He'd have spoken before, but she'd needed time to absorb the news about Con, and then she'd left to visit her family in Liberty while Rob was gone.

The job at the ranch suited him, something he hadn't expected. He'd accepted it on a temporary basis, glad to free Rob to search for his brother. It seemed doubtful that Con would turn up alive, however. Nick could attest, from what he'd known of the man, that he would have wasted no time in going after his sister. That he hadn't shown up at the Cheyenne village meant that something had stopped him. The only things Nick could think of that could do that were death, illness, or becoming lost, none of which boded well for Con's survival. He'd kept his opinions to himself, though. Bry and Rob needed to cling to hope, and for all he knew it might still prove warranted. The only thing he could say with certainty was that if anyone could survive adverse circumstances, it was Con.

He tried to sleep again, but the anticipation of seeing Bry kept him awake. When the first glimmer of dawn appeared outside the window, he gave up the struggle and climbed out of bed in the cabin Rob had given for his use. He put on the work clothes Shane had provided when he'd first arrived in the valley and went out to set the traps and saddle Tavo. Afterward, he took a bath and shaved the stubble from his face. He put on the same clothes but packed the fine trousers, linen shirt, and string tie which also had come as a gift from Shane, into his saddle bag. He would put them on when he arrived. Along with his leather vest and hat, these clothes represented what Shane had called his 'Sunday best.' Nick donned his buckskin jacket and stepped into the saddle.

The weather had cooled into autumn, and now the first hint of winter chilled the air. The trees had turned shades of yellow and orange. Their leaves danced in the breeze, bright against the evergreens' deep hues. He rounded a bend and surprised a bull moose. Paying little attention to him, the hunchbacked creature continued to pull down willow leaves. It was a little early for mating season, when a bull moose might attack someone who ventured too close. Nick gave the animal a wide berth anyway.

He was unprepared for the emotion that choked him when the crossroads came in view. This time he turned the right direction. The broken schoolhouse windows had all been replaced. The blood that had soaked into the grass had vanished, no doubt washed into the earth by rains. He stopped in the place Kicking Horse had died, remembering.

Bry turned away from watching Nick from the window beside the schoolroom balcony. It hurt to see him mourning the brother he'd never had, especially now that it seemed possible she had lost her own. She could be thankful Con had shown her only love. If the worst had happened, she would comfort herself in that knowledge.

She had come over to help organize the potluck food before the service began, but now she could think of a dozen reasons to return to the house. None of them had anything to do with Nick's arrival, of course. Well, all right. She wanted to see him. Giving it no more thought than that, she hurried outside.

Nick was leaving the barn. He waved to her, and she caught

up with him. They stood together in the sunshine. "You look well," he observed. "That's my favorite dress. You're beautiful in it."

It took her a moment to react. She smoothed the blue calico of her skirt. "Thank you." It was nice to know he admired her, but he'd never commented on her appearance before. Nick's manner toward her had definitely shifted. The way he was looking at her sent warmth curling through her. "How are things at the ranch?" she asked to move the conversation into safer channels.

"Apart from a few predators worrying the cattle, all is well."

She frowned. "Why are there always predators?"

He shrugged. "It's the way of things."

He took her hand and coaxed her with a smile. "Walk with me?"

A funny pang shot through her stomach, equal parts longing and joy. She smiled and moved into step with him. He guided her down the road toward the heart of Liberty. Fields and farm holdings gave way to closer dwellings until the space between buildings vanished. A wagon trundled down the broad street and stopped in front of the mercantile. Otherwise, the streets lazed in the same sun that kissed Bry's face with welcome warmth. They walked down the main street in comfortable silence and found more farms and fields.

Bry knew they should turn around but couldn't bring herself to suggest it. The sky spread its wings above blue mountains that rose above trees dressed in autumn finery. Birds sang in celebration of a perfect day.

They stopped at a bend in the road. "We should go back." Nick's voice held regret.

She nodded.

Neither of them budged.

Nick turned to her. "Before we do, I need to make an apology."

"All right."

He took her hands. "I've blown hot and cold with you, which must have confused you. Truth to tell, I've been confused myself. I needed to understand some things about loving others, which

Shane was happy to teach me."

Touched by his obvious discomfort, she opened her mouth to set him at ease.

He shook his head. "Hear me out, if you will."

She waited for him to continue.

"I told myself that my leaving was best for you, but I was thinking more of myself than anyone else. Can you forgive me?"

She gazed back at him, caught in a moment of truth. She could pretend that he hadn't hurt her or risk revealing her feelings. She managed to nod.

A look of peace settled over his face. "Thank you."

She found her voice. "You're not the only one who should apologize. I haven't always been kind to you."

"Never mind." He drew her into his arms and kissed the top of her head. "That's all behind us now." He pulled away. "I know how to go forward from here, if you're willing."

She smiled up at him, more certain of her answer than of anything in her life. "I am."

He lowered his head and touched her lips with his in a whisper of a kiss. Bry met him willingly, yielding to his touch. She curled her fingers into his leather jacket and clung to him while waves of longing swept through her. She forgot everything but the feel and taste of him. Her hands strayed behind his head, and she held him fast while every barrier that had separated them came crashing down.

He lifted his head and smiled down at her. "I've been wanting a repeat since the last time I kissed you."

"I felt much the same." Her face heated at how much she'd admitted.

He touched her cheek. "If I'd known that, this would have happened sooner."

She laughed. "If you'd said as much, I might have told you."

"Is that so? I can see that we need to talk more. Shall we start like this?" His lips caught hers in a lingering caress.

Bry pushed away at last, breathless. "Stop while I collect my wits."

He grinned. "I'll confess the need for that myself. You are a desirable woman, Bry." He captured her hand. "Would you allow me to court you?"

She frowned. "I'm not sure what Rob will say."

"I think he'll be pleased."

She stared at him, startled by his change in attitude. "Con might not be."

He pulled her into his arms and kissed her forehead. "Together, we can deal with any problem that arises."

She'd never heard him speak with such confidence before. "What's caused this change in attitude?"

He gazed into her eyes. "Loving you, Bry."

She placed her hand on his chest and felt the thump of his heart beneath her palm. "I love you too, Nick."

His lips claimed her mouth in a kiss that promised many more to come.

Author Notes

World Building for a Historical Romance Novel

As a multi-genre author, I can say that world building for a historical romance and a fantasy novel are remarkably similar. In both cases, the author creates a world that doesn't exist. With historical fiction, you have clues and records to guide you, but it takes a lot of imagination to fashion such details into a world that feels authentic to the reader. In some respects, fantasy is easier. I align my medieval fantasy to a past era, but if I don't know a fact, I can just make something up. When this happens with historical fiction, I have to research until I find the truth.

A Special Note

My father was half-Meskwaki (also known as the Fox-Sauk tribe). His black hair and dark skin stood out among his classmates, who were not always kind. He was jeered at and made to feel that he didn't fit in. My father's account of the prejudice he suffered informed this story. I remember attending powwows with my family, and Indian decorations adorned the walls of our home. However, my father's attempts to connect with his heritage bore little fruit, both at the reservation and among my grandmother's Scottish family. I could sense his feeling of not quite belonging to either world. I based Nick Laramie's struggles on those of my father.

I'm glad my parents raised me to respect all races. I based my story on the historical accounts that I found and did my best to give even-handed treatment of the Cheyenne tribe and the settlers who came West. I am grateful that the Lord Jesus Christ died on the cross for all of us, no matter what the color of our skin.

A Bit of Trivia About the Story

An excellent editor who reviewed an early draft of this book advised me that I needed to make Phoebe's character more sympathetic. He suggested that readers should be in tears when she died. You see, Phoebe originally died in the stampede. I incorporated his suggestion into this story and wept myself when I wrote the scene in which Phoebe perished. I learned of my success in making her sympathetic when my publisher informed me that Phoebe's demise had traumatized her. After consideration, we agreed not to put readers through such a sorrowful event. Little Phoebe was saved! One problem remained, however. The theme of the book called for an innocent character to die at that point in the story. Poor Natty was minding her own business as a minor character when she was forced to die. It was all in a good cause, Natty.

True Historical Events in the Book

A deep feeling for history sustained me during my research. There is nothing so thrilling as discovering something about the past I didn't know. I suspect, dear reader, that you feel the same. I based *Cheyenne Sunrise* on these actual historical events.

• I derived some of the details of the wagon attack, kidnapping of Bry and Maisey, the subsequent journey to the Cheyenne village, and the women's captivity, on a true account of events in 1864 by Fanny Kelly entitled *Narrative of my Captivity among the Sioux Indians.* The Sioux and Cheyenne were allies and had similar cultures. Fanny Kelly's narrative makes for interesting reading.

• Kicking Horse's threat to put Bry and Maisey on a wild pony for target practice echoes that of the old chief enraged at Fanny Kelly for discarding his pipe. Fanny avoided this dreadful fate accidentally when, fully expecting to die, she distributed the purse of money in her pocket among her captors. This pleased and placated them, and they forgot their deadly intent.

- I invented the town of Liberty, but Fort Owen existed. Major John Owen, a sutler, or provisioner, for the army, came west and settled in the Bitterroot Valley to run the fort as a glorified trading post. He was appointed special agent to the Flathead Indians and given the honorary title, 'Major.' His fondness for Nancy, his Shoshone wife, probably made this position natural for him. Major Owen was himself beloved by the Indians. It is telling that he never had to use the fort's defenses. I consulted his diary for local details and quoted a statement he made in his diary about the recklessness of the young Indians in the text of Cheyenne Sunrise.

Thank you for reading this story. Please consider leaving a review on the Amazon page for Cheyenne Sunrise to help this story reach more readers. Don't forget to claim your reader bonuses and sign up for my historical fiction reader club at

http://janalynvoigt.com/cheyenne-sunrise-readers.

Cheyenne Sunrise Book Club Questions

1. In the beginning of the book, Bry decides to shut herself off emotionally. Why does she do this? Have you ever had a time where events in your life were too painful and you needed to do the same? What did you do to overcome this?

2. Nick wants to shield Bry from the conflicts in his life. Was he also trying to protect himself? If so, from what?

3. How did the Cheyenne tribe feel about the encroachment of the settlers and how did this view inform their actions?

4. Kicking Horse exercises restraint when Nick confronts him in battle, citing their mother's love for his step-brother. Did he hold back for reasons of his own?

5. If you were held captive against your will, would you react with Bry's determination or Maisey's hesitancy? Why? Are there factors in your life that have shaped you to react a certain way and are there things you can do to overcome your past?

6. Did Rising Bird make a mistake when she gave Nick back his horse? Have you had times in your life where you questioned a decision after you made it?

7. Should Bry have told Rob about Thad's abuse? If you knew someone in the same situation, what would you do?

8. What did Nick learn about himself by returning to his parents' cabin?

9. Which emotions did Kicking Horse give in to when he followed Bry and Nick?

10. Bry struggles to understand why God allows bad things to happen to good people. Maisey explains that this is because we have free will and live in a fallen world. What would you advise Bry to believe? Have you ever struggled with this same question?

Now, a Sneak Peek at Book Three
STAGECOACH TO LIBERTY
Releasing December 1, 2018

CHAPTER ONE

ELSA GRIPPED THE RAILING ON THE riverboat's hurricane deck and stared at the city beyond the dock. Independence shone in the afternoon sun, a sprawling metropolis with wide streets. She'd come a long way from her family's cottage in rural Germany. Hopefully, she'd find the promised fortune here in America, or at least enough money to send home to help her mother and the young ones put food on the table. She sighed. Leaving home had been a hard decision, but she'd made it for her family. If only Peter had taken it better, she wouldn't have this pang in her stomach.

"Come along." Alicia Peabody tugged her arm. Her words had sounded impatient, but she softened them with a smile. Alicia's white teeth and creamy complexion were only part of her beauty. She reminded Elsa of the porcelain dolls she'd begged for as a child after seeing them displayed in a store window. That was before she'd grown old enough to realize that no amount of begging could divert money for such a luxury from the constant struggle to fill their bellies and keep shoes on their feet.

Grateful for the distraction, Elsa picked up her valise and joined the other young women traveling with the Peabodys. Red-haired Adele Wargel, who had been her neighbor, grinned at her. "You were daydreaming." She spoke in German.

"I suppose so." Elsa answered in the same language.

Adele walked beside her as the small group turned toward the stairs. "Thinking of Peter?"

"I can't figure out why he thought we were promised." Elsa lowered her voice.

Adele laughed. "Maybe it was the way you flirted with him during that sleigh ride at Christmas."

"Oh, that." Elsa frowned. "I won't deny that I admired him, but it went no further. I have no idea how he came to the wrong conclusion."

"Truly?" Adele's eyes danced.

She arched an eyebrow. "A person might expect to remember something so important. No, Peter chose what he wished to believe. I'm only sorry he's hurting."

The breeze off the water whisked strands of hair into Adele's blue eyes. She clawed them away. "Peter broke his own heart, from the sound of it. I wouldn't worry about that one. He needed humbling, if you want my opinion."

Ida Henkel, a tall blonde girl who had lived across town from them, turned back at the head of the stairs. "What are you two gossiping about?"

Adele shrugged. "Nothing much."

"English, please, ladies!" Alicia's voice held a decidedly miffed note. "And you'd better keep up with the rest of us. We don't want to keep Mr. Peabody waiting."

Ida rolled her eyes and turned down the stairs behind Alicia.

Adele moved closer to Elsa. "I'm beginning to wish I hadn't signed that contract."

Elsa could offer no reassurances since she shared the same feeling. She pulled in a breath and mustered a reply for them both. "It's too late for second thoughts. We'll have to make the best of things." She squared her shoulders and followed the others.

At the foot of the stairs, Miles Peabody waited with ill-concealed impatience. Alicia and her brother were both blond, but there the resemblance ended. Miles was elegant and handsome but lacked Alicia's fine features. The two differed in other ways. Even in the short time Elsa had known Miles, she'd become familiar with his peculiar habits. One in particular annoyed her. Alicia always met her eyes when Elsa spoke to her, while Miles glanced away as if neither Elsa nor anything she could say were worth his time.

Miles watched his sister approach with a smile that didn't include Elsa or any of the other women in his charge. He picked up twin valises at his feet and tipped his head toward the gangplank, which was thick with passengers. "Shall we?"

He had not behaved in so rude a manner when persuading her to sign a contract to play her hurdy gurdy and dance with miners in a gold rush town. They'd approached her after seeing her perform as a way to draw attention to the brooms her family made. Other girls from her village had come home from Frankfurt with lots of money and their wares all sold, so she'd decided to try it. Miles and Alicia had offered to pay her passage to America if she signed their contract.

Elsa treaded with her newfound companions down the gangplank, wondering if she'd made a mistake.

Bry stretched, having just risen from bed, and pulled back the chintz curtains at her bedroom window. In the early morning with the sky washed clean from the night rains and the river glowing with soft light, she could believe in a world where miracles happened. The new school for Indian children would do more good than harm. The town of Liberty, local settlers, and the ranch would stay safe from attack. Her brother Con still lived.

She rested her head on the pane and blew out a breath. "God, please watch over my brother." With no one to see, she let her tears fall.

The door behind her opened and boots thumped on the carpet. She straightened, but her husband must have seen her moment of sorrow.

"Come here, you." Nick enfolded her in his arms and kissed

her neck. He didn't ask what troubled her, having comforted her often enough to know.

"How much longer must we wait to find out what had happened to Con?" She dried her eyes with the back of her hand. "A lifetime?"

"As long as it takes."

She turned in her husband's arms and lifted her face to gaze into the warmth of his eyes. "What would I do without you?"

A smile dented the corners of his mouth. "God willing, you won't have to find out." He smoothed her cheek, then lowered his head for a kiss that brought her more thoroughly awake. "I love you, Mrs. Laramie."

She laughed. "That's best, since we're married."

His eyes gleamed. "I need no reminder of that."

She treated him to a flirtatious glance. "I hope you don't mind being stuck with me."

He tightened his arms. "Look at me like that again, and I'll settle your mind on the matter."

She smiled but refrained. "I have a thousand things to do today."

"Shouldn't your husband find a place at the top of that list?"

"Of course." She walked her fingers up his chest. "Don't *you* have a list?"

Nick captured her hand and kissed each of her fingers in turn. "Mine can wait." He claimed her lips in a caress that left her breathless, but then released her. "I came to tell you that Rob is back from Liberty."

She smiled. "He's remembered to tear himself away from Maisey, has he?" Although Rob wouldn't admit it, he was clearly smitten with Bry's friend who taught children from the local tribes in the town of Liberty. Rob had traveled to Liberty a great deal since the thaw to help build the cabin in which Maisey would live.

"He'll be in after he tends his horse. Seems like he has something on his mind. He wants to talk to you particularly."

"What can it be about, I wonder?"

"You'll find out, I'm sure." He gave her a wolfish smile. "Dress yourself, woman, and meet us downstairs."

With Nick's footfalls dwindling down the hallway, Bry topped her linen chemise with a soft dress made of green wool. Remembering Con's disparaging remarks about the unflattering widows weeds she'd worn as a servant in Boston brought a smile to her face. He'd thereafter lavished clothing on her. Her smile vanished. After being kidnapped by the Cheyenne, she'd lost the trunk. Con had bought her. She'd had to start over in so many ways, including her wardrobe. Almost a year later, the memories were still rough, the worst being when Con took an arrow and fell from his horse.

Pushing her thoughts away, she went downstairs and found Rob pacing in the parlor. Nick watched him from one of the leather armchairs scattered throughout the room. Against walls covered in a beige fleur-de-lis pattern, her brother seemed utterly masculine and, after his journey, rather unkempt. The ginger hair, so like Da's, lifted in peaks, and red shot his blue eyes.

She sank into a blue cushioned chair across a small table from Nick. "What brings you so early in the day?"

A sheepish look crossed his face. "I left Shane's house later than I should have. I could have arrived yesterday but figured you wouldn't want me barging in at midnight, so I made camp before sunset instead of pushing on."

"Very sensible." Shane saluted him with his coffee mug. "Night travel holds too many dangers."

"Yes, well. I almost did it anyway." Rob ran a hand through his hair, a habit that probably explained its rumpled state. "You see, I made a decision while on the road."

Bry exchanged a glance with Nick. From the expression on Rob's face, she already knew what he meant to do. "Oh?"

Rob sat down abruptly in the chair across from her. "It's late enough in spring that I should make it through the passes."

"I'd feel better if you went in summer." What with Indian unrest, road agents, natural disasters, and predatory animals, many perils faced a lone traveler in the wilderness. "Why go at a time of year at risk for avalanches?"

Rob jumped to his feet and began pacing again. "We've already waited too long. If I'd gone after Con sooner I might have found him before the snow set in. I don't want to make the same mistake twice."

Bry put a hand to her stomach to quiet its churning. Rob was right, and she knew it. *Please, God. Don't let me lose two brothers.*

The man called Reilly stood outside the homestead as light ebbed from the sky. Why should the reluctance to go inside take hold of him? He should welcome an evening spent in the company of the Fitzgeralds. After the accident that had stolen his memory, this family had taken him in. Finley felt responsible, since it had been his freight wagon that had thrown him when it overturned. Reilly shook his head. Whatever the cause, he couldn't deny the feeling he should be elsewhere.

The lighted window framed Keira, the oldest of the Fitzgerald daughters. Black-haired and lovely, she possessed blue eyes that had been, as the saying went, put in with a sooty finger. Whatever she was talking about lit her face with excitement, but then Keira always seemed to embrace life with enthusiasm.

He should go inside. At the back door, he stamped the mud from his boots, and reached for the knob.

The world slid away, and he stood in another location, reaching for a different doorknob. A brisk wind stirred the leaves of the cottonwoods behind him, and a mourning dove raised its lament somewhere in the trees. He paused with his hand on the knob and glanced around with a feeling of pride. He'd built this ranch from nothing but his love for the Bitterroot Valley.

A dog barked, bringing him back to the present. His hand shook as he turned the doorknob and went inside.